THROUGH A VEIL

DARKLY

BROKEN VEIL
BOOK 3

MARIE ANDREAS

OTHER BOOKS BY MARIE ANDREAS

The Lost Ancients
Book One: The Glass Gargoyle
Book Two: The Obsidian Chimera
Book Three: The Emerald Dragon
Book Four: The Sapphire Manticore
Book Five: The Golden Basilisk
Book Six: The Diamond Sphinx

The Lost Ancients: Dragon's Blood
Book One: The Seeker's Chest
Book Two: The Finder's Crown

The Asarlaí Wars Trilogy
Book One: Warrior Wench
Book Two: Victorious Dead
Book Three: Defiant Ruin

The Code of the Keeper
Book One: Traitor's Folly
Book Two: Destroyer's Curse

The Adventures of Smith and Jones
A Curious Invasion
The Mayhem of Mermaids
An Intrigue of Pharaohs

Broken Veil Trilogy
Book One: The Girl with the Iron Wing
Book Two: An Uncommon Truth of Dying
Book Three: Through a Veil Darkly

Books of the Cuari Trilogy
Book One: Essence of Chaos
Book Two: Division of Chaos
Book Three: Destruction of Chaos

Magic and Sorcery Chronicles Trilogy
A Touch of Magic
A Slice of Sorcery
A Dash of Devilry

ACKNOWLEDGEMENTS

I LOVE TELLING STORIES, I have ever since I was a kid and I only shared them in my head. Being able to share them with all of you is an amazing thing, and I count myself extremely lucky.

I'm also grateful for the people who have helped me with these stories. Beta-readers/editors: Lisa Andreas, Patti Huber, and Lynne Mayfield. They help make the words, and the worlds themselves, shine. I appreciate all you do! And my proofreader extraordinaire, Ilana Schoonover—thank you for working your magic once again! Any remaining goofs or errors are my fault alone. Or due to that massive issue we're having with the veil between words.

Thank you to the Killion Group for the print cover formatting and interior formatting

And extra thanks to my cover artist Aleta Rafton!

Thank you to everyone for following these adventures!

CHAPTER ONE

A ISLING SWORE AS the window into her world closed, leaving her alone and bloody on the wrong side of the veil. The closing of it was a stab to her soul, but unless she could get to her feet and find a safe place to go, she wouldn't last long. Every part of her hurt and even adjusting how she was sitting caused a stab of pain.

She'd been pushed through the veil—literally—and was now stuck on the other side. There was no way to know if her friends were alive or dead, as her last sight had been of them collapsed on the ground unconscious.

Tears and rips covered her clothing, bloody welts under them. She'd gone through a massive window prior to going through the veil. Every part of her felt beaten and achy. Her head was pounding loud enough that, had there been anyone around, they would have heard it.

Being shoved through the veil to the world her people had fled thousands of years ago wasn't as much fun as it sounded.

Calling in magic to heal herself failed the first time. After three more useless attempts, she stopped. Her magic had been changing after being released from the block her mother had placed on it for most of Aisling's life—but healing magic had always been hers. Until now.

She swore as the pendant the vallenians gave her sent a wave of heat. A quick glance revealed that the spell hiding it was gone, so all the colored lines encircling it now showed. And it was glowing in the dim light around her.

"You did nothing to stop them from shoving me through here. And now you're making me a target for any of the monsters on this side. Happy now? We're on your side of the veil." There was no response from the pendant. It, and the unbreakable chain it hung from, had been a gift of sorts from a vallenian who had crossed the veil to come to Earth. Her brother Harlie had called it a ghau pendant—something of great power on this side of the veil ten thousand years ago when the elves and the rest of the fey races still lived here. To be fair, it *had* helped her a few times, and there had been thoughts that maybe the vallenians were actually not evil.

But while the pendant had defended her against her mother, and completely freaked her out in a way Aisling had never seen before, it hadn't done anything when the skeletal invaders slammed her through a plate glass window and into this side of the veil.

She'd gone through her life thinking of herself as a moderate level magic user, a healer of smaller injuries. Then she'd found out that her brother Harlie had blocked her magic when she was five at the orders of their mother. Once he released the block, she had a lot of magical power at her command.

Until now. No matter how hard she tried, she couldn't bring up the spells that would heal her. It was as if her magic had been cut from her when she went through the glass and the veil. Not a cheery thought.

Slammed through the veil and left bloody, bruised, magicless, and weaponless. Not that she really thought her gun would work here, but it hadn't crossed over with her even though she'd had it before she was pushed through.

Getting to her feet still wasn't an option, so she focused

on something else—maybe if she distracted her mind she could fight her way to her magic. Not a great theory, but she wasn't sure what else to try. She attempted thinking about Reece, Maeve, and her brothers Caradoc and Harlie. The problem was they'd looked in bad shape when she last saw them, so that just notched her terror up and didn't bring her magic back. She needed to get angry. Her mother did that well.

She hoped her mother was dead. In her last sight of the other world, there was nothing left where her mother stood as she betrayed Aisling and the rest of the world except a puddle of blood. Whatever shoved Aisling through to this side had friends that went after her mother. And were possibly rampaging throughout the English countryside as she was stuck here unable to even get off the ground.

They'd been just outside of London, a London that had just been freed from almost certain destruction at the hands of an insane elf named Nix. There was no way, after what everyone had gone through, that they'd be ready for another invasion from beyond the veil.

There was nothing she could do to help them. She couldn't even help herself.

It was her mother's fault. All of it. Her mother was responsible for the deaths of thousands, if not millions, of humans and fey. She'd been involved with altering humanity to massively reduce their ability to reproduce at the time the fey were supposedly saving humanity from the Black Death.

She'd killed Aisling as a child to further her own goals. Someone from this side had made a deal with a lot of high-ranking fey families—a deal that involved them each sacrificing one of their children. All of whom were born the same year as Aisling.

Aisling recently found out about the deal and also realized that she *had* died at her mother's hand—then been brought back. Apparently, whoever called for the killing of innocent children had been misled about her return from death. Somehow beings from this side had been crossing over to Earth—and they hadn't been happy once they realized who Aisling was. It was hard to tell which was worse—that her mother killed her to appease powers beyond her—or that when she had Aisling brought back, she lied to those same powers.

Whatever game her mother had been playing, it appeared she'd lost. Aisling had a feeling that those powerful beings were the ones who went after her mother in the base she'd just been dragged out of.

A flood of fury washed over Aisling and her injuries slowly closed. The magic felt odd, not her normal type of healing—but it should let her get up.

The numbness in her limbs was slowly replaced by pain—but that was an improvement. It meant the healing, weird as it felt, was working. Being in the land the fey had fled from thousands of years ago and injured wasn't a good idea—especially without functioning magic.

The veil between worlds was supposedly impenetrable from either side. Yet in the past year, not only had beings gone back and forth, but a massive building had been sucked through to this side and pieces of it had been falling back to Earth. With horrific consequences.

It was twilight, or what passed for twilight here. Or perhaps that was just how the sky looked on this side of the veil. The sky was getting darker, and she was in some sort of forest. One filled with massive hundred-foot tall Hewlith trees. If she didn't already believe that she was on the other side of the veil, the trees would have confirmed it. They were rare on Earth, only growing in one small area of northern Wales, where the fey first made entry into that world.

Taking a deep breath, she forced her legs under her and started to rise. Only to fall over on her side as her legs buckled. They were mostly healed, but the energy wasn't there.

Falling wasn't as bad as the high-pitched giggling that surrounded her. She'd thought there was no one around; obviously she was wrong.

The laughter that echoed around her sounded hollow and deadly.

There were many beings who had been left behind when the rest of the fey abandoned this world. From what the stories told, none of them were pleasant. Aisling stayed where she landed and tried to think back to her school days—to the tales of what was left behind they were told as young ones. The world beyond the veil was taught to grade school fey children as a cautionary tale. Be good or the vallenians will come and snatch you out of existence. Tall, gaunt beings wearing all black, including elaborate black hats, they were able to remain invisible until they wanted to be seen. Seeing one was cause for death—or so the stories said.

They were also supposedly unable to cross the veil.

Aisling had several run-ins with the almost mythological beings on Earth, but so far, they hadn't destroyed her. In fact, they might have been trying to help her—including giving her the ghau pendant.

The giggling around her intensified, becoming maniacal and rising almost out of her range of hearing. Swearing to herself, she realized what they must be. Hel-pixies. Unlike the human-sized pixies, winged fey who had crossed the veil thousands of years ago with the elves and the others; hel-pixies were tiny, horrific beings who made brownies look like altruistic saviors. No more than two inches high, with fang-filled mouths about half the size of their bodies. They attacked in massive swarms and supposedly could render a body to bone in minutes.

Her brother Caradoc had spent an entire week tormenting her with stories about them when she was little. Caradoc was the closest to her in age of all their siblings, but he was still eighty years older than her.

She tried to think of what could stop a swarm of hel-pixies, but the massive headache she'd had since she was pushed through to this side intensified. She needed to focus. Her mother was a class A bitch, and that was before Aisling found out that she'd killed her own daughter. But one thing she was good at was focus. If she had a goal, she pushed through and figured it out.

Hel-pixies were small. And small creatures usually had enemies, often ones that wanted to eat them. As a kid she had a book of mythical beasts—most of whom were not mythical on this side of the veil. Loghlins. Loghlins liked to eat hel-pixies. Massive bear-like creatures with fangs, four-inch-long claws, and very little in the brain department, they had massively wide mouths to literally suck in hel-pixies.

The picture books had freaked out young Aisling even more than the hel-pixies had, so Caradoc had chased her around making the call of a loghlin. "I really need to even the score with him; but right now, I'm grateful." Aisling braced herself, took a deep breath and yelled her best imitation of a loghlin.

The giggling stopped. Then she heard hundreds of tiny wings flapping and crashing through tree branches away from her. They had surrounded her, but their mass exit was a single direction.

Aisling took a deep breath and focused on getting to her feet once silence filled the area. It wasn't graceful, but she did it. She doubted that the hel-pixies would stay away once they realized there wasn't a loghlin in the area. But this gave her a chance to find somewhere to defend herself when they returned. Unfortunately, she had no idea where to go. Mostly the creatures left behind on this side of the veil were vicious simplistic beasts, or even more vicious non-simplistic beings. Also known as the Old Ones, who wouldn't try to speak to her before they killed her. She needed a place she could hide until she regained her strength—and hopefully the rest of her magic.

As she struggled to her feet, her pendant got twisted in her hair. She swore and freed it, but kept it in her hand. Maybe she could use it to reach the vallenians. They had a way through the veil, so they might be able to get her home. She wouldn't call them friends, but it did seem like they had been trying to help her out. Sort of.

"I need help." She kept her voice down just in case there was anything in the forest that she didn't want to hear. The pendant had done a lot of things since she'd put it on, but right now it was just sitting there. It wasn't even warm and glowing anymore.

No response, no sudden glowing from the pendant, no whisking of her back through the veil. She held it for a few more moments, then let the pendant drop to her chest. She wouldn't give up; it might take a while to reach them. Which meant that she was back to being on her own.

Aisling gave herself a final brush so she didn't look as ragged. She'd been able to pull in enough magic to heal herself, but not fix her clothes. Then she looked around for anything that could be used as a weapon.

Her search ended abruptly when a swamp goblin popped out from behind a tree. Short and gray green, they usually hunted in packs, or so the stories claimed. A thin gray lightning bolt came from its hands. It hit her, but all she felt was a tickle. The swamp goblin scowled and ran at her with his hands out.

She flipped him over her shoulder.

He took one look at her pendant, which had come out again, and ran. Not slowing down when he hit a tree or two.

She picked a direction and slowly started walking as she searched for a large rock, stick, or anything she could use as a weapon.

The only weapon she found was a club-like tree limb. It had fallen on its own so she felt it might be okay to pick up. Even so, she nodded to the tree closest to the branch. "I thank thee for this gift." It had been a long time since she'd practiced the archaic way of speaking, but she hoped she could recall the greetings. If there was anything here who didn't try to eat her as soon as they met her, she really didn't want to offend them. Trees, especially Hewlith trees, had deep souls.

The woods around her all looked the same, but the hel-pixies had flown left. The goblin had been scrambling, but he appeared to have gone that way as well. She went right. So far, she hadn't heard or seen anyone else. The grayish-green skeletal being who shoved her through the barrier between the worlds must have stayed on the Earth side; it had been focused on grabbing her mother.

Shoving her through the veil hadn't seemed to be intentional at first, but maybe getting her out of the way was part of the plan. Hopefully her friends weren't seen as a threat.

"Friends? Who has friends?" The words were light and airy. And the voice was all around her. And was responding to words she'd thought, not what she said. Great.

She raised her club and pulled in a spell—or at least tried for one. As a healer, her best defensive spells were if she could touch her opponent. She didn't think she wanted to be that close to anything on this side of the veil. And her magic still felt like it was gone. Again.

"Who's facing me?" Although she didn't see anyone, the phrase was acceptable for all the Old Ones.

"All face you. All fear you. Take off your pretty trinket and come play." There was an edge to the breathless voice now, but even without that, the fact it wanted her to take the necklace off meant that even if she could remove it, that would be the last thing she did.

"That's not going to happen. Who faces me? I request a name." Always request, never demand—dealing with the Old Ones was a messy, difficult thing in the tales that Caradoc had read to her as a child. "I could call the maker of this necklace if you want it off." It was a risk if whatever was around her was friends with the vallenians. But since they wanted the necklace off before they approached her, she doubted that.

"Names…why need names? Come with us." A bright light; a will-o-wisp, appeared ahead of her, darting in the trees. Then two more, crossing the trees on the other side. Considering that the tiny lights often lured inexperienced travelers to their doom, there was no way she was following. Will-o-wisps were one of the few beings who had crossed the veil with the first crossing, then who were sent back within a few years. Humans were young and awkward in those days and easy prey. The will-o-wisps might be working with an unseen foe. Will-o-wisps couldn't speak out loud.

"Not following that, nor you. *For the final time*, give me your name." That phrasing was important. While she was fairly sure whoever the voice was behind the will-o-wisps wasn't on her side, nor could they actually help her get home, she needed to establish that she was giving them a final warning. According to the beyond the veil rules, the other party couldn't complain if they refused to answer her question and then she fried them with a spell. If she could use a spell.

"Unfun." The voice rose to a shrill note, then vanished. The will-o-wisps circled the area she was in, but didn't approach before darting off.

"Damn it." Maybe she shouldn't have pushed so hard. There was no one in the woods that she could sense, but she closed her eyes and tried to reach out.

Her searching brought nothing. But there was no way to know if it was just that she wasn't skilled enough, the land beyond the veil was blocking it, or she truly had no access to her magic beyond the bit she'd used to heal herself. If it *was* her magic that did it. She thought that she'd healed herself, but it could have been that an Old One did it. She wouldn't make good prey if she was too injured to move. Hunting was important to them.

That wasn't a reassuring thought.

A shuffling sound came from where the first will-o-wisp had been. It was more of a groaning in pain than anything threatening. Lifting her club, Aisling carefully moved forward.

The closer she got the more it sounded like groans and a few bits of muttered swearing.

"Step out slowly, I am not in a mood to be trifled with."

She swore as the person rose to his feet.

Chapter Two

ISLING LOWERED HER club as a battered gnome came slowly out of the bushes. There were bloody marks all over him, like Aisling had received on her trip through the veil, but he also had a lump on his head. Gnome heads were notoriously hard to damage.

"Bart?" Bart was her sort of boss, an internal affairs agent from Area 42 who'd taken lead fighting back against the mess that Nix had created. Short and scruffy looking, it appeared to be him, but he hadn't been anywhere near the room her mother had set up as a trap. In fact, she had used his voice to get Aisling and her friends there.

"Aye. Aisling? Good to see you. We need to get back inside; your mother is up to something nasty." He looked around as if seeing the massive Hewlith trees and wilderness for the first time. "There is no way this is a British forest. Where in the hells are we?"

Aisling helped him get out of the shrubs; however he'd come in, he'd landed in the middle of some nasty sticker bushes.

"We're on the other side of the veil." She filled him in on what had happened with her mother, and then the rest. Bart's injuries looked bad, but that didn't stop him from stomping around and swearing when she finished.

"How did she do it? I know she gave birth to you, Caradoc, and Harlie, but that woman has to be stopped.

Permanently." His fingers twitched as if he needed to crush something.

"I agree and I know my brothers would as well. I don't know that she did this, though. I was thrown through a window by some skeletal monster. But it was almost as an afterthought, the creature was focused on attacking her. What's the last thing you recall?"

"You all had just left the battle zone of London for that recovery base. Been gone maybe ten minutes? We were staging clean-up. Then your mother showed up. Strode through like she owned the place. I followed her to the side of a building." He shook his head with a wince. "Next thing I knew, I was here. Just woke up in a pool of pain when you called out." His eyes went wide and he patted his sides. "Damn it, she took my guns."

"She didn't send me here and my weapons are gone too. It might be the veil itself."

"How did she send me through? Or how did whatever sent you through do it?"

"I don't think she sent you through. If she had that ability, she would have done it to others. But she might have called in whoever did it. Someone or something besides Nix was working with her." She looked closer at his head. Her magic had barely healed the worst of her injuries, she didn't know what power she had left right now. "Are you okay?"

He grimaced and rubbed his head. "No, I'm not. But being over here is worse than some cuts and bruises. Being out in the open makes it worse. We need to seek shelter." He looked up. "We don't want to be outside when true night falls."

"No, you don't." The voice was soft and at first seemed to come from nowhere and everywhere. Then a slim form came out of the trees. The tree-like being appeared female and was a foot or more taller than Aisling. "You need to hide. I will help you, for a price."

Aisling's veil lore failed to identify this one, but there was no mistaking where the person was looking. Her eyes were fixed on Aisling's pendant.

"We do need help, but I'm sorry, I can't take this off." She held the pendant in case the slim creature tried to grab it.

She didn't. A lovely laugh came forth and her smile lit her entire face. "No, one does not remove the ghau. I would ask to hold it for a short while." A sad look of longing replaced the laughter. "Once we are safe."

Aisling shrugged and looked to Bart. He'd studied veil lore in his younger years, maybe he had an idea about this being. She looked like one of the dryads, but according to the old stories, they were lost long before the rest of the fey fled to Earth. His eyes narrowed as he watched her, but then gave a short nod.

"Agreed. But you need to keep us safe while under your care and not dispatch that care to any other." Good thing Caradoc read those stories to her when she was little. There were a lot of ways to be tricked by the beings left on this side of the veil.

The tree-like being smiled and bowed her head. "You are wise as well as beautiful. I promise to abide by the agreement. Come this way." She turned and slipped down a thin path between the massive trees.

Once they were following her it was clear it was a well-used trail. Even with her elven eyesight, Aisling would have been hard-pressed to see it until their rescuer put them on it. She almost asked the fey her name, but that was risky outdoors. She'd already accidently exposed Bart's name—but hopefully, since it was a nickname and not his full true first name, nothing bad would come from it. Ears were everywhere in the forests, even back home. Here even more so. Names could be weapons if the wrong creatures got them.

The tree-like fey led them in what felt like circles, but

eventually they came to a small cave. Aisling knew the beings left behind would probably be living closer to the earth, but the cave was surprising. Until they went inside.

The rough cave exterior was misleading. The interior was more like an old-fashioned cottage, complete with a roaring fire, than a cave. The smoke from the odd peat fire vanished into the upper part of the place, but Aisling couldn't see any chimney.

Probably better not to ask.

"Please sit, we are safe here." Their new friend nodded to the open cave mouth and a door appeared. "It will always be open from the inside, never fear." She looked carefully at both of them. "An elf of a royal line and a gnome of the leafy realm. What brings you both to this side and how did the ghau come to you?"

"I would like to know what to call you before we tell our tale. We will tell you our names and our story." Aisling kept her voice even, but this would be a turning point as to whether this being would help them or not.

The slender fey scrunched up her heart-shaped face and finally nodded. "I trust you both. I am Neasa of the northern peoples; a dryad. I live far from my village in hopes to bring light back to it. So far, I have failed." Her voice wasn't much louder than it had been, but a sound like wind through the trees followed her words.

Aisling had no idea what she was talking about, but Bart appeared to.

He gave a short bow. "I am pleased to make the acquaintance of one of the northern peoples. I am Barthlinio, and I would be your friend. There were tales that your people had been lost long before the crossing."

Aisling was watching Neasa, so she saw the flash of pain, sorrow, and anger that crossed her face. It was gone almost immediately.

"We were…not lost. But left. Tricked by those who crossed." She shook her head. "If we become friends, I will take you to my village and you will learn all." She turned to Aisling expectantly.

"I am Aisling, and I was given the ghau by a vallenian on the other side of the veil. I don't believe I have royal blood though." Her family line was high-ranking, thanks to her mother. But had they been of actual royal descent, Aisling knew her mother would have taken full advantage of it.

Neasa nodded slowly, but watched Aisling's face carefully. "It is there. Might I see the ghau?" She stayed seated, but her slim branchlike hands were twitching toward Aisling.

Aisling held out the chain for her to see the pendant.

Neasa shyly came forward and took the pendant in her hands. Green tears started falling down her face, but she was smiling. "The power in this might be enough. It sings of freedom." She looked up. "Can you hear it?"

Aisling shook her head. "I'm afraid not. And I have no idea what power it wields." It had come to her defense more than a few times, but she didn't understand how it worked. "I can't even get it off."

"Oh, no." Neasa's laugh was lovely. "You won't be able to until the ghau has completed its task. But maybe it can help my people along the way? Perhaps the paths run together?" She wasn't talking to Aisling, but to the pendant itself. It glowed lightly green in response.

"I haven't seen it do that before." Aisling didn't pull it back, but almost felt like she should. "But I think it likes you."

"It is the parts of it completing the whole and they are part of this place." She continued to stroke the pendant and murmur to it. Aisling looked over her head to Bart, who just shrugged.

"Are the vallenians around here?" Hopefully they could help get her and Bart back home.

Before she and he went crazy like Nix had.

Neasa frowned and released the pendant. "No, they stay far from here. Some say they are bad, but I didn't believe so. And they gave you that ghau pendant to bring you here to save us, so all is good."

"Save you?" Bart stepped up on that one. "You want to go to the other side of the veil?"

"No, save us here—save our world. Your world is fine, I'm sure, and my people should have been there. But this is our home now. Once it is fixed, it will be full of light again and my people will thrive. There are beings from the forbidden world who want to destroy us. They must be stopped."

Aisling wanted to ask what the forbidden world was, Harlie had once mentioned multiple worlds, but Neasa didn't look willing to talk about it. She'd ask her brother if they got back.

"I'm not sure if Bart and I alone can save a world. And it's dangerous for us the longer we stay on this side. Isn't this place full of horribly scary things? They tell us that when our people fled, this world was dying."

Neasa threw her hands in the air. "That was wrong. They speak wrongly. Do you know how old I am? Guess." She rose to her feet and spun in a circle.

"Twenty?" There was no way she looked that old, but Aisling was completely unaware of her species.

Neasa laughed so hard she fell over. "More like three thousand." She shrugged. "I stopped counting after that. I was alive when the rest of the fey fled this world. But it was not a bad place and when my people questioned the reasons for the leave taking, we were tricked and left behind."

"That is *so* not what I was taught. I am only two hundred years old, so I was born on the other side." Aisling studied Neasa, but she'd have to take her word for it about her age.

"I'm closer to five hundred and a few, but also born

past the veil." Bart shook his head as he studied Neasa. "As I said, all of our stories said your people were lost before the rest fled to the other side."

"No, they tried to destroy us. They tried to destroy the full trees we live among. Fire came. But we survived and then they were gone. Over time we have lost some of our magic, this world was bright and magical because of all of the peoples who lived here. When they left, they broke this place." She smiled. "But you are back. We have an elf and a gnome to balance the dark."

"We'll do what we can, but we have to get back home. There's a danger to us here, and something was attacking people I care about on the other side."

"You look like him." Neasa appeared to have been listening, but was again holding the pendant and looking dreamy as she smiled at Aisling.

"Him who?"

"King Filthian. He was a good king, until he and his queen fell against duplicitous friends. His youngest son survived, but the royal connection was determined to be gone. The royal line fell to another. But you carry his face. And eyes." She nodded as if this was common knowledge and made sense. Again, Bart didn't seem to know what she was talking about either.

"I'm sorry, but I don't recognize that name. But I guess thank you that I remind you of him?" Aisling had no idea what she was talking about.

Bart was staring at her with narrowed eyes, then smacked his head. "The lost prince. Another story we were told. The only surviving child of King Filthian and Queen Loacia was lost not long after the rest of the family fell. That's what was in our stories."

"No. They removed his memories of who he was and gave him a new life. He crossed the veil with your mother." Neasa kept smiling and cooing at the pendant even as she spoke to Aisling and Bart.

"He's a friend of hers? That can't be good—nothing associated with my mother is good. And how did you know who my mother is? I didn't give you my family name." Aisling didn't think her magic was back and if it was, it probably wouldn't work well. But Neasa wasn't on their side if she knew her mother. She removed the pendant from Neasa's grasp.

"Oh dear. I knew who you were when I came out to get you. But I wasn't supposed to say anything. *They* like keeping secrets." Neasa chewed on one of her long fingers. "They know who you are. They know who your mother is…and they know who your father was supposed to be."

A chill went through Aisling's soul as a whole lot of pieces dropped into place. "My father was this lost prince?"

She nodded sadly. "And he doesn't even know. We have no royals left on this side, or had none. Now we have you."

"Look, we can't stay here. Even if my father was royalty a few thousand years ago, he's not now—and that means that I'm not either. And I can't rule anything. I have a lot of older brothers and sisters, if anyone is in line for a non-existent throne, I wouldn't be it." This revelation was a shocker. Did her mother know? Her mother had always worked closely with the High King and Queen and the rest of the High Council, surely one of them would know? Her father was meek and unassuming, and did whatever her mother demanded. If he did have any connections, her mother certainly would have exploited them eons ago.

Unless either she didn't know—doubtful—or her plan was far longer planned, and it was more important she not be the consort of the king for some reason. Or for a time.

"See? I speak the truth." Neasa walked to a wall where

a painting hung. It was a darker painting in a dimmer part of the cave-cottage.

Aisling and Bart moved forward and she started swearing. It was a picture of her father as a young man, his almost black hair swept to the side, and his flashing green eyes peering out. Her hair was her mother's, but there was no denying his face was like Aisling's. In the picture he looked like a dark-haired, male version of her.

"Okay, so hypothetically, maybe my father was royalty. But we can't stay here whether he was or not. The fey who have crossed the veil are changed, we can't live here now."

Neasa nodded earnestly. "They want to meet you." She nodded to Bart. "Both. They didn't see Barthlinio come this way, but they now want you to join as well."

"I can't meet anyone until you help us find a way home." Aisling wasn't sure what her best defense spell—a healer spell gone wrong with skin-on-skin contact—would do against someone who was basically a walking tree.

"Then we are settled." Neasa laughed and clapped. "You are home."

A thin vine shot out from Neasa's hand and looped around Aisling's hands and then shot over and did the same to Bart. Aisling was fast, but that vine moved faster than she could see.

"Now, you will follow me." Neasa started out a back doorway, then turned. "Oh, I wouldn't use any magic, if I were either of you. My vines don't like them."

Aisling never took other people's word for things—especially when it involved her being tied up. She twisted her left hand so that her fingers grabbed a piece of vine and sent her anti-healing spell into it.

And was flung backwards with enough force to knock the wind out of her and take Bart to the ground.

CHAPTER THREE

A ISLING SHOOK HER head. Her brains now felt scrambled, like the worst nectar hangover she'd ever had. Without the fun part of getting there.

Neasa stood over her, shaking her head. "I warned you. Another reason not to utilize your magic—it doesn't work the same here as it did on the other side. You could have blown all of us up. Now, I will let you get up, both of you, but you must promise to behave. There are important people for you to meet, and I would feel bad if I had to say I'd lost both of you."

Aisling automatically tried to get up and found she couldn't move. Neasa gave her a look of "I told you so." At Aisling and Bart's nods of agreement, she let them up. The vines were still in place and seemed warmer than before.

"Who are you taking us to? I did some studies of the world beyond the veil years ago." Bart was trying to keep things light, but the tone of his voice showed how concerned he was.

"The dryad council of this region. They know everything. They were the ones who told me who your mother was, and to watch for you. They said I might have to kill you if you had too much of her in you." Neasa smiled but instead of making the comment seem less threatening, it made it more so. "But you have more of the lost prince in you than her—that will make them happy." She continued walking and the vines that still wrapped around them ensured Aisling and Bart would follow.

Aisling silently followed. A glance back said Bart was behind her, also silent, but he was studying everything they passed like a student who'd missed class all year and was now facing finals.

The forest they went through on the other side of Neasa's cave was far older and darker than what Aisling and Bart crashed into when they came through the veil. Still almost completely made up of Hewlith trees, these were so tall their tops were lost.

Aisling stepped closer to Neasa, it felt weird to talk among these trees. "Are the trees impacted by the closeness of the veil? The ones on the other side of your home felt less…aggressive than these."

"This is true. The veil leaves behind an impact that no one on this side can miss. It wasn't this way before. The leaving of so many fey changed it. And us. The weakening of the veil has made things worse." She stopped in front of another cave, but unlike hers it looked more cottage-like on the outside rather than cave-like.

The vines binding Aisling and Bart withdrew back to Neasa. "I will present you both, but I can't stay. This is a council meeting and they must make the decisions alone."

"As to whether they can help us leave?" Bart was more optimistic than Aisling was.

"As to whether you will be allowed to help save us and live, or be left to die." Neasa's smile was sadder. "This way." She might have removed the vines, but Aisling still felt a pull to follow the dryad into the cave. Bart was right on her heels. There was no thinking of running; they'd get caught. And she figured this might be the only chance they had to get home. Hopefully before they went crazy.

The homicidal Nix had come back from time spent on this side far more powerful, and far less sane, than he'd started.

This cave was misleading as well, unlike Neasa's cottage-cave, this was a massive hall. Dozens of different types of woods lined the inside, along with stone and gems. Aisling's pendant started to tingle.

"I think it likes it here." She raised her necklace, but the pendant wasn't warm this time, it was just tingly. Maybe as part of the deal to get home she'd let the dryads have it. If they could get it off her without killing her.

"I present the daughter of the lost fey prince, Aisling, and Barthlinio, a scholar and protector of the other side realm." Neasa didn't bow, but did nod as she stepped aside and motioned for Aisling and Bart to come forward.

"Protector?" Bart said under his breath as they moved forward.

"You are a super spy-cop. And you are trying to protect people." Aisling was impressed that Neasa hadn't given their full names. Names held control, and while these might be Neasa's people, she was withholding information. Interesting.

"I could see that." He nodded slowly. "As long as they don't expect me to put on armor and ride a massive steed in their defense, I should be okay."

The image of the less than four-foot-tall Bart riding a warhorse brought a smile, but she quickly dropped it as the dryads looked down at them.

"You have come to stand trial for actions against our realm. How do you defend yourselves?" The speaker was old. He was also massive and could probably easily pick up and crush both she and Bart with one hand.

"What?" Bart stomped forward. "We were brought here against our will, and only sought shelter and a way home. How can we be on trial for anything?"

"You both represent people who abandoned us to

this world, after they themselves caused its troubles. You answer for your people."

"After thousands of years? And wasn't her father a good guy? It wasn't his fault his wife is a sociopath and he doesn't know who and what he was. Shouldn't that give us some leeway? We're the good guys." Bart scowled at all the council members.

The giant, tree-like being leaned over to the slightly smaller one to his right and they spoke too softly for even Aisling to hear. Finally, they sat back up.

"If you do not wish to be held responsible, then you both must pledge to be our proxies on the other side. This is our world now, and your kind are no longer welcome here. However, damage from magics on your side, along with unauthorized intrusions, are weakening the veil. That massive building you sent through to our side destroyed a small village. No one in the building or the village survived and every time a piece was pulled back to your side, the veil weakened, and more damage was done." He leaned forward. "If you do not want to stand trial, then you two must find a way to close the veil forever."

Aisling stepped next to Bart. "But beings from this side of the veil have invaded and attacked our world as well. Not in defense, but attacking and killing people. Some of them were tall skeletal beings who had massive strength. They seemed to come from underground. I believe one of them threw me through the veil. Not everyone on your side is good, unless you meant to send those creatures after us?" The memory of those things going after the frozen Londoners and ripping them apart would stay in her mind for a long time.

His face darkened and his eyes went black. "Those do not act for the rest of us. Nor are they part of *this* world." He leaned back with folded arms but didn't say more.

Aisling glared back. "If they're not from our side, and

not from your side, then where did they come from? Look, I'm sorry for what happened when my people left here. It was never taught to us, and the damage done to the humans when my people went there has been as bad or worse. But those monsters didn't just come out of nowhere."

"Now I see your mother. Yes, we remember her." It was the smaller, older tree person. She squinted at Aisling then turned her head. "This is what she did to me when we tried to stop them." There was an old deep burn marring the side of her face that she'd been keeping in shadow. "I say we kill them. No trial needed."

"No! I can't be held for what my mother did to anyone. She killed me, her own kin, to suit her needs. Trust me, I hate her too. And you can't hold us responsible for all the bad things done by people on the other side of the veil. The vallenians gave me this, it must have been for a reason." She grabbed her pendant and held it up. "It's a ghau pendant—one that survived being on the other side of the veil." Hopefully the importance of that wouldn't be lost on the dryad council.

The larger tree man stood. "The vallenians you say? They have not served our people well. They could have stopped the rest of the fey from leaving. Halted the destruction that came before and after, as our world became unbalanced, but they didn't. And they don't help us now. I would see this pendant." He waved his hand and Aisling had to hang on as the pendant, chain, and herself all flew up to him.

Bart ran after her, but Neasa stepped forward and blocked his way. "This is not for you, protector. You must wait." Neasa looked like a thin tree, but from what Aisling could see she was easily holding Bart in place. Although Neasa had said she couldn't stay for whatever this was, she'd apparently changed her mind, and no one had stopped her.

The dryad giant was even more imposing up close and had an odd, but not bad, forest loam smell to him. He glared at her and the pendant. "Release it. You do not fear I will kill you, but you fear I'll take the trinket?"

Aisling let go of the pendant. "I was hanging on because you were strangling me. This hasn't come off since they put it on me." She held her hands out. "Go ahead and try though."

He lowered his brows and held out a hand toward the pendant. It bobbled forward but wouldn't come over her head. His scowl grew and he focused tightly on the pendant. Aisling felt his magics buffering her, but that chain would not come over her head.

"If needs be, we will remove your head and take it that way."

"That will not be necessary. But it will not come off for you." An extremely tall vallenian appeared in the entryway and held out his hands. The pendant tugged, then lifted over Aisling's head and dropped into the vallenian's hand. "This was to bring help to you and your people." He tilted his head toward Aisling. "You needed more protection than we can otherwise provide on the wrong side of the veil. You should have stayed over there."

The dryad released her on the ledge next to him. Aisling debated trying to climb down to the floor where Bart was, but there weren't really steps, at least not on this side. And trying to jump down didn't sound like a great idea. "We didn't have a choice. My mother, or someone working with her, threw Bart there through the veil somehow, and some weird skeletal creature threw me through. Then it attacked my mother. But I had no way to stop it. We just want to go back."

The vallenian looked up sharply at the main dryad. "Calik, is this true? Some of the ghanlough have crossed through the boundary of the veil? How did this happen? You were to keep them secured from all."

"We have kept them guarded. These must be new ones. What do you care? You and your kind stay far away and ignore the rest of us." Calik, the leader of these dryads, was trying to sound fierce. But even Aisling could hear the tremble in his voice. It was one thing to talk poorly of the vallenians when they weren't around, another when one was standing in front of him.

"We stay away because you and yours won't look at the larger issues and want things to stay how they were. Show me the ghanlough." The vallenian's voice rumbled so deeply the ground under the chamber rattled.

Aisling glanced to Bart. She'd heard very little from any vallenian whenever she'd run into them. Maybe this one was different from the ones that had visited her, but he certainly didn't have a problem speaking. Nor did he seem to care that the dryads were getting angry.

"You can't come to our lands and demand—" Calik's words were cut off as he slowly lifted in the air. Considering that the vallenian was only about a foot and a half taller than her and Calik was easily five feet or more and twice as wide it was interesting that the vallenian didn't seem to be straining as he lifted the dryad in the air.

"I can and I will. Without us your people wouldn't have survived after the others left. Now the beings you were to guard have escaped. Is it any wonder that the veil grows thinner and weaker? Show me the prison of the unforgiven, the ghanlough were to stay there forever." He nodded to Aisling and waved the necklace toward her. "This needs to stay with you."

Aisling didn't even see it happen; one moment the pendant was in his hand and the next she felt the weight hit her chest. She knew without pulling on it that it wasn't coming off on its own.

Bart's eyes went wide as the vallenian flung his hand toward him as well. Then his hand dropped to his chest.

A bit smaller than Aisling's, it looked like he was now also the reluctant owner of a ghau pendant. He also didn't look happy as he pulled on it.

"Stand down there. Together." The vallenian motioned toward the floor.

Aisling found herself floating to the floor and landing next to a slightly freaked out Bart. She figured it took a lot to freak out a major player in the weird Area 42 world, but a vallenian bestowing ghau pendants seemed to have done it.

Calik's eyes had also widened when the second ghau dropped onto Bart but said nothing. The vallenian pulled him to the floor as well.

"No one move if you please. We will be back." The vallenian and Calik vanished on the last syllable.

Leaving Aisling, Bart, Neasa, and four extremely old dryads staring at each other. Aisling ignored the dryads and looked at Bart's pendant. "Welcome to the club."

Even though he knew about hers, he continued to try to pull it over his head. "There's no logical reason for this not coming off."

"Duh, magic?"

"I know that. And no one knows much about the vallenians. But I can sense most major spells. I don't pick up anything with this thing." He looked at the pendant. "They are pretty though, aren't they? Wish I knew why they're just giving them out."

Neasa looked over but carefully did not make a step in any direction. "He is trying to guard you. Both of you. It is a very great honor." She looked around and dropped her voice. "The vallenians are truly amazing, but most of my people don't think so."

Aisling tucked her pendant back under her shirt. "Do you know what these creatures are they were talking about?" She doubted it, Neasa seemed to be on the low end of the power scale here—but she wasn't asking those other dryads. Especially the one who suggested killing her and Bart.

"Not really. There are more than two sides to the veil. The two primary sides," she held up her hand and flipped from one side to the other. "Are like this. We are prime one, your world is prime two. Then there is the underworld, the Isfyden." Her brow wrinkled. "There might be more prime sides as well, but people stopped searching after your families left here." She nodded to herself.

"What about this Isfyden?" Bart pitched his voice to be warm and soothing. "Some people on the other side say this world is the underworld." Mostly undereducated humans, but he was partially right.

"The Isfyden is here." Neasa frowned as she waved at the space under the hand she was using to represent their worlds. "It was originally cut off from the prime worlds, and was used to keep bad beings away from us. But over the last few years it has been making connections. Bad ones. There are theories that those on that side want to slam all the prime worlds together and feast upon what's left."

"That's cheery." Aisling didn't deny that if those monsters who had attacked her and her friends and who had also invaded the temporarily frozen London were from the underworld, they weren't something anyone would want invading anything.

But at this point she also hadn't seen evidence that they *weren't* from this world.

A crack of what looked like gray lightning split the air and the vallenian and Calik the dryad reappeared. If a tree-based person could go pale, Calik was pale. He also seemed to be cowering in on himself and appeared a few feet shorter.

It wasn't hard to guess where those creatures who had

attacked London and her friends came from. Clearly, Calik liked having power but wasn't up to doing what he needed to do to keep it.

"The ghanlough have escaped the prison." The vallenian announced to the dryad council. "Your people had a job, a simple one assigned to you as you were closest to the veil. Keep the ghanlough locked up, because they could not be returned to Isfyden. You will have to fight to survive as is your way when failure has fallen upon you. I must confer with my people." He nodded to Aisling, Bart, and Neasa, and then vanished.

Calik was shaking but lifted his voice into a loud roar. The rest of the council did as well, but Neasa noticeably didn't. She did step closer to Aisling and Bart. "Stay with me, I will try to protect you."

"From what?" Bart asked in-between the roars of the dryads.

Neasa looked at the door then grabbed both Aisling and Bart. "It would be better if we were out of the way." She brought them to a corner and pulled them close as more furious looking dryads came racing in.

"Are the vallenians attacking?" Aisling was still sorting out who was on which side and what had set the dryads off.

"No, they don't fight." Neasa looked terrified. "They don't need to; they will send others to deal with this. The ghanlough might have crossed under the veil, but they are still here also. They were held by my people for thousands of years. That they are out now doesn't bode well." She nodded solemnly. "Stay behind me and I will keep you safe until they rend me apart. Remember me." Her tragic face clearly showed that she might be thousands of years old, but she was still young for one of her kind.

"Now, you've been helping us out, the least we can do is help you." Bart sounded like a kindly old grandfather as he patted Neasa's arm. "Besides, we're protected by these, right?" He held up his pendant. Unlike Aisling's, his started out with five or six different lines of color. Then again, it hadn't had to fight through the veil.

Neasa nodded slowly. "But you have to be careful, your magic might act differently here."

"I thought you said it *would*?" Aisling was trying to stay calm. If these unforgiven, ghanlough, whichever term, were coming to fight, she had no idea what she, Bart, or Neasa could do against them.

"It would…but I'm not sure what the ghau pendants will do. They could protect you."

More dryads armed for war came in. "It's not the ghanlough who are coming. The alari are coming." One of the larger newcomers yelled as they raced in.

"Oh. That's…maybe better?" Neasa forced a smile.

Aisling figured that wasn't really an improvement. Plus, she had no idea who the alari were. She looked over to Bart, but the tightening of his face in terror indicated that he did know. And it wasn't a good thing.

"I need you to help us understand what we're facing." Aisling might have felt foolish at one point talking to a pendant, but not after the past few months. She had to raise her voice as a windstorm raced through the place. The pendant felt warmer, which she hoped was good. She reached over to Bart and shook him out of his shock. "Talk to your pendant—make it a part of you."

He blinked a few times, then reached down to his ghau pendant. His mouth was moving but the words were lost as the windstorm increased.

Neasa was still trying to protect them, but by spreading her arms around them she ran the risk of being torn apart by the wind. "You need to curl up, drop low and curl your arms and legs around yourself." Aisling was yelling at the top of her lungs now.

Neasa shook her head. "I will die protecting you."

Aisling spun as one of the wind tunnels slowed down. A wind dervish, that's what the alari were. They would make perfect opponents for dryads, as trees would be terrified of the wind. When they got out of this, she was having a serious talk with the vallenians.

The alari looked almost like a shorter elf and was a sub-category of elven fey. One far too destructive to have made the crossing through the veil when the rest of the fey fled. The one in front of them paused and tilted its head at Aisling. "Out of way."

"Not happening. Go away." She stepped further in front of Neasa when the alari made a sudden move.

"You not want. They pay."

"She wasn't involved." Aisling dove for the alari and pushed it out of the wind tunnel. With one hand on her pendant and one on its slender arm, she focused on unhealing magic. Unlike her prior attempt at magic on this side of the veil, this time it worked too well.

The alari screamed, then exploded.

Bart had been watching the dervishes while clutching his pendant. He dropped it now, and stepped closer to Neasa.

The fighting around them stopped.

Aisling raised her voice and added a haughty snarl. "I am the daughter of the last prince of this realm. He who should have been king. You will not fight in my presence." She held her head high and channeled not her father, but her mother. The dryad council failed their duties, but she didn't think all of them should pay because the vallenians were too lazy to sort it out.

Not to mention she really wanted to go home. "You saw what I did, *on this side of the veil*. I can destroy all of you."

The alari stopped their winds, bowed as one, then vanished. The dryads had mostly all been injured, including Calik, but a younger one stepped forward.

"Thank you. Most of the council had no idea what had happened. The ones who were aware shall be dealt with." He bowed low. "Hail Queen Aisling!" The cheer went through all the dryads and a chill went down her back.

"As long as this gets us home, go with it," Bart whispered as he stepped next to her. He'd lost some of his terror about the alari, but still looked shaky.

Aisling nodded her head. "My friend and I must leave. You must treat Neasa as you would me, as she will be in my stead."

Neasa's eyes went impossibly wide. "If it pleases the council, I will get them through the veil. They need to return home." She didn't seem to know what to make of the looks coming her way. But at a nod from the younger council member, she spun both Bart and Aisling away from the council building.

"You could stay and rule us, you saved my people." Neasa kept her voice low as she hurried them down the path.

"We have our own home that we need to get back to. What will happen when the vallenians realize that I stopped the fight? They won't send those alari after you again, will they?"

"I don't know. No one has ever stood against the alari and won." She sounded stunned. "The vallenians will probably find you."

"Good, I have more than a few things I want to discuss with them."

They continued in silence until they reached the edge of the forest.

"This isn't where either of us came through." The forest opened to a meadow. "Are those buildings?" Broken and familiar looking pieces of a building stuck roughly out of the ground.

Sections of the lost Area 42 of Los Angeles.

"Yes. Crossing is hard for most beings, but when these

came through, they left a trail out. They weakened the veil badly."

"I don't think we can ride them back to our side of the veil." Bart had been silent but seemed to have recovered from his fear of the alari.

"I agree," Aisling said. "Those building pieces don't land well. Not to mention neither of us fly."

"You won't need to. I can open the veil for just you two—the pieces out there simply mark where the veil is thinnest—they can no longer move. You should end up close to where you left." She frowned. "Sort of. Stay safe and I look forward to your return, Queen Aisling." She bowed.

"I'm not a queen, nor will I be back."

"You will be. And you will be back." Neasa gave them both a soft smile and suddenly the world spun around them.

The time she'd been thrown through the veil from her home side had been brief and painful. This time it felt like she was floating through clouds. Bart tumbled alongside her with his eyes closed and a steady stream of swearing coming from his lips.

It seemed to take a while and still nothing but clouds. Then they cleared. They were in the air above the London countryside and coming down hard.

CHAPTER FOUR

REECE SWORE AS he looked around the dug-up dirt pits. They were clearly created by someone. Something had dug up the ground in this field recently for a reason. It looked like massive trees had run through the ground, tearing things up with their roots.

Stella was certain this patch of dirt was somehow related to Aisling and Bart coming back. She'd been almost frantic as she dragged them all out to the countryside that morning.

That all of them were still here three hours later, and no one had found anything, didn't help his temper.

"I know I felt them here." Stella scowled at the dirt. "There's nothing else here and this was where I felt they would be." She gave the ground an angry stomp. Being a petite changeling who looked like your favorite auntie didn't really go with the foot stomp.

Harlie nodded. "I felt it too. They will be here."

"How long do we wait?" Maeve wasn't used to this waiting business, and it showed. Her satisfaction at having killed Nix, the real one this time, vanished when they realized Aisling had been taken. Reece was keeping an eye on her—he was scared and pissed, but she could fly off the handle if pushed too far.

"I think they are right…here." Harlie looked up as two small rocks descended upon them. He reached out and grabbed them, only to laugh and gently place both on the grass in front of him. "Oh, my, that's an impressive spell. Step back everyone." He waved to the others as the rocks grew and changed into Aisling and Bart. They were standing as they changed, then both collapsed.

Reece ran and grabbed Aisling and Jones ran to Bart. The rest stayed between them.

"Was that the spell I think it was?" Stella grinned at Harlie as she patted Bart's hand.

He nodded. "A transformative relocation spell. Tricky magic and something only theorized to exist."

"How did they…what did they?" Maeve shook her head and looked toward Caradoc.

He shrugged. "Don't ask me, weird magic isn't my strong point."

"It's also known as a lieran spell. Certain classes of dryads could create them in the old world. They could go wherever they wanted by shrinking and transforming, and using their own magic to travel through air tunnels." Stella looked around and shrugged. "That's about all I know, so don't look at me for answers. Someone on the other side of the veil sent them back."

<hr>

Aisling heard her friends' words and felt someone holding her, but opening her eyes was too difficult. She'd heard what Stella said about the spell Neasa had used and she was going to suggest no one try it. She had no idea how Nix had come back, but this landing felt like having your brain squished into a tiny sewing thimble. Speaking was even harder than opening her eyes.

"Aisling? Please, talk to me?" Reece's voice was in her ear, she wasn't surprised that he was the one holding her. He sounded more freaked-out-relieved than she'd ever heard him.

"Hello?" She forced her eyes open.

Reece gave her a powerful kiss—one she appreciated and responded to. He finally broke it off but continued to hold her.

"Is Bart okay?" She tried to see him, but everyone was in the way.

"I'm fine, have a whopper of a headache though. You?"

"Same here." She wasn't surprised to see concern on the faces around her—but they were far more concerned than they should be if she and Bart had only been gone a few hours. "How did you know where to find us, what's with all the dirt, and how long have we been gone?" She stayed seated in case she didn't like the answers. Besides, it felt good to lean on Reece.

"Stella knew, long story, she can explain it to you." Maeve held her right hand and didn't look willing to let go. Considering that Reece had a similar grasp on her left hand and looked the same, things could be difficult when she decided to get up.

"The dirt was churned up to save you if we didn't make it here in time." Harlie's eyes looked like he'd been crying but his smile was huge. "We didn't do it though. I think it was magic from the other side of the veil."

"You've been gone for a month," Reece said softly. His gray eyes held emotion and pain.

"What?" Bart yelled.

"That can't be right, we were gone less than a day. Felt longer, but I'm pretty sure that we would have slept had it been a month. Neither of us slept." Aisling wasn't sure how else to prove it, but their time had been hours, not days.

"It was a full month. Almost to the day." Caradoc had been standing but dropped down to sit in the dirt. "My baby sister. Fights off monsters, defeats our mother, then gets shoved through the veil." His light blue eyes were bright with unshed tears. "I thought I'd lost you, sister mine."

Reece moved back as Caradoc dove in to hug her.

"Not this time, brother mine." Aisling fought her own tears, then gave up. She knew how she'd feel if any of these people had been missing for a month. "Wait, how'd you know we were beyond the veil?"

"Didn't know about Bart, we found out he was missing when we called for backup after you vanished." Jones looked uncommonly happy to see them both, he even had a small smile. He still looked like what he was—a highly trained assassin-secret-agent. But the smile softened things a bit.

"As for you, we were conscious although paralyzed during the attack. We saw those skeletal things run in and one shove you through that window." Caradoc pointed to Harlie. "He traced what happened, but we couldn't find a way in. The passageway shut completely once you went through. Mother is still missing, and hopefully dead, and the city of London is pretty much back to normal."

"In a month?" Bart got to his feet without help, and dusted himself off.

"Yup. It's London, they bounced back in a few days." Maeve had a lot of pride in her voice. A born Londoner, she obviously wouldn't have expected anything else. Never mind that Nix had frozen the entire city in goo and then let monsters loose to feed on the population. It would take more than that to keep them down.

Reece had been watching Aisling closely, but he finally turned to Bart. "Area 42 was going to declare you missing-in-action-at-risk in a day. Good thing you came back now."

"What? They have no right to do that." Bart started stomping around, pulled his cell phone out, swore at it, and looked around. "Jones, let me use your phone. Mine's dead."

"You were gone a month. Your phone batteries knew

even if you didn't." Harlie nodded. "Dailten is back at the London Area 42 office yelling at them about it."

Bart tilted his head away from the phone he was holding. "She's not Area 42 at all."

"And you think that would stop her?" Stella laughed. "My lad, you have some learning to do about harpies. She can't fly yet, wing still has some holes in it thanks to Nix, but she made sure her wings, and those lovely sharp points on them, were out when she went down there."

Dailten was a full harpy, a precog, and a friend of Harlie's. She was also possibly more stubborn than Bart, in Aisling's opinion. Might be what was needed now. Area 42 was a super-secret organization in place to take care of crimes the rest of the world shouldn't see. But they'd also been infiltrated by Nix's people. Bart, Jones, and Reece were all technically Area 42 agents, but were currently keeping their distance.

Bart shook his head and went back to stabbing numbers into his borrowed phone. Then he stomped off across the tossed earth. And started yelling a moment later, which defeated the entire bit of walking away.

"Are you okay to get up?" Reece got to his feet along with Maeve and the two pulled her up when she nodded.

"I can't believe we were gone a month. I'll need to fill you all in about what happened over there, but I'd rather not do it outside. Where have you been staying?" She had no idea where they were, beyond not being in London proper. She swayed and both Reece and Maeve grabbed her. "I'm fine. Just recalled our landing. We were flying, or rather falling, through the clouds. Just threw me off."

"We've rented rooms in a small town not far from here, Flian. It has one of the best fey universities in the world." Maeve said. "And the university has a massive library of veil tectonics. They know us all on sight now." She grinned. She wasn't a massive research person, but clearly even she'd joined in. She continued to look like she might hug Aisling again at any moment.

Bart stomped back to them as they headed toward a group of cars. "They need to verify that I'm really myself. Even with all my passcodes. That's *why* we have passcodes."

"You *were* gone for a month," Reece said. "You're lucky they didn't declare you dead."

Bart shivered. "That would have been much worse. Funny thing though, I'm feeling exhausted. They said they'll wait until tomorrow. I think food and rest are on the agenda at this point. And you filling us in."

Caradoc leaned over toward him as they walked. "Is that a ghau pendant? It looks too small to be Aisling's."

"It's not hers." Bart stuffed it under his shirt. "I now have one. No idea on the size difference, nor why they stuck it on me. And I don't want to talk about it." An exhausted and annoyed Bart wasn't someone to be messed with. Caradoc nodded and stopped trying to peek at it.

They sorted themselves out and got to the cars. Aisling was beginning to feel even more drained than when they arrived, but she knew they needed to know about what was happening on the other side of the veil. Nix might be dead, her mother missing, but there was still plenty of danger. And a lot of weirdness. She wasn't sure about how to deal with her father's status—or rather—former status. That could wait.

"Okay, so what was it like? The other side." Maeve drove the car Aisling and Reece were in, and Caradoc looked back from the front seat.

Aisling shook her head. "Nope, not explaining things multiple times, you just need to wait. So, no signs of *her*?"

Caradoc's grin fell. "Aside from testing that the blood left behind was hers, nope. Our father came out here, stayed for the first week of searching, then went back to

California. I don't think any of our siblings even made that much effort."

"Probably busy fighting over who gets to take her place," Aisling said. She loved Caradoc and Harlie, but didn't really know well, nor care, about the rest of their brothers and sisters. The ten of them were hundreds of years old, and had spent their entire lives being clones of their mother. If Aisling never saw any of them again, she'd be fine.

"You're fading." Reece held her up before she noticed that she'd been leaning on him.

"I have a feeling that my body might be catching up on the entire being awake for a month. I'm also ravenous."

Reece's phone rang before he could respond to her. He laughed at the caller's comment. "Aisling was just saying the same." He looked up. "Everyone want Italian-Chinese-Mexican? Jones can swing by and get food on the way in." He grinned at Aisling's response. "Trust us, it's an odd combination, but they make good food."

"All I care is that there's a lot of it. And tea, strong tea. I have a lot to tell you all and the sooner the better." She covered her mouth as an enormous yawn hit her.

Reece responded on the phone then hung up. He looked into her eyes as Maeve and Caradoc bickered about which way back was the shortest. "I thought I lost you." There was a lot of emotion behind his gray eyes.

Normally Aisling avoided looking directly into them. They had determined that he wasn't exhibiting siren traits, but his eyes had always had an odd effect on her. Even when she hadn't liked him.

"It was only a day for me, but I can imagine how it felt for you."

"Now, you'll love this place we found. We have a full apartment floor with multiple rooms, huge living area, the works." Caradoc said at the perfectly wrong moment.

Aisling laughed at the timing. "Sounds wonderful." She sighed.

"You are sometimes a jerk, my friend." Reece laughed.

"Oops, sorry." The tone of Caradoc's voice said he wasn't. He and Reece had a history of irritating each other—mostly Caradoc annoying Reece. It started when Caradoc had snuck into Reece's car during a car chase and gun battle and had continued from there.

The driveway they turned into was posh with a fair amount of green around it. Aisling had been busy dealing with Reece and missed the drive in, but Flian looked like a nice village from what she could tell. They drove around the back to a carpark and everyone got out.

"What was this originally?" She'd seen an elaborate hotel sign out front but it didn't look like any hotel she'd ever seen.

"It was a manor house. Owners fell on hard times, sold it, and now it's an exclusive hotel." Harlie answered as he and the others got out of the second car. "All expenses paid by a certain rich tech guy." He nodded to Caradoc.

"Money needs to be spent. And Area 42 was going to dump us in a hovel. Mark my words, I'm never helping them out again." Caradoc casually dropped his arm around Maeve's shoulders as they walked up to the building.

That was definitely something she would be grilling Maeve about. Aisling knew they had mutual crushes, but for a pair of extroverts, they'd taken a long time to do something about it.

The place was possibly more elegant now than it would have been in its manor house days. Aisling looked at her torn and grimy clothing as they walked in, then shrugged. She was too tired to worry about it.

The man at the reception desk smiled as Caradoc and Maeve walked by, then looked confused at Aisling and Bart. But the smile only wavered a little once he realized they were all together. They probably could have been wearing togas as long as Caradoc and his money were with them.

That was another interesting change in the last month. Caradoc never denied he was rich. Unlike their siblings, his money was all earned on his own, not given to him by their mother. But she'd never seen him flaunt it like this. Not that she was going to complain. This could be a nice lifestyle.

The stairway was broad and so thickly carpeted that she could probably fall asleep right on the stairs and been more comfortable than in her prior apartment's bed. A wide double door was on the first landing to the left. Caradoc waved his key card at the sensor and both doors opened.

"You found them!" Mott Flowers came running down the entrance corridor like a small child who'd been left with the babysitter for too long. He hugged Aisling and then Bart. Although Bart looked confused by it, he still patted him on the back.

Mott was an elf; he'd even gone to primary school with Aisling and had worked with Caradoc. He was shorter than Aisling and looked more like one of Bart's gnome relatives than a pure elf. He was also terrifyingly smart. He scowled at Aisling after he hugged her. "Things have changed. The veil changed you."

Aisling narrowed her eyes. That was more a Harlie or Dailten thing, or even Stella. While Mott was genius level smart, he wasn't into the mystical side of things.

He grinned. "Kidding. I have no idea, but we are so glad you're both back." He peered at Bart. "Did you get a necklace too?"

Bart swore as he shoved the pendant back into his shirt. "Yes, but I think that can wait until we tell the entire story. Is this everyone?"

Jones and a mountain of to-go bags followed them in.

If the smells were an indication, that food was wonderful.

"Well, it will be once you all come inside proper." Dailten stuck her head into the entranceway hall from a larger room. Harpies were often cranky, but for the most part she was an exception to that. But something had gotten her upset this time. As they came in, Aisling noticed that Dailten's smaller feathers up near the base of her neck were raised. Her massive gray wings were folded behind her and tucked into the special jacket she wore, but those smaller feathers were a good indication of her mood—and it wasn't good. She quickly hugged Aisling and gave Bart a pat on the head.

"Sorry. It's not your fault that you work for complete idiots who couldn't find their arses with both hands, a guide map, and a full searching spell." Dailten snorted and marched to a large chair and pointed to the broad table. "Everyone grab some of that food Jones brought in, then we need to hear about what happened." She paused and tilted her head at Bart, her sharp blue eyes narrowing. "I assume they stopped trying to declare you dead?"

Bart nodded as he went to the spread of food on the massive dining table. "I was able to get a delay until tomorrow. My passcodes weren't good enough to stop it completely. I take it they refused to listen to you?"

"They threatened to throw me out. It was only when I pointed out that I had helped save London, and probably the rest of the world, that they backed down." Dailten picked at some grapes near her chair. "It's an odd thing, those Area 42 people. They seem to feel that the threat is gone and everything can go back to normal—yet they were clearly in a high-threat-watch status. Something bad is going on, and they don't want anyone to know."

CHAPTER FIVE

———◆———

"AGREED, I CAN feel it." Stella put together a pair of plates from the mass of to-go boxes and chased Aisling and Bart into reclining chairs. "But first, we'd better get some food into these two. They have been on the other side of the veil this entire time."

Dailten's eyes went wide. "A month? Oh my."

Harlie nodded. "We'll have to watch them carefully. Bart, when you go to your people tomorrow, take one of us three along. Just in case there are any aftereffects." He motioned to himself, Stella, and Dailten. They were all various levels of precogs.

Aisling didn't like the look in any of their eyes. Those three were the mystic side of this odd team. There was no way that them freaking out about her and Bart being gone this long was a good thing. "It was a *day* on the other side. Not even a full day." She held up her empty plate. "Could I get some more food before we start talking about it though?" She was ravenous and, looking at Bart almost licking his plate, he obviously felt the same.

"It's the delay, the time bubble that functions between here and the other side. It's good in that it indicates the veil is still functioning." Harlie brought them more food and tea but stayed close to Aisling, peering at her as she ate. "The ghau pendants probably helped you two avoid the worst of it. But basically, you're catching up on a month of hunger and lack of sleep."

Caradoc nodded. "What he said. Probably better to tell us what happened soon, before you both collapse. Tea can only do so much."

Aisling finished another plate, then nodded. She quickly told them about arriving on the other side, her lack of magic initially, and finding Bart. Together they told them about Neasa and the rest. Except the bit about her father. He was Harlie's and Caradoc's father too and she wanted to tell them in private. At least at first. Most likely their father's status would play into whatever mess was still going on, so she'd have to tell the others soon enough. But first family needed to deal with it.

Reece and Jones watched Bart and Aisling during the various parts of their story.

"I'd say there are parts missing." Jones frowned. "And that's something Area 42 isn't going to like. If I can tell, so will they." He held up a hand before Bart could protest. "Not saying they need to know everything. They've been completely useless trying to find you two, aside from taking credit for stopping Nix. But you might want to see if some of our magic users can do something before you meet with Area 42 tomorrow."

Reece brought Aisling another plate of food and nodded. "Might be a good idea. Whatever was wrong with the agency before is still present. There are moves of personnel all over the place as more of Nix's plants were discovered."

"There are things we need to talk to individuals about first." Bart shared a look with Aisling. "The rest of you will know soon enough. But you are correct about Area 42. I have a feeling that's the real reason they didn't accept my passcodes. They want to screen me." He pulled out his ghau pendant and held it toward Harlie. "Making it invisible would probably just trigger more questions, but could you make it less noticeable and mask whatever power it has?"

Aisling held up her necklace as well. "Might as well do mine again, too. I'm not one of their agents, so I shouldn't be called in, but better to be safe."

"And you not being one won't stop them from questioning you," Bart said as Reece and Jones shared a look.

Reece spoke. "If it wasn't that Bart was being declared missing-in-action-at-risk, I'd say we get the hell out of here until we figure out what's going on with the veil. And with Area 42. But we can't afford to have them after us about Bart."

Aisling wasn't the only one looking at him in surprise. Stella came over to Reece and reached around him for a hug. "I knew there was a rebel in there somewhere."

"I agree. And that's even rarer than Reece going off— him being up for going against Area 42." Jones had been pacing but stopped and turned to Aisling and her brothers. "The at-risk part means that they officially assume that the real Bart is dead and therefore any sighting of Bart will be considered a copy and should be taken or killed on sight." He shrugged at Bart. "That's what you get for being so high up the ladder."

"There is a lot going on, none of it good." Reese turned to the rest of the room. "Normally it would take at least three months to declare an agent missing-in-action-at-risk."

Harlie had gone to Bart and was peering carefully at his ghau pendant. "We'll have to sort it out when they aren't suspicious of you, but your pendant is different from Aisling's in more than size." He spoke a spell and the pendant changed to a round disk. "A simple, non-denominational, fey charm. I thought it best that you and Aisling don't have the same pendant. I've also put a look away spell on it, so even if someone wants to look at it closer, they won't feel comfortable doing so." He grinned and released the pendant.

Aisling held out hers, but he stopped when he got a good look. "It changed again. I didn't notice before, but there are far more lines."

"I didn't notice, but we were running for our lives a few times." Aisling tried to look down but Harlie's head was in the way. "Can you hide it for now again?" She wasn't sure what the original lines had been for, let alone what new ones meant. However, now that the food was hitting her system, she was fading fast. The caffeine from the tea wasn't even putting up a fight.

Bart was fighting harder than her, but he was blinking longer and seemed to be leaning in his chair.

"Yes, yes, but…no, you're right." Harlie started leaning sideways, then Aisling realized it was her sliding, not him.

Maeve grabbed her and pushed her back in the chair. "I think she's done."

Aisling's yawn took over any words she might have wanted to say. They were right, like the food, her missing sleep for the past month was hitting her hard.

"The pendant is disguised, let's put them both to sleep." Harlie's voice was the last she heard before well-muscled arms picked her up. She recognized Reece's scent as she leaned against his chest while he carried her, but couldn't wake up enough to say anything.

The next thing she knew, she woke up in a long nightgown in a strange bed. For a moment she feared they hadn't gotten out of the other side of the veil. Then the events came back to her. She sat up as sunshine peeked in through the drawn curtains and tried to figure out where the weird nightgown came from.

There was a soft knock at the door, followed by Maeve's

head. She grinned at the nightgown. "Sorry about that, that's a guest nightgown they offer for sale here. We have your things right over there, but Harlie felt it would be rude to dig through them. I changed you, by the way. And don't think I won't tell your brothers about those scars. They appear to be healing, but there are a lot." She folded her arms and gave her best, 'don't mess with me,' look.

"They're from that thing shoving me through the glass and the veil. I couldn't heal myself at first. But I promise to tell them." She swung her feet out of bed and went to her luggage sitting near the closet. "More important right now, is what's up with you and Caradoc? Bonding over me being missing?" Best way to distract Maeve was to threaten to expose something.

Maeve's dark skin always turned a lovely deep rose when embarrassed. Which didn't happen often—she was in full rose as she answered. "Sort of. I mean, I think he's attractive, funny, smart…it's hard to find fault."

Aisling laughed as she went into the bathroom to shower and change. "Oh, I could give you a list, but it's more fun for you to find out on your own."

"It's not going to be weird, is it?" Maeve called out from the bedroom. "I mean me shacking up with your brother?"

Aisling was enjoying the hot shower. "Are you planning on breaking his heart?"

"Of course not!" Her British accent came out loudly on the last word.

"Then I'm fine. Besides, I won't have to worry about what weirdo you'll be dating—it'll be one I already know."

"Okay, then. I did have a bit of a worry about how you'd feel—jokes about your mother as an in-law aside— we hadn't seriously talked about it."

Aisling would have stayed in the shower longer, but

there was a lot to catch up on. She came out of the bathroom changed and towel drying her hair. "I was serious about it. I think you two make a great couple. You won't put up with any of his shit. A lot of women can't look past his persona or his wealth."

Maeve dropped onto the corner of the bed. "For me that wealth was almost a deal breaker. I made jokes about him buying that fancy plane in London, but the fact is, I've never trusted the rich."

"Which is why you're good for him. He needs people who know he's rich and don't care."

"I hope so. Reece became a bulldog while you were gone, by the way. That bit about him willing to jump the Area 42 ship? He's been that way since the second day you were gone. Of course, it didn't help that his beloved agency blew him and Jones off and wouldn't help find you. You were, quote, 'collateral damage lost during a hostile attack'."

"That probably would have been different if they knew Bart was on the other side of the veil as well, but only because they wouldn't want to look bad." Aisling shook her head. "I think you and I lucked out that Area 42 didn't decide to recruit us, even without body snatching copies, they're not good." She paused. "Reece's okay though, right? It's odd, when we first got back, I seriously thought it had been a day for both sides, and was surprised you were able to get out of London and set up that fast. But now, like food and sleeping, I'm feeling the time." She didn't want to say it, not even to Maeve. But when Reece had been carrying her last night, he felt like Reece, smelled like Reece, but at the same time he felt like a stranger. Even a month separated shouldn't have done that.

Nix had come back a changed man in more ways than one when he went through the veil. Had she changed somehow as well?

"He was a bit hysterical about you being taken, I'm not going to lie. He went aggressive on anyone he could find who should be helping. No one could help us. Then Harlie, Stella, and Dailten started calling in their sources. They pinpointed this location and we've been here a week waiting."

"Okay, let's go face the troops. I have a bad feeling we're not done with the mess Nix and my mother left behind." Aisling also needed to pull her brothers aside and tell them about their father.

Everyone was gathered at the table eating.

"Did you save some for me? I'm still catching up on a lot of missed meals." She noticed Bart had mountains of food around him.

Reece pulled out two chairs. "What would you ladies like?"

Maeve immediately filled two cups with black tea. "Toast and eggs, please."

Aisling looked at the buffet. "I'll have whatever Bart's having, please." She turned to where Harlie, Stella, and Dailten were locked in a whispered debate. "Any updates?"

Harlie looked up blinking. "Some? Maybe? A strong perhaps."

"Did you go to sleep last night?" She noticed that all three looked out of sorts, and while she wasn't entirely certain, as last night was foggy, they seemed to be wearing the same clothes.

"They didn't," Caradoc said as he and Reece brought over food. "At least not what I heard. But they said they'd tell us all once you were up and fed."

Bart slowed down his eating, took a long drink of his tea, and nodded. "And Area 42 canceled my appointment for today. Well, rescheduled it for tomorrow. I'll be going down there today anyway." He smiled at the three huddled together. "With an escort or two."

Jones was working on a pile of toast and what looked like a pot of black coffee. "I think I should go with you also. Just in case there's something beyond the mystical to deal with." Tall, slender, with short dark hair and an angular face, Jones always looked like a trained assassin. Especially if his skills might be needed.

Bart looked ready to argue, then shrugged. "Might be good to have a non-presumed-dead Area 42 agent along. The rest of you staying put?"

"I am. Still feeling out of sorts." Aisling looked briefly at Caradoc and Harlie—hopefully they'd get the hint. She wasn't trying to keep their father's situation from everyone, just until she spoke to them.

"I believe I will. Stella and Dailten make a more impressive impact than me. I want to keep checking Aisling for residue as well." Harlie turned to Bart. "I'll check you before and after your trip, if you don't mind." His tone said there wasn't much of a choice.

"I think anyone not going to London should stay in today, people probably noticed us out in that dirt." Caradoc smiled. "Besides, Mott has some new toys to show me. He just got here from L.A. yesterday and was helping us pin your location."

The rest of the breakfast continued quietly.

Reece kept watching her.

"Did I grow another head while I was over there?"

He leaned back with a laugh. "Sorry, staring is rude." He glanced around the table. "I really thought we'd lost you. Even went so far as to try to look for ways to cross the veil." His smile dropped.

"We stopped him," Maeve said as she broke away from a conversation with Caradoc and Mott. "It was close for a while though." The way her light eyes narrowed as she looked at Reece pointed out she still thought of him as a flight risk.

Aisling needed to talk to Maeve about him further. She hadn't mentioned this when they'd chatted before.

"No one should go to the other side. *No matter what.* I still feel off and have no idea when that will go away. Nix was changed when he came back. We have no idea of the lasting impact on Bart or me due to our time there. Promise me that you won't go through. Ever." Reece was already an aberration—he was a human-fey mixed breed with fey powers—something supposedly impossible. All hybrids were magicless—or so they'd always been told. The High Council would lock him up in a heartbeat as he was. They'd done it before, but always denied the existence of the person, and often their family members as well. And if the veil changed his powers? Not going to be good.

Reece tried to flash his charming grin, but Aisling folded her arms and glared. "I'm serious."

He raised his hands. "I promise not to cross the veil unless you are with me. How's that?"

Since there was no way in hell she was ever crossing over again, she nodded. Then turned to everyone else. "I want all of you to promise not to go through. There're some weird things going on there that we need to stay out of." Then she and Bart filled them in on the ghanlough and the Isfyden realm. Somehow, most likely fatigue, neither had brought them up the previous night.

Harlie, Dailten, and Stella hung on every word and scribbled notes.

"I was intrigued when you said the dryads were still alive, but not shocked. But this…" Harlie looked ecstatic as he nodded. "The unforgiven, ghanlough in the old tongue…yes, those things were both in the locked down London and back in that place where they attacked you. They fit the description."

Dailten scowled. "But the Isfyden realm isn't supposed to be accessible to anywhere else. Someone opened it."

"Nix? Damn it, can we resurrect him so I can kill him a few more times?" Maeve had a bad history of dealing with the late elven gangster when she still worked for the British government—it got worse when he tried to destroy Los Angeles, then her beloved London.

"It could have been him, or other forces behind him, right now there's no way to be certain," Stella said.

Reece nodded. "Nix was a bastard, but he wasn't smart enough to pull off half of what he did."

The conversations broke down and Stella, Dailten, and Jones escorted Bart out of the apartment to go antagonize the London Area 42 office. Mott dropped into one of his projects and wandered down the hall to his own room.

"I need to speak to my brothers, if you two don't mind." She figured that Maeve and Reece would be the first to hear the news after she told Harlie and Caradoc—but even with those two, she wanted her brothers to know first.

Both nodded.

"No worries. Believe it or not, I have research to do." Maeve patted a pile of books. "You two are back, but I don't think we can afford to ignore the veil anymore."

"Myself as well. Harlie turned us all into researchers." Reece's smile almost reached his eyes. He was still clearly worried about her.

She didn't blame him. Thinking of how she'd feel after a month of him being lost, she knew she'd be doing the same.

Harlie and Caradoc shrugged and got up to follow her. She held the door for both.

Aisling shut the bedroom door and slowly turned. Harlie looked curious; Caradoc looked suspicious. "I found out some information on the other side of the veil—about our family." She had gone over what had been said about their mother the previous night. Now was the fun part.

She had to repeat the information twice as Caradoc just stared at her blankly the first time.

Harlie, however, looked thoughtful. "That would explain a few things from when I was an only child. The dynamics between our parents were vastly different. From what I recall of the story of the lost prince, our father would have only been ten or eleven when his parents were killed. If the other fey took his memories of who he was, our mother might not have known any more than he did."

Aisling nodded. "That was my thought as well; not his age, I didn't know that, but that our mother married a prince and didn't take advantage of it? Not in this lifetime." She waited for any sort of twinge concerning the missing and presumed dead status of her mother. Nope. After what she'd done to Aisling, to the humans of this world, and the fey left on the other side of the veil—she didn't deserve consideration.

Caradoc grinned and leaned forward. "So, they called you Queen Aisling, eh? You told them you had stunning older brothers, yes?"

"I did. I also pointed out that if the royal line had ended with our grandparents, then none of us were royals. I wanted to tell you both before we told the others." She tilted her head as Harlie was furiously writing.

"Yes, they should know. It could be important later. I think after this I need to go to the university library. They have some amazing ancient history books." Harlie looked ready to jump to his feet and run there immediately.

Clearly, the admonishment to stay inside the apartment today only held when there wasn't information needed.

Caradoc put a hand on his shoulder. "Easy there. You might want to shower and change before you charge over."

Harlie gave a look at his crumpled clothing. "Ah,

probably a good idea." He stood and bowed to Aisling. "If thine Majesty will excuse me."

"Funny. I expected that from Caradoc, not you."

"Eh, he beat me to it. I hate repeating gags." Caradoc paused as Harlie opened the door and left the room. "But Maeve and I might go with him, we have our own projects, and the return of the missing royal sister doesn't change that things are going seriously into the crapper."

Aisling followed him out. Reece had printouts and books piled around him and looked up at Maeve, Caradoc, and Harlie. "You're all going? I can stay and keep an eye on Aisling, Mott, and the place." He kept his voice light but there was tension in his face as he looked to Aisling.

Harlie, Caradoc, and Maeve bundled their things and headed for the door. Maeve gave her a supportive smile as she shut the front doors behind them.

"Is everything okay? You and your brothers have a secret conversation and they run off." Reece leaned back in his seat.

"I think they were trying to give us some alone time, which had nothing to do with what I told them." She sat down at the table next to him and filled him in on the family secret.

He gave a low whistle. "That's wild. So, what now? Can they reinstate your father?"

"From what it sounded like on the other side, no. Not that it stopped them from going against that and calling me Queen Aisling." She saw the smirk on his face and grabbed his hand. "No. That is not something anyone should call me. Not unless they want to see what new magic tricks I can do."

"I promise. I'll be good. But there's something else, too."

Aisling sighed. There wasn't going to be an easy way to say this, and she'd hoped to hold off for a few days in case the issue went away on its own. But better now instead of trying to dodge the others to let him know. She gave a quick glance down the hall to Mott's room; door still shut.

"You know I care about you. A lot. I love you." She squeezed his hand at the wary look on his face. "I still do, trust me. But everything feels off. My relationships with everyone all feel distant, removed. It's less noticeable with my brothers than with the rest, but it's still there. You're all the people I know, but at the same time, you're not."

He watched her for a few moments in silence, then nodded. "I didn't want to say anything, but you feel different too. I wouldn't say distant, but something has changed. You might need to ask the others as well." He rubbed her hand with his thumb. "Most likely it's just some weird aftereffect from going through the veil. Twice. I'm sure it'll go back to normal soon."

"Thank you. I wasn't sure how to tell you. I—" Her words were cut off by frantic pounding on the front door. This apartment was large, but she and Reece were at the front door immediately.

Reece peered through the peep hole but swore and shook his head. He drew his gun as Aisling called a spell and stepped behind the door.

He nodded and cracked open the door. He had his foot keeping it in place, but quickly stepped back and motioned for Aisling to drop her spell.

Surratt and Garran, both of whom should be running one of Los Angeles' largest police stations, strode into the entryway.

Garran looked down the hall to the living area. "We have to find Aisling and Bart. Things are getting ugly."

CHAPTER SIX

———◆———

"YOU CAME ALL the way here from Los Angeles to find me?" Aisling hadn't come out far from behind the door as they'd passed into the apartment. Nor had she completely released her spell. There had been people copied before, and these two shouldn't be in the UK.

Surratt was tall with neat dark hair and a beard trimmed so perfectly it would make angels weep. He also looked human, but was actually a changeling like Stella—something few people knew. He had been her boss back in L.A. Then he'd had to go into hiding when someone tried to have him killed and almost succeeded. Garran had been her coworker and semi-boss, when she and Maeve weren't being sidelined anyway. Then Bart came along and snagged both out from under him. Technically, Aisling and Maeve weren't Area 42, but nor were they LAPD at the moment.

It was complicated.

"Aisling?" Garran spun around and scooped her up in a hug, spell and all. "They didn't tell us they found you." His smile dipped as he set her back on her feet. "You're different."

Garran was an old fey, one who had some sort of mixed fey heritage but wasn't going to discuss it. He was tall and solid with a mostly shaved head and huge sharply pointed ears.

"It's a very long story and yes, I was across the veil." She saw the question on both men's faces as Reece closed and locked the door.

"Bart is back also, but currently on his way to London to stalk Area 42." Reece motioned for everyone to go to the front room. "They tried to have him declared missing-in-action-at-risk. After only one month. Which they claimed was due to his stature within the organization."

Garran snorted his opinion of that as he came into the room. "I'm sure nothing to do with him being internal affairs and them wanting a chance to take him out." He rubbed his forehead. "No offense, Larkin, but those Area 42 people are messed up and a big reason we're out here."

Surratt stayed at the entrance to the living room, but kept watching Aisling. "Good to see that you're back." As usual, figuring out what was going on in his head was impossible.

"You look healthy." She didn't step closer to him either. He'd played off his injuries before, even going so far as to let Aisling think she'd watched him die in the hospital. She still hadn't completely forgiven him for that.

Reece looked between them, shook his head, and then turned toward the living room. "Let's get comfortable. The only people here right now are us and Mott and he's in the middle of something."

"Are you all making a compound out here in the English countryside? Nice place to do it I guess." Garran sat near Aisling as he glanced around the floor-sized suite.

"Helps having a super-inventor as a brother." Aisling smiled, but like everyone else in her life, these two felt odd. Not a good thing if she came across someone who really wasn't what they seemed—she might not be able to tell the difference.

"What's brought you two here that you couldn't call

us about?" Reece was still watching them both carefully, possibly picking up on Aisling's feelings. Or his ability to see what might happen in the near future trick was kicking in again. He was at least a partial precog, but as human-fey breeds weren't supposed to have fey powers, he kept trying to ignore it.

"Aside from trying to help you find Aisling and Bart, not much beyond the possible end of the world. Which will wait in telling for now." Surratt scowled and folded his arms as he focused his glare on Reece. "You could have let us know they were back."

"Bart and I just came back yesterday. For us, we were gone a few hours. Needless to say, we had some sleep and food to catch up on." Surratt was often an ass, something she'd later found out was in part to keep people in the station from thinking that she and he weren't working on a secret agenda.

Which they hadn't been, until not too long before he'd almost been killed. Apparently, he felt he needed a few years build up. But he seemed even more prickly than usual right now.

"I would love to hear about that experience. We left when I was a child, I don't recall much of the other side." Garran's grin was wide—he'd never admitted being old enough to have come through the veil before. "But I think what we have to tell you might be as important, if not more so. I'd prefer to wait for the others to come back though."

"They literally left less than an hour ago. The ones not going with Bart are at the University, researching things. I'll get some tea and coffee and let Aisling tell her tale. Might as well get it out of the way." Reece got up and went to the kitchen.

Aisling nodded to Surratt. "I'll tell you, but for the love of everything, why are you being such a jerk? You're oozing with it." She leaned back and folded her arms.

She'd kick him out if it wasn't that he and Garran might have had a justifiable reason for coming here. End of the world scenarios usually were something they needed to know about.

"I told you she'd notice." Garran shook his head. "Surratt, like myself, was worried about you. Unfortunately, admitting things like that, even to himself, makes him cranky."

Surratt's scowl deepened. He ran his hand through his hair. "Okay, yes, I was worried about you. Your mother is a crazed sociopath. Our theory was that she kidnapped you and took you to the other side of the veil. I'm glad to see you're alive." His smile was closer to a real one and Aisling shook her head.

"I get it, it's okay, don't get mushy. We have no idea what happened to my mother, but I never saw her on the other side. Bart was just waking up when I found him, so I doubt he did either." She nodded as both pairs of eyes widened. "Yeah, he was over there too."

Reece came back with tea as she started the story from waking up on the other side. Both faces grew darker as she told them of the freed ghanlough, their connection to the attack on London, and the vallenians setting the alari on the dryads for failing to keep the ghanlough locked up.

Garran shook his head. "I was young, but I recall being told the tree people all died before we left. There was a huge fire…" He drifted off and then shook his head.

"One possibly set by my mother." That had come to Aisling last night. A while ago, before the trip to the other side, she'd had a dream/vision of being in a forest, in her mother's body or with it, and flames sweeping through a forest. She knew in her soul her mother had been destroying something. Or, as it turned out, some ones. "That woman has too much to be held responsible for."

"Agreed," Surratt said.

"Regardless. Bart and I were sent back here using an odd dryad spell. Reece, my brothers, and the rest figured out where we'd land and rescued us." Like the tale she and Bart had told the rest of them, Aisling wasn't mentioning the entire royalty situation.

"And Bart now has a ghau pendant?" Garran let loose a low whistle. "Those vallenians are up to something. They might not be the killers we heard about growing up, but I don't think they're on our side either."

"The one we saw had no compassion when he left the dryads to their fate." Aisling winced. She'd gone over that part quickly and hadn't intended to point it out.

Surratt leaned forward. "What stopped them? I'd always been told the alari were unstoppable, at least in the children's tales."

"Nothing is unstoppable. You just have to find what breaks it," Mott said as he came out of his room and down the hall to the living room without anyone noticing. He took a cup, poured some tea, then sat as far away from Surratt and Garran as possible.

Mott had issues with authority figures.

"True," Garran cut in before Surratt could respond. "But something stopped them."

Aisling pulled out her pendant. "I did." She had an odd feeling that outright lying would be bad, but she wasn't lying. She did stop them. She was implying that it was solely because of the ghau pendant—but she wasn't saying it. "They left quickly. In gratitude, Neasa sent Bart and I home."

Both men nodded and sipped their tea, but she knew at least Garran wanted to ask more questions. The fact that he didn't, was almost more disturbing than if he'd grilled her for hours over what really stopped the alari.

Mott watched the dynamics as well and she could almost see his mind whirling. Great. At least she got to tell her brothers about this royal tie before everyone else. But Surratt and Garran were just going to wait until everyone found out.

Reece turned to Mott. "Any progress?"

"No. I know there is a frequency that will do it. Just can't get the right harmonics. I will though." He looked around. "We need cookies." He immediately jumped to his feet and jogged toward the kitchen.

"I didn't even ask, but what is he doing?" Aisling usually wasn't sure she wanted to know. Mott was scary smart, but didn't have the same filters others had. And he often failed to realize what the repercussions could be of some of his inventions.

Technically, he'd been the one who led Nix to the creation of the fey killing drug, Iron Death. Mott thought he'd been working on a chemical to help deep space astronauts. Not a compound that would send iron directly into a fey's bloodstream. He needed to be watched.

"He's been working on finding a way through the veil." Reece leaned back in his seat.

Garran shot Reece a confused look. "What? That's impossible. There are odd openings, ones like what Nix used, but you can't just pop it open where you want. At least not from this side."

"I'd say from the other side as well. But if Bart and I are back, why is he still looking?"

"For the sake of science." Mott came back with armfuls of cookie packages. "They call them biscuits, but they're still cookies." He dumped them on the coffee table after selecting a few for himself. "Not to mention, we need to be able to advance when they invade." He shoved a chocolate sandwich cookie into his mouth and chomped happily.

"We, what now?" Aisling got the words out first, but the others looked like they were thinking the same. She knew that Reece had most likely been the motivating factor in finding a way to open the veil and rescue her—but even he looked startled at Mott's words.

"Oh yeah. There's going to be an invasion and if we can't go back and forth on our own, we're trapped. And we'll lose. I'm getting closer, but haven't found a way through yet. This might not be a great area for veil application even though you two came back here. We may need to relocate."

"Mott, where did you hear this?" Reece was keeping his voice calm and level, but from the look on Surratt's face that might not be an option much longer.

"Harlie, Dailten, and Stella. I overheard them talking to some of the other people like them a few days ago. There's an invasion coming, has something to do with the veil and things getting through. Bad things."

"Did they ask you to do anything?" Garran was better at handling Mott than Surratt and spoke like he was soothing a scared wild animal.

"Well, no. They were talking about it more as a theory. But with Aisling being lost over there—I wanted to do something. I know she's back now, but there could still be an invasion."

Reece gave a small smile. "And you hate to see a project unfinished."

Knowing Mott, there might not have been any conversation related to an invasion, but he did like finishing things.

"Well." He shrugged and ate another cookie.

"I didn't see anything that looked like an invasion on the other side. And wouldn't anything able to break down the veil on this side, also make it easier for the other side to come here?" Aisling really didn't think messing with opening the veil in any way was a good idea. They should be finding ways to strengthen it, not weaken it.

"It could. I was still working on that part. I do believe I'd need to move to one of the great henges to really do a good study. The veil construction being more tenuous in those places." He looked around. "They never taught that in school, that the henges are veil focuses? The great stone circles? No? I must have learned that on my own. Anyway, they are. Some, like Stonehenge, are more tightly focused. But ones like the town of Avebury are broad and deep. If they open, entire armies could come through." He nodded sagely. "So, if that's where they'll come through, that's where I need to go. Stonehenge won't work, too tight and too well known. But maybe we could get a small place in Avebury, on the edge on the great henge…" He drifted into muttering to himself while Aisling and Reece shared concerned looks with the other two.

"Mott, we don't need to open the veil. That's a bad, bad, bad idea." Aisling kept her voice stern. Mott didn't have a crush on her per se, but he did fixate on the fact that the two had been in second level primary school together almost two hundred years ago.

"But…fine." He folded his arms and shook his head. "So, what do we do now?"

The door opened and Caradoc, Maeve, and Harlie returned. Both Caradoc and Maeve paused at the entrance of the living room when they saw Garran and Surratt. Harlie kept going.

"When did you get here?" Maeve glared at both, but most of the weight was on Surratt. He'd been her boss too, and she hadn't dealt with his behavior any better than Aisling had.

"Why does everyone hate us?" The tone in Garran's voice was 'hate me.' Surratt thrived on having people annoyed at him.

"Well, you kicked us off the force for one thing. Why are you here?" Maeve didn't sit down nor move further into the room.

"They were looking for Bart and me and claimed they

had some important information. But we're waiting for everyone else to get back."

Caradoc shook his head as he walked through the living room. "Stella called me, they're in Area 42's waiting room hell just for Bart to ask someone a question. If there's no response in an hour, they'll come back. That was about fifteen minutes ago."

Harlie hadn't glared at anyone, but nodded as he continued through and down the hall to his room.

"Is he okay?" Aisling thought he looked fine, but it was hard to tell with him sometimes.

"I think so? We didn't find much, but he jumped up suddenly and said we had to leave. Then just kept muttering to himself the entire walk back." Caradoc moved into the room and sat down. He still shot Surratt a few glares, but not on Maeve's level.

If Maeve folded her arms any tighter, they'd snap.

"Look, things were done because that was how we had to play it. As I recall, I was never notified of your MI-6 still active status." Surratt gave a twitch. That probably pissed him off when he found out. "We need to work together now; things are too serious not to."

"Fine. But I'm still mad." Maeve stomped to the sofa and flopped down next to Caradoc. "Now what?"

"Cookies?" Mott waved a hand toward the pile.

"Great idea. A good biscuit and tea will take the edge right off." She poured a tea for herself and Caradoc before he could move and dug out some cookies.

"We were going to wait for everyone, but we might not be able to," Garran said, "we'll tell you, then repeat it to Bart when he and the others get back, if we're here. If not, you tell them."

"That wasn't ominous at all." Maeve continued to glare; it was just now being done while sipping tea.

"It's the truth." Surratt looked around to all of them. "We came here to help find Aisling and Bart. The Area

42 people in L.A. are useless and wouldn't say anything. Since we came here three days ago, we've been stalked through Heathrow from the moment we got off the plane, and hunted on the tube out of town. That's one of the reasons we weren't here sooner. Our stalkers became aggressive and had to be dealt with." He held up his hand. "Don't worry, no one followed us here—I can guarantee that." He glanced to Garran, but he just gave a closed mouth smile.

"Why?" Reece had his elbows on his knees as he leaned forward. "Did someone follow you from L.A?"

"There were a few odd situations, but nothing like this. The only reason they haven't caught us is that the powers behind it still have to be circumspect and I have a few more abilities than I ever officially listed." Surratt's smile was brittle. Few knew he was a changeling; it shouldn't be surprising that he was also a strong magic user.

"Okay, so who's after you?" Aisling didn't feel like playing guessing games.

"Close confidants of the High King and Queen of the fey."

CHAPTER SEVEN

AISLING FELT A chill. Was there a connection between what she'd found out on the other side about the lost prince and the current fey royals? She looked over and saw that Caradoc's bright blue eyes were worried as well.

"And while that's shocking, Aisling and Caradoc look more worried than surprised." Garran looked to both, then turned back to Aisling. "Something happened, or was exposed, during your visit to the other side. Are the high king and queen working with the creatures left behind the veil?"

Aisling rubbed her forehead. "Okay, yes, something did happen, but I have no idea if anyone on this side of the veil knows about it." She looked to Reece and Maeve. "I wanted to tell my brothers first, but would have told you today once everyone got back. No easy way to put it. Our father was the lost prince of ancient fables. The dryads even have a painting of him before his parents were murdered, it's my father as a young man. His memories were destroyed and he became a new person with no memory of being royal. We're not even sure if our mother knew."

Reece pulled back. "You three are royals?" He hadn't been happy finding out who her parents were initially. This was a whole new level.

"Technically. I doubt it could be enforced though," Caradoc said. "Our father was declared dead and even he doesn't know who he really is. I doubt that a bunch of dryads from the other side of the veil can step forward in a royal court and give testimony."

"That was why the alari backed off. I did have the ghau pendant, and managed to destroy one of them with a spell, so maybe they reacted to that as well—but I identified myself as Queen Aisling." She shrugged. "They left and Neasa sent us home."

"This could be more important than we think. We weren't sure what drove the people following us, but we had been asking some questions about Aisling and the battle of London." Garran got up and started pacing behind the sofa. More of a Surratt move, but obviously they were rubbing off on each other. "Even though we were cautious, our questions got to the royal powers. The minotaur assassins we had to dispose of tried to claim royal clemency."

Mott continued his cookie demolition but watched everyone. "Not only was she accepted as Queen Aisling over there by the dryads, it was enough to make the alari, terrifying creatures from my research, back down. Knowing full well that the vallenians—also horrible— had set them to a specific job—they ran away." He swallowed a few cookies without chewing as he looked around the room. "That could have been relayed to the royals if they have maintained any sort of information gathering from that side." His nod said he knew they had.

There was a connection of some sort between Nix and her mother. And also between her mother and the fey royals. There was a very good chance that the royals were far more informed about their former homeland than anyone knew.

Mott's point about the alari was also true. It was clear that the vallenians were in control of the other side. "The alari were more frightened of me and what I might do, than of the vallenians? That's hard to believe." And more than a bit terrifying.

"They might be afraid of something you could become," Surratt said. "And if that information — that a queen of the lost line was coming back into power — got to the high king and queen's ears, they could have something to fear. Whether or not a bunch of dryads were willing to come over here and testify. The high king and queen, or someone close to them, must know of a way to prove it and are gathering intel. Although the minotaurs did try to kill us, the other followers seemed bent on capturing us."

"They were going after you because you asked about me?" Aisling felt the blood drain from her face. "We have to get Bart and the others back." Area 42 might or might not be aware of her hypothetical status, but they couldn't take that chance.

"I agree." Caradoc got to his feet and went to knock on Harlie's door. The door opened and a tense conversation ensued. Then the door shut and Caradoc came back. "He's coming with us, he's the best magic user we have; no offense to the rest of you. He's also going to add a shield to everyone, going back to London or not." He shook his head. "I know, I don't get it either, but I believe him if he says he can do it."

Harlie came out with a small bottle of greenish liquid. "This will be absorbed through the skin and will block any searchers who are tracking any of us. I was working on it this past month, but it won't last long, and I only have enough for this round. Hopefully it will be long enough to break any spell links following us."

Reece looked around, then shrugged and held out his hand. The drop on his hand spread out and quickly vanished. Harlie quickly dropped some on everyone, although Mott first refused.

"I could just stay inside all the time. No one would know." He kept both hands behind his back.

"We can't stay here forever, and didn't you say your studies would do better at the henge in Avebury? Can't do that if you're inside here. Will you please let him protect you?" Aisling understood his trepidation, but if Garran and Surratt were right, and they probably were, they needed to protect everyone—even if this was just a short-term solution. She didn't need to know how Harlie's odd concoction worked; she just knew it would.

"Since you asked." Mott smiled and held out his hand.

"You do realize Harlie's faster than you, right?" Caradoc asked. He'd known Mott better than the others, having worked with him in a think tank as well as Caradoc's research company. Before he sold it. He knew Mott better than anyone here.

Mott shrugged and rubbed his hand even though the liquid had vanished. "Yes, but I like to be asked, even if it would have happened anyway."

Harlie shook his head and pocketed the bottle. "This really wasn't ready, but I sensed a spell on Garran and Surratt." He nodded to them. "It's blocked now, but those assassins might have been trying to get close enough to tag you both. And I'm not bragging when I say that I am more magically powerful than our high king and queen."

"So, we find out what high powerful magic user they have in their corner and take them down. Or just take down the entire royal group—fey and human." Maeve nodded as if that was a solid plan.

Aisling turned to her. "I thought you liked the English king?"

"I do, but you never know what any of them are really up to, do you?"

Part of that feeling was directed at finding out that during the Black Plague, the elves had saved humanity at the cost of their reproductive abilities. Less than ten percent of humans could currently have kids. And they'd theorized that, based on certain actions over the centuries, the rulers of the world were fully aware. Even the human rulers like the current English king.

Surratt and Garran were both on their feet. "We're going with you to London but will probably separate after we get Bart. Now that we know Aisling and Bart are safe, we should get back home."

"How bad are things back there?" Reece looked up as he added another gun stashed on his person. He usually wasn't as heavily armed as Jones, but he wasn't taking chances this time.

"They're mostly just odd, not potentially catastrophic like over here. Aside from Area 42 shutting everyone out, it's almost as if crime has come to a standstill. There's something big brewing, but getting you two back was bigger. It might be better if you all split up after London. At least some of you," Surratt said.

Maeve and Reece both stepped next to Aisling, with Maeve being a step in front.

"I'm not leaving her."

"Me either." Reece had finished his weapons collection and handed Aisling her gun back.

Surratt shrugged and turned for the front door. "Do what you want, but a larger target is easier to hit."

Mott did stay behind in the flat. Harlie put a spell of unseeing and warding on the entire place as they readied to leave.

"Under no circumstances do you open the door or any window. Keeping the shades and drapes down will also help the spell." Caradoc tilted his head at Mott. "Even if you think it's one of us. We have our own keys." He handed a key to Garran. "Even these two."

"I promise. After I make lunch I'll go back into my study. I think I'm going to switch to looking at what or who is helping the royals though."

With the sound of multiple physical locks behind them as they shut the door, everyone except Mott left the flat.

"How long will this mojo on us last?" Aisling asked Harlie as they went outside.

"A few hours, I'd hope."

Obviously Garran and Surratt had taken the tube… or not. The two walked to a low-slung, bright red coupe parked along the curb. "I thought you said they tried to get you on the underground?" The car looked like Surratt, but Garran went to the driver's side.

"They did. After the third attempt we rented this baby." Garran grinned and patted it. "You have cars, right?"

"Might have thought to check before we got down here." Caradoc clicked a small fob and a fancy black car blinked its lights.

"Black again?" Aisling laughed. Caradoc thought black cars looked cool, until a few months ago when they ran across a bunch of bad guys—all driving similar black SUVs like him. She had been out of it when they brought her back yesterday and hadn't noticed.

"Not the same, it's not an SUV."

Reece also clicked a fob and a dark green SUV flicked on. "I kept the SUV idea, but avoided black." He slid into the driver's side.

Harlie stood between the three cars as if weighing the meaning of life. Eventually he nodded and came to get in behind Aisling in Reece's SUV.

"Am I in danger? Is that why you picked this car?" Aisling figured he'd say something if that were the case, but Harlie was often in his own world and forgot others didn't live there.

He blinked a few times. "What? Oh, this." He grinned and patted the seat. "I was just deciding which one would be more comfortable." With a grin he leaned his head back and was softly snoring before Reece started following the other two cars.

"Damn, I wish I could doze off like that." Aisling laughed. "Okay, when I've not been awake for a month that is." She watched Reece's face as he took the narrow lanes that led out of the village. "I'm sorry I didn't tell you about the whole lost royalty thing sooner."

"Eh, your mother being the evil thing she is was more of a shock."

"True. I know I said I thought she didn't know about my dad, but I can't help feeling that she did and couldn't find a way to make it work in her favor. And there's still a chance she was working with the blessing of the high king and queen this entire time." That was chilling. Just as soon as she thought she'd seen the worst of her mother, there was more.

"Things still feel weird?" His voice was low, but she wasn't sure if it was because of the topic or his focusing on navigating through the narrow hedge-sided road.

She wanted to say no, that she felt like her old self and she felt normal about her friends and family. But she wasn't up to lying.

"Things are still weird. You're you. I know how I feel about you. But…"

"You just don't *feel* it." He held up his hand. "Not like that, but it's like I'm a memory of me. Or you're a memory of you to me." He glanced over.

"Damn, that's what it feels like. I wonder if it's the same for everyone else? And if Bart's noticing it as well. What did that veil do to us? Are we going to go crazy and have wildly dangerous powers like Nix?"

"He started off unbalanced and powerful. The veil just made him worse. But I do think it's something to watch—just to make sure." The smile he flashed her wasn't as reassuring as she'd hoped.

"I really thought that once we'd stopped him, and my mother was out of the picture, we'd go back to L.A., our regular jobs, and spend weekends having barbeques."

"I thought you didn't like barbeques?" He followed Caradoc and Garran down an even narrower road. The hedges would hit the sides of the SUV if he made the slightest turn.

"I don't. But the concept is still sound. I just want to go back to a normal life of catching the bad folks. I'm a good cop." She missed the feeling of being something other than her mother's daughter. She'd worked hard for years to separate herself from her family. Only to have it all snap back and hit her in the face. Even if her mother *was* gone, the issue about her father wasn't going away any time soon.

"You are a damn good cop. Even Surratt said it a few times." He reached over and squeezed her hand. "We'll get through this."

"But who will we be then?" She squeezed his hand back and shook her head. In the last year, Reece had gone through changes as well—ones that would be of great interest to the fey royals if they knew. "We can't let them find you."

"What? Where'd that come from?"

"You're the first fey-human I know of who is showing fey powers. We know what the High King and Queen will do if they find you. Hell, there might have been many more over the years—we didn't hear about them because they were *taken care of.*"

"That's a thought that has been in my head for a while. My gifted swimming was something I just accepted. Saving you and Jones in the ocean was the first time that it had become more than that—and I'd actually changed. As for the clairvoyance issue," he shook his head. "I really thought I was simply great at understanding patterns of behavior. So, yeah, I'm still freaked."

"Sorry. If you hadn't met me, maybe you'd have never known."

"No way. That's not a trade I'd be willing to make.

Besides, what if I'd been found out and I had no clue? This way I know who I am and have a better chance of defending myself."

"Okay, fine. I'm still not sure—" Aisling's words ended in a scream as a massive tractor came plowing through the hedge and slammed into the front of the SUV.

CHAPTER EIGHT

H AD REECE BEEN driving faster, the tractor would have driven right over them. Its tires were taller than their car.

Harlie jerked awake. "Out. We must get out of here." He paled when he leaned forward and saw the tractor. "Now!"

Aisling felt a rush of magic flow from him and the tractor tilted away from them and off the SUV, then crashed backward.

They scrambled out of the smashed SUV with Harlie magically, but not as quickly as could be hoped, leading them through the hedge. There was no movement from the tractor yet, but it was doubtful that would last long.

Aisling called Caradoc. "We were just ambushed by a massive tractor cutting through the hedge. Keep going, we'll find you."

"Damn it! We're coming back."

"How and why? Even you can't turn around on these roads. Let Garran know, and keep going." She cut the call and shoved the phone in her back pocket as she caught up to Reece and Harlie.

"I think they're coming out of the tractor!" Reece yelled as he glanced back.

Aisling looked back as well. There was movement in the field of bright yellow plants they were running through, but no sign of who or what was causing it. The pungent smell of the flowers as the plants were crushed made her sneeze.

What was after them? Dogs? Was it just a case of a farmer losing control of his tractor and they were being chased by mundane farm dogs?

Her laugh caused another sneezing fit. "What are these plants? If whatever's chasing us doesn't get us, these things will." The field they were running through was huge and filled to the far border with these lovely, but bad smelling, plants.

"Rapeseed oil." Reece wasn't sneezing yet, but he didn't sound happy.

Whatever was chasing them let loose an odd cry. Confirming they weren't just farm dogs.

"I might suggest running faster. That sounds like an anghenfil cignoeth—we do not want them to catch us." The level of fear in Harlie's voice as he increased his speed got Aisling to forget sneezing and pick up her feet. She'd heard the term, horrific dog-like monsters who lived to eat. Everything.

Reece was fast, but not as fast as the two elves and slowly fell behind.

Both Aisling and Harlie dropped back to him, each grabbed an arm, and they took off running at full elven speed. Reece was smart enough not to fight. They reached the far hedge with the anghenfil cignoeth dropping back—only one had given the odd cry, but there were obviously far more of them in the field. Fey creatures who would have never been brought to this side of the veil. They were deadly sprinters, and the field was too long for them.

Aisling, Reece, and Harlie still needed to get over that hedge quickly in case there were other things out in the field.

Harlie threw a spell at the hedge like he had on the other side, but it bounced back. He tried twice more before finally waving at it and sending a heavier spell. A set of stone steps appeared.

"Go!" He stayed near the steps, sweat dripping down his face as he almost threw Aisling and Reece up them. He ran up after them and all three jumped to the other side and another narrow road.

"Very nice. Not many people can outrun anghenfil cignoeth, and that's why they guard my land. Now, extremely slowly, put your guns on the ground and kick them away from you." A large wolf-headed fey faced them with a massively modified shotgun aimed at Aisling's head. "I really don't want to destroy her good looks."

Aisling and Reece did what he demanded, but Harlie didn't carry weapons, so he just stood still with his hands straight up.

"I should charge you for ruining my plants. It takes a long time to grow those right."

"Rapeseed? It's everywhere here." Reece locked his fingers over his head.

"Not my kind." The fey winked. "Special blend. Now if you three had just been run over by the runaway tractor as I'd planned, I wouldn't be in this pickle. Three Americans, running in my field…what do I do with you?"

"For starters, I'd drop your gun before I blow your head off." Garran snarled from the hedge on the far side of the road. He was hidden so well that Aisling hadn't noticed him. The start by Reece said he hadn't either.

Harlie grinned and lowered his hands. "He will do it. Even though I would love to know what you did to those plants, he will kill you."

"Seriously? What are you doing Lathen? You used to be a good mate." Maeve stepped out of the hedge as well, also with her gun drawn. She might know this fey, but her gun didn't waver.

"Maeve? What in the hell is going—"

His words ended as something fired from the same hedge that Garran and Maeve had stepped out of hit him with what looked like a small paintball, and he dropped like a bag of rocks. Caradoc stepped out with a grin.

"I wanted to test my kjoli gun, good of your friend to give me a chance." Caradoc smiled at Maeve then walked to Lathen and removed his rifle. "Should keep him stunned for a few hours at least."

"I wouldn't say he's a friend, he was always a bit of a prick. But he was on the good side ten years ago. Low level MI-6, more office support than agent, but still working for the right side." She peered down at him. "And definitely not the farmer type. Were there really anghenfil cignoeth in that field?"

"Your guess is as good as ours, we never saw anything. Heard some weird howling, but nothing visual." Reece pulled out a zip tie and bound the farmer's hands.

"I knew what they were when they howled." Harlie glared at the hedge as if he could see beyond that. "We can't leave them there. They shouldn't even be on this side of the veil."

"If they're as bad as the stories said, how in the hell did he get them?" Surratt glared at the unconscious farmer as he stepped out of the hedge as well. He had a nasty looking low-gawn pistol in his hands. Rare, deadly, and expensive as hell.

"Why are all these evil things, who should be on the other side, popping up here? I know how hard it is to cross the veil, but apparently if you're a deadly creature you can just walk through?" Aisling looked around the group but didn't expect an answer.

Reece nodded to Garran. "How'd you know where we'd come out?"

"Direct line from where I picked up your crashed SUV on my scanner." Caradoc grinned. "I extrapolated the best place to catch you based on the assumption of a direct run. Our cars are on the other side of this hedge—I put a walk-through spell on it, like the one around my house."

"I want to see these anghenfil cignoeth." Harlie was still glaring at the hedge they'd climbed over. "That race should have worn them down." He started to magically build another set of stone stairs.

"Seriously? You're just going to wander over and what, talk to them? I don't think they're the kind of creatures for talking." Aisling put her hand on Harlie's arm. She agreed they couldn't just leave them running free, but he couldn't take them out on his own. Not that he wouldn't be powerful enough to probably destroy however many creatures were out there, but he might get lost in research mode and forget they were savage killers.

Anghenfil cignoeth, like so many things that had been popping up lately, were hunters from the other side of the veil. They worked in large family packs and were mostly constructed of powerful legs, teeth, and sharp claws. They were more a combination of a cat and a dog than belonging to either group. Another creature she only knew about because Caradoc used to tell her scary stories of them.

"Maeve and I can keep watch on her friend," Surratt said. "You go disable those creatures."

Maeve shrugged and kept her gun focused on Lathen.

Harlie tilted his head and magically created another set of stairs over the hedge. Aisling stayed right behind him with her gun in one hand and a spell ready in the other. Most of her spells required touch, but not all of them. The release of the magic block she'd had most of her life was opening a lot more magic to work with. She called up a spell that should be strong enough to send any number of anghenfil cignoeth flying a mile into the air.

There were no signs of anything other than the trails the three of them had made through the bright yellow plants to where they stood. Harlie paused, then marched forward. He wasn't as obvious, unless he wanted to be, about having a spell at the ready. But he had something ready to go this time.

"How long will they stay down?" Aisling walked between Harlie and Reece and kept her voice low.

A whining growl rumbled through the field ahead of them. "Not a scientist, but I'd say not long." Reece whispered and calmly held out his gun. Caradoc held his new invention, but also had a regular gun. Not to mention, he was easily the second strongest magic user behind Harlie. He just wanted to go beyond a magic reliance and would only use it if there was no tech option.

Garran went wide around the rest of them, his gun also tracking the small movements in the yellow flowers.

"Try not to kill them!" Harlie yelled, as twenty anghenfil cignoeth, with greyhound bodies and lion heads, complete with mane, charged toward them. But those four-inch fangs weren't from any current animal on this side of the veil.

"Not sure that we have that option, Harlie," Caradoc said as he slowed down. "My kjoli gun *is* only for stunning. But it might not work on creatures from the other side."

"They can't stay on this side of the veil, Harlie." Aisling also continued forward, but it was as if the creatures were drawing her forward one step at a time. "Are they twisting the veil? Or is the veil so twisted now that it let them through?" She grabbed her head as a sense of wrongness flooded her. The anghenfil cignoeth were glowing from within. That same odd green color she'd been seeing too much of lately.

An energy shield snapped around the anghenfil cignoeth as Garran fired at them. Aisling dropped to her knees as the circle around the anghenfil cignoeth twisted inside out, and they vanished.

She didn't throw-up, but it was a near thing. She did collapse to the ground completely and lie on her back with her eyes closed

"Aisling! Were you hit?" Reece yelled as he slid down next to her.

Aisling squinted open her eyes as Reece was followed by Caradoc and Garran, all with the same looks of panic.

She fully opened her eyes and looked around. Harlie had wandered to the center of where the anghenfil cignoeth had been and walked around it in a circle, muttering under his breath as he went.

"I'm fine. Well, not fine. My head still feels inside out—but not hit by anything. That was brutal." She looked around at their collective blank looks. "None of you felt that?"

"Felt what?" Reece slowly pulled her into a sitting position.

"The twisting of space. Right there. Visual too, I think that's what made me sick." She shuddered.

"Nope. That weird bubble covered the creatures, Garran shot, then they vanished, and you grabbed your head and dropped to your knees," Reece said. "Then went over on your back."

"Sorry, I saw what pretty boy said," Garran said.

Caradoc looked out across the field, then turned back. "I didn't see or feel any of that, either."

"She's gone through the veil and back; it changes things on different levels." Harlie continued walking his circles, but now held out his arms at his sides. "Oh, this would be fascinating if it wasn't being used for evil. There was a time twist here. Those anghenfil cignoeth didn't cross the veil; they bent it. Or rather, someone bent it for them." He finally looked up. "A special trick of magic that allowed them to interact here, but not actually be on this side of the veil. A tricky and difficult bit of magic indeed."

"So, they couldn't have hurt us?" Reece asked.

"Oh, they could have. Someone called them here on a spell. Probably Maeve's friend. But then they were brought back to the other side of the veil as we approached them. There's a lot of veil residue here."

Garran pulled out his phone. "Surratt and I promised to report anything weird to our local Area 42 and police. Even though they've been just this side of useless. This is something they get to deal with." He nodded to everyone, then turned to move away to make his call.

Harlie's face fell.

Caradoc went over and patted his arm. "You can't be everywhere at once."

"I know, but I can see the temptation Nix faced of being able to do that." He'd been looking at the trampled plants, but looked up suddenly. "Not that I would do what he did…I would only use it for good."

Aisling laughed. "I think we all know that, but good to remind us." She rubbed her arms as a chill wind drifted into the circle. "But I'll say it again, no one should try going to, or pulling things through, the veil." She narrowed her eyes at both of her brothers. "No one."

"Never let us have any fun." Caradoc holstered his weird kjoli gun.

Before Aisling could respond, the yellow flowers around them burst into flame. Then turned to dust. The entire field didn't all turn to flame at once, but the crop was gone in moments.

Harlie jumped as the final patch to go was where he'd been pacing.

"What was that?" Reece looked wild-eyed. A streak of soot dusted his left pant leg.

"I have no idea, aside from someone destroying evidence." Garran walked back to them, his phone was still in his hand, but dark. "I got through to Area 42, was telling them they had a damn problem, then the line went dead and this happened."

"You think Area 42 is behind this?" Aisling asked as she watched as Harlie and Caradoc scooped up as much plant dust as they could get. Reece stood nearby with a large evidence bag. Always good to have those on hand.

"I think someone in London knows something and is covering their asses. I think we also might want to grab our prisoner and get the hell out of here." Garran nodded to the scraping going on. "Grab what you can, whether they were involved with whatever was growing here, or just aware of it—this field will be scrubbed completely by Area 42 in a short while. The flaming must have been a remote spell already placed on the field."

Caradoc and Harlie sealed the bags they'd collected and dropped them into the larger bag Reece held. "Do you want it?" He held it out to them.

Caradoc looked to Harlie who gave a nod and took it. "I'll take it, can't do anything with it until we're back to the flat."

They quickly walked back to the hedge, where Harlie set up the stairs again. Aisling still felt a chill even though the wind had vanished. It was more disturbing than the flames.

"Let's get up there. Things to do, move along." She held back and watched the field while motioning for the others to go up the stairs.

"Why do you get to stay?" Caradoc was the last to go up.

"Because I'm special." Aisling swore as a giant bird of prey, similar to a smaller pterodactyl from long ago, but found only on the other side of the veil, appeared and dove for Caradoc. And went right through him.

"What?!" Caradoc looked around halfway up the stairs at Aisling's muffled yell—he hadn't even felt the thing fly through him. There were more ghost-like images coming from the center of the field—and no one else was reacting to them—not even Harlie.

"I'll explain later, but we need to go." Aisling ran up on him, making him jump to the other side. She waved to Garran down on the road. "We need to leave. Now!"

Garran nodded, grabbed the prisoner, and threw him over his shoulder. He was even more secured along with a mask over his eyes and a gag in his mouth. He still appeared unconscious.

"What happened?" Maeve put her gun away as she came over.

"Lots of things, but we need to leave." The creepy feeling was getting worse. Aisling was thinking of running if they didn't get into the cars soon enough.

"Come on, Garran and Surratt have our friend, we'll take you three." Caradoc jogged to his car. Then he hit a few buttons and it shifted. It was now the size of an SUV.

Aisling had been walking over to him but stopped. "You rented a Claniare car shifter?" One of the most exclusive and expensive car companies, the Claniare line outdid itself with a car that could literally shift forms.

"No, you can't rent those." He shrugged and held open the back door. "I bought it. Thinking of buying a place over here when things are settled. Want a ride in comfort or not?"

Aisling hadn't been looking forward to trying to squish all three of them in the back of the coupe, but this backseat could fit four easily. "Anytime." She climbed in, with Reece and Harlie climbing in next to her.

Maeve took the front passenger seat and Caradoc gunned the engine and raced after Garran and Surratt.

A trail of dirt from the road lifted up as both cars went far faster than recommended on the narrow road.

Aisling was surprised at how quickly the others had taken off. They must have felt something even if none of them mentioned it. "Move faster." Aisling felt a trickle of sweat. They weren't going to make it.

Garran picked up speed and Caradoc stayed on his tail. Even though Aisling expected something to happen, the entire farmland behind them flying a mile into the air, then slamming back to the ground in tiny pieces was not it.

CHAPTER NINE

H ER PHONE RANG and she had to unclench her hand enough to answer it. The good thing was the freezing-creeping-out feeling was gone.

It was Surratt. "You all okay back there?" He sounded more concerned than Aisling had ever heard.

"I think so. The car doesn't seem to be having troubles either." Considering how close they'd been to whatever that explosion was, that was a miracle.

"It better not. I paid extra for that protection!" Caradoc yelled back as he stayed on Garran's tail.

"You can slow down, superhero. Garran's swearing a blue streak at you," Surratt said.

"Fine. Sorry, things were weird." Caradoc dropped to a full car length behind them.

Reece looked at Aisling's phone and she handed it over. "Are we all going into London and Area 42 with our prisoner?"

"Change of plans. Garran and I are going back to your flat, we don't want to be dragging him into London— especially if there's a chance Area 42 was involved with that farm. You five go hunt down Bart and his crew. We'll wait for you in your flat and see what information we can get from this Lathen guy. Maybe even let Mott try to talk to him." Mott's talking was scattered at best, but if you gave him a prop, a switch or something that looked like he might use to blow things up, he went from mildly confusing to terrifying.

"Understood." Reece held out her phone, but Aisling shook her head. He shrugged and put it back to his ear. "We'll check-in once we get them." He ended the call and handed the phone back to Aisling. "I hope this tricky car of yours can fit four more people. We're on our own."

Caradoc's grin was wide. "Easily."

With any luck, Bart, Stella, Jones, and Dailten were sitting around back in the flat having cookies with Mott. Of course, luck didn't seem to be favoring them as of late. Or at least since Aisling had gotten pushed through the veil.

Garran's car made a sharp left at the next intersection and Caradoc kept going straight.

"I'll feel better when we're back on a motorway," Maeve said. "I'm not a country girl and these little roads bother me."

"Your wish is my command. Motorway in ten minutes." Caradoc tapped the wide GPS in the middle of the dash. Like the rest of the car, it was changeable. Right now, it was at the maximum size and Aisling could easily see exactly where they were going without leaning forward.

"What did you see that freaked you out? Back on those stairs, you saw something." Caradoc looked up at her from the rearview mirror.

"I'm not sure." Aisling ignored the looks around her. "Okay, it looked like a Flothian eagle from the old world, or a smaller, twisted pterodactyl from this one. It flew right through Caradoc's head. There were more things out there—just vague and ghostlike."

"Which might have been why Area 42, or whoever that was, blew it to hell." Reece swore under his breath. "They were probably counting on us to move slower."

Maeve turned to the back seat. "I know they've got

issues, but you really think they would have killed us?"

"Yes." There was a lot of bitterness in Reece's voice. "Even the ones who haven't been corrupted. I never saw how they were before, but it's clear now that they don't care about collateral damage or deaths. Or that sometimes the end doesn't justify their means."

"So, you're really out?" Aisling turned to Reece, but he was staring out the window. At least there were no more hedges crowding the path, but, like Maeve, she'd be happier once they were on a motorway. Growing up in L.A. meant not a lot of exposure to narrow roads.

"Both Jones and I have been on leave since London. I don't know about him, but even if they clean everything up, I don't want to be a part of them anymore." He leaned into Aisling. "Think Garran will hire me as myself for the L.A. police force?" When Aisling met him, Reece had been disguising himself as a member of the narcotics squad—sort of a CI cop—in order to catch a senior officer who'd gone bad in the narcotics division. Aisling hadn't known about it until she had to work with him in his disguise. The cops in her precinct weren't fond of annoying FBI agent Reece Larkin, but they got along great with his undercover persona.

"Maybe, but I think the people in my station liked Dixon better than you. You did a very good job alienating people." And herself. Reece had been an attractive pain in the ass as far as she was concerned for the first year that she knew him. He flashed his Fey Bureau of Investigation badge around as he stomped on all the interesting cases. Until the Iron Death drug showed up and she saw who he really was.

"Maybe everyone can just move over here. Form our own detective agency." Caradoc sounded too sly yet excited about the idea—clearly he'd been thinking about it for a while.

"A big gang racing around solving mysteries?" Harlie had appeared to be lost in thought, but looked up with a grin. "Do we get a bright van too?"

"Ha, ha, ha. I think it's a great idea." Caradoc went to the onramp for the motorway.

"Harlie, what could have caused what I saw? Were they just hallucinations? Residual from the other side?" Aisling was concerned whether they were real or only in her head. The only reason she'd pushed Caradoc to move faster was that they might have been real.

"I'm not sure. I've been going over what we saw in the field and what you saw as well. There was something going on at that farm, but I'm not sure how much of the cleanup was from people on this side."

"You think that someone on the other side of the veil blew up that farm," Reece said.

"It's possible." Harlie patted his vest pocket where the dust from the rapeseed flowers was. "I need to analyze this. But I believe the flowers bursting into flame and disintegrating was from Area 42 or whoever they are working with. I'm not sure who tried to blow us up." He looked around the car. "And don't doubt for a moment that whoever blew up the farm was hoping to kill us as well as destroy the evidence. I'm not sure who it was, but I know their intention."

Reece watched Harlie, but when he wasn't going to give anything else away, opened his phone and dialed. Then frowned and dialed again. "Trying to reach Bart, but the call says the number has been disconnected."

Caradoc looked in the rearview mirror. "Is that an Area 42 issued phone?"

Reece swore as he shut the phone off and was about to throw it out the window when Harlie reached over and stopped him.

"May I? It could be useful to search when we're in a safer location. I can remove the problem until then."

Reece handed him his phone. "I can't believe it never dawned on me that I could be giving info to Area 42. And that it was a bad thing."

Maeve held up her phone. "Mine is free, clear, and unlocked. Dial away."

"Thank you." Reece had to pull out his number pad, a small digital way of storing numbers off a phone for security, and then punched in a number. The sound of a disconnected phone filled the car. He entered another number. It took two times, but then a low voice responded.

"Damn it, Jones, I can barely hear you. I'm putting you on speaker."

Jones' voice was still low and the connection crackled. "We're under attack. The entire complex, but I'm not sure who is behind it. We can't find Bart, either."

"We're on our way down there. Where are you?"

The coordinates whispered by Jones made no sense to Aisling, but Reece nodded. "I know where that is. Stay put. See if Stella can disguise you three. Nothing fancy, just not what you look like normally. We'll be there in," he looked past Maeve to the GPS. "About a half hour." He hung up, then handed the phone back to Maeve. "I assume Caradoc has some of his toys on this thing?"

"Yup. Might have even have kept them from accessing your phone, but now isn't the time to test it." Caradoc stayed focused on the motorway as they passed an insanely bright yellow, and expensive, sports car. Looked like a Maserati.

Aisling and Harlie shared wide-eyed looks at Caradoc's words.

"Since when have you been cautious? Are you sure the bird I saw didn't actually hit you in the head?" Aisling loved Caradoc, but caution was never a thing for him. However, there was genuine worry in his blue eyes as he glanced back.

"I might have had an epiphany or two while you were gone on the other side. Seeing that thing take you and not being able to do anything got me thinking."

Harlie squeezed Aisling's hand. "We all felt it, but Caradoc decided that it was his fault. He's been, and I quote Stella on this, 'a little old lady' for the past three weeks."

"I have not." Caradoc's shoulders slumped. "Fine, yes, I was afraid that my way of doing things might have led to you being taken. I know, the rest of them talked me out of it. But I still think caution is a good idea."

They passed the bright yellow Maserati again.

"Isn't that the same car we just overtook?" Maeve watched the car in the mirror as it drifted back into the mass of cars on the motorway.

"And the same as the one up there?" Reece pointed to a bright yellow car ahead of them.

"What the hell? Nice to make themselves so noticeable, but what is going on?" Caradoc changed lanes, but the yellow car that had dropped back did as well. It was managing to stay within traffic but dropping speed in the right lane next to them.

Caradoc quickly switched lanes three more times, earning a few annoyed looks from the other drivers.

Harlie closed his eyes and reached out his hand toward the yellow car. Then his eyes flew open and he grabbed the back of Caradoc's seat. "Don't let that car go past us again. Get out of here now!"

"Why? Never mind, there's something creepy going on." Caradoc looked around, then hit a few buttons on the underside of his dash. The car bounced, almost feeling like it was changing. Then it lifted off the motorway to a cacophony of angry honks.

CHAPTER TEN

———

"IS THIS THING flying?" Aisling stopped her scream from going past her lips, but was hanging on to the back of Maeve and Caradoc's seats so tightly her knuckles were white. The car was bouncing more than actually flying, but after the second bounce, and narrowly missing a car, it managed to stay up in the air on its own.

Not well, and it didn't go high, but it was slowly gaining altitude.

Reece was the only one in the back seat who looked excited instead of terrified. He was also the only one not related to Caradoc and was also a serious car nut. "How did you do this? I know these cars, and they can do a lot of things—but not this."

"I got a prototype and did some tinkering on my own." He swore as the car dipped. "Okay, it still has bugs, and we need to set down somewhere for a while. Then Harlie can explain to all of us why I just flew off a motorway."

"I've got to check this thing out once things settle down." Reece was almost drooling.

"I forgot about you and cars." Aisling shook her head, one of the first things she'd learned about the real Reece was that he loved fixing cars. She gave a shudder. Cars should drive, planes should fly, hovering over the countryside like some sort of deranged drunken helicopter wasn't either of those.

Caradoc landed on a field not too far from the motorway. "Did anyone see where the yellow Maserati went?"

"It sped up as we lifted." Maeve seemed fine with this weird flying car and had been watching as they'd flown away. Of course, she also knew what to expect.

"Let me just check a few things," Caradoc said as he started to get out. He turned to Harlie. "But you can explain while I work. I think the odds of three yellow Maseratis on the M-5 motorway at the same time is slim, but you were really disturbed."

Everyone got out of the car and Harlie nodded.

"There was a psychic presence in that car. On its last appearance, I knew it was the same vehicle."

"How? We passed it multiple times, was it using off-ramps to get ahead of us?" Aisling stood back from the engine, but Reece and Maeve were both watching Caradoc's checking of all the various parts with way too much interest. Maeve had never been a huge car person, most likely being around Caradoc too much in the last month had changed that.

"I think it's a ghost car." Harlie shrugged as he said the words. "I know, it sounds unbelievable to me as well. But there was something far more sinister than it just drifting past us. Had it passed through the third time, we might have died."

Even Caradoc looked up from his car maintenance at that.

"You can't just leave that hanging, mate," Maeve said.

"More explanation, yes." Harlie nodded and started pacing. "There is something happening to the veil, a weakness that I believe has been orchestrated by both sides. For different reasons, but mostly power."

"And there are beings from the other side driving ghost Maseratis?" Reece asked with only a little bit of disbelief in his voice.

"Yes and no." Harlie scowled as he marched around some more. "There are creatures called the Biotáille olc. They—"

"Do not tell me those things are here and driving expensive sports cars." Aisling almost jumped out of her skin when Harlie said that term. Her friend died because of them—and Garran almost died as well.

Maeve came to her side and rubbed her arm. It was before Maeve had become her partner, but she'd told her about it on more than a few nectar-filled nights.

"Okay, what are they?" Reece moved back toward Aisling as well, even though she hadn't ever told him what happened—and didn't plan on ever doing so. It was a horrible summer solstice and the reason she stayed home during them now.

Harlie watched Aisling, and then he resumed pacing. "The Biotáille olc are nasty spirits who got pulled back to the other side once they died. Nix would be a great example, except that the power to create new Biotáille olc is long gone from the worlds. They look for times of weakness of the veil. Some days, like solstice or imbolc, when the veil is thinner, they try to come through. But they can't do it on their own. A powerful magic user has to pull them through to this side. Sacrifices and rituals must be made. They occupy bodies of people on this side and let evil reign. Cryptic, but truthful." His brown eyes were sad as he looked to Aisling. "The last attempt on record was over fifteen years ago, during the summer solstice in Los Angeles."

"Oh damn." Caradoc looked ready to hug Aisling, but she held up her hand.

"Not talking about it, still too close. But yeah, Garran and I were both involved in that. Surratt too. You can ask him when we're back at the flat."

Both Reece and Maeve kept their arms around her.

"Agreed, this isn't the place." Harlie nodded. "I'm

not saying one of them is driving that car, but there is something not of this side of the veil involved in it. It might not even have a driver, but it had powerful magic of some sort. I believe somehow it was connected to the Biotáille olc."

Caradoc scowled. "Of course, it did…although with the heavy tinting, I didn't see one. Okay, then what would the ghost people have done if we passed them a third time?"

"If my feelings at the time were right, it would have merged with this car and sent our souls beyond the veil. I believe they are drawn to the ghau pendant, but they know it will eventually destroy them."

Aisling pulled out her pendant. Thanks to Harlie it again looked like a silver Celtic knot. "This thing is drawing creatures from the other side? Can you block it?" Even though she knew it wouldn't do any good, she tugged on the chain, trying to lift it over her head. Nothing.

"I *am* blocking it." Harlie walked closer and narrowed his eyes. "But maybe I can do more." He said a few dark-sounding words and the pendant felt heavier. It looked the same though. "This should hold for a while, but we need to block Bart's as well. I doubt it's a coincidence that he's gone missing at this time. I think we need to call in the Draoi."

Caradoc and Aisling gasped at the term, but Reece and Maeve looked confused.

Aisling responded first. "The Draoi are a fey group of hermits, also known as Alc mages. They don't hang out together really, they're far too powerful to take that risk. As strong as Harlie is, he's nothing compared to them. Or so we're told. Surratt called at least one in when the issue fifteen years ago took place. I didn't meet them."

"They are truly powerful, and as such live in extreme areas of the world. Ones less likely to have repercussions if their magic goes wrong. I believe once we get Jones,

Stella, and Dailten back, we should try reaching out to them. Stella knows someone in the Alert, Alaska Draoi compound." Harlie stopped where Caradoc was just closing the hood. "If you don't mind? I can make it difficult for anyone to track this vehicle. Both from the other side and this one."

Caradoc stepped back with a shrug. "Go ahead, I just wanted to make sure everything went back into place. This was the first emergency use of the flying element."

"Thank you." Harlie closed his eyes, muttered a few words, then nodded. The vehicle looked the same, but he nodded. "Now, we probably want to get to London and get our friends back. Before…" He dropped his sentence and scrambled back into the car.

Caradoc swore. "I hate it when he does that. Get inside folks."

"We're in, what were you saying?" Aisling was in-between Harlie and Reece.

"That we need to move, now. Right now. Zoom zoom." Harlie was behind Caradoc and tapped on his head.

"Damn it, you need to tell us why." But Caradoc still started the car and got on the road. He was quickly back on the motorway. Everyone was looking for a bright yellow Maserati.

"Because there is something that is going to happen here. Well, where we were." He looked at his watch. "Very soon. Drive faster."

He wasn't asking Caradoc to fly, but there was an unusual tenseness to his voice.

Caradoc punched it and zigged through traffic. There was a muffled explosion behind them, and Aisling saw a cloud of smoke go up.

"What the hell was that? Could we have stopped it?" She twisted around but after the initial cloud the smoke was dissipating.

"It was a minor explosion. A car blew a tire coming down the off-ramp and blew up."

"I know you're a precog, but you could tell that?"

"No. It was predicted a while ago. Hard to explain, but someone wanted that car to blow up. At that time and at that place. It may or may not have been related to us."

Reece looked as frustrated as Aisling felt. Getting answers out of Harlie was getting more difficult.

"We will talk about it more once we get our friends."

Maeve jumped as her phone rang. "Hello? Hold on." She handed it back to Reece. "Jones."

"What now?" The tone of Reece's voice as he answered wasn't good. Jones was definitely the type who wouldn't call unless things had gone in the crapper. "Damn it, get out of there. We'll get you, then work on getting Bart back." He listened for a few more moments, then hung up and gave the phone back to Maeve. "The entire Area 42 London branch has been closed down due to an industrial accident. Toxic cleaning supplies were spilled."

"And we know that's not the case?" Harlie asked.

"Dunno, did you see a future image of it?" Reece had some precog abilities, but nothing compared to Harlie.

"I did not, but I see what you mean. The likelihood of such a coincidence is rare."

"Just tell me where to go." Caradoc kept up his speed. They weren't to London proper yet, but it wouldn't be long.

"Whoever was attacking the place vanished not long after I spoke to Jones the first time. They got out of the building." Reece gave him directions to a warehouse. "Stella currently has the three of them disguised as homeless people on a side road. They still didn't find Bart."

Harlie had been scowling as he contemplated something, then smiled. "We can use Aisling's ghau to track Bart's ghau."

"Isn't it supposed to be hidden?" Maeve turned back as Aisling lifted her pendant out.

"Yes, and it will remain so until we get back to the flat. But I believe there is a connection between the two pendants. We will have to break into the Area 42 building however."

"What if there really is a chemical spill?" Aisling didn't trust Area 42, but she also knew things could happen.

"I've improved my masks," Caradoc used his mad inventors' tone. "Full body now, totally invisible, and should block anything they've let loose."

His masks had saved many from the toxic fumes when Nix attacked London. Caradoc's inventions usually worked. Hopefully that continued to be the case.

Aisling's phone rang. "Am I safe to answer it? It's not issued by Area 42." But she also had left it behind for a month.

Caradoc nodded. "I kept it secured while you were gone."

Aisling nodded, saw who was calling, switched to speaker, and accepted the call. "What's wrong, Garran?" She knew he wouldn't be calling just to tell them he and Surratt made it back to the flat. Caradoc had given Garran his own key, so there would be no trouble getting in.

"Mott's missing. We just got here. The front doors were busted open, there's a mess in the kitchen, and he might have been throwing lunch items at whoever broke in. No sign of blood, but he's gone."

"Damn it." Aisling briefly told him about their issues. "We have to try to find Bart."

"And we'll see what we can do to track Mott. Our prisoner has been dumped in the tub in one of the bathrooms and Surratt and I are fixing the front doors. Keep in touch."

Aisling ended the call. "Did my return trigger these

events? Well, mine and Bart's, although it seems that no one knew he was through the veil."

Harlie studied her for a few moments, then shook his head. "I don't believe so, at least not in the way you're thinking. I believe that you were not expected to return, and the situation would have been far worse had that been the case."

"But was there any weirdness like this going on while I was gone?" She really didn't want it to be because of her.

"No," Harlie said, then grabbed her hand and made her look at him. "But I believe it was building. We've no idea if pushing you through the veil was planned or simply an opportunity for those ghanloughs when they came after our mother. Everything that's happened in the past year, and probably before that, has been building to something. I fear we're seeing the start of it now."

"And taking out Area 42 one way or another would help with that," Reece said. "I'd agree this has been in the works for a while."

Aisling looked at the serious faces around her. "So, what do we do? Beyond picking up Jones, Dailten, and Stella, finding Bart, and rescuing Mott?" She had no idea, even if they got Bart and Mott back, how so few could win against whatever was going on.

"We will need more allies. From both sides of the veil."

Even though no one looked to her at Harlie's words, she felt like they were. "I'm not going back through the veil. Besides, the dryads have their own issues."

"Which makes sense." Maeve turned to the back seat. "Not the helping part, but the being under attack. If the veil is weakening on both sides, then the forces behind it want to destabilize both sides."

"Which brings us back to what do we do about it?" Reece looked around. "We can't do anything until we get the others back."

London loomed ahead of them as Reece gave Caradoc

the coordinates for where Jones, Stella, and Dailten were. They got off the motorway and drifted through several smaller roads. Each time the GPS would have to adjust. Caradoc seemed to have an idea where he was going, he just wasn't following whatever the GPS was telling him.

They eventually got to a more run-down part of the city, still one or two nice buildings but most hadn't been taken care of in the last few hundred years. After some loops around different blocks, they found a group of three down on their luck gnomes.

The tallest one stood as they approached and peeked in on the driver's side. "We aren't all going to fit there." It was Jones, regardless of the illusion that Stella had put on him.

"Ah, ye of little faith." Caradoc grinned, then looked around before he hit a button. "You might all want to wait outside the car, this baby's been doing a lot of changes today."

They all scrambled out as Stella dropped the illusions on the three of them. Dailten was back to looking ready to break off arms and beat the previous owners with them. She was a spiritualist and precog like Harlie, but right now her normally cranky harpy nature was overriding everything else. She was pissed and hadn't found anyone to hurt yet.

Caradoc's car shimmied and at first it looked like it was done transforming. Then, with what almost sounded like a burp, the car reformatted into a massive SUV.

Aisling peeked inside. Yup, three full rows of seats. "Do I even want to know how much this thing cost?" She knew Caradoc was rich, but between this thing and that full floor flat he'd rented, he was burning through it fast.

"Nope, you don't. It's also bulletproof. Couldn't find a way to make it safe from monsters beyond the veil yet though."

"Okay, folks, get inside." Harlie was twitchy and kept

glancing at the tall buildings. "We need to move before we try to scan for Bart." He climbed in and sat in the back row. Dailten joined him and the rest filtered in. Once the car was loaded, Caradoc took off.

Aisling turned back to the others and told them about Surratt, Garran, and Mott.

"I'd like to know why there were people after Surratt and Garran." Jones looked around with narrowed eyes.

Aisling sighed and briefly told them about the lost-prince connection.

"That's not good, none of it. Especially Mott being taken." Stella frowned. "Let me call Grundog."

"I thought she went back to the states after the battle for London?" Reece sat next to Aisling, but he was watching the streets as they passed.

"That's what they wanted everyone to think. Most of the trolls who came over from California have now joined the Ckiong and are staying here. They've been lying low though. But if anyone can track Mott—they can." She dialed her phone, explained what happened, and hung up. "Message. But she'll get on it."

"You didn't tell them where he was taken from."

"Nope, they knew where we were." Stella put her phone away. "Now, how are we finding Bart? The Area 42 people separated him after we talked to you. We should have left when they tried that." Stella was a tiny woman of a certain age. But right now no one with any sort of brain would go up against her—even without knowing she was a magically powerful changeling.

"Bart still believes in Area 42—at least enough to not want to be declared dead," Reece said.

"And having a target on his back as a missing-in-action-at-risk would be a bad thing," Jones added from his seat next to Stella. "But part of me agrees, we still should have left the moment they tried to separate us. I can see taking Stella and Dailten out, but even on leave,

I'm still part of them." From the tone in his voice, like Reece, that statement might not be true for much longer.

"I agree that all of you should leave them." Harlie's voice was low and he seemed to be calculating something on his phone. "But first we need to get Bart back. Aisling? Can you hold your pendant out in front of you and repeat these words? Hyithalin nothaer tribusrt."

The pronunciation of all three was tricky, and she had no idea what language it was as it was nothing like she'd heard before. But after four tries she felt a warming from her pendant. And a tug. "It's warmer going that way, and it's pulling that direction." She held it more to the left and moved it back. "Definitely to the left."

"We should have put you in the front seat," Maeve said as she grabbed the dash at Caradoc's sharp left turn.

Aisling shrugged and directed Caradoc through several side streets. "Not sure if it's good or not, but it's getting warmer." The pendant didn't look red, but it was quickly getting too warm to hold. She grabbed it by the chain instead. Then an image flashed in her mind. It was more like she went to the place. A side park with a steep hill. Bart was tied up and unconscious at the bottom.

"Here! Stop here!" Still holding the pendant by the chain, she jumped out of the car before Caradoc came to a complete stop. Reece followed her into the park. "He's down there, I saw him." She heard the others running after them as she raced into the small park. It was the right park, but it took a moment to orient herself. Then she saw the hill. "There."

"Who are you people? This is a private…" The elf shouting at them dropped his complaint when Reece, Jones, and Maeve all flashed badges and guns. In fact, he nodded and ran out of the park.

Aisling would ask them just what badges they were using after they found Bart.

He was where she'd seen him in her mind, but facing

the wall at the base of the hill. There was no blood that she could see as she skidded down to him and gently rolled him over. His eyes were closed, but his chest was slowly moving. "Bart? Do you hear me?" He appeared to be unconscious, but it couldn't hurt to try. No response and she was just reaching to untie his hands when shouting came from the direction of Caradoc's car.

"Aisling! No! That's not me!" A battered and stumbling Bart came racing down the hill behind the others. Jones and Reece grabbed him as he tried to pass them. He didn't fight, but kept yelling. "Don't touch its skin!"

Aisling had been about to check his pulse but froze. Instead, she rolled back on her heels and stepped away.

The Bart on the ground flashed his eyes open—they were red except in what would be the whites—they were a bright green goo color.

CHAPTER ELEVEN

"EVERYONE GET BACK!" Aisling yelled as the fake Bart easily ripped through the ties binding his hands and feet, then removed the tape over his mouth. His movements were fast, like elven fast, but jerky.

"It's a doppelganger. The people that grabbed me created them. There's another in the Area 42 holding area…unless it already attacked everyone." This Bart's face was a mass of bruises, and he wasn't standing well. His shirt was torn open at the neck and there were scratches all around his pendant.

"How do we stop it?" Jones had his gun aimed at the thing's head. Reece, Maeve, and Caradoc did the same. Stella was stalking toward it with a spell crackling from her fingers. Dailten just stood in place with her arms folded and her eyes hooded.

"Harlie? Ideas?" Aisling didn't know if guns would hurt it, and she was pretty sure that both Stella and Dailten intended to physically touch that monster in order to rip it apart. Which, while she wasn't sure about the beat-up Bart's claim, she figured would be a bad idea.

Harlie stood calmly at the back of the group, then nodded and walked forward. "That is a copy, a Xilen, very close to a true doppelganger. And it is deadly. Don't shoot unless you have no choice, but everyone should start taking steps backwards." Even as he spoke, *he* continued moving forward.

Aisling stayed where she was. "Not moving. Someone has to back you up." None of the others moved either, aside from Dailten spreading her wings. The wicked hooks on the end of each were extremely noticeable.

"You are an extremely stubborn group." Harlie appeared relaxed, he sounded relaxed, but as he passed Aisling, she saw the tension in his neck. Whatever spell he was pulling up, it was a strong one.

He cast his spell at the same moment that the fake Bart leapt forward. The real Bart was on the other side of Harlie and grabbed hold of his pendant. Aisling did the same and both pendants flared and sent something alongside Harlie's spell. The world spun, then the evil Bart vanished in a puff of dark smoke.

And Harlie dropped to the ground, looking stunned.

"Harlie!" Aisling ran up to him; her pendant went back to normal the instant the Xilen vanished. Or exploded. It was hard to tell what happened to it.

"I'm okay. Those ghau really pack a punch. It was helpful they were along, as it turned out," Harlie sounded weak and wasn't making a move to get off the ground. "But my spell was surprised when they joined in."

If it were anyone else, Aisling would question the person acting as if their spell was sentient, but with Harlie it was just part of who he was. "Was that fake Bart destroyed?"

"Yes, but I would have rather contained it to find out who called it. Xilen are difficult to create." There was more he wasn't saying. "This one wasn't done right, or its eye color wouldn't have changed."

Aisling turned to Bart, who'd also fallen to the ground. But he was just sitting.

"Damn that hurt." He rubbed the area around his pendant.

"Are those marks from it? Mine got warm, but didn't hurt me."

"Most of these are from the bastards who snagged me out of an Area 42 office the instant I was called back. They grabbed me to get the ghau, but it wouldn't come off. But that spell Harlie flung hurt like hell." He looked around the park. "And I think getting out of here would be a damn good idea." People were being drawn to the park from the explosion, slowly, but it wouldn't be long before a crowd showed up.

"Agreed." Reece came forward and he and Jones helped Bart to his feet and supported him as they walked back to Caradoc's car. Stella and Dailten climbed in the very back with him. Both were making tsking sounds as they started healing some of his injuries.

Maeve stayed with Aisling as the others went back to the car as well. "What's wrong? Well, more wrong?"

Aisling shook her head and kept her hand on her pendant. It was cool now, but there was a weird feeling in the air. "I can't explain it. I don't doubt Harlie that the Xilen is dead, but something's changed. Like this was a test of some kind." She gave a shiver then turned toward the car. "But Bart was right about us getting out of here. And now I hear sirens." She knew her hearing was better than Maeve's and grabbed her friend's shoulder, spun her, and ran for Caradoc's car.

"All in? I think we should go." Aisling patted the back of Caradoc's seat.

He mumbled about pushy little sisters, but got them away from the park before the police arrived.

"How is he? And why were they after the ghau? And how did they see past Harlie's shielding to know that it was a ghau pendant?" Aisling looked back, but with two new seat rows between her and the rear window it was hard to see anything. She'd have to trust in Caradoc's assorted toys to warn them if they were being followed.

"*He's* going to be fine, thank you very much." Bart was already back to sounding like his curmudgeonly self. "As for the shielding on this thing, no idea. I was escorted to a waiting room and left alone. Four thugs in masks showed up the moment the outer door was shut, dragged me out a side door, and into a van. They took some blood, then worked on forcing this pendant off. I overheard that they made two copies, I assume they meant of me, then were debating cutting off my head to get the pendant."

"How'd you escape?" Reece still had his gun out and a close check showed that Jones did as well.

Aisling didn't blame them—this could be another fake, just better disguised. Although she'd felt his ghau pendant. Not to mention Harlie looked exhausted, but not worried.

"I think they knew you were coming. They got something on their radio, freaked out, and rolled me out of the van as it moved off." He looked to Reece and Jones and gave a deep sigh. "Not that I blame you, but you boys can put away your weapons. I'm me."

Harlie had been looking out the window, but turned back. "It's the real Bart and the real ghau." Then he went back to watching the road.

Caradoc looked back in the rearview mirror. "If no one has any other ideas, I'm going back to Flian to regroup. Maybe Garran and Surratt have leads on Mott." He was ignoring the fact that had they found anything of use, they would have contacted someone in this car.

Reece and Jones both put away their guns. "That's a good idea," Reece said.

"Wait, what?" Bart sat up, causing Stella to push him back in his seat while she worked on him. "Why are they here and what happened to Mott?"

Aisling jumped in first with the updates and caught him up before Caradoc got back on the motorway. She only briefly mentioned the issues they'd had with exploding farmland and mysterious animals coming over.

"That's not good, none of it, and I know you're not telling me everything."

Stella and Dailten finally leaned back and nodded that they'd finished healing Bart, so he buttoned his shirt back up.

"We'll give you the rest on the road, just watch for yellow Maseratis." Maeve turned around from the front seat. Before he could ask, Reece launched into that explanation.

The trip back was quicker, no expensive cars stalking them. The GPS sent them a different way since the road they'd almost been blown up on was now listed as closed.

Bart grunted at that. "No question, Area 42 is involved. And I seriously doubt that none of the agents in that office knew that I'd been taken. I'd love to know who or what was attacking you three in the station, by the way."

"So would I," Jones said. "They had everyone pinned with spell-fire, but I couldn't see them. Once we realized the way to where they took you was blocked, we left."

"Oh, phone?" Dailten held her hand out to Bart. "We're making sure anything that might have connections to Area 42 is shut down."

Bart didn't hesitate as he fished in his back pocket for his phone and handed it to her. She passed it up to Harlie. Although he was still watching the road, he took the phone, held it in both hands, then slipped it in a pocket.

"I'll run more of a check and get some high-level security on everyone's phones when we get back." Caradoc got off the motorway. Still no sign of a yellow sports car or anyone else following them.

"How long has Mott been missing?" Bart asked. "I don't need to tell any of you that what he has in that brain of his is more dangerous than anything all of us together know."

"We have no idea," Caradoc said. "He was gone when Garran, Surratt, and their prisoner got there, which was almost an hour ago. But whoever took him probably broke in not long after we left. They said he'd made a mess in the kitchen and he had been planning to make lunch when we left." There was a low-level growl in Caradoc's voice.

Mott was his friend, and he was obviously upset about him being taken. But Aisling knew he was probably equally upset that someone had broken the protection he'd set up around the flat. Caradoc was a powerful magic user, but didn't use it much. When he did, he expected it to work as well as his tech. Having both bypassed wasn't making him happy.

Everyone stayed lost in their thoughts as they pulled into the lot for their flat. Caradoc waited until everyone was out then clicked a few buttons on his key fob. The car shrunk back to a normal sized sports car, glowed green, then vanished.

"Nice hiding." Aisling stepped forward to touch it. "It still has a physical presence. What if someone pulls into this spot?"

"Ah, sister of little faith." Caradoc grinned and hit another button. A beat up old four door sedan appeared. "And if anyone should see through the disguise, the alarm on this thing is loud and aggressive."

Reece was the only one suitably impressed as they walked back to the rental flat. The front receptionist waved Caradoc over. He nodded a few times, then came back as they went to the stairs.

"She just wanted to say how sorry they were about the break in and they hope nothing important was taken."

"They don't know about Mott?" Aisling asked.

"No. I doubted Garran or Surratt would have said anything, and clearly they didn't. The front desk was more concerned about potential damages. I told them my insurance would take care of it." The stairwell opened to the flat entrance. From the outside, the door and frame looked just as they'd left it, but the tingle she felt as they walked in told her it was a spell.

The front room looked pristine, but everyone spread out to check the entire flat, just in case. Since she doubted that Garran or Surratt would have taken time to straighten things, it looked like whoever broke in only wanted Mott. A quick peek in the closest bathroom showed the beat-up farmer, Lathen, in the tub. Bound, gagged, and still asleep.

The kitchen was a mess. Not only were there assorted lunch meats, cheese slices, and bread thrown everywhere, every knife was thrown. Including dull ones. Judging by the wild places they were sticking, Mott might be brilliant, but he didn't have good aim.

Harlie stuck his head into the kitchen, looked around, then went back to the front room.

"Should we fix all of the phones before we try to call Garran?" Aisling asked Caradoc.

"Yeah. Damn, he put up a fight. He should have been safe here."

"It wasn't your fault, we all thought he'd be safe here." Maeve patted his arm.

"He should have been," Reece said from where he and Jones were looking over a knife pattern in the corner. "We're playing too much catch up on this, we need to figure out who's behind everything."

They all went to the front room where Harlie had taken apart two phones. Most likely Reece's and Bart's, unless he'd started pickpocketing people.

Jones dropped his phone next to Harlie, then sat further down the table. Caradoc sat next to Harlie and pulled out his tool and gizmo kit. Everyone who hadn't already slid their phones toward the brothers did so—even Maeve.

"I thought your phone was fixed?" Aisling sat next to her friend at the table.

"So did I, but Caradoc has new additions." Maeve shook her head, but the look on her face as she watched him was adoration. Then she turned back to Aisling. "What's that smirk?"

"Not a single thing," Aisling said. "Just glad for you two."

It took Harlie and Caradoc ten minutes to fix all the phones, which was akin to a few hours work for anyone else. They'd been working together, passing the phones back and forth. Harlie spelled them, and Caradoc added new tech to each.

"Okay, who wants to call Garran?" Caradoc slid everyone back their phones. He kept the question open but was looking pointedly at Bart.

"Fine, as long as you're both certain this won't give us away." He looked around the room. "Not to mention that we're in a compromised flat."

"I already checked for any stealth devices; Harlie checked for magical ones. We're good for now." Caradoc gave a sigh as he looked around. "But you're right, we can't stay here. Call Garran first, then we'll see where to go."

"I'll keep it short, since we don't know if their phones are compromised." Bart punched in the call, then set the phone on speaker.

"Good to hear from you." Garran had a low level of annoyance in his voice—they hadn't found Mott yet. "It's been a slow day."

"Got you on speaker with the group, same here. Phones might be compromised. Any luck?"

"Not a thing. We're coming back in."

"See you then." Bart hung up the phone and got to his feet. "We need to get out of here asap. Everyone grab what you need to keep."

"What? I thought they were coming in?" Maeve asked, but everyone else looked ready to do the same.

Bart was already heading for his room. "They are staying put for now, we can call them when we're out. Garran and I used to work together a few lifetimes ago. Slow day is code for everything's gone to hell, get out of wherever you are."

CHAPTER TWELVE

"WHAT? DAMN, YOU'RE calm." Caradoc shoved everything back into his tech box and ran to his room.

Aisling shook her head. She hadn't seen it, but she could imagine how much tech junk he had spread around in there.

"How much time do we think we have?" Harlie got to his feet. He didn't look as totally wiped out as he had after destroying the Xilen of Bart, but he still seemed tired.

Bart shrugged as he headed for his room. "Not sure. But slow day is things are going into the crapper—get out. Dead day is get out immediately. Since he didn't pick that, I'd say we have time to get what we need."

"What are we going to do with Lathen?" Maeve pointed toward the bathroom where the farmer who'd attacked them was tied up in the tub.

"I think we have to leave him behind," Bart said. "I understand that he was involved in the attack at his farm, and those illegally modified rapeseed plants you told me about, but we can't haul him around with us."

"I can make sure he forgets the last twenty-four hours." Harlie paused outside of his bedroom. "Rather, I can help Aisling do it. My magic is taxed after securing this place and the phones." He didn't mention what he'd done to the duplicate Bart, but Aisling knew that spell had hit him hard.

Caradoc and Aisling both looked at each other. Neither of those activities should have wiped him out, even after dealing with the Xilen Bart. But they couldn't deal with it now.

"Let's do it, I didn't get a chance to unpack much, but I think we want to get out of here sooner rather than later," Aisling said as she and Harlie went to the bathroom.

"What do I do?" Aisling knelt next to the tub. While she agreed that hauling him around wouldn't work, she hated losing a connection to whatever was going on. She had a bad feeling that when they got a chance to look at the rapeseed plant dust, no one was going to be happy. Without intel from Lathen, there was no way to tell if any other rapeseed fields were also compromised. And there were a lot of those bright yellow fields around.

"Just hold both of your hands directly over his forehead. Then cast a level two cleansing spell."

She scowled as she tried to recall that one. It was one of the newer ones he'd taught her. She finally found it and cast it. The spell felt tingly in her fingers and it seemed like he'd twitched as she cast it.

"Okay. Now how do we know if it worked?" Short of waking Lathen up and asking him if he knew them, she couldn't think of a way to check.

Harlie bent down and closed his eyes. Then finally stood back up. "It worked a bit too well. From what I can tell, you removed his memories from the past week."

"Damn. That's a scary spell." Aisling got to her feet. "Let's not have me do it again unless it's life or death, okay? At least until I get more control over it."

Harlie nodded. "Did the pendant get involved?"

Aisling was ready to say no, then she noticed that it was warm. "It might have. It's felt different since we crossed back through the veil. Like it's sentient." That was an extremely disturbing thought that she wasn't even going to pursue—at least for a very long time. The damn thing already freaked her out.

"It's changing." Harlie narrowed his eyes and scowled at the pendant. "It would make sense that going back and forth through the veil did something to it. Tell me or Bart if anything else happens."

Aisling nodded, then they both went to pack.

Aisling was the first one back in the front room—it helped that the majority of her things were still packed and she hadn't been here for a month adding to them.

"How are you feeling?" Reece came out at the same time Jones did, but after dropping his bags in the front room, Jones went back into the kitchen.

"Tired, yet also edgy?" She shrugged. "That spell Harlie had me use took out a lot, but at the same time I feel ready to fight something." She held up the ghau pendant. "I think this thing is messing around. I hope we find a way to get it off without removing my head."

Honestly, knowing these pendants, even taking their heads off still might not do it. She needed to speak to a vallenian and figure out what was needed before these things caused more trouble. That whoever grabbed Bart knew he had one on, even though he'd just come back, it was shielded, and tucked under his shirt, wasn't good.

"That would be a good thing, I'm fond of that head of yours." He looked ready to say more, but a shout from the kitchen cut him off.

They both ran in to see Jones up on the counter, looking at one of Mott's flung knives. "I think I know where they went, or at least where Mott thought they'd be going. Avebury. Might be Stonehenge, but the circle of knives is too wide."

"Besides, Mott said Avebury was where he wanted to go. The veil will be thinnest in the middle of all those standing stones." Aisling looked at the knives and was amazed that Jones picked up anything out of the apparently random knife throwing.

"How in the hell did Mott have time to throw all of those knives while obviously being overwhelmed?" Reece studied the knives as Jones jumped off the counter. "And how did you pick up Avebury from them?"

Jones grinned and held up a slip of paper. "This was on the knife in the ceiling."

It was an advert for a café in Avebury that had been ripped from a magazine.

"He's a champion knife thrower and was carrying around a snippet of where he wanted to go?" Aisling took it and shook her head. "But how do we know that's where whoever took him went?"

"Probably because whoever took him wanted to know about the veil. He might not have been sure that was where they were taking him. But he was telling us that was where he was going to tell them they needed to go." Caradoc had come in. "It could be something other than the veil, but I think we agree everything is connecting to that."

"So, we go to Avebury." Reece shrugged. "I would like to get another car though, no offense to your super vehicle, but it is extremely noticeable."

Stella popped her head in. "Dailten has one you can use. We were tooling about this past month in it, didn't take it to London because she hates driving there."

They all left the kitchen. The front room was full of belongings and one of Caradoc's gizmos was whirling in the middle of the table. Three antennas bobbled out of the top. Aisling was going to ask what it did, then decided it would just hurt her head to find out.

"We might even want more than two," Aisling said. "There's a lot going on, and if we're all targets, we should be as spread out as possible." Part of her felt safer having her friends and brothers around her—the other part pointed out that a single target was much easier to hit than a bunch of them.

"I agree, we're too vulnerable like this," Reece said. "Stella, Dailten, and Jones take Dailten's car. Aisling, Harlie, and I can get a rental; Caradoc, Maeve, and Bart go in Caradoc's."

"Nice splitting, we should have magic and firepower represented with each group." Bart looked up from a discussion with Dailten. "I think we're going to need more people. But not yet. I have calls out to three people I still trust in Area 42, one of them being Narissa Jhali, the flyer who helped during the London crisis. I just want to keep in touch with folks who might help."

Maeve nodded. "I heard from MI-6, or rather the Closen, the supernatural offshoot I'm tentatively assigned to. Basically it was to lay low and that there were more problems with Area 42. Not very helpful, that. I don't know that we can count on either group for support."

Reece was fussing on his phone and eventually hung up. "I got a rental car. The other one I had was registered as destroyed in an industrial accident. And it wasn't reported by me." He didn't look happy. "I went with another car rental company."

"Most likely Area 42 cleaning things up," Bart said. "It wouldn't be that hard for them to track it down just by the license plate. I wish I knew who else had been involved with it."

"And that we'd had time to check that plant dust before running off again." Caradoc nodded to Harlie. "Still have it?"

Harlie patted his pocket. "Yes, I believe the veil has been opening to this side more than we thought and we'll find evidence in the dust once I can take a longer look at it."

They picked up their things and headed for the door.

"Isn't us leaving Lathen going to be a problem? We abandon our flat after being attacked and there's a bound and unconscious body left behind?" Maeve asked. She had far more with her than her usual light travel supplies—it looked like Caradoc's collection had flooded over to her.

"I've taken care of that." Caradoc nodded toward the bathroom door as they passed. "He's currently untied and should wake up in an hour or so. I'm going to call the front desk at that point and say there was an intruder alert in my flat."

"Aren't they going to think it's odd we're all leaving with everything?" Stella asked.

"Not really. I've paid for the flat for the next two months—they don't care beyond getting their money."

They took the stairs with Caradoc carefully leaving the front door barely ajar. Since there were no other flats on this floor, no one should notice it until he called it in.

"I'll take the lead and hit the car rental place first." Caradoc extended his car back into the full massive SUV version—but this time it was for room for his stuff.

"What did you do while Bart and I were gone, rob a tech store?" Aisling, Harlie, and Reece took the last row once their luggage was squished in.

"No. We needed this stuff to find you two." He glanced back as he took the driver's seat. "Okay, I needed it. But I still think we need it. There're some crazy things going on and if we have to go underground, I can't be running out for supplies." He waited until Stella, driving Dailten's car, pulled up alongside them, then took off.

"Is it a good idea to have Stella driving? She kinda has a bat-out-of-hell technique." Aisling looked behind and from what she could see through everything piled up, Stella was right on their bumper.

"Better than Dailten." Harlie didn't look back but nodded. "She drove us around to check a few locations before we settled on that flat. She doesn't use brakes much."

Aisling could imagine. Harpies were often high-strung and excitable. Dailten really wasn't as bad as most, but she also didn't seem to be patient.

Caradoc was pulling into a large car rental station when the radio came on with an alert. "Stand by for a message from the High King and Queen." He parked, but they all waited.

"Due to dangerous inconsistencies within the British government, as well as that of the United States, the High Queen and King will be assuming rulership over both lands—for human, hybrids, and fey. This will certainly be temporary until the crisis has passed." The speaker wasn't either of the two royals, but spoke so fast that it took Aisling's mind a moment to catch up.

"I know we were gone for a while, but what crisis? And can they really do that? The US government leaders and the British Parliament are elected." The British royals, and even the Prime Minister, were mostly figureheads since the fey royals kept their primary home in Northumbria. But the Americans were fiercely independent.

"There isn't an emergency or crisis that we've heard of. But this goes in keeping with however they are involved with what's going on with the veil." Bart started to dial someone, then shut his phone down. "I'm not even sure who to reach out to."

Reece got out of the car and went into the rental office.

Aisling and Harlie got their stuff and Reece's from the back of Caradoc's car and waited near the trunk.

"Have the High King and Queen ever done this before? Like ever?" Aisling watched the people passing on the street, many were glued to their phones or sitting in their cars in shock. It was good to know she wasn't the only one.

"Never. Not since immediately after the Black Death ended," Harlie said. "They did take over during it, the human governments were in shambles at the time. But once things settled they ruled in conjunction with the human rulers of all the lands."

"After they'd made sure we couldn't out-populate them, you mean." Maeve got out of the car. "There must be a reason for them doing this now. They picked off the two strongest countries, the European Empire will be next. Unless they're bold enough to go after the Asian conglomerates."

"I doubt that it will take long to pull in Europe. As for Asia? Depends how confident the High King and Queen are feeling. But there is no way the Asian stronghold would go down without a serious fight." Caradoc stayed in his car, but kept the door open. "I wonder if our mother is involved."

Stella had parked Dailten's car alongside Caradoc's and nodded when she heard him. "You said is, not was. Do you think she's alive?"

"I won't believe she's dead until I see her body on a funeral pyre. And watch it until it is nothing but dust." Caradoc shook his head. "We can't assume she's not involved otherwise."

"Do you think this has anything to do with what I found out about our father?" Aisling wasn't sure how they could be connected, but if she had her murder board this would be a giant knot of twisting lines crossing over each other. "Odd question, what happened to my murder board briefcase?"

Caradoc had made her a portable version of her long destroyed white board. It had taken some getting used to, but it did help her sort things out. It hadn't been in her things, but she hadn't thought of it either.

"It's in my massive pile of gadgets." Caradoc grinned.

"Don't worry, I kept it safe for you." His grin fell. "I'm not sure what's linked to what. But if there is something going on between both sides of the veil, and if our father's true status is well known on the other side, we have to assume it's connected. And not in a good way."

CHAPTER THIRTEEN

"I THINK THAT WOULD be the best assumption. We have no idea what's connected now." Harlie kept his small duffle bag next to him. As far as Aisling could tell it was full of everything that he'd brought with him from Nepal when he came to Los Angeles a few months ago. Which wasn't much. "I wish it was safe to contact our father. But I don't know how we could get his memories back."

"*You* think your mother is alive as well? I saw the photos, that was a lot of blood," Dailten said.

"I don't know. I can't sense her, but she is a powerful magic user and whoever took her would have been powerful also. I don't trust any of my siblings beyond Caradoc and Aisling. With our mother missing, at the very least they would have closed ranks at the compound. Our father would be in the middle."

Reece came out of the rental walking quickly and looking behind him. He jogged to a small SUV, gunned the engine, then started toward them.

Two dark garbed men came out of the rental office as he got to Caradoc's car.

"Get in now, throw in the stuff." Reece stopped, but didn't turn off the engine.

Jones got out of Dailten's car and stood behind Reece's

rental car with his gun drawn. "Those two are coming up fast." Not as fast as fey, but they were moving quickly.

Caradoc started his car, Maeve and Bart jumped in. Harlie and Aisling threw their things in the back of Reece's car, moving at full elvish speed. Jones waited until they were in, then got back in Dailten's car.

Before the men got to them, all three cars raced off.

"Did you steal this thing?"

"No. They already killed the owner and took his place, but I didn't realize it until I was leaving. No idea who they are, but they were up to something." Reece looked into the rearview mirror. "And we're being followed. White coupe. I can't tell if there are more people than just those two in it though."

Aisling's phone rang. "What?"

"Get ahead of us, my car is more bulletproof than yours." As Caradoc spoke, Stella zipped ahead of them all.

Reece didn't argue, just passed Caradoc and dropped in behind Stella.

"Who are they?" Aisling kept looking back but Caradoc's monster car blocked everything. "You rented this from a dead man?"

"I don't know, but I had a weird feeling as I walked in. One of them came out, pretending to be the owner. I should have listened to my gut—it said run."

"Why didn't they shoot you then?" Harlie asked from the back seat. "Not that I want them to shoot you. Or us. But it doesn't make sense."

"I…I'm not sure." Reece picked up speed to stay behind Stella. This was one time when preferring to drive fast was a good thing. "When I turned to leave, I saw the body in the back office, the door wasn't shut completely. I also looked both in the eyes. They froze. I mean not blinking, nothing. It didn't last long obviously, but something happened." He sounded far more upset about that than he would have been had they been shooting at him.

With good reason. As a hybrid, Reece *should* have no fey powers. But he'd already shown a few tricks from his fey ancestors. This had to be a new power that had arisen—and Reece clearly wasn't happy about it.

"They're human?" Harlie was turned to look back even though Caradoc's car was only a few feet behind them.

"Yeah, or hybrids, like me." There were a lot of things packed into that statement, but now wasn't the time to address any of them.

"Hang on, Stella's getting on the motorway." Reece continued to follow on her bumper, with Caradoc riding closely behind.

Aisling's phone rang. "Hit the button on the upper right of your screen, the one that looks like a yelling mouth." Aisling hit it, but it looked more like an odd circle. "What now?"

"Let me get Stella's group in too." Caradoc's voice came back a moment later. "We now have secure walkie-talkies. Easier with multiple phones. I think our friends have picked up another car behind us, there's a dark blue one pacing the white one on the left. Keep an eye out if there are more—they must have called ahead to their friends when we went this way."

"I'm seeing three cars slowing ahead of us. Just them, no one ahead of them," Dailten said. Stella switched lanes with Reece and Caradoc following her. The cars ahead of them also switched lanes.

"Are they seriously trying to pin us on a motorway?" Reece was pissed as he raised his voice to be heard by the walkie-talkie phone. "Stella, I'm taking the lead, there's something wrong with those three in front of us. You two stay close behind me."

His rental SUV was new, which was a good thing, as

Reece's maneuvers could have broken an older car. The motorway wasn't that crowded, but he switched lanes quickly, forcing the three cars in front to follow his moves and the ones behind to back off for a moment. Then he pulled alongside the smallest of the three on its right side. "Hang on!" He acted like he was passing them, then veered slightly to nick the other car. At their speed even a tap could cause a collision.

Aisling screamed and grabbed the dash, but Reece's timing was perfect. Their car barely reacted to the impact, whereas the other car swung into the one to its left and then they both smashed into the third. Stella and Caradoc stayed right behind him. The cars that had been chasing them slammed into the growing pileup.

"Damn it, that white car is still coming," Caradoc said.

Aisling twisted around to look back. Yup, the white car's driver had better timing than the other four and hadn't gotten stuck in the smashup snarl.

"I'm getting off the motorway, it doesn't look like any bystanders were hit, but better to get off if they start shooting." Reece moved over and the other two followed.

"Us Brits aren't as gun crazy as you, you know," Maeve said from Caradoc's car.

"Wanna take the chance that they aren't armed?" Reece crossed two lanes to get to the off ramp.

"Nope. That swearing you hear is Caradoc, by the way."

"Yeehaw!!!" Stella yelled as she came tearing down the ramp, passing both of them.

"Still back there." Harlie twisted in his seat to get a better look. "They are most determined. But I don't sense any magic from them. However…." he dropped his words as a new car, a large gray SUV, zipped off the ramp and slammed into the white car in a move similar to what Reece had just done on the motorway—only with a lot more force. "They have magic. Fey. Asian." Harlie closed his eyes as he tried to sense more.

"Lazing?" Reece swore as he turned down a side road. The Lazing were an Asian fey gang, one of the most powerful groups in the world. They worked with their own agenda and had been hunting down Nix for the past year to take care of his still being alive issue.

They'd also brought out one of their highest-level magic users, a shachen mage, in the final battle against Nix to save London. Many of their people had died, but their contribution turned the fight.

So, there was a chance they were still on their side. Or they wanted the men who'd killed the car rental owner to get out of the way so they could take care of Aisling and the rest directly. Their motivations were known only to them, and if it suited them, they'd switch back to being enemies. With Nix gone, there was no way to know their current motivation.

"How many are in that car?" Caradoc was probably thinking like Aisling—were the Lazing here to help or to hurt? A single car against all of them probably wouldn't win, unless it was a full car of Lazing mages. Even if there wasn't a shachen mage with them, Lazing trained harder than anyone else—even their low-level mages were deadly.

"Five. All mages." Harlie was far too calm about this.

"Shit. I'm pulling over. We can't win if they come after us on the road and use magic." Reece turned into a shopping center parking lot. The huge Tesco grocery store had a fair number of cars around it, but Reece stuck to the edge of the lot where it was mostly empty. Hopefully close enough to convince the Lazing not to attack, but far enough not to hurt innocents if they decided to do so anyway.

Stella and Caradoc pulled in alongside and everyone was out of their cars as the Lazing SUV pulled into the lane across from them.

The doors opened slowly and five male elves got out. All in black, all wearing dark sunglasses. No weapons that Aisling could see, but Lazing mages probably didn't need them. They might not be stronger than Caradoc and Harlie, but they would be close. And there were five of them.

They all stood there as if posing for a photo op, then the tallest stepped forward. "Are you Harthinatle?"

Stella bounced in front of Harlie. "Who wants to know?" Her fists were clenched and Dailten came up next to her with her wings open.

"I am. Might I ask who you are?" Harlie spoke as if two little old ladies weren't standing between himself and the Lazing, looking ready to start breaking heads.

"I am Satoshi. We have a mutual friend." He rattled off what sounded like a name but had to have been in an ancient fey dialect.

Harlie nodded. "She was a strong spirit and is missed in this world." He turned to Aisling and the others. "A friend long lost before any of you were born."

"She is my grandmother and her spirit lives on," Satoshi said.

"Kana was never a believer in the Lazing, or their actions." Harlie's voice clearly held disappointment.

"She approved my joining when I was a child. I work for the good of all, not just the good of the Lazing or the empire. I bring balance to the Lazing. You are all in grave danger." His voice was calm, but he watched the parking lot carefully.

"Here? Or in general?" Bart stepped forward. Satoshi might know of Harlie, but Bart was taking the lead again.

"Barthlinio, it is an honor to meet you. I would say now. Those cars were not the only followers. It appears they knew where Larkin would go to get his rental. I know Caradoc Larfin would never let there be a leak in his tech, but there are other ways to follow people." He made another surveillance of the parking lot. "There are fifteen people paying far too much attention to us."

The two mages on the ends of the line of Lazing formed balls of crackling power in their hands, but kept them low.

Bart and Reece both subtly looked around. Jones dropped back and acted as if he were going back into Dailten's car.

"So, we're going to rumble? Here?" Stella was bouncing on her feet and looked too excited about that idea for it to be good for anyone.

"Hopefully, not." Bart shook his head. "This wouldn't be ideal."

"Yet, you picked it." Satoshi held up a hand. "I know you were hedging your bets, and this is a better choice than some. Harthinatle, could you cause a sense of unease among those shoppers?"

"That might help," Reece said as he also stepped back toward his car. Both he and Jones had their guns on them, so Aisling wasn't sure what they were getting. Then she saw they were both using the cars to block them watching the parking lot behind them.

Harlie nodded and closed his eyes. Nothing appeared to be happening as more shoppers pulled into the lot, parked, and went into the store.

"Are we just going to wait for them to attack us? Maybe leaving would be a better idea?" Maeve shrugged. "I like a good fight as much as the next bloke, but seems silly in this case."

"They will continue to follow you. Their drive to get what they want is overcoming common sense. You need to shut them down now, and show them their prey is not easy." Satoshi's fingers twitched as he looked over the parking lot.

Aisling still wasn't completely sure why these Lazing were throwing themselves in on this fight, Harlie's connection to Satoshi's grandmother excluded. But their help was welcome.

Since the Lazing were facing the lot, they had a much better view. They all stepped apart from each other, still in line, and the crackling balls of some potentially nasty spells now appeared in all their hands except Satoshi's.

Slowly, confused shoppers started coming back out of the Tesco, some with bags, some not. They got in their cars and left. A car in the process of turning into the lot, stopped and went back out.

"It's working, Harlie. Are we assuming that the ones left in the lot are the ones after us? Do we know why?" Aisling was grateful for whatever mojo Harlie was using to send people away, but this was still a public place.

"Some, but more are coming." Satoshi lowered his sunglasses and looked between Aisling and Bart. "They are coming for the power of the ghau pendants. One on this side of the veil wasn't noticeable. Two, however, are causing ripples in dark places."

CHAPTER FOURTEEN

"THEY KNOW WE can't get the necklaces off, right? Seriously, even if they take our heads, I'm not sure they'll come off." Aisling had a flash of saying they didn't have the ghau, but that vanished as she glanced into Satoshi's eyes. He knew and denying it would just be a waste of time.

"Do you have any way to contact the vallenians who gave them to you?"

"No." Aisling wasn't sure she wanted to ever reach them. The one on the other side who'd been so quick to destroy the dryads was still lurking in the back of her mind. Yes, so far, they'd helped her—more or less. But she knew it was only because she was somehow helping them and whatever they were trying to do. When that ended, all bets were off. She also had no idea how to contact them.

A group of what could be described as thugs, both male and female, human and fey, started moving toward them across the parking lot. They weren't running, but walking quickly. And trying not to appear as if they were doing so.

"They are all carrying guns." Harlie opened his eyes. "I know we have some as well, but while I can control spells to keep bystanders safe, I can't control bullets."

Caradoc nodded and ducked back into his SUV. He

came back out with one of his triangular gizmos. "Anyone who has a gun on them, you probably want to remove it. This will short them out in a rather painful way. It shouldn't impact any other electronics as I've narrowed it down to the firing mechanism in guns. I've also extended the range and time, so I should," he glanced around the lot behind him, "be able to keep the entire parking lot and the street out front gun-free for about an hour."

"We'll make sure to finish kicking their asses before then." Stella shared a grin with Dailten.

"Is your wing fully recovered?" Aisling knew she'd been gone a month, but Nix had left some nasty holes in her wing.

"More or less." Her smile was almost as excited as Stella's. And as disturbing. "I can do recon if they try to take off before we're finished with them." Her wings had been partially extended, but she stepped away to fully extend them. They easily reached ten feet across. Harpy wings were almost all versions of the same dark gray coloring with thick feathers and nasty hooks on the top bend. Dailten's looked mostly recovered with patches of thin feathers coming in where the holes had been.

Bart, Reece, Jones, Maeve, and Caradoc set down their guns—four of them, in the case of Jones—in their cars. Maeve and Jones were pure human, with no magic. But they were both such experts in hand-to-hand fighting that Aisling wasn't worried. Reece was an expert at hand-to-hand as well, plus whatever weird magic was coming out from his hybrid side. And although he didn't like to use it, Caradoc was almost as strong of a magic user as Harlie. And Bart was Bart. He didn't look at all distressed when he put his gun away. Aisling had never seen him use much magic, but most gnomes had skills. A top Area 42 agent would have massive skills.

None of the Lazing removed weapons. Most likely they considered them unnecessary.

"It might be considered rude to rush things, and this is your fight, but shall we engage?" Satoshi's smile was small, not friendly, and directed at the people behind them.

Bart cracked his knuckles. "Since you did remove that other car for us, we surrender the opening to you." He gave a slight bow.

Satoshi moved almost faster than even Aisling could see. He hadn't been armed with a spell ball as the others were, but he let loose with a lightning strike as he darted around Caradoc's car. A pair of jack-trolls spun back as the lightning hit. One of them raised his gun as he flew backward.

Caradoc made a tsking sound and hit the button on his gizmo. The loud screams and swearing all around the parking lot was good. Their opponents were now disarmed. Not so good, there were a hell of a lot more people against them than expected. At least thirty were shaking their hands as they moved in.

The rest of the Lazing followed Satoshi in a blur of black suits.

Stella and Dailten were the first after them, but Jones and Reece weren't far behind.

The few non-combatants who remained in the lot ran back into the Tesco and it looked like barricades were being put up. Aisling wasn't sure what a few racks of potato crisps and snack cakes could do to stop attackers, but at least it was something.

She, Maeve, Caradoc, and Bart followed the others.

"I'll stay here to protect the cars," Harlie said. It wasn't that he couldn't fight, he could without ever touching his opponent. But he was more peace driven than the rest of the family. And he had a good point about the cars. It would suck if someone else got near them.

When Bart nodded, Harlie put up a shield over all four cars, then leaned back to watch from the hood of Caradoc's vehicle.

Aisling found herself facing a pair of elves, both had burn marks on their hands but didn't look like that was going to stop them as they blocked her from following the others. She knew her ghau pendant was hidden, but she doubted these two were anything more than hired goons. Which would imply they would be trying to disarm and bring her in. Or if whoever was behind this was really an ass, kill her, and bring the body in.

She'd had a lot of adrenaline stored up from her little trip through the veil, so she didn't pull out magic right away, but went for some more satisfying martial arts. The first one went down in a heap when she kicked him in the head. He had to have realized she was an elf, as one himself, so her speed shouldn't have been a shock. But he went down hard and didn't look like he was getting up soon.

The second slowed down his attack and pulled out a knife. He didn't say anything but charged forward. His speed was impressive, and against a non-elf might have gotten him a good strike on her. She grabbed his arm as he came close and swung him. She'd only meant to throw him off his stride, and she was possibly as surprised as he was when he went flying fifteen feet in the air.

Maeve had been near her and choked her opponent, a minotaur woman, into unconsciousness. She was just getting up as Aisling's flung elf flew over her head.

"What kind of spell was that?" Maeve's dark eyes were wide.

"No spell. Weird, must not know my own strength." Aisling shrugged it off as two gnomes, a man and a woman, charged her and Maeve. It had been shockingly easy to throw him. He was at least six inches taller than her, and outweighed her by a lot. But it had felt like she was tossing a towel. She didn't have time to think of it more as both gnomes came for her.

All that did was piss Maeve off and she yelled and swung out at the man's legs.

Aisling again avoided a knife thrust, and grabbed the woman gnome. This time she paid more attention when she flung her and took out two human women stalking toward the larger fight.

The Lazing had all sent their spells, variations of the lightning spell Satoshi had used. But instead of calling up more magic, all five were fighting hand to hand.

Stella and Dailten appeared to be having the most fun and were staying on the outer edges of the fighting, keeping everyone inside. They took turns darting in, zapping an opponent or two, then darting back to the edge.

Caradoc was using magic, but mid-level spells only, and seemed to be having no trouble keeping the attackers at bay.

"Is it just me, or does it seem like they're not very good?" Maeve stayed back-to-back with Aisling, but no one was coming at them for a moment. "Granted, they were probably counting on their guns and numbers, but it's kind of disappointing that this is all we're worth. We need to find a better class of villain. Whoever is behind this is seriously lacking."

"I have to agree." Jones had ended up closer to them as another round of attackers came forward. "They might be testing us? But they really aren't good."

"Or they're delaying us." Reece was also closer than before and he scowled at the new wave of fighters. They were coming from behind the Tesco. "Let me see what Satoshi is picking up."

He jogged away, then increased speed as an enemy elf started following him. He ran past Caradoc who slammed the elf as he passed with a spell to his chest that dropped him. Reece nodded his thanks—he was faster than a normal human, but not as fast as an elf unless he was in the water.

The hair on Aisling's arms stood up and an odd feeling went down her back. The sky was mostly clear with only a few white clouds drifting by, but it felt like there was a thunderstorm coming. The Lazing were all using lightning-based spells, but it was more than that.

"Do you feel that?" Maeve asked as she looked up at the sky.

"I do." Aisling shook her head as three attackers, one of which was yet another jack-troll, charged her and Maeve. Jack-trolls were an offshoot of the true troll lineage, and unlike Grundog's mixed status of troll and minotaur, were considered their own sub-species. They had small lower bodies, wide shoulders, and arms that went to the ground if they bent forward. They mostly lived in massive underground warrens and rarely came out except at night.

Seeing two out during the day was startling, three was creepy.

She and Maeve fought the three new attackers. Aisling was holding her own against the jack-troll as whatever was increasing her strength kicked in, but she was tired of the fight, so she flung a spell of holding on him.

And not only froze him but shoved him back into another group of fighters.

"Damn girl, that was a bit overkill."

"Yeah, I noticed." Aisling scowled at her hands. Wherever the boost was coming from needed to give her some warning.

Reece came running up and it appeared the Lazing were moving back as well. As they and the rest of Bart's group moved toward the cars, their attackers grew more aggressive about pushing them.

And still more were coming from behind the Tesco.

Reece looked around. "Satoshi agrees, something we

don't want to deal with is coming this way. He and Bart believe that we need to leave immediately."

Aisling heard a yell behind them and saw Harlie shooting out a spell as five elves charged the cars. His shield was holding, but spells crackled along the surface as the elves fought to break it down.

The going was slow, as more opponents continued to enter the fight. They were still at the same skill level as the initial ones, throwaway thugs, but there were enough of them to make it difficult to get back to the cars.

The feeling of impending doom, or at least something nasty and magical, coming their way increased.

"We need to get out of here." Aisling yelled.

Bart came running up. "My idea completely. Shall we?" He held out his hands to the growing group that was blocking their way to the cars.

Aisling felt her pendant warm, clearly it was involved in whatever her recent increase in strength had been. Something to be dealt with later. "Let's show them what we have." Not a great idea, but if these people were after them because of the ghau pendants, it wasn't worth keeping them hidden. Not to mention that the feeling of impending doom was about to make her start screaming and seeing how far she could run.

She and Bart stepped in front of their friends and let loose a firestorm of magic aimed at the people blocking their way to Harlie and the cars. Aisling wasn't even certain what spells she was casting; they flooded her mind so quickly it was hard to grab ahold of them. She'd be freaked out about that later, right now she just needed to get the people she cared about the hell out of here.

The attackers fell before them, but there was still a group of six, heavier magic users from what it felt like, that were focusing on Harlie.

Harlie didn't look worried, but he kept looking up into the still mostly blue sky. "Hurry!" he called out as he set another spell toward one of the attackers. The closest elf flew backwards a few feet and was getting up when Aisling ran to him and threw him as hard as she could behind her.

Bart gave her a lifted eyebrow as the elf slammed into the front of the grocery store. "Impressive."

"Shit." Maeve's eyes were huge.

Aisling ignored them both for now.

The other elves continued to barrage Harlie's shield until they were all removed by Bart and the rest. The Lazing were behind them, cleaning up as they came forward.

"Do we need a prisoner to question?" Stella asked as she and Dailten joined them. Dailten was flying about ten feet in the air and was holding an unconscious minotaur in her hands.

"No. I think we know these were just fight fodder," Bart said. "They probably don't even know who they were really working for. We need their higher-ups."

Dailten shrugged and dropped the minotaur, then landed near Stella.

Harlie released his shield. There were still a few fighters in the parking lot, but no more were coming from behind the store and the ones left were running toward the exit of the lot.

"Are they running away?" Reece sighed. "Or do they really think they are going to stop us from leaving by standing in front of our cars?"

Aisling agreed, that was a bad idea—Caradoc's monster car probably wouldn't even notice them as he ran them over.

"Or they're trying to distract us." Satoshi pointed up as his crew got into their car.

The formerly mostly clear sky was being overwhelmed by jagged black clouds, crackling with reddish lightning.

They were disturbing enough, but then Aisling

collapsed as a horrific stabbing pain crashed into her skull, and she saw Bart go down as well.

"Grab them! We must leave!" Harlie's voice was distant as Aisling felt people pulling her to a car, tossing her inside, and slamming the door. She didn't have the energy to lift her head up, so she had a nice sideways view of the back of a car seat. Forces like she'd never felt before were pulling at her mind.

"Go. Leave." Those words were possibly the hardest she'd ever had to say. She felt as if she was falling in a pit between two massive energies and they were tearing her apart.

"Those people won't get out of the way," Reece said as he swerved his car. "Damn it, I tried." The thuds and crunches weren't good to hear. But Aisling knew they were all going to die if they didn't get away from the lot immediately.

"Keep going, follow Caradoc." Harlie was up front, which made sense.

The pressure inside Aisling's head continued to grow. "Faster!" She felt like she shouted it, but could barely hear her own words.

"We are, you just focus on getting your mental shields up." Harlie's cool hand reached back and took her own. "I can help, but *you* need to cast them."

Crap. Shields. She still wasn't great at them, and trying to pull up the spell when her entire being felt like it was being ripped in two wasn't fun.

A scream of tires and she almost fell off the car seat, but Harlie held her in place. She took a few deep breaths, then concentrated on a shield. Nothing else, just a shield to block her from the barrage of dark magic invading the world at this juncture. A brief feeling of tree branches brushed by her, but suddenly the pressure in her head eased.

"Don't drop your shield. We're not out of danger. You

might need to go faster, Reece." There was a tiny note of concern in Harlie's voice, which would be screaming-level terror in anyone else.

Clearly Reece understood that as well, as the car increased speed.

"Keep going, we'll catch up." Caradoc's voice came through one of their phones in the front. Him sounding freaked wasn't as surprising as Harlie, but still not common.

"Dailten knows another route that will get us out of here sooner. And a place to recoup." Stella's voice crackled through the phone and Harlie's hand kept Aisling in place as Reece swerved again.

A minute later the world cracked open.

CHAPTER FIFTEEN

R EALITY CAME UNDONE.
That was how Aisling would describe it later. Right now she was part of that unraveling reality and didn't know if she could speak. Shapes, sounds, feelings, and images flowed through her vision—even when she closed her eyes.

"Focus! Concentrate on the world you know."

At first Aisling thought it was Harlie, but then she blinked. It was a vallenian. He shouldn't be able to be inside this car, but he was there, mostly transparent. *"You must stop this. Now."* He reached out toward her, but her mind was already trying to discount him and the rest of the images she was seeing. His hand touched her stomach and pain stabbed through her.

"Good. Focus." Then the vallenian vanished.

Aisling gasped as shooting pain came from where the vallenian struck her and a wetness trickled down from her stomach to the car seat. But she focused on the world, this world, not the other. She bent over in pain as more blood came from her wound. Then the feeling of whatever had been trying to tear into this world vanished.

The pain in her stomach didn't.

Reece was slowing the car and she heard him drive over gravel or rocks, then stop.

"Aisling!" He got out and came around to the back seat along with Harlie.

"I think I stopped things, with help. But a vallenian stabbed me." The good thing was that her mind was clearing, the bad thing was the massive amount of pain in her stomach. And a weird smell of burning fabric.

"Get her out, and get some water on that seat." Bart's voice was just beyond Reece and Harlie, at least whatever took her out hadn't gone after him aside from the original attack.

She looked down as she was gently lifted out from the car. A small burn mark the size of her ghau pendant had eaten its way through a layer of upholstery on the car seat.

"Get her inside, this cottage hasn't been used by my family in a while, but it's more secure than it looks." Dailten wasn't visible but her words sounded great to Aisling.

There were at least four sets of hands carefully moving her into a room. She couldn't see much beyond the ceiling but the pain in her stomach was getting worse.

"Put her here, I need to look at the injury. Harlie, I'm going to need your assistance." Stella's voice was serious now. She was the closest they had to a healer.

"How did a vallenian stab you inside the car?" Caradoc's voice, but Aisling kept her eyes closed.

"Not. Sure." Those two words felt like hell to get out.

"Not now. We need to stop the bleeding and fix the damage. I need everyone except myself, Harlie, and Reece to go into the front room or outside. Go see what our Lazing friends know." Stella might be the tiniest one of all of them, but she wasn't messing around.

Aisling heard the others leave, but was focusing on her stomach and couldn't turn to look. On the inside it felt like her entire stomach had been sliced, but only a small amount of blood seemed to be coming out.

"Okay, Reece, I'll need you to hold her still." Stella was all business now. "I have a med kit, but the sedative in it isn't made for elves, it'll help some, but she'll burn through it quickly. Harlie, hold her other hand and chip in when I ask for magical support. Nothing fancy, just support."

Even though he didn't act like it, Harlie was the oldest of them. Aisling saw his deep nod toward Stella though.

"Why did they attack her?" Reece kept a steady pressure on her hand.

"He wanted me to focus," Aisling said around a yawn. Stella might have said the sedative wouldn't last long, but it was working now. Aisling wasn't asleep, but extremely groggy.

"Shhh, we'll talk about that later." Stella patted her other hand.

Cooling magic flowed over Aisling's torso. She was aware of Reece's hand, the coolness, and that was about it.

"*Did you survive? I can't reach out to you like this. Or shouldn't. But the Malifithri was going to kill you all.*"

Aisling would have thought the words in her head were simply leftover hallucinations. But she recognized the voice as Neasa and she wasn't sure those hallucinations hadn't been real. Plus, the feeling of tree branches could have been the dryad trying to reach her earlier.

"*I am here. We survived. Thank you.*" Speaking in her head was like talking to herself, only aimed at another being.

"*It is good. The battle will come. Must go.*" Neasa's words were faint now.

"*Wait, what can you tell me about what's coming?*" Either Neasa had ended communication—however she was doing it—or she wasn't able to answer that as there was only silence in Aisling's head.

"The wound isn't bad, but aimed to cause pain." Stella's

voice was low and the cooling feeling from her continued. "Harlie? Can you help me close this?"

Aisling felt magic flow into her stomach and Reece's hand tighten. But she didn't feel pain.

"There we go, all closed up." Stella sounded pleased. Aisling opened her eyes to see Stella's face peering closely into her own. "How are we feeling?" The look on her face was as if she'd just asked her if she wanted apple or brambleberry pie for dessert.

"Brambleberry." Aisling laughed at the confused looks around her. "Sorry. I feel stiff, but not like parts are going to come out anytime soon." Reece helped support her into a sitting position. She looked down at her bloody shirt. "Ruined that one though. But no hole. Damn sneaky vallenian."

"Can we come back in?" Caradoc asked as he and Maeve stuck their heads in the doorway.

"The patient appears to have recovered." Stella went to the sink, washed up and put everything back into the med box.

"Am I laying on the kitchen table?" Aisling looked around, there were a number of sheets under her, but by the location, it looked like a huge kitchen table.

"Sorry, our options were limited." Reece helped her spin around and get off the table.

"Any idea about this tiny, invisible vallenian?" Maeve asked as they and the rest came in the room. Luckily this place, while rustic, was large. Sitting options in the main room consisted of two huge l-shaped sectionals and several chairs.

"I have a big family," Dailten said as she motioned for all to sit. "Let me see if there's still fixings for iced tea." She went back into the kitchen and Stella followed.

"I'm not starting my short tale until they get back out here." Aisling leaned back against the cushion with a sigh.

Satoshi and his Lazing didn't sit. Neither did Jones.

"Is this a trained assassin thing? Should we all stand?" Maeve had flopped down next to Aisling, but looked annoyed at the wall of trained killers. Aside from not being fey, nor Asian, and not wearing a suit, Jones fit in perfectly.

"This place is not as secure as we'd like. But we won't stay long, regardless. You have your job, so do we." Satoshi smiled. "But hopefully we will now be allies."

Dailten came out with Stella and glasses of tea. "Made from frozen tea and some magical assist but refreshing. She looked at the Lazing. "Not staying? Did you want tea?"

Satoshi tilted his head toward her. "Thank you, but we will have to leave. I would like to hear what happened to Aisling, however. That thing that opened over the parking lot was meant to destroy us all and rip a hole in the veil. Somehow, she closed it."

Aisling took a long sip of iced tea then put the glass on the coffee table. She filled them in on her strange strength in the parking lot, the flood of spells in her mind, and the vallenian.

Bart had nodded along until that part. "The first two, yeah, although my strength wasn't as increased as hers. But I definitely wasn't visited by a vallenian." The relief in his voice at that was clear.

"Yeah, you were lucky. His attack forced me to focus and shut down the Malifithri. He was a small projection, but still packed a wallop."

Satoshi stiffened. "Did the vallenian say that was the Malifithri?"

"No, that was later. On the other side of the veil, Bart and I met a dryad named Neasa. She kinda spoke to me in my head, like the vallenian had, after everything was done. She used that word to describe what had been trying to open over the parking lot. She said it was stopped now."

She didn't like the look that Satoshi shared. "What does it mean?"

Harlie had been the only one aside from the Lazing to react to the word, but he looked inquisitive rather than angry.

Satoshi stayed silent, but Harlie responded. "The end of times. The shattering of all that stands between rational thought and utter chaos. The walls of the veil collapse, and all realities merge. Not well, I might add."

"We just faced off Armageddon?" Maeve had been in the process of taking a sip of iced tea but set the glass down carefully instead.

"Sort of. It's complicated, but that is a very old term, and it holds many meanings." Harlie still didn't look concerned, but the thoughtfulness on his face was becoming worrisome. It was his, 'I really need to research this' look.

"We will be alert for any signs of Malifithri. And I will let our shachen mages back home know what has taken place here. The fact that a vallenian and a dryad from beyond the veil were both reaching out to stop it indicates that was a true event." Satoshi's emphasis on the word 'true' elevated it to something terrifying.

"We will keep in touch as well." Bart held up his phone, they must have exchanged details while Aisling was having her stomach repaired.

With a bow to all of them, including a slight pause at Aisling, Satoshi and his Lazing left.

"Anyone else think they know way more than they're telling?" Maeve waited until the Lazing drove away, but kept her voice low.

"Far more," Jones said as he took a seat and sipped his iced tea. He was far more relaxed now that the Lazing had left. For him, anyway.

"To be fair, Satoshi needs to speak to the heads of his order, the other one he belongs to besides the Lazing."

Harlie nodded and got to his feet. "Is there a place where I can work in private?" He went to his duffle and retrieved a small laptop in a well-padded case.

"There are six bedrooms, help yourself. But there's spotty reception out here." Dailten waved down the hall.

"Don't worry, I have my ways." Harlie flashed a smile at Caradoc and slipped a small round disk on the top of his laptop. Then he vanished down the hall.

"It took me until now, but I've heard that term as well, the Malifithri. My aunt spoke of it. Said it was coming but never clarified what it was." Stella's aunt had been a troublemaker and had asked too many questions of the wrong organizations. She'd been killed under mysterious circumstances in a forest in Slovenia ten years ago.

Stella had just assumed she'd been making up stories until things she spoke of started appearing in the past year.

"I'm not sure if I'm more disturbed about the term or the fact that Neasa just spoke in my head. Through the veil." Aisling drowned her issues in her iced tea.

"Or that you're now some super strong wonder woman." Maeve grinned.

"We should see just how strong you are, and how much Bart is affected too," Caradoc said. "It must be coming from the ghaus. I've never seen some of the spells you two were throwing when we were getting back to Harlie."

"Me either," Aisling and Bart both said at the same time.

Aisling laughed. "Yeah, most of them went in and out so fast, I couldn't tell you what they were. If the ghau pendants were stepping in, they, as well as the vallenians, aren't happy about the veil being under attack."

"Which indicates they aren't involved in the attack, but who is?" Reece looked pointedly at Bart. "I'm not an expert on the veil, but it seems to me if it were under attack, both sides would have to be involved."

Bart shrugged. "True. However, my expertise, as it were, is quite old."

"Could the attack have come from someone in the Isfyden? That third plane?" Aisling knew the others who'd heard of it had insisted that nothing should be able to come through from there—but they were finding that a lot of supposed absolutes were vanishing.

Dailten and Stella both scowled.

"I'd say no, but there are too many odd things going on." Dailten nodded. "When Harlie comes back out, he, Stella, and I can look into it."

Reece ran his fingers through his hair and leaned back. "What now? Do we just keep going to Avebury and hope we can find and rescue Mott before things completely fall apart? Normally I'd say this veil issue is something for Area 42."

"And we can't trust them." Jones nodded. "I'm sure there are some agents who are fine and who they claim to be, but many were replaced without anyone knowing. Also, that attack on the London branch left more questions. The agents we saw were all young—too young in my mind. Many of them ran once the attack began."

"Well, we can stay here as long as we need. It's off all grids with magical reinforcement." Dailten shrugged. "Some of my family had legal issues. But it's not going to solve anything, or get Mott back."

A soft knock came from the front door, but Aisling couldn't see anyone through the thin curtain.

Reece and Jones beat everyone else to the door. With guns drawn, they slowly opened it.

"No one." Reece called out as he stepped further out the door. "But we have another elven family box."

Aisling jumped to her feet as Jones and Reece moved back into the house. One thing about the vallenian visitor she had in the car, he hadn't left one of the first family's ancestral boxes with her.

In the past year, the vallenians had been using them as calling cards. Or clues to a puzzle that was still missing too many pieces to solve. So far they had three, no, four. They were keeping them locked up and apart from each other and hadn't told the families in question that they had them.

One had been from Aisling, Caradoc, and Harlie's parents.

That their ancestral boxes were missing should be a big thing with high-ranking elven families. It would also be something that they'd never admit to anyone.

Aisling looked at the box at her feet and held out her arm as everyone came to the door.

"It's another Hewlith tree, family box." She knew Reece had just said it, but she felt it needed to be said again. This was annoying, dangerous, and cryptic.

"Are we just going to look at it from a distance? Seems rude, since your friends brought it here." Maeve leaned forward. Unintentionally on her part, the vallenians had used her as a carrier for one of the boxes back in L.A. She hadn't been pleased when she realized what it was and that having the boxes could cause serious issues if the families ever found out.

"I'm working on it." Aisling kept her arm up with a spell as she looked around. She hadn't seen any of the surrounding area on her way in, but it was mostly grassy fields with ancient, short stone walls dividing them.

She seriously doubted a vallenian would duck behind one of those walls to hide. With a sigh, she lowered her arm but grabbed the box before anyone else could move. She flipped it over to see the family, then almost threw it across those lovely fields.

"It's the High King and Queen's family box."

CHAPTER SIXTEEN

"OH, SHITE." MAEVE pulled Aisling and the box back into the house. The rest slammed and locked the door, then Dailten pulled heavy curtains to cover the cute sheer ones. She did the same in the kitchen window.

Aisling stood there trying very hard not to hyperventilate. The urge to throw the box, now into a roaring fire, was still there. But mostly she was fighting down the terror of it being here at all.

"No one would admit their family box is missing, right? So, the royals won't start a search for it because they'd have to admit it was gone." Aisling drummed her fingers on the warm wood but stopped once she realized what she was doing. "Why did the vallenians take it, and more importantly, give it to us?"

"You." Reece gave a wince. "Sorry, but you are their focus, like it or not. Can someone get Harlie? We might need him to get it out of her hands."

"Ha." Aisling walked to the coffee table and gently put the box down. Part of her didn't want to let it go, and her fingers twitched as she released it.

That couldn't be a good sign.

Harlie came out, pushed by Stella and Caradoc, but he looked unfocused. "I was in the middle of something which could prove to be exceedingly...hello? Is that another box? One with the royal seal on it?" He came close to the box, but kept his hands tightly behind his back.

"Your vallenian friends are playing hardball now. They stole *the* royal family box? No one else should be able to touch it." He took a step back but continued looking at the box.

"They aren't my friends. And maybe it's not real. Could it be a joke? We didn't see anyone outside after all." Aisling looked around, but it was clear no one else believed her any more than she believed herself. "Damn, it had to be them. This one was different, aside from the obvious because of who it belongs to, there was an odd tingling to it. I didn't want to let it go."

Caradoc peered down at the box, then grinned at Aisling. "Maybe you really do want to be queen." He waggled his blond eyebrows.

"Funny. No, I don't. Not now, not ever. But there is something weird about that box."

"Could the royal family have any sort of security within the box itself?" Jones was doing his regular standing rest. Arms locked behind his back and legs relaxed. Placed halfway between the threat of the front door and the troublesome box. He would leap whichever way danger came from. Reassuring, and a little scary.

"They shouldn't have. Each box contains something essential to the family, but beyond that it shouldn't be tampered with." Harlie stepped forward again but also continued to keep his arms back. "The royal crest is there, a lion rampant. Standard forest scene. Interesting. Caradoc or Aisling, do either of you remember our father's crest? Our mother made hers the dominant one for our family, but he had one."

"That wouldn't be something I'd have a clue about." Aisling had never cared anything about her family, aside from staying as far from it as possible.

"I actually might." Caradoc turned his head to the side like he did when trying to access a memory. "A unicorn. I remember it because I thought that would have been cool. Mother pointed out that our official deer was far better. Why?"

"Look closely in that corner." Harlie stepped back to allow both Cradoc and Aisling to move in.

"That's a unicorn." Aisling probably wouldn't have noticed the animal if it hadn't been pointed out, but now that she'd seen it, it was clear what it was.

"Not only that, there's blood on it. On its sides and on its horn," Caradoc said. "It's been attacked, but it fought back."

Aisling shook her head, "That's a wild guess, don't you think? Not to mention, if our father was this lost prince, and the current royals were fully aware of that, why would they put his symbol on their box? Even if they weren't aware, why would they put his symbol, and a bloody one at that, on their box? The boxes were made after they crossed to this side, right?"

"Yes, they were. They magically grew the Hewlith forest, in what is now Wales, and took the wood to make them within the first five years of arrival," Harlie said as he watched the box in case it was going to do tricks. "As for the why, I have no idea. That *is* a unicorn, it is bloody, but still standing, clearly it damaged its attackers. And it is carved into the High King and Queen's family box."

"Which we now have." Like Harlie, Caradoc didn't have his hands anywhere near the box. He was far more tech guy than magic or history guy, but he seemed fascinated. And concerned.

"No offense, but you can't leave that here." Dailten also watched the box, but from the far end of the kitchen. "I have little respect for our royals, but they are our royals. I can't risk any of my brothers and sisters by it being found here."

"I have a bag we can put it in." Stella bustled over to her luggage and pulled out a silky black bag.

"Not sure how a fancy pillowcase will help hide that thing, but I agree it needs to be hidden." Jones had no magic. But the box was clearly weirding him out too.

"This, my fine friend, is not a pillowcase. Well, it's not *just* a pillowcase." Stella's grin went feral. "It's a shatil bag. It'll block any magic from any source outside of it. It will also keep anything that happens to be casting spells inside of it, null." She leaned down to glare at the box. "You hear that? I'm not sure what you're doing, and you probably shouldn't be doing it, but this bag will settle you down." She glanced up and tossed the black bag to Aisling.

Aisling waved the bag. "One, aren't these illegal in most countries? And two, why are you all insisting that I be the one to touch that box? If it does have some familial connection, it might be better if someone not related touched it."

"They're only illegal if you get caught and can't talk your way out of it. Hasn't happened yet, and my aunt gave me that one almost a hundred years ago," Stella said.

"And, let's face it, you're the one they're bringing them to." Caradoc shrugged.

"I wouldn't touch it any more than necessary, but you shouldn't use anything to help get it in the bag." Harlie gave his best helpful-big-brother grin, then held up both hands and brought the tips of his fingers together in a pinching motion. "Just use the tips if you can."

"None of you are helpful." Aisling glared around the room. "Fine. If something happens to me, just remember this was your fault."

"Nothing happened when you carried it in," Maeve said.

"That was before I realized it was a weirder than normal box with a bloody unicorn on it." Aisling shook out her shoulders, then grabbed the box with the tips of her fingers and thumbs and moved it toward the shatil bag.

And was suddenly in a forest. The bag was nowhere to be seen, and neither was the box. And a quick glance down told her she was dressed in black and green. Still had the damn ghau pendant on though.

A tiny old woman peeled herself away from a shattered tree. Long, silvery white hair was looped around her head and she had kind, dark brown eyes. She looked oddly familiar, and was wearing a cloak similar to the one Aisling now wore. "Oh, you shouldn't be here now. Well, not at all really, but especially not now. It's not your time. Nor really is this your reality. Sort of. It might be, might not." She walked around Aisling, shaking her head.

A loud explosion came from beyond the trees and Aisling realized that they didn't look like the other side of the veil had looked before—they weren't Hewliths, but she wasn't sure what they were. She didn't think she was in Neasa's woods—or anywhere on earth.

"Where am I? How did I get here? And who are you?" It was weird, even though the box wasn't wherever she was, Aisling felt like it was nearby. Its presence felt like a ghost.

"Too many questions. You need to go back. *It* needs to behave." She patted Aisling on the cheek. "And do give my love to Stella, and hand this to her as well." She pressed a small metal object into Aisling's hand.

Before Aisling could respond, she was flung back into Dailten's front room, sliding on her ass to the far wall from the force of whatever pulled her back, and wearing her normal clothes.

"What just happened?" She got to her feet slowly. The box and bag were still on the table and her friends were all watching her closely.

"You were putting that box away when you yelped and went flying backwards," Reece said.

"There was more than that." Aisling stalked over to the box. "Was that you? Where did you send me?" When the box didn't respond, she held her breath and snapped the bag over it. "Damn box, I think it did it." She held the bag up and Stella handed her what looked like a simple tie.

"Don't worry, nothing's getting in or out once you set it."

Aisling tied the bag up and dropped it into her luggage.

"Now, what happened that we didn't see?" Reece steered her toward one of the sofas to sit and everyone else trailed behind.

"I was in a different place, a different time maybe? There were woods, twisted ones, but they weren't Hewliths like on the other side of the veil. I was wearing weird clothes, including a cape. The ghau was still on. A woman came to me, said I shouldn't be there, and a few more unhelpful things." She looked up at Stella. "Then she said to give you her love. And this." Aisling held up the small thing she'd been given, a tiny key, like one would have on a music box.

Stella looked like someone smacked her on the side of her head, but gingerly took the key. "I lost this key when I was a child." There were tears in her eyes as she looked to Aisling. "Describe her?"

Aisling did as best she could, but the image was already fading from memory as if it was designed to do so.

"That's my aunt. You spoke to my Aunt Jilan." Stella slid down into the sofa. She looked like she'd seen a ghost. Or rather, like Aisling had seen one.

"I thought she was dead?" Reece asked.

"She is. Or was. This is most disturbing." Stella no longer looked like she was going to cry, but like she had a new mystery to solve.

"Ya think? Seeing your lost aunt was weird, but only second to me being pulled out of this place and time, interacting with her, and being flung back here in what was really only a moment to all of you. You didn't notice I was even gone." Aisling looked around the group, but mostly watched Harlie. "What in the hell happened? I'm assuming it was because of that box?"

"I don't know. But Dailten, Stella, and myself will investigate. Along with everything else. But we must assume that where you went had something to do with the box, the royal family, or our father." He kept looking toward her luggage. She knew he wanted to look at the royal box more. She also knew that wasn't a good idea, even though she couldn't say why.

"Or my aunt didn't actually die, but was pushed somewhere else. If there is this third plane, the Isfyden, maybe there? Did she seem like she was expecting you?"

Aisling thought back. It might not have been more than a moment here, but it was still fast wherever she was. "Not really. But she wasn't surprised and told the box to behave."

"I thought it hadn't gone with you?" Caradoc asked.

"It didn't, but I still felt it. Obviously, so did she."

Harlie gave a sigh. "As I said, we'll have to work on sorting it out, but for now we keep that box in the shatil bag." He didn't look happy about it, most likely because he really wanted to find out its secrets. "I haven't been able to find out much about the Malifithri, but I can research in Avebury as well as here."

"We should go after Mott quickly. If he did convince whoever grabbed him to go there, he might not be able to stay long." Caradoc was up and looked ready to head out.

"Let me see if Garran and Surratt have any new information." Bart pulled out his phone and dialed. It took two times to get through, but Caradoc just nodded.

Part of his new security apparently. Not helpful if there had been an emergency. Garran's voice was clear as Bart put him on speaker.

"We're not getting anywhere on finding Mott, there's no clues. Hopefully Harlie, Dailten, and Stella can crack something on the metaphysical end of things. We do have a lead on what happened to you at the London Area 42 that we're going to check into."

Bart nodded then told them about the Malifithri and the Lazing. Even with enhanced security, he wasn't going to bring up another family box, especially this one. Aisling figured they might need a code word for it to even discuss it in person. Just to be safe. At least the shatil bag was managing to block the weird feelings she had been getting from it. She still wanted to dump it somewhere. Like an active volcano.

"We'll keep an eye out for both, but I have a feeling that if the Lazing don't want to be seen, they won't be. And if the Malifithri is as bad as they told us in school—I don't want to see one anywhere. Keep in touch." Garran ended the call.

"Good he's keeping things short which will help stop folks tracking them. I wish I could update their phones though." Caradoc's fingers twitched.

"Are we leaving for Avebury today? It's already getting late." Maeve pulled back the heavy curtains.

"We could, we're only an hour away. But I think it might be better to stay here and get there first thing." Aisling had been looking out the window as she spoke, but turned to find most of the others looking at her. "What?"

"Just wondering if that trip you took made you more in touch with *things*?" Caradoc asked.

"Funny. No, no weird feeling about the future. But I'm tired. Fighting, getting stabbed, being zapped to who knows where—I'm wiped." The drive might be short, but there would be the tromping around looking for Mott. The places to stay in town weren't large so they'd probably split up—but that would be another thing, looking for places to stay.

She also had an odd feeling. But it wasn't concrete enough for her to share. Mostly she was just tired. Stella's magic had healed the wound, but a lot of the energy to help heal had been her own.

"I think it might be the best," Dailten said from the kitchen. "While sleeping here won't be a problem, unless all anyone wants for dinner is tea, dinner will be. We'll need to head to the Tree and Hound, a nice pub not far from here. We can even walk." She paused. "Which might be better if any of us need a drink or four after today."

"I vote for staying and walking to the pub. Haven't been to a good pub in too long." Maeve grinned.

"Just bring me back something." Harlie got to his feet. "I want to do more research…not to mention, pubs are busy and noisy."

Harlie had been coping with the outside world far better than Aisling would have expected, considering that he'd spent the prior two hundred plus years in a small cave in the mountains of Nepal. It made sense that he needed some downtime away from people.

"I'll get you something, never fear." Dailten looked at Harlie closely as if she was debating what to bring back—or what not. She'd known him through mystic groups they were in online. But she constantly looked at him like he was going to waste away in front of her. To be fair, harpies were mostly stocky and solid. Harlie was six foot nine and rail thin. He seemed fine with it and ate all the time.

He nodded and went back into the room he'd been using.

Aisling looked at her clothes. "Let me get a quick shower and change. Blood isn't a great look and we don't want to upset the locals." She grabbed her bag and went for the hallway.

"Take the second room on the left, has its own bathroom," Dailten said.

A quick shower and change and she almost felt normal. Staying home and waiting for some food to come back, providing she didn't fall asleep, first sounded tempting. But it would be nice to just go to a normal pub with her friends.

Not to mention she didn't want Harlie to drag her into his research.

Dailten was right, the pub was a nice walk. There was a walkway alongside the short walls that marked off the driving lane, and evening was just falling, so it was quiet and peaceful.

Aisling kept waiting for something to happen. Maybe it was some sort of time delay from her being gone a month, but she was far twitchier than usual. She'd ask Bart if he'd been noticing anything odd, but he was up front with Dailten and Stella, comparing recipes for meat pies it sounded like. She'd ask later when they were in the pub.

Reece and Jones were at the back of the group discussing something about Area 42 that Aisling had no interest in. She would love it if everyone she knew got as far away as possible from that organization.

Caradoc and Maeve had been walking together, then he started fussing with a gizmo about the size of a cellphone and Maeve dropped back alongside Aisling.

"How are you doing?" She held up her hand. "I know I keep asking, and I will keep asking until I'm certain that you're okay. And weird shit stops happening to you."

Aisling laughed. "I'm as fine as I can be, given all the weird shit that's been happening around *us*."

"Yeah, I'm not the one who slipped into another reality, or seems to be buddies with killers from beyond the veil. But I was also asking about how you're *feeling*." She glanced back where Reece and Jones were still in their conversation.

Aisling watched Reece for a few moments, he still looked the same, sounded the same. But there was still that distance. She felt it with everyone, but only when she thought about it. "The same. I have only been back a short time, maybe it's just reentry back to this side of the veil."

"Nothing new from the pendant?"

"Not really. It went with me on that little trip, but I don't think it caused it."

Maeve let out a sigh as she looked around the fields. "I do love being back in England, even if I was more of a city girl. But I would give a lot to be back in L.A. right now, just chasing regular perps, and listening to Surratt bitch at everyone. How did everything suddenly go so sideways?"

"I don't think it was sudden. I think we just weren't aware of things changing. Think of my mother—some of the crap she pulled was before the fey even left the other side of the veil. And I think whatever she did then trickled down to the current time. It sounds heartless, but I hope she's gone." She hadn't thought kindly of her mother for decades, and that was before she knew the extent of her evilness.

"Not heartless at all, with what that woman did to humanity and her own family."

They dropped into silence for a few moments and then a building appeared as they rounded a bend. An old-fashioned sign of a massive tree and a large hunting dog dangled from a post at the front. It was a large pub, but many pubs also had inns attached. The two story whitewashed building had a warm light coming from the windows facing the road. It wasn't cool enough to need a fire, but it looked charming. The inside was just as expected. Low beamed ceiling made of dark wood, the same dark wood making up the walls and most of the furniture. A pair of large screen TVs on mute were playing a repeat of matches from earlier in the day. There were a few folks around, most eating dinner more so than drinking heavily, but they had the relaxed look of regulars.

Dailten might not live around here anymore, but she still knew a fair amount of people and greeted those who shouted her name. A large table in the corner, rather two tables put together, was quickly made ready for them after a few words to the half-giant behind the bar.

"Do you trust me? They have a great selection of local ale." Dailten asked all of them as a waitress came over.

Everyone nodded as the waitress gave them menus and Dailten ordered a round of Hawk's Red.

Aisling spotted fish and chips, one of her favorites, on the menu and then leaned back on the bench and watched the room.

Watching a room was habit as a cop and she doubted she'd ever stop doing it. Even if she never went back to the force. That was a disturbing thought. But her world had gotten so messed up that she didn't know what she'd be doing when things settled. The world wouldn't be the same and she had no idea who she'd be then.

A pair of korbins, thin, short, almost like four-foot-tall bipedal rats, came into the pub. Unlike the others here, they didn't seem to know anyone, but the bartender nodded toward a table for two in the back.

Bart watched them, then leaned over to Dailten. "Are korbins common down here? I thought they preferred the northern areas."

Dailten had been in conversation with Stella—still apparently about meat pies—when the pair had come in, but she narrowed her eyes when Bart pointed them out. "No, they aren't common. We're too warm down here, and for some reason my people make them uncomfortable. There are a lot of old harpy families in this area." Her grin was feral.

Aisling looked from Dailten to the two korbins. Considering that Dailten looked like a giant hawk when her wings were out and the korbins looked like rats, she could see why they wouldn't want to live in a part of the country that was known to have a lot of harpies.

"Are they casing the place?" Maeve leaned forward, then sat back as the waitress brought out their ale and took their food orders.

"That's what it looks like." Reece pointedly didn't look at the two korbins.

"I was kidding about catching perps by the way," Maeve said to Aisling as she took a long sip of her ale. "Good stuff."

"I told you. I'll never lie about alcohol." Dailten swallowed half her glass in a single swing and Bart did the same.

"They don't seem to be doing anything, maybe just traveling through." Caradoc looked up from his newest toy long enough to watch the korbins, take a drink of ale, then go back to focusing on his gadget. He had a small tool kit out and kept shocking himself as he tested whatever the thing did. It wasn't stopping him though.

"Could be, I'm not one to judge," Maeve said even though she had been the one to point it out.

Aisling kept watching the room with perhaps a few more glances toward the korbins, who were now deep in conversation. After all her years on the force, she was more than aware that if something looked odd, it probably was.

Judging from the cautious glances from the rest of the people in the pub—this was odd. Most fey got along with each other, but there were definitely groups who were more wary toward each other.

Her thoughts vanished when the waitress and two more

servers brought out the massive piles of food. Aisling's fish was as long as her forearm.

Food and more ale became the focus for everyone, and it wasn't until the fish and its mountain of chips and side of mushy peas were history that Aisling looked over to the korbins. There was now only one. He was leaning against the wall and didn't appear to be breathing.

CHAPTER SEVENTEEN

R EECE FOLLOWED TO where she was looking when she had a sharp intake of breath, but Jones beat him in getting to his feet.

Jones silently weaved toward the table where the korbin sat and tapped him on the shoulder. The korbin collapsed to the table. Jones looked around the pub. "Has anyone seen the other one? This man is dead."

Considering most of the people at their table were cops or agents, almost all of them got to their feet. Reece changed directions and went to the bar.

The rest of the patrons looked concerned but weren't worried. Either extremely jaded or they felt the missing korbin—a stranger—had killed this one, also a stranger, and therefore had nothing to do with them.

Aisling had seen that attitude in some of the smaller communities in L.A. It wasn't always right. She stayed back at their table to watch the people in the pub.

Bart started to go over to the table with Jones and Maeve, then instead went to the bar to join Reece.

"I might not be involved with the law, aside from hanging out with all of you, but they know me, let me go talk to some folks." Dailten nodded and also went to the bar.

Aisling stayed with Stella and Caradoc, although he put his gizmo back in his pocket and nodded to the table with the dead korbin. "Think we should call in the local police? I know several of you are police, and Maeve technically is still MI-6 adjacent, but I think the local police might want to be included."

"The bartender is on the phone, probably who he's speaking to," Aisling said. "I'm sorry that korbin was murdered, but for once it's not something relating to us. Or the veil." She said a silent prayer that it stayed that way. Issues and threats were piling on each other and there wasn't a sign of any solutions.

The sound of sirens echoed down the road behind them, and stopped directly in front of the pub. Aisling watched as the two cops, one human and one elf, walked in. The way the other people in the pub called out to them, they might as well have been there on a social call.

And they were acting like it too. They stopped by each table, greeting people by name but not showing any indication or concern about a dead body in the place.

Her eyes narrowed. There was casualness and then there was weirdness—this was the latter. She reached out with a spell where Jones and Maeve were still looking around the table, but not touching anything.

"What's wrong?" Stella wasn't a cop or agent, but she was a diner owner—she could pick out wrongness like a hawk.

"There's a spell over that body. It's blocking others from remembering it's there." Aisling swore as Bart and Reece came back looking vaguely confused.

"I don't know what—" Aisling cut Reece off and grabbed his hand and released a light spell as he came to the table, then looked to Bart's confused face and grabbed his hand too. "There's a spell over the table where Jones and Maeve are." She forced Reece and Bart to see beyond it.

"What the hell?" Reece went for his gun, then stopped. "Can you break that spell for everyone here? The cops think they're on dinner break and the bartender's getting them drinks."

Aisling expected the spell she'd used to rip through the one blocking the body, or rather obstructing reactions to it. She couldn't recall what the obscuring spell was called but knew what it did. People would recall what they were really seeing if they glanced over there for a moment—then it vanished the instant they even slightly looked away. She had to slide her spell breaker alongside the original spell. It took a few tries, but swearing all through the pub and both cops running to the table indicated it worked.

Jones and Maeve flashed badges and Dailten came over and spoke to the cops. Even though she didn't have a badge, they knew her and listened to her more than the others.

"We need everyone to stay here until we get a coroner out." The elven cop turned to Aisling and the others at their table. "If all of you will wait, we'll talk to you first." He dismissed Jones and Maeve, clearly not impressed with their badges. Since both outranked him, that was disturbing.

Jones watched the cops the entire way back to the table, a feat in navigation to be sure.

Maeve shrugged it off and slid into a chair. "Local cops in a small town, they all have tiny wand issues—regardless of species or gender." She finished her ale while she scanned the room.

"It felt like more than that." Jones continued to watch the cops. The human officer was in the corner calling in someone, the coroner most likely, the elf was using his phone to take pictures.

"Hard to say. I didn't even feel the spell on that body." Bart was also glaring at the two cops. "There's something bigger going on. To kill that korbin and mask it in such a way that some seriously heavy magic users didn't even feel it? That's not normal level let's kill-my-partner-in-a public-place situation. And it seems like no one saw the other one leave. Including us."

"You mean the killer?" Maeve kept looking between the cops and the rest of the bar.

"They might not be the same person." Reece was seated but leaning against the wall as if he was just working on his ale. "Nothing against korbins, but they aren't known for having a lot of heavy magic users. Whoever pulled this off was Caradoc's level or higher."

Stella nodded. "I'd say higher. But why?"

"That's my question," Dailten said as she joined them. "This town is too low-key for any serious trouble." The coroner and his assistant arrived and were taking the information they needed before moving the body. The two cops were heading toward their table. "I don't know either of these two officers personally, but just be your usual charming selves."

The elf cop took the lead, stepping ahead of the human. They were of the same height, but the elf had his old-fashioned long hair tied up in the back and the human was bulkier.

"You saw the killing? Did you mention you were law enforcement?" He flashed Aisling a stunning smile. "Or some of you are."

Maeve got to her feet and leaned on the table. "As we told you back at the crime scene. I'm MI-6, three of these are Interpol, and the rest are agencies that I can't discuss. No, mate, we didn't see the murder. Whoever did it had a hell of a lot of magic running through them and blocked everything. You two came in thinking you were on a coffee break." There was a serious snarl in her voice.

Aisling wasn't sure that was the best tactic, but interestingly, the human cop grinned and put a hand on his partner's shoulder.

"Good to see you, Maeve. Wasn't sure that was you when you flashed your badge." He nodded to his partner. "I wouldn't mess with Maeve Halithi. Regardless of the lack of magic or the badge she's under, she's one of a kind."

"Marcus?" Maeve's eyes went round. "Marcus Littleton? Damn! You shaved!" She went around the table and hugged him. "Didn't even realize it was you."

He laughed, ignoring the scowl from his partner. "It's been almost twenty years since the academy. I went clean shaven about eighteen years back. You went hardcore, MI-6?"

"Among other things. We're just passing through, heading north." She quickly introduced everyone by first name only. "Dailten here was a local."

Marcus tipped his head to her. "I've heard of you and your family, ma'am. And nice to meet the rest, but not under these circumstances."

The elven cop had relaxed a little, but still looked annoyed. "Which one of you broke the spell?" He even flipped out an old-fashioned notepad and held his pen ready.

"I did. Aisling Danaan. Los Angeles. Cop." She wasn't sure if she was still on the roster at this point, she'd been officially on leave when Bart commandeered her, Maeve, and Caradoc.

Bart nodded. "And working on assignment with me. As they all are." He flipped his badge open and whatever it said, both cops stepped back. "We can tell you what we saw, but it wasn't much. Two korbins came in, looked edgy, sat down. We ate, looked up, one korbin remained and there was a strong spell on everyone."

"We're going to need more than that." The elf was recovering. "I need—" his words were swallowed by screaming and the sounds of pans, a lot of them, being thrown in the kitchen. Two cooks came running out.

Both were bloody, but they were able to run out the front door.

"Monsters! There are monsters coming in from the walls!"

CHAPTER EIGHTEEN

THE BARKEEPER STARTED to go into the kitchen, but the cops blocked him and started setting up a perimeter by pushing back tables.

"Not in my town." Dailten raced forward, ignoring the cops as she barreled to the kitchen.

Stella shrugged. "Can't hurt to check." She tore after Dailten.

"Damn it, we need to stay out of things that don't involve us," Bart muttered to the rest, then flashed his badge to the cops as a reminder. "We've got this, might be rogues," he yelled, then followed Dailten and Stella with Jones on his heels.

The cops didn't look happy, but neither they, nor the barkeeper, tried to stop them.

"Caradoc, can you and Maeve stay and make sure nothing weird happens out here?" Reece checked his gun then nodded to Aisling. "You look like you want to go see."

"Not really, but I think we might need to." She beat him to the door before Caradoc and Maeve agreed to stay put. The door was a thin swinging one, but no sound came out from the other side. She held up her hand. Stella had taught her a shielding spell when they were dealing with the situation in Noth—but it wasn't as consistent as she'd liked. "Stay behind me, and duck down. My shield is limited." Reece was a few inches taller than her and she wasn't sure if her own shielding would deal with that.

He narrowed his eyes, but nodded and bent down, keeping one hand on her shoulder and the other on his gun.

Aisling grabbed a powerful disrupt spell, secured her shield as best she could, and swung open the door.

A bolt of gray lightning shot toward her and bounced off her shielding. Damn it, she recognized that lightning, even if she couldn't see the one doing it. Dailten, Stella, Bart, and Jones were all frozen in mid-run in front of her. Considering what strong magic users Dailten and Stella were, that wasn't good. None of them were bloody like the cooks had been though. Maybe whoever was behind this came up with a second strategy when the cooks fought and ran.

Another bolt shot out at Aisling and Reece and this time the one firing the spell bolts briefly appeared—a swamp goblin. Another bolt shot out as a second one appeared. They couldn't keep hidden and use their magic. Aisling swore, they were far stronger magically than the one she'd faced on the other side of the veil—the going invisible was a new and unwelcome trick too.

And they shouldn't be on this side of the veil.

Luckily, Aisling didn't need to hide as she fired a blast spell at the first one, then at the second. The ghau pendant heated up, but she didn't have time to check if it was glowing or doing anything else. Her spells should have obliterated both swamp goblins, but all they did was singe them and push them back against the kitchen wall. Someone had amped up the magic of these two when they pushed them over to this side.

She felt Reece reach around her, and stayed close as he fired his gun at both. The first one exploded at the first shot to the head. The second collapsed as it was hit, but then vanished. They were defended against magic, but not bullets.

Her friends all unfroze, but unfortunately, Dailten and Stella ended up with a bunch of splatters on them. Swamp goblin insides were as nasty looking as their outsides.

"Damn it! What the hell was that?" Dailten shook herself off, but she and Stella would need to be hosed down. Not to mention the entire kitchen would have to be shut and cleaned.

"Swamp goblin," Aisling kept her voice low; it sounded like the cops and the barkeeper were coming in. "Yeah, from the *other side.*"

The door swung open with the elf cop in front with a stun gun. "What happened?"

Bart stepped forward. "My people were injured and contaminated by a rampaging water sprite. She had to be taken out by Agent Larkin and it wasn't pretty." He spun to the barkeeper. "I don't need to tell you what those things have in them—you need to shut this pub down immediately and get a full decon team out here." He put his hands on his hips when no one moved. "*Now.* Get your witness statements for the korbin killing outside. This place needs to be sterilized."

Both cops nodded and pulled the barkeeper away.

"I need to be clean." Dailten spoke through gritted teeth as she stalked out of the kitchen. Stella was by no means happy about her condition, but didn't look ready to kill someone as she followed her friend.

"We'll get a decon team out here; you need to wait." The elven cop was in full command now; he'd already gotten the pub patrons to go outside.

Dailten stomped up to him and partially unfurled her wings. "*I need to be clean. Now.* You can send people after me, but messing with a pissed harpy isn't a wise idea." She marched away without his response, only lowering her wings to get outside.

Stella grinned. "I'm with her." She nodded to Aisling and Bart as she went for the door. "Don't worry, the *water sprite* remains should clean up fine." There was an emphasis on water sprite. Most likely Stella had magically modified the remains in the kitchen, or disguised them enough that no one would be able to tell what they were if they checked. It wouldn't be a good idea to have swamp goblin guts being found here.

"You can't let them walk off; they have evidence on them." The elf cop turned to Bart.

Bart just shrugged. "It was a deranged water sprite, there's nothing you need from them, or us. You saw my badge. It covers *all* my people. Most of what we do is need to know only—and you don't need to know at this point. I'll be back in a few hours for the korbin autopsy. You probably want to keep an eye out for the second korbin as a person-of-interest as well."

"I…Fine." The elf cop backed down and went outside to make sure the rest of the patrons were gathered.

Marcus nodded toward the elf cop. "Tell Maeve I'll keep her updated. He can be a jerk." Then he headed outside, but away from where Maeve waited.

"Dailten and Stella are already heading back, Jones and Caradoc went with them," Maeve said as they approached. "I feel bad for anyone who tries to ambush that group."

"You really think the second korbin stuck around?" Reece asked Bart as they walked away from the pub.

"I think the second one is dead and they both killed themselves or the first was killed by the second—without a fuss." Bart's voice was low and he kept looking around. "I only felt the edge of it before I was frozen, but someone cast at least one, possibly two, death spells to bring those two…things…over to this side of the veil. I think those korbins were sacrifices."

"I didn't know that was possible." Aisling swore. People could use death to bring over monsters from the other side? There were extremely few necromancers among the magic users here—because any that were found were killed on sight. There was no way to know how many were on the other side.

"It is, but I've only heard of one case. It was a thousand years ago, and I read about it in my veil research. I'll see if Harlie has more information and can find the article. Obscure journal, one that I don't recall now." Bart looked pale and was still checking every tree and wall out for lurkers.

"Could that way of crossing over make them stronger?" Aisling automatically lowered her voice to match Bart's. "Or anything else that could make them stronger? I faced one of those swamp goblins on the other side, before I found you. It was annoying, but nothing like these two. The one I faced used the same weird gray lightning, but all it did was sting a bit."

"I don't know." Bart took a long look down the road as they crossed. "I'm really hoping Harlie has a clue."

Aisling wasn't happy about the swamp goblins being here or what they'd been able to do—but Bart's twitchiness disturbed her more.

Dailten and the others were already out of sight and she'd only seen them in the distance once—they were moving fast.

She, Reece, Bart, and Maeve turned to go into the driveway to the cottage. All still lost in their own thoughts.

Then screeches came from the back of the cottage.

Reece, Bart, and Maeve drew their guns, and Aisling readied a blast spell as they ran around the corner.

The screams turned to laughing as Harlie aimed a garden hose equally at fully clothed Dailten and Stella while they slowly turned. Jones and Caradoc stood off to the side holding out huge robes.

"Sorry, there was no way I was setting foot in my

cottage with that stuff on me. My family would never forgive me." Dailten stretched and made sure the water got all her feathers. It was doubtful any exploding swamp goblin got anywhere near her wings, since they had been folded up behind her. But Aisling didn't blame her for wanting everything clean.

Bart put away his gun. "We should have saved some of the mess—there was something odd about those things beyond the fact that they shouldn't be here."

"Ha! Harlie scooped up a dozen samples before he even considered picking up the hose." Caradoc held up the first robe as a shield and Dailten stepped behind it. She flung all her clothes off to the side, then took the robe and wrapped herself in it.

"I'm burning those." She glared at the pile of clothes.

Stella duplicated her moves, looking lost in the much-larger-than-her robe. "Agreed. Just for the memories, even if they were washed a dozen times. Shall we go inside?"

Night had already fallen and Harlie had magically lit the backyard to hose down Stella and Dailten. They trooped inside and worked through what had just happened at the pub.

Harlie kept shaking his head. "Swamp goblins are minor nuisances; they shouldn't have been able to do what they did. Especially against magic users like Dailten and Stella, let alone the rest. Something is very wrong."

Since Dailten was still in her robe, Maeve went and got tea for everyone.

Aisling shook her head. "And they shouldn't have been able to hide like they did. The one I ran into on the other side of the veil was hiding behind trees, but it wasn't invisible. Those two were invisible until they released their spell. And why didn't my magic take them out? It was like I'd pushed them with a feather."

"That's another issue. I'm glad I could stop them, but

only one exploded when I killed it. The other did a weird vanishing trick," Reece said.

Stella tilted her head. "I was aware during that. The second one was dead as well, but someone pulled it back through the veil. I really hope it exploded on whoever that someone was." She gave her hair a furious scrub with a towel.

"We have to assume it did have something to do with us." Bart settled in with his tea.

"True, not sure why or how, but agreed," Caradoc said. "If it's weird and in any way associated with the veil, it's probably about us. I feel like a magnet for mayhem."

Harlie didn't have much more information about the Malifithri, but he had been checking some of the occult websites and he confirmed that Mott was in Avebury. "I know he left the clue back at the flat, but his kidnappers still could have refused to take him there. But there are a lot of odd occurrences popping up in the Avebury area. Weird lights above Silbury Hill that vanish if anyone comes close to them. Plus, these codes." He held up a handful of paper notes. "Okay, not easy to sort but when put together they say, 'Count Alessandro Volta is here, now I need a beer.' Okay, the last part might not have been him." He scowled at the pages.

Caradoc laughed. "But Count Alessandro Volta is him, one of his secret names. Do I want to know how you got that out of all those pages? Are you sure you aren't a tech guy?"

"It was a logical deduction based on words he'd been using. I'm not turning into one of you." Harlie put the papers away. "Is our recent situation going to cause an issue? We really should get to Avebury tomorrow."

Bart nodded. "It shouldn't be a problem, and I don't want to stay here if we don't have to. But I still want to see if they find the second korbin. Maeve can put the pressure on her cop friend to make sure we get cause of death updates. But I have a bad feeling the second korbin killed himself."

"Agreed," Harlie said. "I'll look up that information, but I feel you are correct. We're looking at a necromancer who is using people on this side to pull in creatures from beyond the veil."

"They're trying to break it down." Stella looked around the room. "My aunt had a theory that to destroy the veil you wouldn't need one big thing, just a lot of little events. The cumulative reaction would destroy it. I think that's what we're looking at now. And have been for a while, we just didn't see what it was."

Everyone dropped into their own thoughts on that until Dailten spoke. "Nothing more is going to be done tonight, and I'm tired." She got to her feet. "I say we get some sleep. Sort out the beds, these sofas fold out as well. Just keep in mind—the walls are extremely thin." With a nod, she marched down the hall and soon a shower was heard.

"I'm going to keep working in that room, maybe get some more answers." Harlie collected his bits of paper and started down the hall.

Stella got up as well. "Let me shower and change into something less comfortable, and I'll join you. I'm feeling more connected to my aunt, maybe I can find something. I'm not ready for sleep." She pulled the massive robe close, grabbed her luggage, and darted into a bathroom.

Jones went for the door. "I'm going to patrol. I don't need a lot of sleep, and those swamp goblins were nasty." He nodded and left.

Aisling turned to Reece. That was the closest she'd seen Jones get to being freaked out. But Reece just shrugged as his friend left.

Bart's phone rang, causing everyone still in the room to jump. "Hello?" There was a hesitancy to his voice. Whoever it was they hadn't shown on his caller ID. "No, we didn't know. Thank you for telling me." He hung up. "It was Maeve's cop friend. He felt my number might be more secure. They did find the second korbin, his throat was slit and he was behind the pub in some bushes. They found two knives in the bushes as well, both bloody. It appears he killed his friend, but then someone else killed him. Marcus said a few patrons mentioned there had been a third korbin standing outside when the first two came in. He also said a dead korbin was found down the road from here about a half-hour ago with self-inflicted wounds."

"Wait, so if those korbins killed each other or themselves in order to bring those two swamp goblins to this side. If there's a third dead one…" Aisling let the rest drop.

"There's probably a third swamp goblin. One with the same weird powers the first two had." Reece he went to his luggage and pulled out a second gun and added it to his person.

"We need to warn Jones." Aisling got to her feet, then got her own gun from her luggage. "I know he's tough, but he won't be expecting a swamp goblin and they were able to freeze him before."

Bart, Caradoc, and Maeve all got to their feet.

"It's Bart's call, but I think it would be wiser to have you three guard here. Harlie and the others need to be protected. And Jones couldn't have gotten far," Reece said.

Bart scowled, then gave in. "I'd like to disagree with you, but you're right. However, if they're after Aisling, she needs to stay here too."

"I think they're after all of us right now," Maeve said. "They know we're closing in on whatever in the hell it is they're doing. They want all of us."

Bart frowned. "You might be right. Go find Jones, get him back, and make it quick." He sat down and then Caradoc and Maeve did as well.

After Maeve gave Aisling a serious glare. Aisling owed Maeve one for supporting her.

Aisling gave her a quick nod, then she and Reece went into the dark. Reece's odd hybrid status didn't extend to great night vision, so Aisling took the lead. Of course, following an assassin in the dark, in the country, wasn't easy even with elven eyes.

The area was silent as they followed the road. Then Aisling saw a path branch off that appeared to go a distance around Dailten's cottage. If Jones was patrolling, he wouldn't be sticking to the road, even if it was a narrow backcountry one. Aisling nodded toward the path, then she led the way.

Reece was close behind her, but so silent if she didn't know he was there, she wouldn't have heard him. She worked on keeping her own steps quieter.

A bunch of broken branches on a tall shrub to the right of the trail brought her to a stop. She bent down as Reece kept watching around them. They were recently broken. She crouched to the path and saw it was roughed up. She hadn't done wilderness tracking since she'd lived in Alaska as a rebellious youth, but even she could tell this was fresh and looked like a scuffle. She stood up and whispered as much to Reece. He nodded and she turned to follow the broken branches away from the path they were on. There was no sign of Jones, but no sign of any attackers either.

Jones was the most efficient human killer she'd ever seen—that something might have taken him out before he could damage or kill whoever attacked him was bad.

A few more broken branches, larger ones this time, indicated they were on the trail of something. There was enough moonlight to see a small field with a low dividing wall just past the trees and shrubs. And two dark forms silently fighting in front of it.

CHAPTER NINETEEN

—◆—

THE TWO PEOPLE were both so soundless that they looked like an odd game of charades. The taller one turned so his face was briefly noticeable—Jones. He twisted toward his gun lying on the ground near him, but a flash of gray lightning—not coming from the person he was fighting with—hit the gun and shattered it.

Then the swamp goblin who'd attacked with the lightning, vanished.

Reece readied his gun.

"Keep an eye out for that swamp goblin, I'm going to try stunning whoever Jones is fighting." When Reece nodded, Aisling moved closer to the fighting. She did have her gun, but whoever this was, was taller than a swamp goblin, and catching them might give them a lead as to what was happening.

It was difficult to tell who Jones was fighting, but the fact that the being was so silent, and seemed to match every move Jones made, caused the hair on the back of her neck to stand up. Clearly, there was a dampening spell over them. She was watching them, and not the ground, and snapped a small branch when she stepped forward.

The swamp goblin flared into view, then fired off a bolt of gray lightning, which bounced off her shield. Reece fired at the swamp goblin while it was visible.

The swamp goblin collapsed, but as it did, a patch of

swirling gray nothingness appeared behind Jones and his assailant. Jones looked away just long enough for the shadow person he fought to hit him in the head with a rock, toss him over its shoulder, and dive into the swirling void.

Reece yelled and tore after them with Aisling on his heels. She had no idea what was on the other side, but just as Reece wasn't letting Jones go, she wasn't letting either of them go. She hit the shrinking void just as Reece did and grabbed him as they both dove through.

And looked up into a mass of familiar trees. Aisling wasn't a tree-elf, nor one that lived outside of cities, but even she knew that these trees weren't the same as where they'd just been. But she did know them. They were Hewliths.

"We're on the other side of the veil." She stayed on the ground for a moment to let the slight bit of dizziness vanish, then got to her feet and looked around. Nothing but more trees.

"Where did they go? They were right in front of us." Reece was already on his feet and still had his gun out. "Wait, what did you say?"

"These are Hewlith trees, and it's not Wales. We're on the other side of the veil. Although this was a much less painful way to get here than my first trip. Aside from the dizziness. And this time I have my gun and phone." She had no idea if either would work here, but it was comforting to have them.

"Damn it. You shouldn't have followed me." He holstered his gun and pulled out his phone. His swearing told her what she'd feared—they both had their phones, but they wouldn't do any good in this place. She could see the black screen on his from here.

"*You* shouldn't have followed Jones without waiting for me. We shouldn't have been able to do that. Harlie said the portals between the worlds had to be opened for a specific person."

"He also said that going back and forth repeatedly wasn't good for anyone." He took her arms and looked into her eyes. "Do you feel anything odd?"

"Nothing more than annoyance. Either they, whoever they are, want Jones for some reason, or they were aiming for more of us." It was obviously a trap of some kind. Just not clear for whom.

Reece looked around the thick forest. Like her prior time here, the sky was an odd twilight—not that much could be seen through the trees. "I'd say they were looking to get more of us. I know Jones' fighting, and they'd already done something to him to slow him down when we found them. Pretty sure they wanted someone to find them and follow. We need to get you back to the other side."

"First, *we* have to get Jones. Second, just *how* are we going to get me back anywhere?" Aisling spun around the forest. "Bart and I only got home the other time because Neasa decided we were on the dryads' side, and she used her mojo to send us back through." She pulled out the ghau pendant. It was giving a soft golden glow. One that grew stronger when she was facing to the left of where they'd landed. "This, however, is new." The pendant had briefly glowed when she was here before, but it was more focused this time. It went completely dark as soon as she turned away from the specific path to the left. "It wants us to go that way." Would have been exceedingly handy when she'd been trying to figure out where to go the first time.

"You can't stay, it's too dangerous." Reece folded his arms and glared as if by will alone he could push her back through the veil.

Aisling smiled at his concern. She was worried as well, but there was no way she had been willing to let him cross without her. "The danger is in the actual crossing back and forth, not how long someone is on this side. Did Harlie mention anything about being here causing a problem that I missed?" She knew he hadn't around her, but she needed Reece to back down on this. If he was concentrating on her, he wouldn't be focusing on staying safe himself.

He ran his fingers through his hair and looked off into the woods. "Not that he said."

"Then it makes more sense that as the only full blooded fey between us, and the only one who's been here before, I stay." She held up the ghau. "And we go that way."

From the frown on his face, Reece was as happy about that as he was her being here.

Aisling gave him a quick kiss and then turned and followed the ghau's direction.

"Fine." He stalked along beside her, then started swearing after a few minutes. "There's something behind that rock." His gun was out and pointed to where a foot could be seen. A long, narrow, green foot.

She followed him as he silently walked behind the rock.

A dead swamp goblin. Non-exploded, but with a distinctive bullet hole in its head.

"Well, you got him. But whoever was fighting Jones still dragged him through the veil. And whatever that was, it wasn't a swamp goblin." The dark being had been as tall as Jones or more. Jones was a few inches past six feet tall. Swamp goblins were more in the four-foot range.

Reece dropped down and studied the swamp goblin, but didn't touch him. "He's disintegrating." He jumped back to his feet and stepped back.

Aisling watched as the body slowly turned to liquid. It was as if the ground was absorbing the body in tiny bits.

"Okay, that's just weird. And we probably want to be further away in case it does something to the ground beneath it." There wasn't any blood, just body matter turning to a murky liquid and soaking into the ground. It was more disturbing than if the thing had been bleeding.

They continued backing up as the ground around the swamp goblin collapsed. Then the entire body vanished, except for a bullet lying on the soggy ground.

"Great. I think we should leave now." Reece gave a shudder and turned to go.

Aisling started to turn toward the bullet. "Might not be a good idea to leave that there."

Reece grabbed her arm. "You might not know all the human stories of tricky fey, as you are one, but I do. Something wants us to grab it. It's another trap."

Aisling shook her head and the urge to take the bullet vanished. "You're right, they have a spell on it." That she'd almost fallen for that simplistic trap indicated she was still off her game. She held up her pendant. "It's changed direction though." Where it had appeared to lead them down a wider trail, the pendant was now heading to the right.

"What about the dryad who helped you?" Reece asked as they started down the new path. "Can we find her? I know the vallenians haven't gone after us directly, but especially with that last box of theirs, I feel like they're setting us up for something nasty. I don't want to see if this is part of their plan."

"Agreed. And the vallenian I did run into here wasn't helpful. Not to mention that I might have pissed him off by stopping his planned slaughter of the dryad council." She looked around. While the trees looked familiar, they also all looked the same. She had no idea if they were near Neasa's home or a thousand miles away. "I don't know where to find the dryads."

She kept following the ghau, hoping that it would lead them to Jones and, ideally, a way out. The dead swamp goblin, while disturbing, was also a good sign. Whatever had grabbed Jones probably came this way. She mentally tried to reach out to the ghau pendant—some artifacts had sentience. But either it wasn't aware on that level, or it was ignoring her. Most likely the latter.

The trail they were following grew narrower as they went. The trees closed in tighter, almost as if they were leaning toward her and Reece. Aisling studied each tree as they passed. Some of the dryads from the council had looked very tree-like until they spoke. If they were herding her and Reece in a specific direction, she needed to know.

"Maybe I'm going about this wrong." Aisling stopped in front of a massive old tree. They needed to find Jones, and while the ghau was helping, there was no way to know where it was sending them.

Reece watched as she held the ghau in her left hand and put her right hand on the bark of the ancient tree. She didn't speak out loud, but mentally asked the tree where Neasa was. Getting involved with the dryads so soon wasn't a great idea in her book. Until she'd chased off the alari dervishes, they'd been ready to try her for the crimes of her mother from thousands of years ago.

But Neasa might be their best chance to find Jones and get home.

Reece didn't say anything, but out of the corner of her eye she saw him step closer to her, pull out his gun, and face toward the woods. She figured he was just being cautious; if he'd heard or sensed anything, he would have said something. He might not like being one, but he was a precog.

The tree she was touching didn't respond, so she continued mentally asking about Neasa. Even sending mental images of Neasa. Still nothing.

Then a groaning sound echoed around her.

But it wasn't from the tree she was touching, or rather not *only* from that tree. The sound came from all around them. It was as if a hurricane-level wind was whipping through the trees. Without any wind.

She opened her eyes and let go of the tree she'd been trying to talk to. Nope, the sounds kept coming. Groans, but just on the edge of being low, drawn-out words. In a language she didn't speak. And, unless she was hallucinating, the trees were also starting to rustle. Again, as if there was a wind. But nothing could be felt.

"What's happening?" Reece kept his voice and gun low as he slowly surveyed the area around them.

"Not a clue." Then Aisling raised her voice. "We come in peace. I am looking for the dryad Neasa. I am her friend, Queen Aisling." The queen part stuck in her throat; she wasn't a queen and she knew it. But the dryads had called her such, and at least Neasa had been impressed with her heritage.

The rustling of the tree branches around them grew louder, then all went silent except a single row of trees. The same direction the ghau pendant pointed.

"I guess we're going that way and hoping it's not sending us to our doom." She lowered her voice again. She had no idea how well trees heard.

"You lead, I'll back up." He smiled and nodded for her to go first, but he didn't put away his gun. They still didn't know if the guns even worked. Testing it could call unwanted attention. Worst case, he could throw it if someone attacked and the gun didn't fire. Aisling left her gun in her holster; she needed both hands free if she needed to throw a spell.

Aisling followed the direction of the ghau and the thin line of rustling trees down another side path. They'd stopped the groaning sound; if it was how they spoke, they must have figured out that she and Reece were clueless. But the rustling was consistent and focused. Aside from a few fantasy books, she'd never heard of trees doing either behavior, but they had to go somewhere and this direction held promise.

They'd been walking for about ten minutes, the woods silent aside from the rustling of the trees, when they and the ghau pendant stopped. No amount of turning in a slow circle brought either back.

But she did feel an odd pressure closing in, like a massive weather front.

Reece must have felt it as well as he stepped back alongside her. "What happened?" His voice was barely a whisper, but in the silence of the woods sounded painfully loud.

"I don't know. However, something is coming this way. I think whatever it is stopped our path." What had started as just an odd pressure, was now becoming almost painful. She wanted to run, but she wasn't sure that wouldn't make things worse. Nor did she have an idea where to run to.

The crackling sound was gentle at first, echoing gently around the woods. It wasn't a fire sound, nor a rustling like the trees, but more reminiscent of static electricity.

"Stay behind me. I'll put up my shield again, but not sure how well I can cover you." Or how well it was going to work. But she kept that to herself. It had worked in the pub, she had to believe that it could work here.

It felt like the shield was working, but also almost like it was a living thing that happened to be covering her and Reece. Hopefully.

The crackling sound increased and fifteen swamp goblins materialized in a circle around them. They hadn't cast any magic, so they were appearing because they wanted to. Now that she could see them for more than a few moments, she noticed how different they were from the one she'd seen on her prior trip through the veil. They also looked larger than the ones she'd seen back home. These also looked far more fighterish than any of the others she'd seen. All had dark clothing, simple but effective. Most had bandoliers of throwing stargas—nasty sharp three-pointed throwing weapons that she'd only read about in history books. Half also had short daggers. The crackling stopped, but she had a feeling they could bring it back at any time.

Providing her shield was in fact working over here, it should hold against one or two of them throwing their lightning. But fifteen attacking were an entirely different thing. She had a bad feeling that many would easily overwhelm her shields even if they'd been back on Earth.

"What do you want?" Reece still had his gun out, but kept it pointed at the ground. Trying to appear like he could defend them if needed, but wasn't going to attack.

"We come for the queen. Danger here. Protect." The swamp goblin who spoke was taller than the others and had a small golden pin on his chest. He was too far away to see what it was, but the way it glinted indicated that there was a jewel of some kind on it.

"I didn't need protecting until your people attacked us on the other side of the veil and took one of my companions." She almost said 'friends,' but then recalled that some older fey had no concept of friendship— usually the more aggressive ones.

"Those not ours." The one who appeared to be the leader spat off to the side. The rest did similar motions after he'd finished.

Great, were they in the middle of some kind of swamp goblin civil war.

"You didn't take the man who had been with us? The human who was attacked and brought over from Earth just a short time ago?" Reece sounded calm but he was close enough that Aisling saw how tightly he held his gun.

"No. We do not welcome interference from the other side." The swamp goblin leader's language skills were improving rapidly. "We'll help you, to make you go back. The way must be sealed." He nodded to Aisling as if that had been profound.

She had no idea what he meant by sealing the way, but if they could help them get Jones back and get home, she was all for it. "Once we get him back, we'll leave. If we can. That's why I was looking for the dryads, they helped me leave last time." She didn't want to bring up Neasa's name in case these swamp goblins didn't like dryads either. She'd seen a lot of fractions between the dryads and others last time.

"Dryads have their own problems. They let the ghanlough free. But we can get your human back and get you home." He tilted his head and watched her with narrowed his eyes. "For a cost."

Considering that his heavily armed, and probably magic using, people were still surrounding them, she'd pay whatever the cost was to get Jones back and keep them all safe. "What?" Even though she knew they didn't have a choice, she did her best to sound haughty and unconcerned. She knew growing up in the family she had would come in handy at some point in her life.

"A blessing." He looked around his people. "We are a smaller troop than the others we face. But with the blessing of the queen, we will succeed." His grin was disturbing as it showed the two rows of tiny, pointed teeth.

That request would be more upsetting if she really thought any blessing from her would help anyone. There was no way to know if this group wasn't really the bad guys of the situation. And she didn't intend for them to stay around long enough to find out.

"I have no idea what I would do to bless anyone." She carefully wasn't saying that she was or wasn't a queen. Hell, if her father really was the lost prince, then it was possible. At least it might get them out of this mess. She and Reece had been here about an hour. The time back on Earth could be vastly different if her prior visit was any indication. They needed to find Jones then get back soon.

"You will know when the time comes. I will hold you to it. The blessing must come after we have completed our task." He looked around sharply, as if he heard something behind him.

Aisling had excellent hearing, but heard nothing.

Or maybe that was it. The bird and small animal noises had come back once the swamp goblins appeared. They were gone now.

All the swamp goblins drew weapons and about half raised their hands as if preparing a spell.

"The ghanlough are hunting. The dryads failed their watch and now they roam freely. Stay close to us, we will protect you if we can." He tilted his head to the sky and let loose a deep roar—one that didn't sound like he was large enough to create. Not a good idea if they were trying to be secret, obviously he believed that the ghanlough already knew where they were.

Aisling swore as they started running. The term ghanlough translated from the old tongue to the unforgiven—those skeletal beings who'd attacked the frozen people of London, taken her mother, and shoved her through the veil. The ones that the dryads were almost killed over because they failed to keep a watch on them.

Reece put away his gun and ran alongside her. Like her brothers and the rest of her friends, he'd been frozen by her mother as the ghanlough attacked. He knew what was after them. Aisling hoped their guns worked, but she'd count on her magic first.

The swamp goblins fanned out around them, keeping Aisling and Reece in the center. They must really believe in the value of the hypothetical blessing from Aisling.

The leader of the swamp goblins dropped back to her

and Reece. "We will protect you, but we need to run faster to reach a safe haven." He glanced to Reece. "Not-human-and-not-fey, can you run as your ancestors from this side did?"

Reece gave him an odd look at the swamp goblin's description, but nodded. "I will go as fast as I can. If you must leave me behind, do so."

Aisling shot him a glare. "Stop being heroic, it freaks me out." Then she nodded to the swamp goblin. "We're not leaving him behind. We will go as fast as we can to keep up." Reece was a hybrid human-fey, but his fey ancestry was from the water end of the world rather than land. Still, she knew he could run faster than a pure human. And she wasn't leaving him behind. If she had to carry him, she would. This over-heroic bit of his was going to have to stop. Most likely incorrect guilt about not saving her when she'd been shoved through the veil the first time. A month of regret and fear had settled in too well in his psyche.

The swamp goblin bowed his head to her and resumed taking the lead.

Reece didn't say anything, but picked up speed.

"Just so you know, if you try to bail to save me, I'm coming after you," Aisling said as she ran.

"I know what's hunting us."

"So do I. No deal." She held her glare—not easy when they started running through narrowing trees.

The swamp goblins were running toward a glen in the woods. It was narrow and deep from what she could see. But she seriously doubted that it would hide or protect them from the ghanlough.

The swamp goblin leader stopped at the entrance to the glen and motioned for Reece and her to hurry. The rest of his people ran in as well. "Hurry, we can hold this for a while. I have called for help."

Aisling wanted to ask how in the hell a narrow glen

was going to stop anything when she felt a pressure surround her as she passed the leader. There was some magic on this glen, but beyond the fact that it was there, she couldn't tell what it was.

The leader ran behind them, then turned and clapped his hands together while he faced the way they'd come in. The pressure increased, then seemed to settle. But it was still noticeable. It felt as if she went to the edges of the glen and tried to put her hand through it would be like trying to press against a giant unbreakable bubble. She'd have to ask Harlie if he'd heard of that spell when she got back.

This must be a safe spot that the swamp goblins regularly used, but it wasn't where they lived. There was a small cave on the side of the rise that held basic supplies, but nothing more.

"What is this place?" Reece asked as he clearly came to the same conclusion she had. His gun wasn't out but his hand was on the grip.

"It is our place of war." The swamp goblin looked sad for a moment, then nodded toward the small cave where the others were pulling out supplies. "My people realized there was a foulness growing in this land in the last few years, one not felt since before your people left here. We have been preparing." He looked down at Reece's gun. "Your weapon might not work in our protected area, and even if it does, it won't last long. Can you fight with a sword? Either of you?" As he spoke, a swamp goblin brought them each a short sword.

Aisling took it and moved it about in a basic warm up formation. It was a simple blade, not like the fancy ones she'd had at her parents' home in L.A., but it was solid. "I was trained in formal swordplay growing up." She shrugged. "Most of the elves in the first families trained their children in that. Archery as well. It made them feel special."

Reece also took the sword offered to him. "I'm afraid that was never part of my upbringing." He slowly mimicked Aisling's moves. "I might be more of a danger than a help with this."

"Touch the ghau." The leader nodded toward Reece.

"What?" Aisling and Reece said at the same time.

"Hold the sword in your left hand, grasp the ghau pendant with your right." He turned to Aisling. "You will ask it to give him the sword training from your own skills. I have heard of this."

Aisling blinked a few times. That would be a great trick if she could get it to work. "It probably can't hurt?" She held up the ghau.

Reece looked far more skeptical as he came up to her.

She felt an odd rush as he took hold of the ghau and quickly asked the pendant to give Reece the gift of swordsmanship. The ghau grew warm, Reece's eyes went wide, then he released the ghau and collapsed to the ground.

Aisling dropped down next to him, but he shook his head and sat up almost immediately. "Okay, don't know if it worked or not, but that hurt." He rubbed his forehead.

"Fight." The swamp goblin leader folded his arms and stepped back from them. "Pick up your sword. Fight."

Aisling shrugged as Reece reclaimed his sword and stood. She stepped into position and grinned. "I'm ready when you are."

"And I have a massive headache, but okay. Not sure what's in my head, just don't stab me." Reece moved into the same stance she held.

She lunged forward for a simple strike, but Reece blocked her easily. She tried a few more moves, each one getting more complicated. He continued to block her.

"You aren't fighting." The swamp goblin shook his head.

Aisling and Reece picked up their pace. It had been

decades since she'd learned swordplay, but once she started again, the moves came back. It was as if her muscles instinctively recalled the hours of training. Neither could gain the advantage over the other, and both were sweating when they stopped.

"That will do. Keep the blades with you—even when you leave." The swamp goblin stepped away to speak to a small group of his people, but turned back to Reece. "The knowledge isn't permanent—but should hold to get you back home."

Reece held up his sword as the swamp goblin moved away. "The ghau did that? Damn, it was worth the headache. Which is still hanging around by the way. But to be able to pass skills between people like that? That's impressive."

Another swamp goblin approached with two belts and scabbards and gave them each one.

Reece laughed as he fumbled with his. The belt was fine, but his scabbard went the wrong way.

Aisling got hers on and then helped him with his. "Now you're a swordsman."

"I am. How are you feeling about this? Not about me being a swordsman." He laughed.

"It feels odd, but part of me feels like I'm supposed to be here. Don't worry, I'm not planning on staying. But I feel more like myself than I have since I came home." She tentatively kissed him to test her theory. She pulled back with a grin as it became more than tentative. "You seem like *you* now. If that makes sense."

"I'd have to agree. But I also agree that staying here for any of us isn't an option." He gently ran his thumb over her lips. "Glad to have you back though."

A roaring cry cut off her response and all the swamp goblins ran to the highest points in the glen. Mostly the hills surrounding it.

The leader ran to Aisling and Reece. "The ghanlough

are coming and our reinforcements have not yet arrived. The glen magic should hold, but if it doesn't, kill any that attack and run if you can. If we live, we will find you."

Aisling nodded and she and Reece stood back-to-back. The swamp goblin hadn't indicated any place for them to stand, so staying put was best.

Reece kept his sword, but also drew his gun. "If this works, great. If it doesn't, I'll go swordsman on them."

"Good point." Aisling called up a disable spell, another of her newer ones. Even though her magic hadn't worked well the first time here, she wanted to try it over her gun. Besides, this place seemed fluid—she had a feeling gifts and powers came and went as the wind here.

If she hadn't been completely certain that the ghanlough were the same monsters who had attacked her and the others in London, she was now as a group of them charged the opening of the glen.

Rail thin, skeletal beings that didn't carry weapons. But their long, hooked fingers and elongated fangs indicated they didn't need them. They yelled as they ran forward. But they only got a few feet into the glen when the spell around them snapped back and sent them flying into the air.

Another wave ran forward with the same results.

"Are those things stupid?" Aisling wasn't sure what to think. They had seemed very focused when they'd attacked in London, but maybe they worked better with simple concepts.

"Or trying to wear the spell down." Reece added. It wasn't clear if their guns would work, or if their bullets could pierce the swamp goblin spell surrounding them, but he was ready for that spell to fall.

"Damn it, you're right. It even looks like it's strong enough to take some of them down for good, so that's the only reason to keep running at it." A few of the first group weren't getting back to their feet and at least one looked like the force of the swamp goblin spell sent it back hard enough to break its neck.

The attack on the front of the glen went through a few more rounds. The ghanlough weren't going around the glen, and even though the swamp goblins had all taken positions up high, they were all facing the front. Either there was something about this glen that made it impossible to get into from the any other direction, or it was also part of this spell.

Aisling really wanted to learn the swamp goblins' protection spell.

Another group of ghanlough charged and this time they got a good five feet further into the glen before they were flung back. The swamp goblins around them tightened their holds on their swords and stargas as they braced for attack.

CHAPTER TWENTY

"REMEMBER. YOU RUN if you can." The swamp goblin leader silently appeared next to her. "When that shield falls, don't wait."

"But will you be okay?" She surprised herself at her question. But these swamp goblins had been trying to help. That was a rare thing on this side of the veil.

The swamp goblin tilted his head in almost a bow. "Thank you. We will be fine. I know more of our people are coming soon and there's a good chance the ghanlough will be split when you leave. I would keep you here, but we don't have enough people to protect you." He nodded to both. "Stay together. Be careful who you trust. I will find you when I can." As he was speaking, two more charges from the ghanlough pushed the shield spell further in.

"Thank you," Aisling and Reece said at the same time and then they moved to the far left. The ghanlough seemed to favor the right side, and there were more shrubs to the left.

One more charge and the spell shield fell.

As it collapsed, the leader of the swamp goblins and five of his people raced forward. The remaining ten were all on the hillside and already raining down stargas at the ghanloughs.

Aisling and Reece darted out the side. A ghanlough

spotted them and ran to intercept them. Reece shot it. The bullet was oddly slowed, but the creature was hit and tumbled to the ground.

"Guns work. For now," Aisling said as they ran around the rest of the ghanlough. The swamp goblin had been right; most of the ghanlough were running into the glen, but six had turned to follow her and Reece.

Yelling echoed in the forest and Aisling saw a pack of swamp goblins in the distance heading toward the glen—hopefully they were with the group who was under attack and not the bad ones.

"Ideas on direction?" Reece was keeping pace with her and not seeming out of breath. Granted, she wasn't at full elf speed, but it was still a good clip. Maybe the ghau gave him more than just swordplay knowledge. Yet another thing to ask Harlie about.

"That way?" She pointed ahead and to the right with her sword. She didn't want to drop the disable spell in her other hand to grab the ghau pendant to see if it was going to help guide them. They just needed to get out of there.

"You lead." Reece dropped back a step, easier to follow if she changed direction suddenly. And he was probably trying to guard her. Again.

Once they weren't running for their lives on the wrong side of the veil, she was seriously sitting him down and hashing this out.

The ghanlough were keeping pace a good distance behind them, close enough that it would be awkward for Reece to turn and get a decent shot at them without the ghanlough overwhelming him.

And they were trying to force changes in the direction that she and Reece were running.

"Damn it, stick close, we are not going that way." The direction that the ghanlough seemed to be trying to force them down actually looked far more enticing than the one she was going. Had the ghanloughs not wanted them to go that way, she might have chosen it.

Running with a sword out might look great in movies, but not so wonderful to actually do it. Certainly not for any length of time. Aisling slipped her sword into its scabbard, then reached up to grab the ghau pendant. The direction they were going had a warming feeling, but not as strong as when they first arrived. She couldn't take the necklace off, but the way they were going was still stronger than the other routes. She even tried holding it behind her but that way was stone cold.

"They're pacing us too well; they must have more of their kind coming." Reece kept pace. "It's still the original remaining five at this point though."

"Damn it, what are they waiting for?" Aisling didn't know about Reece, but this was making her edgy. She could handle a fight, this chase with no end was getting old. "That." What had looked clear ahead suddenly changed into a solid wall as they crossed a low barrier. The ghanlough, or whoever they were working with, had set a glamor on the wall. "They got us."

Either the trying to direct them a different way effort had been a ruse, or the ghanlough had planted multiple traps.

Aisling and Reece both turned to face the oncoming ghanloughs. There was no way to get out of this trap without going right over the group of them. That had now tripled in size.

"I'll take the left." Aisling threw her disable spell to the left side of the group. Reece fired two shots into the right.

The magic and the bullets both were slow, but not slow enough for the ghanlough to avoid them. Although, she overpowered her spell as it blasted the three she'd aimed at to bits.

The ghanlough behind the ones they killed leaped over

their companions and kept running. Aisling tried to pull in another spell, but there was a weird fog around her magic. She pulled out her sword as the first ones got within striking range far too quickly.

Even though it was a short sword, she was still able to lop off the heads of the first two. Reece fired three more times but was soon overwhelmed. He never put his sword away, so quickly started dispatching as many ghanloughs as he could with it. Even though there was a difference in their heights and reach, he was using her moves—just modified.

Aisling really needed to speak to Harlie about this.

An odd muffling noise came from behind them as they were pushed back a few steps. Aisling leaped out, slicing the three ghanloughs closest to her as she looked behind them.

Jones was sitting off to the side, behind some trees. Tied up, secured to a tree, and gagged, but there.

"Jones is alive and bound behind us. He looks angry."

Reece was holding his own but she didn't want him turning away from the fight. What the ghau had given him was great, but who knew how long it would last.

He didn't turn to look back. "Do you still have your gun?" His second gun was in an ankle holster and hard to get to in tight quarters.

"Yup. You want it?"

"Yes. I can hold them back; you get Jones untied. At full elf speed." The ghanlough were slowing down on their advances. They'd blocked the only way out and probably figured they didn't have to worry.

Aisling wasn't happy about leaving him, but handed him her gun. Then she raced back to Jones, freed him, and removed his gag.

"Have another one of those swords?" Jones was beaten and bruised, but no serious wounds that she could tell. He was, however, exceedingly pissed.

"Take mine. I have magic." She hoped. It felt like the weird fog surrounding her magic was gone.

Jones yelled and ran into the ghanlough with sword moves that she'd never seen before—but they were effective.

He obviously wouldn't need the ghau education transfer.

Reece had shot six more Ghanloughs and was now using his sword as well.

There were only six of the monsters left now. They needed to kill them and get out before more showed up.

One of the ghanloughs got close enough to Reece that they were able to strike him. Reece yelled but then swung his sword out and cut the ghanlough's head off. Aisling ran to Reece. The strike had cut across his chest. Slicing through his shirt like it wasn't even there. Not a lot of blood, but the skin around the injury already looked gray.

Aisling did a full-strike spell. It was one that Harlie had warned her to practice more before she tried to use it in a fight—and that she hadn't had time to do. It blew apart all the remaining ghanlough, including the one Jones had been fighting. It also almost knocked her back into the wall and left her right arm numb.

Reece gave an odd smile, then he dropped her gun and his sword, and fell. Aisling caught him before he hit the ground, but he was unconscious and burning up.

Jones ran to them. "I think the thing that dumped me is coming back with friends. *Those* aren't them." He pointed to the dead ghanloughs.

Aisling picked up Reece and threw him over her shoulder. Jones grabbed the second sword and shoved Aisling's gun in his waistband.

Aisling grasped the ghau pendant. The direction to go was stronger than before, so she started running. There were no signs of ghanlough, but that could change. Not to mention whatever the thing was that had grabbed Jones was still out here somewhere. She picked up speed.

Although Reece was taller and outweighed her, her elven strength meant she could run while carrying him. It slowed her down some and she knew she couldn't keep it up for long. But his body was on fire everywhere it touched her. Her right arm eventually got feeling back, but she knew a lot more training would be needed before she tried that spell again. "We need a place to hide. He's really hurt." She was slow enough that Jones was pacing her. She tried not to think about what might be running through Reece's body right now.

"*Follow me.*" The words came from the trees, but there wasn't a dryad around. Or if there was, they were well hidden.

Aisling swore but followed the direction the voice said—which did coincide with the ghau. She saw Jones looking at her questioningly, but she didn't have any answers. Reece was possibly dying and she couldn't carry him for too much longer. It was more than just his weight, something else was weakening her. Residual from the spell, or just something about this side of the veil—there was no way to know.

"*More. This way.*" The voice echoed above them, but still no sign of who or what was speaking.

Distant shouting came from behind them. Jones looked back but shook his head. "I can't see anyone but that sounds like the people who took me."

"What were they?" She dodged around a rock and felt Reece spasm. Not good.

"Humans or elves, but oddly cloaked in shadow. I'd say English ones, from the few words they said."

"What? There shouldn't be humans on this side of the veil."

"There are and they seem quite at home. The one who grabbed me had the swamp goblin hit me with a spell before they attacked. Not the full freeze like they did at the pub, but enough to make me punch drunk."

Aisling kept her voice down as she told him what she and Reece had seen.

"Yeah, I woke up when they were tying me to that tree. I overheard their leader, another shadow covered person, say I'd served my purpose, and would make a fine gift. That was right after she ordered her people to beat me up."

"Nothing else?" Aisling adjusted direction again. No words this time but a very focused and distinctive wind was moving the tree branches.

"Nope. Obviously, they were using me to get you here. Those creatures you were fighting were the ones who sent you here the first time, right?"

"Yes, although the first time they sent me here almost felt like an afterthought. The thing just shoved me and then went after my mother."

"*Almost there.*" The voice was ahead of them now.

"I really hope whoever we're following is on our side. I'm running out of energy, and Reece is getting hotter."

"*Here.*" A will-o-whisp appeared in front of them and Aisling skidded to a halt.

"Don't follow it. Damn it." Aisling had avoided the will-o-wisps last time, but she didn't know if she could do it again. She started backing up, not wanting to follow it, but also not wanting to turn her back on it. Not that it probably really mattered—those things never traveled alone.

A tree ahead of them rustled and Neasa stepped out from behind it. "It's okay, Skee is with me. You need to come quickly, you're being tracked."

Aisling nodded and jogged toward Neasa; Jones held back. "It's okay, this is my friend." She nodded to Neasa. "She's the one who got Bart and me home." She didn't want to say Jones' name in the open woods.

Neasa bowed to him anyway. "You must come before they see us." She took off at a pace that Aisling would have been hard pressed to keep up with even if she wasn't weakening and carrying a six-foot-two, well-built man over her shoulder. Then Neasa came back, spoke some words that Aisling didn't understand and lifted her long arms. "Hold on, this might be tricky."

Before Aisling could ask what she was doing, she, Reece, and Jones, all lifted into the air. Only a foot above the ground, but whatever spell lifted them all also pulled them behind Neasa as she resumed running.

Aisling held on to Reece. Jones grinned and looked to be enjoying the ride.

About ten minutes later, Neasa stopped and the spell lifting them gently lowered them to the ground. "This way." She walked toward a clump of massive trees.

"Are we nearing your home? I'd been trying to find our way there."

Neasa looked back to them. "No, we are quite far away. But I'd heard through the trees of an elf being attacked. I took a chance that it was you." She turned and continued into the trees. And vanished.

Jones ran in after her with Aisling tailing behind.

Jones disappeared in front of her right before she got to the trees. The smart thing would be to wait and see if he came back out. But Reece's breath was rattling now. She had to find a way to save him.

As soon as she crossed the line of trees, Neasa and Jones were both visible. Along with furnishings not unlike Neasa's cottage.

"This is a place of hiding. Much of the land here is not safe even for my kind. Please bring your mate here, I can remove the poison."

Aisling wasn't sure how Neasa knew of the connection between her and Reece, but brought him to a high bed covered with leaves and gently put him down. His wheezing got worse and now most of his visible skin was gray.

"A ghanlough struck him. Can I help?" Now that she wasn't running, the terror of the situation hit her. Aside from the rise and fall of his chest, Reece looked dead already.

"I don't know if you can help directly." Neasa turned to Jones. "You are his friend."

"I'm Jones. Yes, we're friends. Can I help him?"

Neasa smiled. "You both care for him very much. That alone will help." She stood over Reece and reached out her hands. "The poison has gone far, but not too far." She swayed over Reece's still body, but his skin seemed to be getting grayer and his breathing shallower. Finally, Neasa reached one of her vines out to the plants along the protected circle of the place and came back with a collection of greens. The vine twitched and the greens became a mushy mess. "Here. Each of you take some and smear it on his face and arms. I will apply it to his wound."

The green mass reminded Aisling of ground up wet lawn clippings, but she felt a magical tingle as she touched it. With a shrug she started smearing it gently on Reece's face, Jones took care of his arms, and Neasa started humming as she covered the gash in his chest.

Reece twitched, then spasmed, and Aisling and Jones stepped back.

"It's just the poison trying to fight back," Neasa said softly as she kept humming. "Keep working."

Aisling went back to Reece and a moment later so did Jones. Concern was clear on his face, but he finished applying the goop. She agreed with the concern, but they didn't have a choice.

Reece's spasms grew worse and he started groaning. But he was also looking less gray.

Finally, Neasa stepped back. "He will recover." She

smiled and collapsed onto a bower built along the tree line.

Reece's eyes fluttered open. "Water?"

Neasa didn't get up, she looked exhausted, but she nodded toward a small fountain in the corner. "There are bowls there as well."

"I'll get it," Jones said. "You hang on to him."

Aisling nodded and took Reece's hand, the tight squeeze he gave back was a good sign. Even if he still looked weak enough that a five-year-old could push him over. She stared down at him. "You had to find a way to almost die. Again. Stop that."

"Only if you stop crying." His smile was almost normal.

Jones came back with a deep bowl and Aisling helped Reece sit up.

"Have him drink all of it." Neasa grinned as Reece's eyes went wide—the bowl was huge. "Trust me. I'm Neasa by the way. I'm glad I could save you."

Jones held the bowl up. "Might as well do what she says, I'm going to keep holding it until you drink it all. You looked like crap. Still do, but you were a lot worse."

"I'm Reece Larkin. Thank you, Neasa, for saving me." Reece ignored Jones' comments and started drinking. Aisling held him up as he drank.

Neasa went to the waterfall and got her own bowl. "I won't make you two drink, but after he's done, you each might want to have a little from the fall. There's a foulness in the air that zaps strength. And Aisling appears to have a serious spell backlash." She frowned. "You both need to replenish."

"I didn't notice that energy drain when I was here before, how recent is it?" There had been some odd things before, and her magic hadn't responded at all in the beginning the first time she was here. But it wasn't the same as this soul draining feeling. This wasn't just her magic, it was everything. She now felt the full weight of the backlash of the massive spell she'd cast—but this was more than that.

"Very. There was a time dilation spell on you and your friend Bart when you arrived last time—I didn't notice it until we sent you back. It was tied to when you arrived but it wasn't something that came from our side. I'm sure you noticed that the time difference between here and your world was great. However, there isn't such a spell on any of you this time." She gave a grim smile. "I know what to look for now. You have been gone five days, and this weakness began four days ago. Something has moved into this world that shouldn't be here."

"Humans? Elves?" Jones took the empty massive bowl back and got two smaller ones for him and Aisling. "I was attacked by one on the other side. A swamp goblin hit me with a spell and they dragged me through to here. There were more here, but they were all cloaked in shadow." He drank some of the water. "Probably to get Aisling back over here. Larkin and I were just bait and collateral."

Neasa scowled. "Neither humans nor elves should be here. None of you should. They could be what's causing the problems. I will have to tell the council."

"The dryad council?" Aisling liked and trusted Neasa. But the rest of the dryads were useless or plain hostile. She honestly didn't think they'd be helpful for anyone.

"No. That group…was disbanded by the vallenians." Neasa normally had a very expressive face. Right now, it was so neutral that it looked more stonelike than tree-ish. She might have an opinion about the situation, but she was keeping it to herself. "There is a multi-species council. One that had been forming over the past year, but that my people ignored. The few of us dryads who remained sanctioned by the vallenians have joined it. They need to be made aware of these developments. You must come speak to them."

"We need to get back home. I'm sorry, but Reece and I

only crossed over to rescue Jones. And if he was taken to get me over here—we need to leave immediately."

"The walls between our worlds are growing thin, and myself and several of the council are afraid that they will fall. Not just the veil between our worlds, but the one protecting both of us from the third world, the Isfyden. There are deadly beings there—the xpenc rule there and they are fouler than anything in either of our worlds. They can never be allowed to escape. I believe that something is forcefully weakening the walls with that intention."

"We have to help them." Reece leaned away from Aisling and swung his feet over the side of the bed.

Aisling nodded. "But if we're being weakened and the energy drain expands? How serious is this?"

"Very, for those who aren't strong enough to hold it at bay. The water you all had will help and one of our wizards has made a band that can keep the decay at bay." She held up her tree-branch-like arm and showed off a deep brown band pushed almost to her shoulder. "Like your ghau, it won't come off. But it might help you all on the other side as well."

"If you two say yes, we go to this council." Aisling looked to Reece and Jones. When both men nodded, she turned to Neasa. "We will tell them what we can. But we need to get home quickly. There have been incursions on the other side. Death driven ones." She briefly told Neasa about the korbins and the evil swamp goblins.

"This is grievous news. I know of the Wolia band of swamp goblins; they are most likely the ones who helped you. The Gful are the ones who probably crossed over to attack. They have become more aggressive in the past year, but they don't have any magic users strong enough to cross, and certainly no one capable of death magic. They must be working with someone extremely powerful." She strode to the opening where they'd come in. "We must go."

Reece reclaimed his sword from Jones, and they all followed.

Aisling hadn't noticed the change in her energy until Neasa mentioned it. Or maybe it was simply more noticeable outside the protection of the tree cottage. But she did feel closer to her old self.

Neasa was lost in her own thoughts, only seeming to remember them when she strode too far ahead.

Aisling kept pace with Reece and Jones and continued following the trail until Neasa would come back for them.

"I do apologize, I forget how frail you all are. We are almost there." She'd just started walking again when screeching hoots came from all around them. "We must run!" Neasa took off with the three of them fighting to keep up.

The hoots grew louder and reminded Aisling of baboons. Combined with a massive jaguar. All in all, not a good sound.

She made Reece and Jones run ahead of her. Her magic felt stronger than it had since they'd crossed the veil and if she was going to cast a spell, she needed things to be clear behind her.

A brief look back showed her what was chasing them. Krilaze. Nasty beings with more fangs and claws than brains. The old stories said they were always controlled by a master magic user because when left to themselves they often killed each other.

Eight legs like a spider which supported a large body, but their faces were like a huge cat. A sabretooth to be exact. They gave their odd call again as she picked up speed.

"We're close to safety, but I fear not close enough," Neasa said. "I have sent a call to the council, but we must defend ourselves until they can get here. The krilaze will run us down and destroy us." She spun and lashed out with her vines, shooting them past Reece, Jones, and Aisling and grabbing the first two krilaze. She smashed them together with such force that both of their necks broke on impact.

Jones raised Aisling's gun and took out two more. They were now out of bullets.

Reece waited until one got close enough then swung his sword in an impressive move and sliced through two legs. The creature spun and Neasa's vines snapped it in half.

Aisling stepped back from the others and prepared a wind spell. Another tricky one that she really hadn't had time to practice. A voice in her head that sounded a lot like Harlie reminded her that using spells unprepared was sometimes worse than not using them. Options were nil at this point though.

She took a deep breath, grabbed the ghau, and released the wind spell. The remaining krilaze all tumbled backwards and exploded. Then a wave of power slammed into her and sent her high over the trees.

CHAPTER TWENTY-ONE

AISLING HEARD REECE and Jones shouting as she flew, and it looked like Neasa sent some vines shooting after her, but the backlash of her spell quickly pushed her far from all of them.

She was starting to descend, and was desperately wishing she'd been born a flyer, when a cushion of air slowed her down. She braced herself, this was still going to hurt, but she probably wouldn't break anything.

Hopefully.

Her landing wasn't graceful, but she hit the ground with a roll and seemed to be fine. She quickly got to her feet and looked around. At first she saw nothing but trees, then three alari wind dervishes appeared. None of them looked happy.

Considering that she'd destroyed one of their people and bullied the rest into not destroying the dryads as the vallenian ordered when she was here last time, she was surprised that it had clearly been their magic that slowed her descent.

The three stared at her, scowling. Then they all dropped to one knee and bowed.

"We serve the true queen of the prophecy." The front one looked up as the other two held their positions. "What would you have us do?"

Aisling had no idea how to respond. The queen thing

was clearly a mistake, but if a prophecy had now been tagged onto it, things were getting worse.

Shouting; more importantly, shouting of her name, delayed her having to deal with it. Mostly. "Please rise. My companions are coming." She channeled her mother and sisters as she gave a haughty nod to the dervishes then turned to see three shapes running her way. "I'm over here. With *friends*." The dervishes appeared to think she was important enough not to hurt—she had no idea how long that would last.

Neasa got to them first and didn't see the dervishes until she was almost past them. She jumped away from them and gave a sound that almost sounded like a hiss.

Aisling stepped between them and held out her hands. "It's okay, we're all friends." She had no idea what to do if one or all decided to fight.

Reece arrived before Jones, but he did have the hybrid thing working for him. Still, both he and Jones were winded when they got there.

"These shouldn't be here." The lead dervish stood up and raised his hand for a spell.

"They are with me, as is the dryad. All are protected by the queen." She couldn't look at her three friends as she spoke—she needed to sound serious.

"We will allow it, as the queen has spoken." The other two dervishes got to their feet.

"Thank you for assisting my landing." Aisling hoped that once she'd thanked them, they'd go away. Reece and Jones were just watching them, but Neasa looked ready to send out her vines and would be aiming for their necks.

"We were coming to offer ourselves in service for the great purge."

Aisling looked to Neasa, but she just shrugged. Great. Not a clue what the purge was—but it didn't sound good.

"Okay, well, that might have been postponed for now. I believe that—" her words were cut off as arrows flew past her and hit each dervish in the chest. Arrows that were almost as long as Aisling's legs. "Run!" She'd just started when she was picked up by a pair of Neasa's vines.

"It's okay, they are on our side." She brought Aisling back as five giants came forward—all armed with massive long bows.

"Thanks?" She wasn't sure what the dervishes had been up to, but as they had saved her from the spell blow back, part of her was sorry they'd died. Unless they were really on the other side.

"They thought you were the queen of prophecy, did they not? That queen is said to bring a rule of darkness to all the lands. You are with Neasa; therefore, you are not her." The lead giant nodded as he spoke.

"There's an evil queen? Good to know it's not me." Aisling hoped he was right. The queen thing was disturbing, that she might be a queen of evil, was far worse.

Reece and Jones came closer to her and looked ready to fight the giants if needed.

The giant peered down at her and nodded slowly. "The queen of prophecy has hair like yours, but a small mark on her neck. A dagger."

Shit. Her mother had an elongated birthmark on her neck. "Like a mole?" When the giant tilted his head further, she tapped the side of her neck, down near the collarbone but close enough to be seen most times. "An elongated black mark. Right here?"

The giant rose back up. "You know of her then. She is a foul beast and will destroy us all."

"Is she here on this side of the veil?" The chill in her stomach gave her the answer. Her mother hadn't died when she'd been grabbed by the ghanloughs.

"They say she has come to this side, but is not at her full strength."

Aisling turned to Reece and Jones. "It's my mother.

She's here and is somehow going to be the one to destroy the world as we know it."

"I'd say I'm surprised, but I really can't. Sorry, but your mother is a nasty piece of work." Reece put his arm around her waist and she leaned into him.

"Your mother is the one who is calling the evil? This is not good. We must destroy her." Neasa looked concerned, but Aisling shook her off.

"I have no problem with that. I thought she was already dead to be honest. She killed me when I was a child, so there's not a lot of fond memories."

The lead giant scowled. "Then you should not be here. She is not at full strength and is using others to regain it. But if you are kin…" He let the last part hang there.

"She siphoned off my power before, she might try it again." Logically, she knew that with the veil already weakened, crossing to the other side, and tracking her there wouldn't be a problem once her mother regained her strength. But emotionally, she wanted to get back home.

"I need them to speak to the council." Neasa nodded to the lead giant. "Thank you for stopping the alari, but might I ask for an escort?"

The other giants were already looking restless. Regardless of species, there was an energy of bored teenagers about them. Once there was nothing for them to fight here, they wanted to move on. The leader was older, but from the way he was watching them, he knew they weren't happy.

"Glin, you take charge of the patrol. Stick to our planned route—engage if needed, but this is also a fact-finding trip." He slowly looked at all four younger giants. "You are all responsible for returning with information." Then he turned back to Aisling, Reece, and Jones. "I am Cloul, I will escort you to the council." He gave a low bow.

Neasa smiled. "Thank you, Cloul." The four younger giants all turned and ran off.

Cloul watched them go. They were surprisingly quiet for their size. "They will learn. Energy is to be spent wisely, and not always on the hunt."

He and Neasa began walking with Aisling, Reece, and Jones following.

"Your mother is the evil queen? Does that make you Snow White?" Reece seemed to have suffered no ill effects from his near-death experience and was trying to keep things light.

Aisling still watched him closely. "Ha, ha. I am glad she's not at full strength. But if she was to be this ruler of prophecy—one I've never heard of—wouldn't she have jumped into it years ago?"

"One would think. Which could mean this is a new development and not one of her making." Jones walked a step ahead of them and although he seemed to be casually walking, Aisling could practically feel his tension as he watched everything around them.

A group of three dryads, all older looking and larger than Neasa, plus two more giants, approached them, then waited. They all held large axe-sword weapons and seemed to be focusing on Neasa.

Neasa had been talking to Cloul, but they both stopped when the other group came to a halt before them. "Thank you for answering my call. My friends and I were first attacked by krilaze, then three alari approached one of my companions to pledge allegiance to serve her—or who they thought she was. Cloul and his scouts removed them."

"The krilaze being about in the daylight is not a welcome situation," the dryad in the front said. "Thank you for watching over them, Cloul."

If Cloul was upset about being dismissed, he gave no

sign. He nodded to Aisling, Reece, and Jones, then turned and went back the way they came.

"The council was about to convene when you called for aid." The dryad didn't introduce himself or his companions and kept looking at Aisling, Reece, and Jones like they were interesting bugs he might have to squish. That he didn't appear to recognize Aisling from her prior trip might be to her advantage. To be honest, she didn't recognize him either. Aside from Neasa, the dryads all looked like walking trees and were too similar to each other.

"Thank you. My *friends*," Neasa put a heavy emphasis on the word as she pointed to Aisling, Reece, and Jones, "have much to tell the council of their trip here."

The lead dryad nodded and turned to walk back the way they came. The four with him silently followed. None of them put away their weapons.

With a nod to Aisling, Neasa walked after them, but stayed in-between the two groups.

The council chamber was a large hall, and far grander than the one the dryads alone had. It was filled with assorted creatures from this side of the veil, all quietly in discussion. Silence fell as soon as Aisling, Reece, and Jones entered.

The beings in the room didn't seem hostile, but they weren't happy to see them either. Wariness filled most of the faces she could see.

"I bring to testify to the council—Aisling, Reece, and Jones." Neasa didn't mention full names and since full names could hand over power with some of the older fey on this side, Aisling was grateful. More for the other two than herself, as she doubted that she would escape without being recognized.

There were far more dryads than she'd expected given what Neasa had said, but the vallenians might have only punished the local group as they had been the ones charged with letting the ghanloughs escape.

"Call them forth." The speaker was a female wispy joli, a distant relative of the will-o-wisps, but not nearly as capricious.

Aisling went first and gave them all the information she had, starting with the korbins' deaths and the swamp goblins attempted invasion, to the alari helping her land after her spell flung her airborne. Not that Reece and Jones couldn't speak for themselves, but she felt the less they said here, the better.

Since Reece had been with her for everything, he didn't have anything to add. Jones stepped forward and gave a brief telling of his encounter.

"You were attacked by a human who brought you through the veil? A human working with swamp goblins?" The joli hadn't introduced herself, but she was clearly the leader. And her disbelief was clear in the tone of her voice.

"I was attacked by a human or elf wearing the glamor of shadow. They weren't stronger than me initially, so I believe it was truly another human. The swamp goblin hit me with a spell when we first started fighting and my energy weakened." Jones locked his hands behind his back and stood at parade rest.

"This is greatly disturbing news. You will wait until we verify this." The joli leaned down to a guflin on her right and whispered something. The small, purple, winged fey took off running out of the chamber.

"We need to get home. The veil is obviously thinning and my world is in danger." Aisling took a step closer to the council bench.

"There are humans and elves running wild in our world, uncontrolled and dangerous ones. Now you say the ghanloughs attacked a group of peaceful swamp goblins. How are we to know that you didn't bring the humans and elves here to invade us during the weakening of the veil?"

Aisling took a moment to mentally catch up on that. "You were already being invaded by these humans and elves before we came here, you just didn't know it. Why would we come to tell you about this if we were behind it? Both Jones and Reece almost died on this side of the veil. We don't want to be here." The tension in the chamber had been slowly growing.

The joli reached out a long, thin arm and pointed a finger at Aisling's chest. The ghau pendant lifted out of her shirt and hung in the air as far as the chain would allow. "The vallenians. You are working for them." Her voice was flat, but it didn't sound like she thought that was a good thing. "I know of you now. There was another so marked with you. Where is he?"

"Look, I didn't ask for this, the vallenians did it on their own. As for the other, he's back home, where he belongs. Please. We need to get back home."

"We will have to—" the joli's words were cut off as the entire chamber shook. The purple fey that had just been sent away came flying back in. He had bloody tears all along his right arm.

"We're under attack! Ghanloughs, swamp goblins, alari!" He yelled as he flew to the joli.

"This can't be, why would they attack now?" One of the dryads sitting near the joli turned and glared at Aisling, Reece, and Jones. "Seize them! They have distracted us!"

Aisling pulled up a spell and started walking backwards to her friends.

"They are trying to help us!" Neasa yelled back as something shook the chamber again.

"To arms!" At the joli's yell, the giants and dryads all ran out of the building. But three small guflins stalked Aisling.

Neasa blocked them. "Friends. These are friends."

A powerful wave of air slammed into Neasa, Aisling, Reece, and Jones. Then three vallenians appeared in front of them. They said nothing, but sent whatever they'd just done to create the blast of air into the guflins and pushed them back.

Then the vallenians returned to them and the air lifted Aisling and her companions high and flung the four of them.

Aisling was pretty sure there wouldn't be any dervishes to catch them this time. Neasa reached out with her vines and pulled the other three close to her. "Hang on!"

There was a feeling like the shattering of glass and all four of them tumbled into a field surrounded by classic British stone walls. It was night. Lightning and thunder filled the sky, and there were fires all along the horizon.

CHAPTER TWENTY-TWO

NEASA RECOVERED FIRST and stood up. She looked at the distant flames in terror, but she didn't release the other three. "Where are we? What is this place? The very air is poison."

"We're on our side of the veil and not far from the cottage," Jones spoke first. "Could you put us down?"

"This isn't right. It's not right!" Aisling yelled toward the sky. The fires in the distance were destroying everything around them.

"*It is what will become if you do not close the veil for good. The worlds cannot continue like this. Use the boxes, the pendants, and your soul. Stop it, or your world will burn.*" The vallenian didn't appear, but his words, and the truth of them, seared through her heart.

"I don't know what to do!" She had to yell even louder as a massive wind hit them. Neasa bent low, but maintained her grip on all the others.

"*You will.*" The images around them changed and the wind and fire vanished. It was still night, they were still in a British field, but the only lights in the distance were of farmhouses and pubs.

Aisling's shakes were bad enough that if Neasa hadn't still been holding her, she might have fallen over. That reality they just saw was too real in her mind. This world would burn and so would Neasa's. She felt that as well.

Neasa released them, but then she started shaking. "Why am I still here? I can't be on this side. I can't!" Her eyes were wide with terror as she took in everything around her.

"I don't know how to get you back, but my brother might." Aisling calmed herself and patted Neasa's shoulder. She had no idea what they would do if Harlie couldn't get her back to her side. She was also clueless about what the vallenians had been up to by bringing the dryad here. She had a feeling that nothing done by them was without a plan.

"Is that another box?" Reece pointed at something in the grass, but didn't go any closer to it.

"One over here too," Jones added from a few feet away.

Aisling took a step away from Neasa. They didn't have much of a choice about ignoring the boxes, but she could try. Then she tripped over one directly behind her right foot. "Damn it." She got up, grabbed the box, then picked up the ones that Jones and Reece had found. "Are there others?"

Neasa got her panic under control and sent out her vines, then shook her head. "Those boxes have a distinct feeling; those are the only ones in this field. Do you often keep Hewlith wood boxes in your fields?"

"No. The first families have them, but they normally stay in secure vaults for each family. The vallenians seem to think they're helping by bringing them to me." Like some deranged dog she wanted to add. And would have if she thought they'd hear her.

"We probably don't want to be out here like this." Reece tilted his head toward Neasa.

"No, we don't. I can't tell how many days have passed on this side, but it feels like about the time I was jumped." Jones scanned the dark field.

"There shouldn't be a time difference this time." Neasa frowned. "Unless the vallenians did something when they threw us here." She retracted her vines and rubbed her arms as she looked around the field in fear.

"It will be okay, my brother Harlie is a powerful magic user, he'll get you back home. But we definitely won't let anything happen to you while you're here." Aisling made Neasa look down at her. "I promise that."

Neasa visibly relaxed. "Thank you. I believe you will try."

Jones started stalking back down the trail they'd come down to find him.

They got to the road and he nodded to Aisling. "I'm going to drop back and to the side, make sure that nothing came back with us." He was the only one of the four who wasn't a magical creature, yet she knew he was the best choice if they'd been followed.

Aisling nodded and kept walking. Neasa stayed close, but she noticed that Reece had dropped back as well.

They came around the mass of trees that blocked Dailten's driveway from this side and Aisling started swearing.

It was pitch black here, all light around them had faded and even with her advanced eyesight, Aisling had trouble seeing clearly. But the cottage looked like a burnt-out pile of rubble. Before she could turn to say anything to the others, the world shifted, literally. She almost fell over and barely held on to the three boxes she carried. By the time she recovered, the cottage looked as they'd left it. The only thing odd was the number of lights peeking through the curtains. It should be three or four in the morning, no one should still be up.

The others came up silently behind her. "What do you see?" She kept her voice low and never took her eyes off the cottage.

"Dailten's family cottage." Reece finally answered. "You saw another vision?"

"Yup. Vanished almost immediately. But as I turned the

corner it looked like it had been bombed a few weeks ago."

"Another seeing?" Neasa shook her head and tightened the grip she had on her upper arms. "They are coming through the veil. It is becoming too thin."

Reece raised his hand to check the handle when the door flung open.

A rattled looking Harlie lunged out and pulled Reece and Aisling in and motioned for Neasa and Jones to follow. If he was surprised at seeing a dryad, he didn't show it.

"Get in, go to the back room, quietly!" The house was far too lit up, but there was no one else she could see. Low voices came from the dining area.

Aisling knew better than to ask him questions with that wild look in his eyes and jogged down the hall with the others. The room was the one Harlie had been doing his research in and had printouts and books scattered about.

Harlie got in the room, took one final look down the hall, then shut the door and leaned against it. He smiled to Neasa. "Hello, I'm Harlie, nice to meet you. I do apologize for the abrupt entrance."

Neasa relaxed immediately and tipped her head low in greeting. "Harthinatle, your wisdom is known beyond the veil. I am honored to meet you. I am Neasa."

"You don't seem surprised at seeing her." Jones folded his arms. "And you rushed us through the front room. Who didn't you want to see us?"

"You three haven't left yet, so I thought it might be less confusing if you didn't see yourselves." He nodded to the three boxes Aisling still held. "Especially with those."

"How could we not have left yet?" Aisling sat down the boxes on the desk. She hadn't realized how tightly she'd been holding them until she shook out her numb arms. "I know time is different on the other side, but it went backwards?"

Harlie ran his fingers through his hair. "I'm not sure, not yet anyway. I just realized that you were all coming a few moments before you arrived." He raised his hand as Reece and Jones both opened their mouths to speak. "No, none of you should say anything more until we're certain that you've left. Time should snap back once the impact of the three of you being in the same place twice has vanished."

Voices came from the front room, then the door opened and shut.

"Me, I presume?" Jones stood nearest to Harlie and the door.

Harlie nodded. "And in a few minutes, Aisling and Reece. I am seeing both timelines up here." He tapped his head.

"You can see the future?" Neasa seemed calmer, but she visibly tensed up at that idea.

"Not really. But it's logical that Reece and Aisling would have followed Jones when they found out about that third korbin. But I do have a bit of a déjà vu phenomenon going on at the moment." He rubbed his head in annoyance. "I believe the snap to the correct time of your return will be hard on all of us." He dropped to the floor where he'd been standing. "You may all wish to sit."

Everyone sat on the bed or floor.

There was more low-level chatting coming from the front room and then a second door opening and closing.

"When will things—" Aisling's words were lost as the entire room dropped out from under her. For a few disturbing moments, it seemed like there was no sight, no sound, no feeling of being anywhere. Then with a pop, reality came back.

"I don't know about the rest of you, but that wasn't fun." Reece's eyes were watering and he was clutching his head.

"I must agree. Are these events common in your world?" Neasa had also taken a position on the floor when Harlie did. It was hard to tell, but she looked paler than before.

Aisling shook her head when Harlie didn't answer. "As far as I know they aren't. Can we leave this room now?" She felt like she needed a massive glass of water and a few dozen painkillers. Aside from Harlie, everyone else looked to be in the same condition.

Harlie shook himself out of whatever thoughts he'd been locked in, got to his feet, opened the door, then went briefly down the hall. He came back and motioned for them to get up. "We can go into the rest of the house. They've all left to go find you three and it's now four in the morning."

Hours after Aisling and Reece left to find Jones.

"Why did they all leave?" Aisling asked as they went down the hall. "I know we were missing for a few hours, but wouldn't some have stayed here?"

"I sent them away," Harlie said. "I had an odd foreboding about you three and now I know why. You all coming out of that room could have been awkward, if not far, far worse. Even without a dryad friend." They'd all gone to the kitchen and Harlie pulled out a flat bowl and raised it to Neasa. "Would you like some water?"

Neasa nodded and accepted the bowl when it was full. "Thank you. I don't mean to be ungrateful, but I don't belong on this side. Can you get me home?"

"I'm sure we can, it just might take longer than we'd like." Harlie nodded to the rest. "I recommend water, and lots of it, for all of you. Time travel can be hard on the system."

Reece had been just about to lift his glass for a sip, but stopped. "You've time traveled before?"

"No, but I've looked at it in theory." Harlie nodded. "I'd love to know how you came back before you left.

Who sent you back? Did you get those family boxes on this side or the other?"

Aisling had left the wooden boxes in his room.

"Unless our eyes were deceived, we were sent back by vallenians." Jones had been silent, but it was clear he'd been thinking, and he didn't look happy. No one was supposed to see a vallenian and live. That he, a pure human, had seen three of them, was getting even to the stoic spy. "We were about to be attacked on the other side, when three of the vallenians appeared in front of us, and sent us here." He shook his head. "I believe that the time issue was something on their side as well."

Reece nodded. "And the images. When we first arrived, there was fire and destruction all around us. And Aisling saw more when she first saw this cottage."

"I also heard the vallenians, or at least one of them, when we arrived. They said this was our future unless we closed the veil for good. And we can figure it was them who gave us the boxes, but they were on this side of the veil." Like the others she polished off another two glasses of water and a pair of painkillers.

"Who were the families?"

"We didn't look, your guess is as good as mine." They'd already gotten the shocker of all boxes—the one belonging to the royal family. The more boxes they got, the better chance of figuring out what the connection was. And the better chance that someone would mention their box was missing.

"I'll check when I go back into the room," Harlie said. "If you don't mind, I'll keep them."

"Go right ahead, you can have the royal one too." Aisling looked to Neasa. "Until we can get her back, she'll need a disguise." There were many different types of fey on this side of the veil, but a walking and talking tree person would be noticeable. According to the old stories, none of the dryads had survived before the fey crossed here.

"I can put something together. But I would like the rest of our friends to meet you as you are, if that's okay?" Harlie refilled Neasa's water bowl.

"That's fine. But you can get me back?"

Harlie had seemed sure before; he didn't look it now. "I will try. But if the vallenians sent you, there must be a reason. I'm not sure that going against that at this point is a solid idea. They wanted you here. At least for now."

"Maybe they were just getting her out of harm's way?" Reece looked better than before but there was still a tightness around his eyes. "We were under attack and she was trying to defend us."

Harlie nodded. "That could be a part of it, but if so, they had another reason as well. Vallenians are turning out to be unlike what our stories said; however they appear to function with their own reasoning and rules."

"Oh, and it looks like our mother might be alive on the other side of the veil and working to take it over." Aisling briefly explained what she'd heard. "It might not be her, but I seriously doubt it. Those alari only saved me because they thought I was her." Maybe she'd have to investigate dyeing and cutting her hair. Anything to keep her looking less like that woman.

"That's not good." Harlie had already started moving toward the front room when the door opened.

"What's not good?" Stella was the first inside, but the rest were right behind her. "We didn't find them, by the way."

Harlie motioned to Aisling and the rest, then walked into the front room. "They are here now. And the not-good information will come once everyone is settled." He looked around as Bart, Dailten, Maeve, and Caradoc came in. "Unless you'd rather wait until daylight and try getting some sleep now?"

"I think we need to know what the hell is going on," Bart said. "Sleep can wait."

Neasa came out behind the other three and her arrival stopped them all in their tracks.

"Oh, we brought a friend." Aisling took Neasa's arm and led her to the large sofa to sit.

"There's no way I'm going to bed right now." Stella smiled to Neasa, then sat down on the sofa as well. "Start talking."

Aisling waited for everyone to sit, then turned to Jones. "You start."

He quickly and efficiently explained being hit with the spell, kidnapped, and then dumped on the other side of the veil.

Aisling and Reece stepped in for their parts, with Neasa filling in the gaps. Everyone was interested, but calm, until Aisling mentioned her mother's involvement.

"That's what I was saying was not good," Harlie said.

Bart's eyes narrowed. "That's far more than not good. The havoc she could cause over there is terrifying."

"Agreed. And there are three new family boxes. The vallenians left them when they dumped us on this side and showed us what the world would be like if we don't close the veil." Aisling didn't argue about their mother being not good, but whatever the vallenians had shown them was possibly worse.

"*Close* the veil? Not just fix the weakness?" Dailten's head was tilted as if she were a bird after prey.

"Yes. They were very focused on that word. I assumed they meant fix the breaches so the wall isn't so thin. That's not it, is it?" For some reason that idea of shutting the veil completely left Aisling cold. She had been through the veil twice, and never wanted to go back. But the other world had always been there, whether they could cross the veil to it or not.

Having it shut was an odd concept.

"Probably the only way they feel they can close off Isfyden. The beings rumored to be there can never be allowed to escape." Stella nodded. "I'm not a fan of the vallenians, but they will do what needs to be done to save the other side." She turned to Neasa with a sad smile. "I believe in their minds you're needed on this side, at least for now."

"You are probably right." Neasa took a deep breath. "I am terrified of being trapped on this side, in this strange land. But if it is what is needed to save both our worlds, I will stay."

Harlie got to his feet. "I will still try to return you to your home, once we are closer to figuring out why you're here. Let me get the boxes they gave Aisling." He left the room.

Maeve gave Aisling a look and shook her head. "You've got to stop running about on adventures without me. I was afraid we'd lost you again."

"I agree. I know you went over to save Jones, but we can't keep crossing the veil," Caradoc said.

"Now I know something is wrong." Aisling narrowed her eyes at her brother. "You? Wanting to be cautious?" He'd shown leanings that direction before, but now he was deadly serious.

Even Maeve gave him a sideways look.

"I know, I know. But I can't control this flitting back and forth." He leaned back and folded his arms. "I tried to reach through the veil when you were gone. Again. I got nothing."

"Thank you." Aisling got up and hugged him. "But until we can figure out what exactly we're supposed to be doing, we're kind of stuck with what happens. Have we heard from Mott by any chance?"

"No," Bart said. "Whoever took him hasn't let him go. Garran and Surratt are still checking leads in London, nothing in the few hours you were gone though."

Harlie came back out with the boxes and he didn't look happy. "I had to translate which families two of these were from, and I do mean translate. They were in an archaic version of elvish. Both were families who died out within the first few years on this side. They are old and I have no idea where the vallenians got them since there are no living descendants of either."

Caradoc looked at the boxes, but didn't take them when Harlie held them out. "And the third?"

"Is almost more disturbing. It's the ancient family line of the Asian empire, the offshoot line that became the Lazing."

CHAPTER TWENTY-THREE

—

"THE LAZING ARE made up of first families? Royal ones?" Reece wasn't even full fey but his face paled at that.

"Yes, it's not well known, as the ruling family currently disavows the connection." Dailten scowled at the third box. "I wish we knew what those damn vallenians were playing at."

"Can I see that one?" Stella reached out her hands and gently took the box. "Can you get the royals box? I know that the two kingdoms rule most of the fey world on this side of the veil, but there is something I recall my aunt mentioning." She put the box on the dining room table.

Aisling retrieved the royal box from the shatil bag, but barely touched it as she also set it on the table. Unlike the three from tonight, that box had issues and she didn't want to get involved.

Stella picked up a napkin and then used it to move the royal box over. She slowly turned the two boxes around each other. "Oh. Oh my. There are more that we need. It's a puzzle." Stella stepped back from the table and even Neasa moved forward to see. The two boxes wouldn't touch, a subtle force kept them an inch away from each other. But the lines of details on their sides were clearly the continuation of each other.

"Do any of you more mystically minded folks have a

clue?" Bart joined the others around the table, but stayed back.

Harlie and Dailten shared a look with Stella, then all three shook their heads.

"The only bit that I have is the fact that the family boxes were more than just ancestral relics. That there are connections. I wish I could speak to my aunt." Stella frowned at the boxes.

"I recognize what they are now. There are stories of those boxes in my world." Neasa had stayed the furthest back and still looked hesitant to come forward. "They are said to be the guides for the afterlife for the evil ones." She winced. "Sorry, that's how everyone who abandoned us is viewed. But our lives are good, or were good before the unbalance came. I fear the Malifithri will engulf both worlds."

That reminded Aisling of Neasa's mental popping in during their fight at the Tesco parking lot. "How did you reach out to me before? You shut down a Malifithri?" Things had happened too quickly on the other side to have brought it up then.

"It can be multiple events, but all will have the same result—the end of everything. I now believe what happened to you was a test, not a real Malifithri. Had it gone through, it still would have destroyed much of this world before it was stopped. However, I honestly don't know how I reached you before. I had a vision that the end was coming and I needed to know you were okay." She gave a small smile. "I now believe there is a reason the vallenians sent me here, whether I am ready for it or not. We all need to work together to stop the Malifithri. And those images the vallenians sent are the beginning of the end."

Bart shook his head and stomped back out to the front room. "If these vallenians are so keen on getting involved, why don't they do something directly? If the stories are true, they are a hell of a lot more powerful than anything on this side."

Neasa followed him away from the dining room. "They are the most powerful beings on our side as well. Yet, they rarely act directly. The council of dryads that I originally belonged to was tasked with controlling the ghanloughs. Even though the vallenians were stronger than my people, they passed that crucial task to us."

"And when they failed, the vallenians didn't punish them, but sent the alari to do so. Who appear to be on the side of the evil queen—aka our mother," Aisling said.

"Maybe they *can't* do anything." Reece looked around the room. "The fey have stories of them being invincible killers, but has anyone seen it happen lately? Maybe they're all reputation. Or maybe something has happened to them in the past thousand years to weaken them."

"One of them did manage to stab me in the gut while I was inside a car just to make me focus. That's pretty intense." Aisling looked around. Granted, that focus might have saved not only herself but a lot of others. But there should have been a less violent way to do it.

"True. But there must be a reason they're making everyone else do their heavy work." Bart turned to Neasa. "On the other side, the vallenians don't get involved directly in anything?"

"No." She shrugged. "Aside from flinging the four of us through the veil. But normally they just demand that things happen. And the rest of us follow through." The lines of worry down her face pointed out that her people, and the rest of the fey on that side of the veil, hadn't questioned the vallenians' control of them. Until now.

Aisling started to ask another question, but a yawn cut her off. That triggered everyone except Harlie and Neasa, into their own round of yawns.

"As the house mum here and now, I say we all go to

sleep." Dailten turned her glare around the room. "No one goes outside, understood? No matter what you hear, see, sense—you wake us all up first. We can continue everything in the daytime." She glanced over to the table. "I'm pretty sure we don't have to worry about the two boxes of the dead families, but that Lazing ancestor box might want to go into the shatil bag with the other royal one." She made no move to touch either of the boxes.

Aisling took the black shatil bag and nudged both boxes inside it. Luckily, nothing grabbed her and sent her to another dimension this time. She did notice Stella watching her as she clipped the bag closed. "Sorry, nothing this round."

"Eh, you never know. My aunt was a feisty broad." Stella grinned. "I have a feeling we haven't seen the last of her."

They filled the bedrooms, luckily most of them had multiple beds, and Neasa chose the sofa. Harlie stayed out with her to talk after the rest went to sleep.

Reece and Aisling were the last two in the hall. He stepped forward. "We *should* check, you know."

"Check what?"

"This." He kissed her gently, then she wrapped her arms around him and intensified the kiss. He felt good.

"I'd say things are better." She smiled and took his hand and led him into the empty bedroom.

"They are. Nice to have you back." Reece tilted his head in question.

Aisling smiled. "We've no idea what will happen in the coming days, or even tomorrow." She pulled him close. "I want this night. We can keep quiet." There was an almost panic in her mind—she needed him now. They'd both almost lost each other too many times already and a battle to save the world didn't sound hopeful.

Reece grinned and followed her in, gently locking the door behind him.

Aisling stayed in bed after she woke up. The warmth from Reece curled against her back almost lulled her back to sleep. She wanted this mess to be over and go back to being a cop. In L.A., without weird crap crossing over to this side of the veil. Well. L.A. had its own weird crap—but it was a lot better than this.

"Are you awake?" Reece's breath whispered along her ear.

Aisling turned to him. "I've been awake for a while. Just didn't want to get out of bed. Ever." Last night had been amazing and for a brief time they both forgot about world destroying invasions. Magic had kept any sounds from escaping the room.

"Me too." He traced her shoulder and neck. Then looked into her eyes. "We will get through this." His gray eyes were full of intensity, but she welcomed it.

Aisling kissed him gently. Leaving this bed seemed like she'd be leaving him.

"We will have to get up eventually." Reece returned the kiss but broke it off before it could go further. "We need to find Mott, save him, and stop the end of the world."

"Well, when you put it that way…yeah, I'll stay here." Aisling snuggled into his chest.

A rough pounding on the door ended the moment. "Aisling, Reece, get out here now!" Caradoc shouted.

Aisling and Reece both threw on clothes and opened the door.

Caradoc's blond hair stuck up in clumps and he looked like he'd just rolled out of bed. He grabbed Aisling's arm and motioned for Reece to follow as they ran down the hall.

The front door was open and everyone else was just outside of it, most still in their sleep clothes. An odd greenish fog covered everything a few feet past where they stood.

Aisling crept closer as a shiver hit. "Is that something we should be breathing?" She and Reece came next to Jones and Maeve. Both shook their heads and blinked.

"I don't think so. Damn it. Everyone back inside." Bart did the same shake and blink and started pushing everyone back in. They appeared to have been under the start of a spell even if the fog hadn't hit them yet.

Neasa was the furthest out and she took another step closer to the fog.

Harlie grabbed her hand, but dryads were extremely strong and she pulled free.

Aisling ran in front of her and reached up to grab the sides of her head. "Fight it. You're strong. Fight back!" Had she been asked, she would have said she had no idea that was what she needed to do. Only that she had to stop Neasa from going into that fog.

"It calls…" Neasa took another step forward, pushing Aisling back a step as she did so.

"I need help stopping her! None of us should touch that fog, especially her." Aisling had no idea how she knew, but there was a cold lump in her gut that screamed in terror at that weird fog. She tried to pull up anything magically that would help, but it was as if her magic wasn't there. And the coldness at her back from the fog was becoming brutal.

Everyone grabbed ahold of Neasa to pull her back, but it was a slow process as she was exceedingly strong. Harlie joined Aisling in facing the dryad and he started whispering. But it wasn't magic. Whatever was blocking Aisling was hitting him too. But his words got Neasa's attention.

She blinked, shook her head, and snorted at the fog. "Get back! That's a baois fog, and it will take our souls!" Neasa looked down and noticed everyone pulling on her for the first time. "Ah." She turned toward the house. Everyone joined her, but Aisling and Harlie stayed at the back of the group. Harlie's face was creased in worry.

Dailten shut and locked the door once they were all inside. "Will it come closer? We can try to stuff rags under the door, but this cottage is over two hundred years old—there are cracks everywhere."

Aisling felt access to her magic come back once they were inside, but the chill lingered.

Stella stalked near the door, then turned as if listening and marched toward the table with the shatil bag on it. "I think our two boxes here are somehow keeping that killer fog at bay. But how did it get here?"

Neasa kept staring at the door. "We removed it from the other side of the veil eons ago. It shouldn't be anywhere."

Harlie watched Neasa and his frown hadn't vanished. "Where did your people send it?"

Neasa pulled her attention away from the door. "I don't know. I've never seen it, just heard the stories when I was young. I assumed that it was destroyed." She saw something in Harlie's face. "It wasn't, was it? They just sent it somewhere else." The last wasn't a question. "They pushed it into Isfyden, didn't they?"

"Your people probably did dump it there, which means this leak in the veil is impacting Isfyden as well."

Aisling looked around at her friends. "How do we get rid of it? My magic vanished when I went out there."

Nods from all the other magic users confirmed she wasn't alone.

"So, this is how the world ends? By fog? That's great that those magic boxes are holding it off, but I hate to tell you folks, we can't live here for long. Not to mention, losing everyone who is still out there," Maeve said.

Harlie scowled at the door. "By the way that baois fog is repressing magic, we need non-magic solutions." He turned to Caradoc. "Your turn."

"I think I might have something." Caradoc raced down the hall before anyone could ask what.

Reece stood near the shatil bag. "I don't understand how these two boxes, in a suppression bag no less, are holding that fog off."

Maeve pulled out her phone and warned her cop friend, Marcus, about the fog. "Oh, well maybe it's just down here. Keep folks away from this area." Then she hung up. "It's only around this cottage, apparently. He hasn't seen or heard anything. Is this magical fog supposed to be targeted?"

Neasa shook her head. "In the stories that I heard, it would encompass an entire area. The good died along with the evil. No one survived."

CHAPTER TWENTY-FOUR

———◆———

"AND YET, THIS one has held off attacking. Even if those family boxes are helping, we should be dead now," Caradoc said as he came back down the hall with a collection of his electronic gizmos. "That's good to know. Tells us that someone modified that fog." He spun to Harlie. "Did you find alopoxilyn hyto in the dust samples from those mutated rapeseed plants?"

Harlie tilted his head. "I did. I didn't get far in breaking the compound down, but that was a part of it."

"Ha!" Caradoc handed out his sheer face masks to everyone. "Same ones that worked in London, should do the same here. Put these on. Neasa, yours will adapt to your face. Go on all of you, that crud is creeping forward as we speak." He tapped his face and his own mask flared. "Alopoxilyn hyto is made up of elements from *this side* of the veil. Therefore, someone created that fog here, to make it look and behave like the baois fog. But it's not the same. We're fighting some tricky bastards, but I'm better." His grin was back to normal Caradoc wattage.

"Then you can stop it?" Aisling put on her mask. As during the attack on London, the thin, transparent, material clung to her face.

"Better than that, sister mine. I can send it back to whoever sent it." His smile dimmed. "Sadly, I can't follow where it came from, and unless they are extremely close to here, we won't be able to know where they are when I reverse it. But they won't be expecting it." He sorted the gizmos in his hands.

Aisling looked them over, but aside from differing shapes, they all appeared to be the same.

Finally, he looked up and nodded. "Jones and Maeve will help me. Sorry, fellow magic users, but it'll be better with them. From what I can tell, even Larkin won't work as well with the half-fey blood he has." Caradoc caught his response before Reece could volunteer. Hybrids weren't supposed to have any magic. Reece did, but the entire group wasn't aware of it.

Jones and Maeve left with Caradoc and the rest clustered around the window to watch.

Caradoc gave Maeve and Jones a pair of the smaller gizmos, then motioned for them to flank him on either side as they spread out and stepped toward the fog.

Even though Aisling had faith in her brother's inventions, she still bit her lip as the three were overtaken by the fog. Reece reached for her hand and she leaned into him.

"Is it thinning?" Neasa was closest to the window and leaned even closer.

"I don't…yes, I believe it is." Stella grinned. "That Caradoc is a cocky one, but he's good."

"He is." Aisling and Harlie echoed each other.

The fog cleared as it swirled in the center between all three of them and their gizmos. Then Caradoc pulled out a larger one and aimed it in the center of the fog funnel. Lightning flicked through it. If it were a living thing, Aisling would say it fought back.

The funnel exploded and reached out to overwhelm Caradoc and the other two. If they hadn't been wearing the masks, they'd be dead—or whatever that fog was trying to do. The name of the original fog translated to death, so the odds weren't good at surviving an attack, even if this wasn't the same fog from beyond the veil.

Aisling and Reece started to run out, but Harlie held them back. "They'll be okay. Let Caradoc sort this out." Harlie was the most anti-tech person Aisling knew, but there was a tone of pride as he watched his younger brother.

The fog lifted away from all three of them, leaving Jones and Maeve standing there with their guns in their hands. Aimed at each other. They both blinked and looked extremely confused as they put their weapons back. Masks or not, something of that fog had gotten to them.

Caradoc increased whatever he was doing with the larger gizmo and the lightning coming from inside the fog slowed down and vanished.

After a few moments, the fog disappeared. Whether it went back to its creators or not, they might never know.

The three held their positions until Caradoc nodded and removed his mask.

Bart was at the door and stepped outside. He nodded to Caradoc. "I really hope that you're as good as you think you are and it is now annoying whoever created it. Although part of me really wants to know how they created it."

"That would be my question as well." Although she'd been watching closer than anyone else, Neasa stayed just inside the doorway when everyone else went outside. "If that wasn't the same baois fog that my people sent through to Isfyden—there's no way to know what it could have done to any of us."

"I think we'll need to be searching for data on this baois fog, even if this was just a twisted copy," Bart said.

Maeve and Jones still looked stunned.

"I don't recall anything of what happened after that fog overtook us," Maeve said.

"Until I saw myself aiming my gun at your head." Jones might have sounded calm to anyone else, but Aisling knew him well enough to know that he was freaked out. Not that she blamed him. That was terrifying.

"Are those plants dead?" Neasa still refused to come out of the cottage, but pointed to the hedges outside of the property. They were brown and seemed to be withering as they watched. "The real baois fog was harmless to pure plant life."

Caradoc went to the closest dying shrub, broke off a piece, and raised it to his nose. Then coughed and almost threw it. Harlie ran out with a sample bag, plucked the dying plant out of Caradoc's fingers, and sealed it up.

"Thanks. That smells vile. Not sure what they did to that poor plant. Or why." He took the gizmos back from Maeve and Jones and everyone went back inside.

Stella nodded. "Now that the immediate threat is taken care of, I'm going to work on breakfast. We expect a full report of what just happened."

Dailten followed her in.

Maeve was leaning on Caradoc and he took care to get her to a chair. Jones stayed on his own, but also quickly sat.

"What happened out there, Caradoc? Did your masks fail? And why weren't you affected?" Bart kept watching both Maeve and Jones.

"I don't know. These masks should have blocked everything, but even I felt a pull to kill something when the fog surrounded us. Even though we can't use magic near the fog, I think my magic ability protected me." Caradoc almost had Maeve on his lap. That she wasn't complaining about it was concerning. Maeve didn't mind public displays of affection, but she did mind if people saw her as weak.

Jones was struggling to stay upright, but he still looked upset. As a trained assassin, among other things, something that almost made him kill a friend was horrifying. He was a master of control.

Stella and Dailten had been making a loud racket in the kitchen, then Stella came out with two cordial glasses. The deep purple contents appeared to be alive. "Don't worry, breakfast is coming. But you two need these." She gave her best harmless old lady grin as she handed one to Maeve and one to Jones.

Both accepted their glass, but didn't bring it to their mouths.

"Now, now. It's not that bad. Just a bit lively." Stella's smile could knock a missile out of orbit. It faltered as both continued to stare at her but not move. "Might need some help. I think they're still under the influence." She kept her smile focused on Maeve and Jones, but she spoke to everyone else.

Caradoc took Maeve's glass and Reece took Jones'. Neither moved.

Caradoc quickly held Maeve with one arm and poured the drink in her mouth with the other. Aisling stood ready to help, but aside from an initial twitch, Maeve didn't fight back. She did fall forward as the last bit was swallowed.

Jones, however, fought back.

Stella darted forward and grabbed the glass as Jones hit Reece hard enough to push him off the sofa. Bart and Stella both held Jones down and Reece finally got the drink in him. He twisted for a few moments, still fighting even as he was passing out. Then he slumped forward.

"Are they going to be okay? I swear, I thought these masks would hold." Caradoc got Maeve into a more comfortable position, but she looked to be asleep.

"They should be." Harlie winced. "They *will* be. Your masks were fighting an unknown foe. None of us could have known what would happen."

Stella looked to Caradoc with narrowing eyes. "I won't

make yours as strong, but it would be best if you had some elderberry too." She turned and darted back to the kitchen.

"Never seen elderberry look like it was trying to crawl out of the glass, but if that's what you say it is." Bart had moved to the door and seemed to be blocking it.

"I'm fine." Caradoc shot a look at Bart. "And I'm not going to run out the door."

"We have no idea what that stuff did to any of you. Maeve and Jones are indicators that the masks didn't work as well as hoped, which means it didn't work as well on you." Stella came back out with another cordial glass, but this one was a lighter purple color and hardly moved at all.

Caradoc looked ready to argue, then shook his head and flashed Stella one of his magazine smiles. He downed the drink. "Am I supposed to pass out too?" Maeve and Jones were both snoring softly.

"Nope. You're not showing any signs, so this was preventative. They should wake up in a few minutes and be fully recovered. Breakfast will be ready in ten. I think we need food quickly, so I might be cheating." Retrieving the three glasses, Stella marched back into the kitchen.

"Not a bad tasting potion, I have to say." Caradoc pulled Maeve closer to him. "But Harlie, you need to figure out what that mutated fog was. I need to adjust my masks." The scowl on his face was directed at the fact his tech had failed him. Not something he took well.

Maeve twitched, yawned, and then stretched as she peered around the room. "Why are you all in my bedroom?"

"Nope, you passed out in Dailten's front room. Couldn't hold your elderberry." Aisling kept it light, but that fog was terrifying. Even with Caradoc's masks, which obviously did something, they still fell victim to it.

Jones woke up alert and aware. Not surprising. "That was a nasty drink. You can let go now, I'm fine." Reece had stayed next to him and had one hand clamped on Jones' shoulder.

"You almost shot Maeve, then went zombie on us. Just making sure." Reece watched him for a few more seconds, then released his shoulder.

"Thanks." Jones still looked disturbed, for him, but he genuinely seemed grateful to everyone. "Is mind control part of the original baois fog?"

Neasa nodded. "Please keep in mind, I only have myths to go on. But yes, it is supposed to make its victims numb though, then destroy them. Not make them try to kill others."

"And it hit the non-magic users harder. Damn it, is this a weapon targeted against humans?" Reece kept an eye on Jones.

Humans and fey had a mostly agreeable relationship—at least after the fey saved the humans from the Black Plague hundreds of years ago. Of course, the resulting lack of fertility in the surviving humans appeared to have been caused by Aisling's mother and a few other high ranking fey. That wasn't common knowledge by any means, but if someone was trying to develop a weapon to have humans destroy each other, there was something going on.

"That's what I hope to find out," Caradoc said, then looked to Harlie. "I think we need magic *and* tech to sort this. And figure out what the connection is to those modified rapeseed plants."

"But first, everyone come eat." Dailten stuck her head out. "And I have an old school chalkboard for tracking down connections." She gave Aisling a grin. Aisling preferred to see weird issues in a large format. Her original murder board had been blown up, along with her townhome, in Los Angeles. Caradoc had made her a new portable one, disguised as a laptop, but she admitted that she missed the old school style.

The meal was massive, but almost everything got eaten.

Stella and Dailten stood by and nodded to each other as they watched.

"Make a note, you investigators, that the pseudo baois fog also attacked metabolism," Stella said. "Both Dailten and I were ravenous and figured it might be hitting you all as well."

Neasa looked up as she finished a bowl of salad the size of her head. "That's never been in any tales."

Caradoc made notes in his phone and Harlie pulled out a small pad and pen.

"But was this a test of their weapon-fog, or an accidental release?" Reece asked.

"Damn good question." Bart got to his feet and moved toward the chalkboard. He drew a circle in the middle just labeled, "Veil failing." He then started adding things, including Lady Tirtha Lasheda Otheralia—Aisling, Caradoc, and Harlie's mother. Several people spoke up when he also added the Lazing.

"They aren't against us that we know of. At least not actively. Satoshi and his people helped us in that Tesco parking lot." Reece looked to the side table where the shatil bag sat. "As long as they don't know we have their family box. I doubt they'd care how we got it, just that we didn't give it back." There was a question in his voice, one that Aisling shared.

"How do we give it back without more questions that we can't answer?" Jones countered with his own question. "Not to mention, I'm thinking the Lazing's family status isn't something they want bouncing around."

Caradoc shook his head. "Nope."

"And I think these boxes were brought to Aisling for a reason." Dailten nodded as she snacked on a carrot.

"They weren't just brought to me…" Aisling looked

around the room with a sigh. "Fine, yes, they have been. Lucky me."

"The lost royal family would have a lot of power on my side of the veil." Neasa glanced to Harlie and Caradoc with a wince, then spun back to Aisling. "They do know, yes?"

Aisling laughed. "That our father, who has never asserted himself during my lifetime, is the missing prince of the former fey royal line? Yes. I told everyone here." It still made her uncomfortable and itchy. As if another target had been put on her back.

"And no offense, but I don't believe it either." Caradoc shrugged. "If you knew our mother, you'd know she'd never let that be ignored."

"Unless she had something else planned." Harlie softly echoed Aisling's thoughts when she first found out about the possible royal status. "I don't think we can afford to believe that she didn't know. Everything she has ever done during my lifetime has been for a purpose. Everything."

Bart waited for more information, then added, 'lost royal and connections' to the board when there was no more coming.

Within fifteen minutes, the board was nothing more than a massive collection of people, places, and events that all had lines tagging them to other lines. None of them seemed to make sense.

Maeve walked over and shook her head. "It's really rubbish. I hate to say it, but I don't think this board thing is going to work this time."

Everyone was looking at the crowded board when Bart's phone startled them. Neasa jumped the highest, but the fact that even Jones gave a start was worrying.

Bart stepped into the front room to answer the call. He got two words out before whoever on the other end started yelling.

"Caradoc, Mott is on the phone." He held his phone out

to Caradoc and shook his head. "He's having hysterics."

"Considering that he's been kidnapped all this time, they might be warranted." Stella started taking the empty dishes back to the kitchen.

Caradoc had to shout to get Mott to be quiet. "Okay, take a deep breath and tell me where you are. We're about an hour out of Avebury." He rubbed the side of his face as, while Mott's volume had decreased, the speed of his words was obviously still fast. "Damn it. I have no idea which standing stone you mean, there are too many out there. Stay where you are, we'll find you somehow. But why didn't you call my phone instead of Bart's?" Whatever Mott said, it was low enough not to be heard by anyone else, pissed off Caradoc, and ended before he could respond beyond sputtering.

He handed the phone back to Bart. "He said that my phone was compromised. He wasn't sure about everyone else's and would call randomly when needed. Pah. Compromised." But even as he spoke, Caradoc took out his phone, popped open the back, and started fussing.

"How did he escape? Why is he hiding around the stones?" Stella looked around the group. "Shouldn't we get moving?"

"He didn't say, just kept yelling to come get him. Damn it, he was right." Caradoc flicked out a tiny green metal dot. "We're not going anywhere until I check everyone's phones. Again. Damn it, how are they doing this?" He didn't use magic much, but he zapped the bug out of existence with it now.

One by one, everyone put their phones on the table.

Neasa watched with interest. "Are they magic?"

Reece shook his head. "Technology. They're handy, but can be used against someone. But speaking of magic, were you going to put a glamor on Neasa, Harlie?" He gave her a smile. "You look fine as you are though."

She nodded. "Thank you. But yes, I agree that I would

be startling on this side. Especially since there would only be one place I could have come from."

Harlie had been watching Caradoc work, but nodded. "I'll do it right before we leave. Which we should do soon?"

"I agree," Dailten said. "Neasa might feel more comfortable in our car than Caradoc's tech vehicle."

Considering that Caradoc's car could transform into numerous shapes, that might be a good idea. Neasa was going to have enough new information to take in as it was.

Everyone left Caradoc, with Neasa watching in fascination, to get their things. When they came back, the phones were closed and there was a small burn mark on the table.

"Sorry, Dailten. I got a bit exuberant with my destruction. All our phones, aside from Aisling, Reece, and Jones, were compromised. Yeah, even yours, Bart. However Mott picked up on mine having a problem, he missed yours."

Once the phones were cleared, and Neasa was disguised to look more like a woodland fey, instead of a full dryad, they left.

"Are you sure no one can see what I am?" Neasa asked as she twisted around to look at herself. "I seem very much as I was."

Harlie smiled as he helped her into Dailten's car. "The woodland fey are a sub band of elves that modified their appearance over the centuries to appear more tree-like. I needed to keep your disguise as close to your true appearance as possible. You'll still draw some looks, but people won't think you're a dryad."

The disguise was impressive. Aisling had seen a few woodland fey when she'd lived in Alaska. Neasa looked like one, but still like herself. Shorter than her natural height, and more elf-like.

Maeve took the front seat, but she still looked off kilter.

"Are you sure you're okay? Dailten said you could stay here if you needed." Aisling was worried about her friend. Jones was either fully recovered or more than likely extremely good at hiding it. But Maeve still looked pale.

"Pish, I'm fine." Maeve smiled then let it drop. "Okay, you know me better than most. I almost killed Jones. There was no thought, no rationale, just kill. And in that flash of awareness, I realized that had he not also killed me, I would have gone after Caradoc next."

CHAPTER TWENTY-FIVE

"WE HAVE TO make sure whoever made that fog can never do it again." Maeve held up her shaking hand. "I'm not sure that I'll ever get over that feeling."

Aisling took her hand. "Deal. But you need to be honest. If you can't continue, you have to say something." She had trusted Maeve with her life too many times to count.

Maeve paused, then nodded. "I promise." She looked out through the car window where Caradoc and Dailten were comparing travel notes. "You have to promise to take me out if I try to kill any of us." Her light eyes were bright with unshed tears when she looked back. "Promise me."

Aisling squeezed her hand and swallowed the lump in her throat. "I promise."

Maeve nodded and settled a smile on her face as she sat back in her seat.

Aisling got into the seat behind her and waited for the others. Caradoc had his car fully extended and was taking everyone except Dailten, Stella, Harlie, and Neasa. Considering that this would be the dryad's first time in a car, having those three with her would help. Although her head was still closer to the roof than would be preferred.

Caradoc got in the driver's seat and Reece climbed in next to Aisling. Bart and Jones took the back row.

"Let's get Mott back, solve the mystery of the boxes, and close the veil." Caradoc started his car and tore out of the driveway with Stella, driving Dailten's car, right on his tail.

"Seriously, you're sounding like a cartoon character." Reece hung on to the seat as he'd still been putting his seatbelt on when Caradoc took off.

"It's all how you look at the world. Things look dire, yes, but we can figure it out. We'll be fine."

"Like your masks?" Aisling didn't want to remind him, and she got why he was trying to be so optimistic. But from the scowl on Maeve's face, she knew it too. Coddling Maeve would just make things worse.

"Okay, fine." Caradoc glanced over to Maeve. "Things suck, but I still believe we can win. We have some serious magic users and brains in this group."

Aisling could only see the side of Maeve's face, but the scowl was lifting.

"Damn right we do. Now get us there in one piece?" Maeve looked and sounded almost normal now.

Bart's phone rang as they got on the motorway. "Yep? You're sure? Okay, come back when you can. I have a bad feeling things are going to get worse." He disconnected the call. "That was Garran. He and Surratt are flying back to Los Angeles in a few hours—something is messing up the west coast."

His phone rang again before anyone could respond. "Yes? Mott, slow down." He paused. "Seriously, I can barely hear you, I'm putting you on speaker." Without waiting for a response, he switched his phone.

"—don't do that! What if they hear? Too late, you did it. Fine. If they get me, it's on your head. Hello everyone and potential killers. You must get me now. They're sending searchers—not ones of this world types." His words were so fast it was amazing he got them all out.

"We're on our way, but we still don't know where you are." Caradoc yelled over his shoulder as he sped up.

There was a pause on the line. "Southwest sector, tenth stone in. Maybe eleventh. Don't know, but I'll try to stay in this sector!" The call ended.

Bart called Dailten in the car behind them and gave her the update. Caradoc again picked up speed.

Avebury was a small village. Luckily this wasn't high tourist season and the road in was almost empty. The standing stones of the great henge surrounded them as they drove in. They'd been put in place by humans long before the fey crossed over from the other side of the veil. Aisling felt an oddness as they drove closer.

"Anyone else feel that?" Reece shook his shoulders.

"If you mean like someone just tripped over all my nerves at once? Yes." Aisling rubbed her arms. The initial feeling had been sharp, now it just lingered.

"I did." Jones and Bart said at the same time.

"Nothing here. Caradoc, did you?" Maeve asked.

"Not a thing. But the four of you have been on the other side of the veil. Damn, that's a good indicator this henge is somehow connected to the veil." Caradoc pulled over down a narrow lane and Stella pulled in right behind them.

Neasa was out of the car before Stella even came to a full stop. "This is a bad place, very bad." She walked over to a nearby standing stone, but didn't touch it. "How did these get here? They're charged with veil energy." She walked around the huge stone slowly. "They shouldn't be here."

Everyone got out of their cars, and Harlie went next to Neasa. "These have been here since before the fey left your side of the veil. Our people didn't bring them here—humans did."

"No. These feel too much like Isfyden. They were brought here."

"Or, were they contaminated because the veil is so thin here?" Mott popped out from behind the nearest stone. "You feel it, don't you? The event will happen here. I'm Mott, by the way." He looked like he'd fallen down a few dirt-filled holes, but seemed to be intact. He didn't come any closer to any of them though and while he'd spoken to Neasa, he didn't ask who she was.

Caradoc stepped forward. "Are you okay? You look a little rough. Who took you? What did they do to you?"

Mott took two steps backwards. "Don't come closer, you might not be who I think you're trying to be." He patted his clothes. "This wasn't them though. The ones who took me didn't rough me up…not yet." He nodded as if that was important. "They were government. Maybe Area 42, MI-6, someone sneaky." He narrowed his eyes. "How did you find me?"

"I tracked you down through your ad." Harlie had stayed toward the back but came a step forward. "Count Alessandro Volta. Caradoc told us that was one of the names that you like to go under."

"Well not anymore! You just told everyone!" Mott crossed his arms and glared.

"You used it so we could find you, right?" Aisling was used to Mott being eccentric, but the weird feeling that hit her when they got here was ramping up again.

"Yes, well. I was desperate. I'm not sure who can be trusted."

"We really need to get back in the cars." Reece looked concerned and was holding the side of his head.

"You know something's wrong, don't you? Yeah, so do I." Mott nodded but didn't come closer.

"Harlie? Do you feel anything?" Aisling asked. Harlie was a stronger precog than Reece, but Reece might be reacting to whatever she, Bart, and Jones were feeling because of their connection of going through the veil.

Harlie looked around the standing stones. "No, but I trust what you feel. Especially Reece. Let's get in the cars." He led Neasa back to Dailten's car.

Mott still hadn't moved from the stone he stood by.

Caradoc went toward him. "You need to come with us, Mott, that's why you called."

Reece bent over and his breathing became ragged. "Now."

Aisling turned to get him back to the car when a stab of pain slammed into her. She dropped to her knees along with Bart and Jones. Reece collapsed completely.

"This is wrong." Neasa was getting in Dailten's car when the pain hit, but she reached her vines out and grabbed the four of them.

Mott ran forward as a massive wind rose up and the sky cracked open.

Or so it looked like from Aisling's pain-narrowed eyes.

"Get in the cars!" Caradoc started dragging people into the car as Neasa's grasp on the others failed. Mott dragged Jones in. Not easy. Mott was an elf, so stronger than most humans, but he was also about a foot shorter than Jones. Jones would probably have a dozen bruises from being dragged to the car.

Aisling tried to get to Reece but couldn't move her limbs. The wind was running through her soul as much as it was pushing her down.

Shapes fell through the rip in the sky as Harlie and Caradoc ran to her side. Somehow, she'd missed that everyone else, including Reece, were back in the cars. Her brothers held her up.

Harlie yelled next to her ear, but she could barely hear him. "Neasa says we must close that rip in the veil. Our mother is involved."

Aisling was only able to sit up with them lifting her, so she wasn't sure what help she could be. But she grabbed both of their hands as she recognized the beings who'd come through. A dozen or so alari.

Wind dervishes arriving on the wind through the veil and using it to destroy everything around them.

Harlie started chanting words—ones that meant nothing to Aisling and judging by the shrug Caradoc gave her, nothing to him either. But at a nod from Harlie, they both echoed him.

The good thing was that whatever spell they were chanting closed the rip. The bad part was that the alari stayed on this side. And all noticed them at the same time. They were moving slowly, either because they had to, or out of wariness, but magic crackled from their fingers as they approached.

Car doors behind them started opening, but Aisling turned and yelled, "Stay there! No matter what you see or hear—stay in those cars!" She tried to get up, but a heavy feeling pressed her down. She pulled at her brother's arms. "I can't explain, but it's up to us three to stop them. Help me get to my feet."

Harlie and Caradoc each grabbed one of her arms and they got her up just as the alari reached them. Both readied spells to throw, but Aisling shook her head and pushed ahead of them. "Follow my lead." Her body hurt like hell at this point, but she pulled up as tall as she could and looked down her nose at the approaching dervishes.

"Who dares to cross here without our permission?" There were close to twenty alari and all were armed with short, jagged daggers. Just in case their natural ability to create winds strong enough to tear people apart wasn't enough.

"You are not she who rules us." The closest alari stepped forward and a whirlwind formed around his feet.

"I am Queen Aisling. Next to me are my brother kings, King Harthinatle and King Caradoc. We guard this world." She channeled her mother strongly in the last sentence, then flung a lightning spell at the closest alari.

Even she was surprised when it blew him apart.

"You don't have power here, go back before we destroy you." Caradoc was getting into the pissed and powerful royal bit as well. Aisling swore he'd managed to make his eyes flash as he spoke.

Harlie didn't say anything, but reached one hand out and lifted five of the alari in the air. As beings who controlled winds, they seemed extremely uncomfortable at having the situation reversed. Unfortunately, one of their kind blowing up and five going airborne against their will, wasn't enough to stop the others and they charged.

CHAPTER TWENTY-SIX

A ISLING CAST HER shield spell, but it was oddly weak and the first alari got a strike through it. He missed her, but it was a close thing. It also indicated that the alari either didn't believe who Aisling and her brothers were, or they didn't care.

Caradoc and Harlie were two of the strongest magic users she knew, but both were struggling to hold the alari back.

The ghau pendant gave a flare of heat, and Aisling grabbed it and held it up. "You can't go against this." The alari paused their attack and gave the pendant more of a concerned look than they did the three of them. Aisling dropped her voice. "Harlie? Can you work some spell mojo through us and the ghau? Something on the level of what you did on the plane?" On their trip to the UK, the ghau had been acting up. It turned out that somehow it knew that a nice big chunk of the destroyed Area 42 L.A. building was about to knock them into the Atlantic Ocean. It took them, and the entire plane, out of this reality for about ten minutes.

Harlie flung the five alari he'd had in the air into the rest and nodded. "We need to be touching each other and we must do it quickly. The spell will be in your minds when I shout." The alari were getting back up.

Caradoc, Aisling, and Harlie joined arms and Aisling

focused on the ghau pendant. If she was going to be stuck with it, she was going to make it work for her.

On the plane, Harlie had cast a spell around them. This time the spell was focused outward, between two distant standing stones. "Now!"

An insanely complicated spell slammed into Aisling's mind, but she managed to cast it even though it vanished as she said the words in her head. The target wasn't the alari, but the space between the two standing stones. A jagged and nasty looking hole in reality opened in the space between them. A push from Harlie, and the alari were shoved back into it.

All but two who'd managed to hang onto a standing stone.

Aisling felt Harlie trying to get them, but the hole he'd created was growing smaller.

"I can't!" Harlie dropped to his knees as the hole slammed shut and the two remaining alari ran out across the fields and quickly vanished in a pair of whirlwinds.

The wind around them dropped immediately.

"Damn it, two got away." Caradoc looked ready to go after them.

"Don't." Harlie got back to his feet, but looked more shaken than Aisling had ever seen. "They will be long gone."

The car doors again opened, and this time everyone ran out.

"What the hell just happened? And why did you trap us in the cars?" Bart stomped over with everyone else trailing behind.

Aisling had wondered why they'd been so compliant about staying in the cars.

"A rip through the veil is what happened." Caradoc still looked annoyed that he couldn't go after the two alari even though, by now, they could be anywhere in the world. "I'd guess either the alari or Harlie trapped you."

Mott looked calmer than before, but was watching Neasa carefully. "I think it was Harlie, those dervishes wanted to rip us up. I knew they would be coming."

"It *was* me, and they would have torn all of us to shreds. We must find a way to capture those last two." Harlie walked to the closest standing stone.

"But you stopped me from going after them." Caradoc followed him as he searched the stones for something.

"I don't think that even you can chase whirlwinds. They've left this part of the country, but beyond that I'm not sure. Also, there are small incursions from beyond the veil taking place all over this world. The two alari are nothing more than what's already happening. If we close the veil completely, the invaders will be destroyed. If we fail to shut it when the battle comes, it won't matter." Harlie looked around, then patted the third stone he stopped at. "I think the area is clear. Shall we find a place to stay?"

Aisling shook her head. Nothing like being reminded of the stakes to rattle one. "There's still a weird vibe coming from all those standing stones. We're tasked with saving the entire world, and you want to look for a place to stay?" She was glad that Harlie looked better, but wasn't certain he had his priorities in order.

"Yes." He started to walk around her and back toward the cars but she stepped in front of him.

"You—*we*—opened a portal to the other side of the veil. Isn't that something we need to discuss?" Maybe she was the only one freaked out about it, but it was something that they shouldn't have been able to do.

"Yes. After we find a place to stay, and maybe lunch for Mott. He hasn't eaten lately." Harlie turned toward Mott just as his stomach rumbled. "We need him fed before we can sort things out."

"Don't bother fighting with Harlie," Caradoc said with

a sigh as he turned to Aisling. "He'll win and you'll just be exhausted."

Harlie smiled, patted them both on the head like kids and went back to the car.

"Shouldn't we be more worried about more incursions across the globe?" Reece asked as he walked with her back to Caradoc's car. He wasn't holding his head, but the continued tightness around his eyes wasn't good.

"Harlie's a good gauge and he's not freaked out. So hopefully we have some time to figure this out and stop it. You, however, look like crap. Your head still hurts, doesn't it?" Aisling still felt the odd pressure that had hit them as they came into Avebury, but it looked like Reece was getting far more than that.

"It's like someone has turned up my abilities." He still hated to admit to being a precog, even if there wasn't a risk that others would hear. "But also kept them oddly muted. There's something big coming, larger than the opening of a breach in the veil."

"Talk to Harlie, he might be able to help." She'd also talk to Harlie just in case there was something she should look for with Reece.

Mott climbed in the back seat with Bart and Jones and was back to his normal chatty and odd self. "I found a good house for us to rent, go down the road a few blocks then turn left. We might be here a few months."

Caradoc had started the car, but spun around at that. "What? Months? I don't think we have months; a lot has happened since you were kidnapped. Speaking of which, you seem awfully calm about your attackers finding you again."

"Maybe weeks." Mott looked around. "Days? I missed things obviously. Oh, they knew where I was, but couldn't find me. And definitely won't now that I'm with you. They're now most likely heading north. I left a psychic-electro-spectral trail that headed north. Bounces around

Edinburgh, and up past Ft. Williams where I made it seem like I was hiding. I had to wait for all of you to get here to let it go."

Caradoc had started to pull off the gravel, but looked back in his rearview mirror. "You made it work? Those things are tricky to pull off. Are you sure?"

Aisling was as confused as the rest of the people in the car. She understood the words, just obviously not what they meant run together.

Mott grinned like he'd just solved everything. "I did. I planted the base near that standing stone I was hiding at, it will keep bouncing them around for at least a month."

"But who are they? You said you knew who grabbed you, who was it?" Bart wasn't one for waiting and he'd been patient so far.

"I thought you knew; it was Surratt and Garran. I think they were working for the government."

Caradoc didn't spin out, but he did take the turn faster than expected.

Bart almost grabbed Mott by the throat. "What? *They* took you? They've been in contact with us, they were the ones who told us you were gone."

"I know. I heard them speaking to you." Mott scowled. "Both are magic users, right?"

"Yes."

"Then those could have been duplicates. Their magic felt off." Mott didn't seem concerned.

"Damn it, were they copies the entire time they were here? They acted like Garran and Surratt." Aisling would have sworn they were the originals. But she'd rather they'd been duplicated somehow than them having gone to the bad side.

"Not sure." Mott shrugged. He leaned closer to the window as they went down the side street. "Yup, that white two-story place. Figured we should stick together for now."

Maeve was leaning over the back of her seat. "Those were the real ones; I'd stake my life on it. Besides, I thought Nix was behind those doubles we ran into before London."

"Someone made the Xilen of Bart. If those were Xilen, I don't know we'd notice unless they made a mistake." Caradoc pulled into the driveway of the house and Stella pulled in next to them. "We need to sweep the house for bugs, then sort this out inside."

"I wouldn't worry, they're gone now." Mott climbed out of the car. He pulled out a large key and waved it as he ran for the door.

Reece was getting out of the car when he clutched his head and stumbled. "Mott! No!"

Jones didn't ask, just tore after Mott, grabbed him, and pulled him away from the doorstep.

"Everyone down!" Harlie yelled as he caught on to whatever Reece had picked up.

A moment later the front door exploded.

Aisling got up once the explosion died down, expecting the entire house to be gone, but it was simply the front door and two windows next to it. "What in the hell? Mott?" The smoke from the explosion was still lingering on the lawn, but Jones and Mott popped up.

"They tried to kill me." Mott stood there as the smoke faded. "I didn't try to hurt them. That's just rude."

Bart looked at the neighboring houses, but no one came out. The odds of everyone on this street being at work or school were slim. And even though the entire house didn't explode, the noise was loud enough that most of the area would have heard it. He jogged to the closest neighbor, and tapped on the door. It swung open. He darted inside, calling as he went, but came out shaking his head. They spread out, with Jones holding on to Mott, but all the houses were the same. Doors unlatched, no one inside. In some cases, there were signs of rapid leaving—dinners were scattered about. Considering it was a little after eleven in the morning, these people had been taken last night.

"Damn it, someone took all these people. And set up the door to explode? Why not wait until we were inside and take us all out?" Maeve turned to Mott. "I think they knew exactly where you were going, whether or not they were really Garran and Surratt."

"I was so careful." Mott scowled around the area.

Stella, Harlie, and Dailten had stayed near Dailten's car with a freaked-out Neasa.

Finally, Harlie joined the other group. "I don't know what was said in your car on the way here, but we believe that Garran and Surratt have gone to the dark side."

Bart filled him in as he continued to scan the area. Where there had been a few cars on the roads when they entered the village, there were now none. The only sound was of sheep bleating in the distance.

"I think we have to leave." Harlie tilted his head. "No, *we* need to stay, *you* need to leave."

"What?" Maeve raised her voice and gestured around. "No one should stay here. Hello? Exploding doors, vanished neighbors, possibly our former bosses behind it? We need to get the hell out of here."

"Actually, Harlie is right." Stella moved over. "I'm not as precog as some of you, but I feel it. The people who were taken are still alive and we must save them. And guard the standing stones from being used as a passage again. The rest of you need to find those beings pretending to be Garran and Surratt." She held up her hand as both Aisling and Maeve opened their mouths. "No, I can't tell you how I know, but those two were not them. We can find another place to go, and we'll keep in touch. But we must split up."

Bart nodded. "And we might be able to track those two alari. Something is—"

His words were cut off by a blast of sound and wind. Aisling swore as the world around them changed. It was daylight this time, but the images were just as horrific. All the empty houses around them were rubble, and flying monsters, the likes of which she'd never even heard of screeched across the sky. The air was dark with smoke and a sickly green color.

Then everything snapped back into place.

Aisling swore as the snap back to reality almost knocked her off her feet. "Please tell me you all saw that?"

"Yes. It is the beginning of the end." Neasa hadn't moved far from the car but was shaking until Dailten and Stella wrapped their arms around her.

"What's that?" Caradoc pointed to a clump of wood near Aisling's feet.

"I think it's just from the front door blowing up." She bent down to pick it up. "Oh shit." She held up a splinter piece of wood. It was Hewlith tree wood and clearly from a family box.

CHAPTER TWENTY-SEVEN

SHE NUDGED THROUGH the pile with her foot. "Actually, I think it might be two boxes. But they feel dead." A chill crept through her. The family boxes were made of enchanted wood, and all the ones she'd touched so far had felt alive. It was too hard to define, but they felt like they walked through her soul, as the stories said. This piece felt like driftwood. Harlie took the piece before she could drop it back in the pile.

"This is familiar." He turned it around, pointing out small markings. "I've seen these symbols before." He handed it back to Aisling then dropped down and rummaged through the shattered wood.

"Should you be going through that? Aren't those boxes sacred or something?" Maeve stepped forward along with Caradoc but didn't come near the wood.

"They are." Stella also stopped outside of arm's reach. "The first families were all elven and those boxes were their heritage. For them to be destroyed is a serious issue."

"There is too much wood to be from a single box, there appear to be the remains of two." Harlie waved his hand around. "I need a bag; we have to take these with us."

"Who do they belong to?" Even Reece was drawn in.

Harlie held up the original piece as Dailten handed

him a bag. "I believe they were the first two boxes the vallenians gave you, the families Hthia and Wolinshea."

"The two that were left in sealed safes in L.A.?" The chill in Aisling's soul was getting worse. Although with everything else the vallenians had been doing, trans-dimensional safe breaking shouldn't be a shock.

"I believe these are the same." Harlie finished gathering the pieces. "I was right about us splitting up, but wrong about who needs to stay here." He looked around the group. "Dailten, Stella, Neasa, and myself need to find a place far from here to examine what is going on at a different level, and away from the influences of this village. Starting with these shards. The rest of you need to find out what happened to the people in those houses and see what you can pick up about the stones."

"But you four are the big woo-woo ones, shouldn't you be working here?" Maeve was used to magic users, but the more mystical side made her uncomfortable.

"That's why they need to be somewhere else." Bart nodded. "Whether the two who grabbed Mott were actually Garran and Surratt or not. Someone knows us too well." He and Garran had been friends for a long time. He hadn't said anything when Mott said who had grabbed him, but the almost constant clenched jaw pointed out that he was concerned.

"Exactly. These boxes could only have been left here by the vallenians. Destroyed by them as well." Dailten ruffled her feathers.

"But what if more shattered boxes show up? Do we think the ones in the shatil bag are safe?" Aisling didn't mention their own family box—which was also in a safe in L.A., hopefully. She also didn't come out and ask what had happened to those two families when their boxes were destroyed. The myths said the boxes kept the families safe—but never from what.

"The shatil bag would keep them safe." Stella fished around in her massive purse and pulled out a round blue box. "We're not sure if Garran and Surratt have been taken over or replaced. And if we're separating, we need to make sure no one else is duplicated." She flipped the case open and took out the scanner and a collection of tiny silver slivers. "I'd hoped we'd never need these again, but I did update them as the ones you had before might have failed. Now who's first?"

The scanner worked as before, with Mott's recorded voice claiming that everyone was who they were supposed to be. Even Neasa. Then the small silvery mark flashed briefly on their cheeks, then faded.

Neasa rubbed her check where the sliver went in. "What is this? Will it stop me from returning home?" She was trying to stay calm, but getting home was still first and foremost in her mind.

"It's to make sure that you're you and have not been replaced. We had a problem a short while ago with people being possessed or duplicated—which is what might have happened to our friends." Stella tapped the box. "This should keep that from happening."

"This probably means our mother was behind it, right? We thought it was Nix, but he's gone," Aisling said.

"Or someone else." Harlie shrugged. "I recommend you stay somewhere outside of Avebury." He hugged Aisling and Caradoc. "Stay safe. We'll communicate when we can."

They loaded into Dailten's car and left.

"Okay, let's go somewhere, this place is creeping me out." Maeve rubbed her arms as she looked down the desolate road.

"How is no one noticing?" Aisling asked as they got back into Caradoc's car. "These people appear to have vanished last night—but no one noticed they didn't go to work? To school?"

Caradoc headed down the road. "Maybe there's no one left."

"Or there's an isolation spell in place." Bart looked back as they left the road. "I didn't feel it, and neither did anyone else, but that doesn't mean it's not there." Isolation spells were powerful magic and rarely used. But when they worked, they kept a area cut off from everything around it. Rather, the section under the spell was still there, but the people outside of it forgot about it.

Two blocks over, everything seemed normal. A small village, with people walking and driving about. And not noticing that people were missing. Whoever pulled off that isolation spell of that block was strong.

"There's a fey and human commune outside of Avebury, that might be a good place to hide. My folks brought us up here a few times when I was a kid," Maeve said.

"Flijian Way?" Mott had his phone out. "It's just two miles away."

"That's the one. Until you said it, I couldn't recall the name."

Aisling thought about what might have happened to the two families with the shattered boxes. It wasn't unusual for the vallenians to make points, but they were becoming more violent about them. She rubbed her stomach. There wasn't a scar, but it would be a long time before she forgot what they did to her. And the fact that they could kill anyone at any time.

A tattered sign, surrounded by a mass of plants, trees, and vines said welcome to the Flijian Way. The road immediately became little more than dirt.

"Seriously, we aren't in some distant wilderness, how did this happen?" Bart scowled at the plants.

"Ambiance." Maeve grinned. "My folks said the first comers to this place created it based on a forest that was here thousands of years ago. I think it's lovely."

"I thought you didn't like the country?" Reece didn't look away from the window, but he smiled.

"I don't overall, give me a city any day. But this place always felt special. They used to rent cabins on the edge of their property. Hopefully they are still doing that."

The road twisted through the forest for no reason other than the creators wanted it to. Eventually it opened on a clump of buildings.

Aisling's heart dropped when one of the doors swung open and shut in the wind. "Damn it, did whatever happened in that street in Avebury hit here too?"

Caradoc stopped the car away from the buildings and everyone got out, after checking and loading their weapons.

They slowly approached the first building, with Bart and Jones going to the back before Aisling, Reece, and Maeve took the front.

"I'd freeze like stone if I were you. All of you. Magic users release your spells." The voice was low and deep. And somewhat familiar.

Everyone froze. But no one released their spells or their guns.

"Oh, come on, seriously? I could destroy you where you stand. And that's just me, not counting my thirty mates that have you surrounded."

"Reg?" Aisling almost turned but stopped. Reg was a troll, one on their side when it worked with the plans of the Ckiong, a group of trolls working together for troll kind. He was also the boyfriend of their friend Grundog.

"That depends. Are you really Aisling? And Reece, Maeve, Caradoc, and short person I don't know? Don't turn around yet, bringing out an expert."

There was a rustling sound and a very old troll woman, so short she wasn't much taller than Aisling, came around to her, holding up a weird gizmo that looked like one of Caradoc's rejects.

"Now hold still. This might sting." The old troll held the gizmo up to Aisling's shoulder, pressed a button, and a shock went into her arm.

"Ow, damn it! What did you do?" Her hands were going numb and within moments, she wasn't moving even if she wanted to.

The troll woman might be old, but she was fast and quickly zapped everyone else.

Except for Jones and Bart.

Hopefully they'd escaped notice and could rescue them. The trolls had worked alongside them when they freed London, but they had their own agendas.

"There we go, all better." Reg came around in front of Aisling. It was him as far as she could tell. "Now, we heard about you vanishing after London. And yet, here you are. Make me believe you're really Aisling."

"When you first found us, you were on walk-about and trying to appear like a cave troll." Aisling saw his eyes narrow, so kept going. "When we came across Reece, you mentioned that Stella had a friend named Agent Larkin but you'd expected more. Sorry Reece."

Reg narrowed his eyes even further, then he finally nodded. "Release them. Including the other two." Four trolls came out from behind the building holding a really pissed off Bart and Jones. "You were right, Grundog." He waved behind them and Grundog came forward. She was a troll minotaur mix, but the only bit of her minotaur heritage that showed was that she wasn't as large or bulky as a full troll. She could still crush a human or elf to death if needed—it just might take her a few more moments.

"Aisling!" Grundog picked her up in a massive hug, pointing out that the numbness from whatever the old troll had hit her with was gone. "Where's Stella?" She went through and hugged Reece, Caradoc, and Maeve. She gave a polite nod to the others.

"Stella had her own work to do. We honestly don't know where she or the others went." Bart nodded to Reg. "Good to see you. Thank you again for stepping in during the London incident."

The Ckiong officially hadn't been involved in freeing London. But Reg and most of his people had fortuitously been working on maneuvers nearby, so came in to help. In reality, Stella had tipped them off. This way, no one felt bounds were being overstepped and the Ckiong weren't official participants.

Reg nodded, then motioned toward the building they'd been heading for. "My people have this complex covered, but still might be better to be out of sight. After you."

Bart took the lead. The building appeared to be a reception area for the compound. A long counter had old fashioned keys on the wall behind it. A wide lobby sitting area with assorted low sofas and chairs was to the left. Bart went into the lobby and took over a wide, comfy looking chair.

Once everyone had filed in, only Reg, Grundog, the older troll, and two guards came in. The rest of the trolls stayed outside. Reg locked the outer door.

"You know, I swear I just felt all of you reach for your weapons and magic." Reg held up the key he'd locked the door with. "I locked that because we just got here an hour ago and have no idea what happened to the people. But here. A copy for you." He handed the key to Bart.

"They're all gone?" Maeve asked from her sofa seat next to Caradoc and Mott.

"Aye, that's what it looks like. We've gone through all the cabins, camps, houses. Everyone is gone."

"It seems like they've been gone for a few days at least," the older troll woman said. "No sign of violence. I'm Fieath, by the way. Reg might sound cultured, but he forgets to introduce his friends." Her accent was heavier than Reg's and sounded more northern Scottish. Reg sounded like he came from the posh areas of London. Which he might have, except trolls didn't really like big cities for any length of time.

"I do apologize. We were busy determining if you lot were evil or not." He quickly introduced everyone he knew to Fieath and the other trolls but stopped at Mott, "Sorry, mate."

"I'm Mott, nice to meet you all." Mott kept looking around the room as if it triggered something, but didn't say more.

Fieath watched Mott carefully. "There was a big disturbance yesterday not far from here. You wouldn't have been part of that?"

Aisling thought she was going to mention the attack at the stones or even the explosion. They were far enough from Avebury that non-magical people might not have noticed the two events. But Fieath almost crackled with magic.

Mott shrugged and wrinkled his nose. "Might have. I don't use much magic, but I needed to get away from my captors." He looked around. "Is there a kitchen here?"

Caradoc laughed. "He does have his priorities."

One of the two obvious guards stepped forward. "I can take him." He made Reg look like a child and might be large enough to keep Mott out of trouble. Hopefully.

Bart started to get up as well, then instead just shook a finger at Mott. "Get some food, stay with him, and don't wander off."

Mott shrugged then followed the troll into another room.

"It's not far, right? Mott can take off easily." Reece watched as they left.

"He is Mott Flowers, the inventor, right?" Reg lifted an eyebrow. "I expected someone more impressive."

"He is, and even smarter than most people know. Also, a known flight risk. He came to us, but I think I'll go help keep an eye on him." Caradoc got to his feet and went through the door Mott and the guard used.

"And you are in extreme pain." Fieath got to her feet and was glaring at Reece. "Why do you try to hide it?"

Reece looked around the room. Every person who knew about his clairvoyance was a possible leak—even if they were all on the same side. At Bart's short nod, he sighed. "I've had a massive precog headache since our fight at the standing stones in Avebury." That he was clearly not fey, and therefore shouldn't be able to have precog abilities, wasn't lost on anyone. But Grundog didn't look surprised like the others.

As Stella's best friend, she must have already been told.

"I think we need to hear of these events," Reg said. "Once Fieath fixes Larkin's head." Reg leaned back in his chair. He'd started at Reece's comments, but obviously was setting the implications aside for now.

"Naw worries." Fieath went to Reece. "Just a bit will block the pain." Before Reece could respond or react, she put her palm on his forehead and pressed slightly.

"Ow." Reece rubbed his head when she removed her hand. "But it's gone now."

"Not hard to do. At least not at that level. But I'll warrant what got inside your head will be hitting all of us if the situation isn't changed." Fieath tilted her head as she watched him, then gave a nod to herself and resumed her seat.

Bart quickly filled them in on everything from Aisling's return to their arrival in Avebury. He left out the revelations concerning the royal status of Aisling and Caradoc as well as everything about the elven family boxes. He also didn't mention Neasa.

Aisling liked Reg and Grundog, but agreed with Bart on those omissions.

"There are so many things to ask." Reg motioned to the remaining guard. "Can you bring tea for all? We might be here a while." When the guard left, he turned back to Bart. "Most worrying is the status of Garran and Surratt. They are well known and trusted allies. Being possessed, duplicated, or going to the side of evil are not good things."

"Very true. What do you know of what happened here?" Maeve leaned forward. "I haven't been here in twenty years or more, but it was always popular. The buildings we saw looked to be in good shape."

"We don't know much aside from all of the people having vanished," Reg said. "It does look like there were over a hundred people here—everything looked recently lived in."

"What about animals?" Caradoc asked and looked to Bart. "We didn't look closely, but there were no dogs or cats on that street we were on."

"Good point."

"It is," Reg said. "And as of our initial searches, there were no animals. No pets, no farm stock."

"Something or someone took their pets along with the people? Why?" Aisling wasn't sure how the others felt, but finding out all the animals were missing was almost more disturbing than the people.

"Since we don't know why these people were taken, the rest is just more mystery," Bart said.

"Even the big farm animals?" Maeve shook her head. "There were working farms out here."

Grundog nodded. "The stables that we found looked recently used, but empty. And I didn't see any signs of livestock or people running away in a panic."

The guard brought tea and biscuits and Fieath poured. Mott wandered out behind him, with the second guard following. Mott seemed lost in his own thoughts though and kept drawing symbols in the air as he talked to himself.

At Reg's confused look, Bart just shrugged. Ignoring Mott in these cases was the best policy.

Jones declined the cup and got to his feet. "I'd like to search the area myself."

Reece joined him. "I'll go as well."

Aisling had already taken a sip of her tea, but sat the cup down. "Me too. The three of us were on the other side of the veil. If this village-wide abduction was veil related, we might pick up on it." No one had mentioned that yet, but she had a feeling there was a connection. Removing a large group of people without anything left behind, would have been tricky for the street they'd been on. For something like basically an entire small village, the odds were astronomical.

Unless they were all pulled through the veil.

The street had been extremely close to the standing stones, this commune compound was a few miles away, but for anything that could reach through the veil, that distance might be marginal.

There were just too many things they didn't know.

Bart obviously weighed joining them, as he was the only other one who'd crossed over. But he also needed to talk to Reg. Whatever was going on, they were going to need allies. The Ckiong wouldn't work directly with Area 42, even before they'd been compromised. But they might work with friends.

"Keep in contact, and stay together." Bart raised his hand when Jones looked ready to argue. "Nope, no one goes alone at this point."

The slight flush on Jones' face was one of the most emotional reactions Aisling had seen from him. It was going to be a long time before he got over being used as bait and being taken through the veil.

Mott continued having a meeting of one, and the rest stayed and tried to figure out what was going on.

"We can split up, you know." Jones pulled out his gun when they'd gotten outside.

"Yeah, no. We can't." Aisling spoke before Reece, but he looked ready to say the same. "We're not crossing over to hunt you down again. You're a deadly killer, armed with a few guns and they got you last time." She didn't want to be harsh, but the reality was, he was one of the most well-trained people she knew. And whoever took him had easily grabbed him before. "Not to mention, the three of us are well-balanced power wise. We're far stronger staying together."

"I'm not arguing with her about any of that. And you know it too." Reece and Jones had been partners long before Aisling met Reece. If anyone understood Jones' mindset even slightly, it was Reece.

Jones let out a sigh. "Fine. Just don't sacrifice yourselves if they grab me. To be fair, I wasn't great bait for them. It got you there, but didn't do anything to help the other side."

"That we know of." Reece didn't look like his head was still bothering him, but he rubbed his forehead. "We have no idea who brought you through, what their goals were, or whether they succeeded."

That was a disturbing thought. Aisling had assumed that because they'd made it back, they'd stopped whatever the attempt had been. The idea that it might have been what was wanted, didn't dawn on her before.

"On that cheery note, shall we?" Reece motioned down the path.

There were a few troll guards in the distance, but Aisling knew there were far more they weren't seeing. The place looked like a rustic campground with a few buildings like the reception area. Cottages, also rustic, were spaced with enough trees and bushes between them to give privacy even though they weren't that far apart.

They took turns entering the buildings first, rotating their order so two went in and one stayed out watching. Every single cottage looked the same. No people, no animals, and no signs of a struggle. But they kept checking them.

"Are either of you two feeling anything odd? I'm not." Reece finally asked after they'd walked through what looked like the last cottage and were heading toward the campgrounds.

Jones shook his head before Reece even finished. He then moved toward the first campsite.

Aisling followed him. "I haven't, but I'm not sure if there's nothing there to sense, or they're getting better at blocking it."

"That's a cheery thought." Reece stayed a few steps behind Aisling who stayed a few behind Jones. Just in case something attacked, hopefully two would be able to fight back. "Do you think they have a way of watching us?"

"It's a possibility. They could have some strongly powered fey there that we don't know about. I have no idea whether there are any myths or legends about lost fey who could see beyond the veil, but we can't discount that."

"This is where Harlie and the others would have come in handy." Reece raised his hand. "I know there were valid reasons for the split, but we're now hindered on the more mystical side of things."

"I think—" Aisling's comment was swallowed as the site they were about to enter began to fall in on itself. A sinkhole opened right under it. Directly in front of her and Jones.

"Damn it!" Aisling jumped back, managing to miss slamming into Reece.

Jones had been ahead of her, but had almost elf-like reflexes and managed to dive to the side of the sinkhole.

He rolled and got to his feet with his gun aimed at the hole before Aisling could blink.

Sinkholes had been appearing before the attack on London and had been ways for the ghanlough to try and get into this world. They all watched it with guns raised for a few moments.

"I think it's just a hole," Reece said as he motioned for Jones to lower his gun.

Jones nodded and lowered his gun. He didn't holster it but stood back as Reece and Aisling moved forward.

"I'm not picking up on anything. Not here either." Reece tapped his head.

Nothing on the precog end, could be good or bad.

The roaring behind them could only be bad.

CHAPTER TWENTY-EIGHT

REECE SPUN TO the creature, and held his arms out for Aisling and Jones to go to either side. The creature they faced wasn't of this world. Nor, would Aisling say, one from the other side of the veil. She was by no means an expert of other-side-of-the-veil creatures, but this thing looked too much like a female elf combined with a krilaze, down to eight legs, even if they weren't all arachnid, to have been only from beyond the veil. Or at least not naturally.

It was easily six and a half feet tall, moving as awkwardly as its horrifically matched body would imply. The tail it lashed was short and looked like it had been grafted off an iguana. There could have been other animals added but she couldn't waste the time to look for them.

The elf's face seemed familiar, but it was contorted both by the massive cat-type head next to hers, as well as intense pain. She also didn't look sane. Her long gray hair had once been braided, but now flew around her like a filthy cloud.

The creature used one of its extra legs to swipe at Reece. It missed hitting him directly, but did cause him to wobble to avoid falling into the sinkhole. He stayed clear of it, and shot one of the legs.

Even Jones was swearing out loud when the leg

regenerated. Not instantaneously, but within a minute, the limb looked just as it had.

Aisling pulled out her gun, and she, Reece, and Jones fired at the creature in the heads and chest. It screamed as it was hit, but kept reaching out one long leg toward Aisling. The elven mouth opened as if to say something, but it could only screech.

In that moment, Aisling realized who the woman was. Or who she had been. "Wait! Don't kill it!" But she was too late and Jones was too good. He'd pulled out a dagger and raced for the monster, sliced its neck, and took one more head shot.

"Sorry, don't think we had an option."

The body was done for but the elven face continued to try to regenerate. Partially. Aisling didn't want to touch it, but she lifted the head so both could see the profile. "This thing is the spitting image of Queen Bellaquora."

"The one who supposedly led the medical battle against the Black Death and probably has a few hundred hospitals named after her?" Reece peered at the face then stepped back. "And who died three hundred and fifty years ago? I will say that it does look like her likeness on the coins. But how and why could that be her?"

"I don't know, but shit!" Aisling felt the tingle in her fingers a moment before the flesh beneath them collapsed in on itself. She jumped away from the body.

The body turned to mush, liquidized, and then was swallowed by the dirt.

"Damn it, just like the dead swamp goblin on the other side. What the hell was it?" Reece got to his feet.

"Not a clue, aside from it looking like someone combined the very late High Queen Bellaquora with a krilaze, set it loose, and it didn't handle being killed well." Aisling took a few photos, but it was mostly just muddy dirt and the sinkhole.

"We need to go through the rest of the campsites. That sinkhole is growing." Jones was now at the edge of the site. The sinkhole swallowed a picnic table as they watched. So far there hadn't been any ghanlough coming out, but there was no way to know how long that would last.

"Give me a few minutes though." Aisling nodded, but moved toward the monster-remains-mud, held up her right hand, and clutched the ghau in her left. She didn't know how much the ghau picked up things going on, but figured helping it couldn't hurt. She focused on picking up on any otherworldliness from the remains.

The ghau flared and she got the information that she needed in a flash inside her head—the body had come from beyond the veil. Part of her had hoped that it had been made of magic. Unfortunately, there was no information in the image from the ghau about how the monster had been created. From an elf long dead, no less.

Then she stepped to the sinkhole and again reached out for the ghau's assistance. The feeling was completely different. This had nothing to do with the other side of the veil. It was from this side, but she couldn't get more than that.

Aside from its plan to destroy the entire compound. Rather, the plan of whoever created it.

"Change of plans, we need to get back to the others and hope someone there can stop that sinkhole." Aisling grabbed Reece and Jones' shoulders and spun them toward the front of the compound.

"But... Never mind. Let's go." Jones had started to argue, looked at Aisling's face, and dropped it.

Reece kept looking back toward the sinking site. But the chances that something vital to their investigation was in those tents was minimal. And the odds that sinkhole was going to swallow everything out here in about forty-five minutes was almost at one hundred percent.

Five troll guards followed them running in, or at least the ones she'd seen. They didn't ask questions, but stayed watchful as they ran behind them.

Aisling hit the door with Reece, Jones, and the five guards behind her. "We have to get out of here." She froze as a pack of swamp goblins stood near her friends and the trolls, with claws extended over each person's throat.

She immediately raised her hands. "Let them go. Your issue is with me." She wasn't certain of that, but it was worth a try. But the largest swamp goblin's eyes flared when she spoke.

Bart opened his mouth to speak and the swamp goblin's clawed hand moved with lightning-fast speed and a thin line appeared on Bart's throat.

"Wait! What do you want?" She kept her arms out, but lowered them. "We can talk." It was interesting in that they weren't casting magic, yet were visible. Maybe their ability differed depending how they crossed the veil. She was afraid that at least some of the missing people from this commune might be dead. Victims of bringing these swamp goblins to this side.

"Home. You brought us, take us back," the goblin near Bart said.

"I didn't bring anyone here; you murder people to cross to our side. Who cast your spells for you?" There was a chance that these swamp goblins didn't have magic, but were sent as a scout force.

"You were the one. Left trap. Can't go home." The swamp goblin seemed paler than before, they all did. "Dying now."

He moved too fast, and only Jones expecting it saved Bart's life.

Jones leaped at the swamp goblin and the others all grabbed their assailants. Aisling joined Jones since that one was the leader, but grabbed his gun when he was about to shoot it.

"No! Wait." She looked around. All the swamp goblins were on the ground, either dead or injured. Now that she'd seen both types of them, she knew these were the ones who'd been after them and who had forced their way through the veil twice. The Gful, as Neasa had named them. However, there was still a chance to gain information.

Everyone kept their swamp goblin pinned if it was still alive, but no more were killed.

"I'm all for shoving them back to the hell they came from," Reg said. "But I'll give you two minutes."

Bart nodded slowly. "I'd talk fast if I were you. While my troll friend said back to the hell you came from, I can assure you, he didn't mean alive. Explain how you got here and why."

The swamp goblin stared at Aisling. "That one. She called us. Said there were riches. Half of my tribe died coming here, we have no magic, and our bodies are failing. She tricked us."

"I didn't…did you see a mark here?" Aisling tilted her head and pointed to where her mother's mark was. She didn't think she looked like her mother, but this was getting old.

"Yes, you hide it now. You told us to take everyone. Through veil. We did." His breathing was labored now. "But no riches. Send home." He collapsed as did the rest of them.

"Get their bodies outside!" Reece yelled as he grabbed two and dragged them out.

Reg looked like he wanted an explanation, but nodded to his people to help remove them.

It looked like an odd Halloween theme with the swamp goblins lying around.

"I think they all died." Grundog walked around them

slowly. "Even the ones we didn't kill." Grundog used to speak with the pigeon accent common to the mountain trolls of California and the Pacific Northwest. That had changed when Reg came into her life. Aisling didn't think Reg cared one way or another, he liked her, not how she spoke.

"Why did we drag them out here? And what were you three running from when you got here?" Bart asked as Fieath checked to make sure the slice on his throat was clean. It was shallow, but who knew what was on those claws. They weren't as nasty looking as the ones on the ghanloughs, but they weren't good.

"Both items are connected." Reece watched the bodies, then shrugged. "We were attacked near the campground and the body turned to a liquid. We saw a swamp goblin body do that on the other side. Thought it might be a trend. And what we were running from was a fast-moving sinkhole with evil intent. According to Aisling."

"They're not dissolving. Are we sure they're all dead?" Maeve walked around the bodies in a counter circle to Grundog.

"They're dead." Fieath tapped each body with a stick. "Why did they think you sent them here?"

"Our mother," Caradoc said before Aisling could. "Some people think they look similar. Especially ones on the other side."

"Could your mother have modified her looks to appear like you?" Bart squinted at Aisling and tilted his head. "There is a similarity, but unless she changed her appearance drastically, I don't see how these beings from beyond the veil are getting you two mixed up." He'd gotten a close look at Aisling's mother—right before she shoved him through the veil.

"She could? Maybe a glamor spell, but those are hard to hold unless you're a changeling. But why? She used to mock me for not looking enough like her when I was young." Aisling had no idea why her mother would be trying to look like her.

"Do any of your sisters look like her or you? I know you don't associate with them, but could they have gotten involved?"

Caradoc bit out a laugh. "I know them better than Aisling, since I'm eighty years older than her. None of them look like our mother, at least not more than Aisling does. And while all are magic users, they never reached our mother's level of power and were content to be her minions."

"Which leaves us with your evil mother, projecting herself as you, while she takes over the other side of the veil and then this world." Maeve folded her arms. "Charming."

The swamp goblin bodies started to smoke.

"That's different, and probably bad!" Aisling yelled as the sound of a million bees filled the area. "Back inside!" Might be leaving them trapped, but the bodies were between them and the car.

Reg yelled for his trolls to get inside, even the ones still on guard duty in the surrounding woods. They'd all gotten into the building when the creatures making the sounds burst out of the swamp goblins.

Massive yellow jackets that were easily as long as Aisling's pinkie finger.

CHAPTER TWENTY-NINE

"WHAT IN THE hell are those?" Maeve kept back from the window. Her gun was in her hands and she looked ready to start shooting.

"They're big, but not sure they're large enough that you can shoot them," Aisling said. "I agree though, what in the hell are they? Let me guess, another thing left out of our stories about creatures from the other side? There's nothing like them on this side of the veil." Caradoc would have harassed her as a kid with stories of these things. If he'd known of them.

"I'd guess they're polit wasps. Yes, from the other side." Mott had stayed quiet during the prior ordeal and remained inside as the swamp goblin bodies were dragged out. He stepped closer to the window now. "I've been doing some studies since I was taken. Garran and Surratt, or whatever those two were, had a lot of data about the other side. They were searching for something and needed my brain to do it. They weren't clear on what they were searching for and I believe they threw in random information to keep me off track."

"Those things were in their files? And why didn't you tell us they had information that we could use? We should go back and grab that information if they left anything behind." Caradoc didn't use magic much, but he loved data.

"Pish, even duplicate Garran and Surratt wouldn't leave it behind. I'm sure once they realized that I was out of their reach, they took or destroyed it all." Mott gave a peaceful smile.

"What did you do?" Caradoc's scowl vanished when Mott just grinned and tapped his head.

"I've memorized a lot of it, took images of more. It did look like they were trying to bring down the veil completely, but I don't think they were working with your mom. Especially since it looks like they might have been in touch with the High King and Queen of the fey. Never did get enough information to sort out who was behind it. But it looked like there may be multiple elements trying to merge both sides of the veil into one miserable whole."

The wasps continued to buzz around the bodies of the swamp goblins. No new bugs came out, but it was still a gruesome sight. At least the bodies stopped smoking.

"We can't stay in here forever," Maeve said as she watched them. "How smart are those wasps, Mott?"

Mott squinted through the window. "If they are polit wasps, then very. They're mutated from a bunch of types of bugs found on the other side. They were used as trackers."

As they watched, the wasps began tapping the windows—from the sound of it, all the windows. They weren't slamming into the glass, but were hitting it softly with their legs.

"Are they looking for a way in? Because that's what it seems like." Reece hadn't put away his gun, and like Maeve, looked like he was debating how much damage a bullet could do to the three- or four-inch-long flyers.

Two of the troll guards had gone to make sure the windows and doors in the rest of the building were also shut. They came back and went to Reg.

Reg shook his head after talking softly with them.

"The good news is, the wasps are still outside and the building is secure. The bad news is, they are trying to change that, and unless we have a damn good plan soon, they will succeed." He motioned to a side window that was along the wall leading into the kitchen.

It was completely covered by the massive wasps—all tapping slightly as they walked on the surface. Soon the rooms darkened as all the windows were covered and the tapping grew louder.

"I assume those things are killers?" Aisling asked as she watched the creatures. It was interesting from a horrifying point of view.

"They are ten times more deadly than the common wasp." Mott also continued to watch, but unlike everyone else, he didn't appear freaked out.

"Mott, if you know a way to stop them, this would be the time," Caradoc said.

"There are a few windowless storage rooms in the back, I'll get my people working on moving everything out. But those things still might get in, and we can't stay in there forever." Reg turned and issued commands and all the trolls, including Fieath and Grundog ran toward the back of the building.

"I think we can get them to leave. They reacted to certain sounds to know when to hunt according to the study I saw." Mott pulled on his lip as he watched the wasps.

"Okay, first, who did a study if they were from the other side of the veil, and secondly, they can hear?" Aisling swore the wasps were tapping in formation. "And thirdly, chasing them off to attack the unsuspecting English countryside isn't the best idea."

"Oh, the study was done a few hundred years ago. By the Anliab brothers. They had been working on ways through the veil. Based in northern Wales, where the veil remained thinnest, they wanted to see the impact of this world on other-worldly creatures." Mott nodded. "They died. But before they and their projects exploded in a fiery doom, they got out a few papers." He looked around. "Don't worry, those wasps aren't theirs."

"Wasps on this side of the veil have fine hairs that detect pressure differences, they work to basically hear." Reg shrugged. "Wasps and bees were a study in primary school. And I agree, we can't chase them off. Unless one of you brainiacs has a way to open the veil and send them back?"

"Not me, that's for sure. Let me try Harlie." Caradoc got his phone out, then swore as an electrical arc zapped him, and he dropped it. "Damn it, there's an electrostatic field hitting the phones." He looked toward Mott.

"Don't look at me, even polit wasps can't do that." He leaned forward, almost with his nose to the glass. "Unless someone modified them. They could be doing it if that were the case. Would mean they were modified for this side of the veil and our reliance on electronics." He was more talking to himself than anyone else and never took his eyes from the wasps on the glass.

"The back rooms are cleared out, but it will be a tight fit." Fieath and two guards came out.

"There must be something inside that head of yours that will destroy them before they can kill us." Caradoc gathered all the phones, but all were emitting odd arcs of electricity.

"I know." Mott chewed on his lip. "You'd think so, wouldn't you?"

"They follow sound and are emitting an electrostatic field. Can't those two points help us?" Jones asked. "And I'd rather not be trapped in those storage rooms without a plan."

"It might." Reece looked around. "My fey side are naiads; sounds carry differently under water, but are finely tuned. There could be a frequency that could damage the wasps, but not us or anyone else on this side. I think those two pendants can help." He nodded to Aisling and Bart.

Aisling was impressed at his way of handling the naiad issue. He was also part siren, but they sure as hell weren't going to bring that up around Reg and his crew.

She wasn't as impressed about pulling the ghau in. The annoying pendant had helped a few times already, but she still had the feeling that could change at any moment. The vallenians weren't trustworthy and their gifts had to be treated with suspicion.

"That might work. The disruptions on the phones are from something nearby and not a frequency I've seen before." Caradoc was waving one of his larger gizmos over the collected phones. "But once we have it, we can try blocking it. Maybe the ghau pendants can give things a lift."

Mott had been watching the wasps with his vacant, thought-processing look. His eyes were open, but there didn't seem to be anyone home. Then he blinked, jumped, and turned. "Yes! We can do it. That frequency messing with the phones is from their wings, they *were* modified. If we can reverse it, it will destroy them."

"Can we do it before they get in here? I have some equipment, but most is back in my car." Caradoc was eyeing the phone collection enough that Aisling had an urge to snatch hers back.

"Yes, we'll need your gizmos, a few things I have, both ghau, and all the phones' speaker systems. Oh, plus Reece's inherent naiad audiological abilities." He frowned. "Probably all of them. Plus, some electrical wiring."

"I don't know how much I can help," Reece said. "I had music classes as a kid, but I'm not a naiad." Again, skirting around the fact that he did have some fey abilities.

"You might be better than you know. First, I'll create an electronic opposite of what they're currently creating."

Mott marched to Reece, spun him to a window, and went forward. "You put your ear up to the glass and let the sound infiltrate to those ocean-living ancestors. While you do that, I need Aisling and Bart to sit here. Just hold the pendants for now." He motioned toward a sofa nearest the window that Reece was now hovering uncertainly around.

Bart shrugged and sat so Aisling joined him.

"Now, Caradoc and I need to work on the parts."

"What do the rest of us do?" Reg watched Mott with a combination of concern and humor. It was hard to take Mott seriously with his hair sticking up and the childlike way he walked around.

"I'd say go to the storage rooms. This very well might not work." Mott nodded then turned, obviously dismissing anyone who was not part of his group.

"I'll send my people in, and Maeve and Jones if they want to go. But I'm staying out here." Reg sat down to emphasize that he was not going to be moved.

Grundog sat next to him and so did Fieath. They didn't say anything, but their view was clear. He glared at both, then dropped it with a shrug.

"I'm not going, either." Maeve stood near Caradoc and Mott with a collection of wires that Mott had stolen from somewhere.

Jones was near Reece, but simply turned and shook his head.

"Fine. Guards, I need you all to go into the storage rooms. Stuff kitchen towels under the doors and wait," Reg called to the rest of his people inside. "If this doesn't work, you'll be the last line to stop those things from escaping."

The guards didn't look happy but nodded when he got to the second part. They still weren't happy, however, they understood contingency plans.

Although, Aisling pretty much figured if Mott, Caradoc, and Reece couldn't stop them—the odds weren't in the trolls' favor.

Caradoc and Mott were moving at elvish speed, just pausing long enough for Maeve to hand them another wire. At least one of Caradoc's gizmos was completely disassembled. It looked like the phones weren't being taken apart, but all had their backs removed.

Reece looked back from his window position, but Aisling just shrugged. If possible, she felt even more confused than him. She raised her pendant toward him. So far, her ghau hadn't even warmed up. She was trying to talk to it in her head, but there was no response.

Maybe there were only certain things the vallenians wanted their magically annoying jewelry to do.

"Ha!" Mott jumped up as he yelled.

"Are you done?" Maeve still had a good supply of wiring.

"Ah, no. I burned my thumb." Mott grinned, shook his hand, then sat back down.

Meanwhile, Reece had closed his eyes and was softly humming. Jones stayed near him but didn't interfere. Fieath did get up and stand close to the window, she also closed her eyes and seemed to be humming. It was so low it was hard to tell.

"I think this might work." Caradoc raised his hands free of the electronic mess. "I need Jones, Maeve, and Reg to come help us with the phones. The rest of you keep doing what you were doing for now."

Aisling wasn't really doing anything and watched the others sort out phones and wires. The wires all had a sticky substance on one end, and the other end was attached to a phone. Bart was leaning over to see as well. It was hard to be in the middle of a life-or-death situation and be stuck sitting out.

Or in this case, sitting on a sofa waiting for a pendant to do something helpful. Aisling still didn't trust it, so doing nothing was better than doing something bad.

Fieath and Reece were humming in counterpoint to each other. It was still soft, but the tone was eerie.

Mott left the sorting of phones to Caradoc and joined them. "I think you have it. Keep humming, both of you." Mott hit record on what at first glance looked like a phone, but was almost the size of a smaller tech pad. The humming from the two came through the speakers. With a few tweaks, an off-sounding wail came from Mott's pad. He quickly shut it down. "We have it!" He ran to Caradoc and they transferred a file to all the phones.

"Now Aisling and Bart stand in the middle of the room and hold your pendants. Think helpful thoughts." The rest of you, attach your phones to the windows with the sticky stuff and hit play when I yell!" Mott ran to the window that Reece had been near, sending Reece and Fieath to two other windows. The phones were all quickly attached to windows. "Now!"

The sounds went through the glass and the wasps immediately lifted away from the windows. Aisling figured all they'd done is piss them off, but the sound followed the wasps as they smashed into each other, attacking one another as they went across the parking lot. They began ripping each other apart, more focused on destroying each other than getting away.

Aisling was about to drop her pendant, clearly, they weren't going to help this time, when a single line of light burst from it, through the closest window, and blew up the remaining wasps. Bart's pendant had joined in, but the light was weaker.

The window the light went through shattered, but it looked like the wasps were gone.

The ghau pendant glowed, then went dormant.

"I really wish these damn things came with instructions."

Bart glared at his before he dropped it back under his shirt. "Stupid thing singed my fingers."

Mott nodded but his wide grin said it had nothing to with what Bart said. "I think we need to burn those bodies though."

"Can we get our phones back? In working order?" Maeve finally holstered her gun.

"Oh, yes." Caradoc had been transfixed by the shattered window and kept glancing back toward Aisling and Bart. "This would be a good thing to tell Harlie and the others."

Reece shook his head. "And yes, burning the bodies, and quickly, would be a damn good idea. Or did people forget there's a sinkhole heading this way?"

"Sorry, swamp goblins, mutant wasps, killer beams coming out of necklaces—there's been a lot to take in." Maeve shrugged as she looked around the building. "I don't see it coming. How would someone create an attack sinkhole anyway?"

"That's a good question." Caradoc handed everyone their phones back. "Mott?"

Mott had been slowly walking around the dead and mangled swamp goblin bodies outside. It seemed that each wasp had burst through at a different spot. "Nope. Nothing I've read about sinkholes. They could be a good weapon if they were fast enough. That one back there might be designed to do something else. If it's moving fast, but not killer fast, if we can still get away."

"Who wants to do the honors of torching the bodies? The sinkhole might swallow them, but we can't take the chance that it doesn't." Bart looked around.

"I think we will." Reg came out with six guards, all armed with torches. "No offense to you magic users, but better to go old school sometimes." He paused in front of the bodies.

Bart shrugged. "I'm all for the old ways. I'd like to see this sinkhole though."

All of Bart's people, except for Mott who was determined to watch the end of the swamp goblins, followed Bart down.

"Do you know any spells that could stop it?" Aisling asked as she walked alongside Caradoc. "Harlie never thought to teach me anything like that." The ones they faced before were shut down with electricity. But they also had parts of the Area 42 building and green attack goo in them. This one had neither.

"Nothing directly related," Bart said. "There's no way to know if this sinkhole will stop when it reaches the edge of this commune. Normal sinkholes stop when the ground is no longer collapsing, but this doesn't sound normal. I take it that you didn't find any of the residents before the sinkhole chased you?"

"No, but we were attacked." Aisling quickly told him about the weird creature that had Queen Bellaquora's face.

"Seriously? How'd you forget that?" Maeve turned around.

"Those swamp goblins were holding you all by your throats." Although Aisling was surprised that she'd momentarily forgotten it. There was no way she'd forget what that creature looked like—ever. She turned to Caradoc. "I used the ghau, the creature was from beyond the veil. Whatever is causing the sinkhole isn't. There were no ghanlough coming out."

"Then what are those things crawling out of it?" Bart had taken the lead, but stopped in his tracks and motioned for the rest to stay back.

Aisling looked around him as skeleton-like gooey things crawled slowly out of the massive hole in the ground.

CHAPTER THIRTY

"GHANLOUGHS. DAMN IT, the sinkhole must be connected to the other side." A few months ago, they'd seen the same creatures crawl out of the ground where a house had exploded in outer London. The ghanloughs had been trapped in place by the local Area 42, and eventually died. Not unlike the swamp goblins they just faced, the creatures were unable to survive on this side.

When Nix attacked London and froze all the people inside a massive dome over the entire city, he'd let loose the same creatures to feed on the population. Like the ones Aisling, Jones, and Reece had faced on the other side of the veil, those had looked far too alive. The London dome had allowed them to survive here.

These appeared sturdier than the ones Area 42 had cordoned off, but not as robust as the ones Nix had brought in. That could work in their favor if the worst creatures couldn't live on this side of the veil for long without protection. Unfortunately, there was no way to know if the dome had been solely Nix's creation. If it wasn't, someone could make a new one.

"A magic user had to pull them through." Reece had his gun out and was already taking aim for the closest one as he stepped to the side.

"I don't think they're going to tell us," Jones said as he

also spread out and readied to fire. "Any objections? I know you folks always want to study things."

Caradoc pulled out a small gun. "I'd say not this time. Bart?"

"Fire away." Bart also had his gun aimed at the creatures.

Aisling felt an urge to use her magic, but it was odd, and not from within her. Like something outside of her wanted her to use magic. Which was enough for her to use her gun instead. A flash of annoyance hit her and she looked around for the source. Seeing no one, she focused on shooting the ghanlough.

The creatures were slower than the ones they'd faced on the other side of the veil, but far more active than the first ones she'd seen in that housing area in London.

They took being shot about the same though. Kept struggling to move forward as they continued to lose body parts. They didn't really bleed, but the green ooze that covered them dripped out faster. They wouldn't stop until they literally couldn't move any more. The fact they all went down with enough fatal hits to kill most creatures was disturbing.

Caradoc swapped his own gun for a scanner and ran it over the bodies. "They're all either dead or dying. But I think there are more coming through." He nodded to the slowly advancing sinkhole. "We have to close it."

Bart turned his scowl to Caradoc. "I know you and your sister are strong magic users, but I'm not, and Maeve, Jones, and Reece don't use magic it all. How in the hell are you two alone going to close that? And I thought you said that hole came from this side, not the other."

"It did." Aisling lifted her pendant up, but it had nothing to add or do at the moment. "This thing said it did. But even if the sinkhole came from here, it could have been created by someone trying to reach through the veil." She stepped back a foot as the ground crumbled before her. "And I have no idea how to stop it."

Caradoc peered over the edge, adjusted his odd scanner, and started nodding. "We shock it. Like those wasps, there's an odd vibration moving this thing. It's not the same as the wasps, but I think a holding spell with a magical charge should stop the earth from moving. The collapsing ground should move faster than the ghanloughs and close them off." He looked around. "With some help from the boulders around here. Could someone get Reg and his people? I don't know that I trust the phones around that thing."

Maeve holstered her gun and nodded. "I'll go. Just don't do anything dramatic until I get back." She took off down the path.

Caradoc went over the spells with Aisling, even tying in Bart for support. Bart wasn't at all familiar with the spells, but more magical support would help even if he wasn't a strong magic user. They were trying to stop whatever was motivating the sinkhole to increase as well as shock the dirt into collapsing into the hole both here and in the veil.

This wouldn't work with a normal sinkhole, but a weird, magically motivated one should shut down after this. In theory.

The spells had seemed simple when Caradoc told her about them, but there were subtle nuances that were tricky. Bart added some magical support, but didn't even try to step in on the actual casting—it was more like he was a magical back-up system.

More ghanloughs crawled out as Aisling and Caradoc worked on shutting the sinkhole down. It might have just been wishful thinking on her part, but they appeared to be slower than before.

Reece and Jones had no trouble stopping them, but would eventually run out of bullets.

The sinkhole was closing, and no more ghanloughs had crawled out, when a wave of dirt rose and crashed on

Aisling, Caradoc, and Bart. It didn't attack them, just the one wave, then the dirt went still.

"Don't let go of the spells!" Caradoc yelled once he brushed the dirt off his face. "The spell is still active."

Aisling shook off the dirt and focused on ending whatever spell was on the soil. In her mind she saw a tunnel, one most likely that passed through the veil. She reached forward, feeling a nudge from the ghau pendant, and crushed the connection.

"Back up!" Reece yelled as he grabbed Aisling's arm.

The ground around them was collapsing, but unlike before, it looked more natural. Aisling had pulled in the veil tunnel and whether it was real, or only existed in the space between the worlds, it was collapsing the dirt.

The ground rumbled, then stopped. Just as Maeve, Reg, Grundog, and six guards came down the path.

"You weren't supposed to bathe in it," Maeve came up and brushed off Caradoc. "Interesting look for you three through."

"Funny." Bart shook himself like a dog, then fixed his hair. "Reg, can your people move those boulders over the center of the sinkhole? I honestly think it's completely shut, but just to reinforce it."

"Agreed, and it never can hurt to be careful. Once they're in place, I can use magic to keep the spell behind the sinkhole dormant," Caradoc said.

"Harlie would be so proud," Aisling said as she and Reece continued brushing the dirt off. "Look at you using all that magic." Caradoc was an extremely powerful magic user, but had tossed it over for technology years ago. He'd probably used more magic in the last few months than he had in the prior five years.

"Ha. Just rusty. But I still have it."

Maeve tilted her head. "Was the dirt bath part of the plan? You three need showers."

Aisling ruffled her hair to get more dirt out. Maeve was

right, providing they found a place to stay, she needed a shower.

"That dirt wave was weird, was it just a last push from the spell?" Aisling asked as Caradoc walked to the edge of the sinkhole. Reg and his people had most of the boulders moved but there was still dirt along the edge.

Caradoc dropped down and ran his fingers through the dark soil.

"Not sure what you're sensing, but it was the last push of an earth-magic spell." Bart stomped around some more. "My people historically were fond of dirt, but even though that was centuries ago, I still have a lingering affinity. I couldn't feel that the sinkhole was earth-magic based, but that flinging dirt over us was. If I believed in such things, I'd say the ground was thanking us."

"With a dirt bath?" Aisling looked at the dark earth dubiously. "I guess thank you?"

"This will hold things? Maeve said you were under attack from ghanloughs." There was a slight tone of disbelief in Reg's voice.

"We were, they aren't doing well on this side of the veil, not without Nix's shield to protect them. And they still don't do well with bullets." Bart stomped around the dirt. "If Caradoc thinks we're good, I agree." He looked past the rocks to the collapsed land past them. "Hopefully we can find what happened to the people who lived here, but they've got some work ahead of them."

They all walked back to the main building.

Reg stopped. "We're going to stay here for a while, at least until more of my people arrive. We're calling in all the Ckiong families—something big and nasty is heading our way. My people have claimed the nearest cottages, but you're welcome to crash here for tonight. It's got a full kitchen, facilities, and beds in the back. Won't be exotic, but you all look rushed off your feet."

"And in need of showers." Aisling held up her hand

as Reg tried to deny that she still was wearing a fair amount of dirt. "Nope, showers, food, bed. The day's already mostly gone; traveling isn't a great idea."

"Especially since we have no idea where to go," Maeve said. "Unless you don't think we need to stay near Avebury?" At Mott's violent head shake, she sighed. "Let's bring the bags in then."

Aisling went out with her. "I thought you liked it here?"

"When it was a charming part of my childhood and not the focus of evil creatures seeking our doom. Swamp goblins, killer wasps, and those…things, is this because of how close we are to Avebury? Shouldn't we evacuate the village and surrounding areas?"

"I wish we could." Aisling looked around the peaceful countryside. Untold number of people missing, spells to keep people from realizing it, and these attacks. And it looked calm and lovely. "How can we? Area 42 has gone off the deep end, and at this point might have declared Bart missing-in-action-at-risk. You said you don't trust MI-6. None of us are even cops over here. Who will believe us?" That was harsh to say and worse to think.

The people around them had no idea what was coming. All Aisling and her people could do was try to save as many as they could. And stop it before it was too late to save anyone.

She jumped as her phone buzzed. Keeping it in her back pocket was handy, for the most part. Harlie's name flashed on the screen. "Hey, what's up?"

"I had a horrible premonition about all of you. Are you okay?"

"Yes. Are you four?" She knew Caradoc had updated all their phones, but they were standing in an open parking lot. It didn't look like anyone was around, but it was impossible to tell. This wasn't the place for a long discussion on what happened.

"Yes, are you sure?"

Aisling grabbed her bag, Reece's, and Mott's. They'd come back for the rest. "We're fine, but things did happen. I'm in the parking lot, probably better to discuss from inside."

"Oh, good point. My head has been hurting all day, and I'm not thinking right. Call me back when you're inside." He ended the call before she could respond.

"That was odd, but instead let's get all the bags in one shot. The hairs on my arms are standing on end."

Maeve grabbed a few bags; Aisling added the rest to her collection. It had been Harlie on the phone, she knew it. But there was something off about him. And the way he thought something *was going* to happen, yet missed everything that had happened here? She looked up as storm clouds raced across the sky. The weather had been cloudy but pleasant before, but the temperature dropped quickly as they ran for the reception building.

The rain let loose just as the door shut behind Aisling. Lighting and thunder decided to show up and the timing between the two was short enough that they were striking extremely close to the area.

"Okay, anyone else think that's odd? I'll be the first to say that our weather can be unique, but that came up terribly fast even for England." Maeve scowled at the rain slamming against the window.

"Better than wasps, though." Mott came out of the kitchen, took his bag from Aisling, and wandered toward the back rooms. "Thanks."

"Don't mind him, he's calculating things, lots of things." Caradoc helped move the bags further in. "Reg and his people left right before the rain hit. Fieath perked up and said a storm was coming, so they went for their cottages."

"She's good. There were only scattered clouds until a few minutes ago." Aisling grabbed her travel bag and looked around. "Caradoc should call Harlie to check in and I need a shower."

Reece laughed. "This way."

Caradoc was already dialing as they left.

Aisling paused as they rounded a corner. There was a bank of single showers in a long, completely tiled, white room.

"This is different."

"We have the same in some campgrounds in the states. My parents used to take my brother and me to Yosemite and Hetch Hetchy when we were kids. Always stayed in tents. These rooms were common."

"My mother didn't take us anywhere, and if she had, tents wouldn't have been it." Aisling watched him for a moment. It was more subtle than before, but there was still a tightness around his eyes. "I talked to Harlie briefly, he sounded off and said he'd had a headache. He also thought something was *about* to happen to us, but didn't act like he knew that something had already gone on. How are you feeling?"

Reece hadn't had anything like a premonition for a while, or at least he hadn't said anything about having one. He was still getting used to the idea that what he thought were just great people skills in predicting behavior, was precognition.

He sighed and rubbed his forehead. "No on recent premonitions. I also didn't pick up on anything that just happened. But there's been a building pressure. Like that storm out there but worse."

"That's not good. You need to talk to Harlie too." Aisling grabbed him for a long kiss that was enthusiastically returned. "Yep, still got it. Go talk to my brother."

Reece grinned, gave her a light kiss, then left.

The shower was not exotic, but at this point anything warm and cleansing was a plus. That dirt felt like it was everywhere. It might have been a thank you for stopping the sinkhole or it might have been making a point of how strong the earth was.

Or if it had been earth-magic the practitioner was making a point. Earth-magic was an ancient form of magic and the spells used were far more based on will and intent than most magics. There had been four elemental forms of magic, or at least the history books said there were. As far as she knew, earth-magic had been the only one to cross over when the fey fled the other side. The number of users shrunk drastically over the years and she hadn't read of a single practitioner since a thousand years before she'd been born.

She was pondering the implications of that, and not paying attention to her shower, when a stream of water wrapped tightly around her. Not strangling her, but tight enough to freak her out.

"What the hell?" She raised her arms, a spell of repealing at the ready, but the watery band dropped and the shower returned to normal. "No. I know what you just did." She reached up to a coldness on her chest. It was the ghau pendant hanging like a lump of ice. The red line was gone and it looked like a blue film covered it. "Are you doing this?"

The pendant didn't respond. Neither did the water. "Damn it." She quickly finished her shower, dried, dressed, and joined everyone else.

"The water attacked me." Everyone had been chatting in groups, except Caradoc who was near the window on the phone with Reece near him. But she figured this was important enough to break in. "Seriously, it wrapped around me and squeezed."

"Water-magic?" Bart looked doubtful. "My people didn't deal with that, ever. But that magic was lost long before we crossed over to this side." He looked over to Reece with a frown. "Your people once had water-magic users. Anyone ever mention it in your family?"

"No. I think mom would have told me if thousands of years ago someone in our family could work water-magic." He shook his head then came over to Aisling. "You're okay?"

"Yeah. But it was disturbing. Oh, and the ghau lost the red line and was like ice." It looked normal now, but that was the first time that had happened. "I don't think it did it, but who knows."

Caradoc nodded and talked faster on the phone. "Harlie said that's not good, and really could be a water-magic incident. Also, they got hit with a weird windstorm a few minutes ago. Almost like a tornado."

"Ask him if his crew have heard of anyone with elemental magic," Bart said.

"Check with Neasa about it on the other side too." Aisling took an offered cup of tea Maeve gave her. She was still oddly chilled. "It seems that a lot of our history of what was really going on over there was complete fiction."

Caradoc listened, not getting any words in though. Then he pulled the phone away from his head and glared at it. "Damn it, the line died. Harlie said Stella thought she recalled something about the elemental magic users, something her aunt used to talk about. He was about to ask Neasa when the line dropped."

"So, hypothetically, we've had earth, water, and air elemental magic, possibly appear. What do we do if there's a fire-magic user lurking out there?" Maeve stepped near Caradoc to look out the broken window.

"Hope they are on our side?" Bart added with a shrug. "So far, they haven't done anything bad. The dirt that was thrown on us could have been a lot worse. And Aisling was startled but not hurt. High winds and fire could be a danger, but only if they're meant to be."

"More importantly, we might have elemental magic back in the world." Mott grinned as he looked up from the three computer pads he was working on. "I always thought it would be cool to control the elements. Like those cartoons." He wiggled his fingers for emphasis.

Caradoc started to respond, then shook his head and turned back to the window and tried to call Harlie again. He shrugged when it didn't go through.

Bart grabbed his phone as it rang, then held up the caller ID to the room. Garran. "This should be interesting." Considering whatever grabbed Mott had used Garran's phone, this was probably them. "Hello?" Bart's voice was neutral and he nodded as the other person spoke. "Nope, still no sign of him. Where are you now?" He listened again, looked at his watch, then cut the call. "Oops. Bastard was trying to trace my location." He disconnected another call as it came in. "Not sure if it's a possessed Garran or a duplicate. But that's not the person I know. He barely sounded like himself."

"If they were duplicates, they could be losing cohesion," Mott said. "Area 42 did studies on the bodies of replicas they found. Their tissues were already dying before they were killed."

"That's great. Did he or it say anything helpful?" Jones asked.

"Not really. Still looking for clues in London, etc. The trip to Los Angeles has been supposedly called off. He kept rambling about nothing which clued me into him tracking my phone." He nodded to Mott. "I'd say they think you're with us."

Mott shrugged.

"Let me do more work on the phones. Just to make sure." Caradoc settled down at the far end of the dining table from Mott and started going through the phones.

There weren't a lot of food options in the kitchen, but they cobbled together a pile of sandwiches and soup. Aisling added a few pots of tea as the storm outside kicked up stronger.

Since Mott and Caradoc had turned the table into a mad scientist's laboratory, everyone just ate where they sat. Jones and Reece had taken advantage of the showers as well, but didn't report any odd water tricks.

"I'm pretty sure Jones had his gun with him, though," Reece said as he took his food to sit next to Aisling.

Jones shrugged. "It might have been right outside to be honest. Not sure what a bullet would do to a water sprite though." They'd all reloaded their weapons after fighting off the ghanloughs. Hopefully they could find more ammunition soon, at the rate they were going through it.

Caradoc had just handed Aisling's phone back to her when it buzzed. She glanced at the ID, then held it up. "It's Surratt this time. Answer, or not?" She knew Caradoc would have gone above and beyond to keep anyone from tracking their phones, but she wasn't sure if answering was a good idea.

"The more we don't answer, the more they'll think we're on to them. If it's safe, we should at least answer occasionally." Reece took his own phone back as well.

"They are safe," Caradoc said. "Well, as safe as possible. Don't stay on more than a few minutes. And come up with a good lie about where we are and what's wrong with our phones."

"Oh! Say you're following my trail and you think I'm heading toward the Outer Hebrides Islands." Mott smiled. "I've always wanted to go there."

Bart shrugged. "That works, and just say our reception is bad, and Caradoc is having trouble with some bugs on our phones."

Aisling hit answer but kept the phone a distance from her mouth. "Surratt? Can—hear me?"

"Aisling! We lost contact with Bart, where are you?" If she'd doubted that something was up with Garran and Surratt, she didn't now. He sounded completely snark-free. She really hoped the real Surratt and Garran were alive and well somewhere.

"—barely hear you. We—stuck—in Scotland. Mott heading— 'ter Hebrides." She grinned to the others. Faking a broken phone call was something she learned when her mother first started calling her. "Phones not— bugs in." That was a trickier one but she assumed he'd figure it out.

"Tell Bart to not trust Mott, he's up to something."

Aisling rolled her eyes, then cut the call. "He had no useful information, but hopefully when Ft. Williams doesn't work out, they'll cross over and take a ferry to the Hebrides." The Scottish islands were lovely and there were plenty of places to hide.

Reece's phone rang this time and he held it up. Surratt again. "I think they have enough information?"

"Yes, they do," Bart said. "And I think we need Mott to write down everything they were having him research. They're panicking."

Reece declined the call.

Then they hit Maeve's phone and she did the same. "Why aren't they calling Mott's phone? That's who they're looking for, right?"

"It might not just be Mott that they're after." Bart turned to him. "Be honest, how hard was it to get away from them?"

Mott had been focusing on something on one of his pads and his hair was more scrunched up than usual when he looked up. "What? It was hard! They had me in a little room under a stable. That I probably should have taken you to, now that I think of it." He waved his hands. "But they took or destroyed everything there. I'm sure of that."

"Getting away? How did you get away?" Aisling came closer.

"I…I got out the door and ran." The look of confusion

on his face wasn't good. "The standing stones, I needed to go to them and they wouldn't find me." That he seemed surer about, but not being able to articulate how he escaped was bad.

"Okay, Mott, it's me." Caradoc sat down next to him and used his talking-to-scared-puppies voice. "You've never been vague about anything in your life. You need to focus."

Mott's brow furrowed and he chewed on the inside of his cheek. "It's like it's not there. Like what happened to everyone who didn't realize their neighbors had been taken. I didn't feel upset about it. I still don't."

Caradoc waved Aisling closer. "I think we need your healing magic."

"He's not sick." Aisling took the seat on the other side of Mott, but didn't touch him. Yes, her main magical ability all her life had been healing, and that was still there even though the rest of her magical skills had been released. "I need something to heal."

"But couldn't him having forgotten memories be a sickness?" Maeve asked. "Healing is restoring to the normal, healthy form, right?"

"You could be right. Maybe a mental healing spell." Aisling ran through her healing spells as Mott started to lean away from her. "Don't worry, this won't hurt."

She reached forward to touch his temple, when Mott screamed and jumped out of the chair.

"No! You can't do this. You'll take my knowledge. That's what you all want." He tapped his head. "What's up here! It's mine!"

He'd been focusing on Aisling and didn't notice when Jones and Reece stepped behind him and grabbed his arms. Mott was shorter than both, but elves were stronger and he put up a good fight.

Aisling darted to him and put her hands on his head. "It's okay. Relax. Shhh. We're your friends." As she spoke, she sent forth a calming spell matched with a healing spell. It was one that worked well on children. "You're okay. You were overpowered by something in your mind. But it's gone now. All of it is gone."

Mott stopped fighting and the tension left his face.

"How did you get away?"

"They let me. Well, the fake-Garran did. He fought with the fake-Surratt about how much they were having me do. The leak in the brain could be real."

Aisling looked up to Caradoc at that but he shrugged.

"So, he just let you go?"

"I was supposed to go to that house, the one that blew up. It would have been at night. But I knew they couldn't go near the standing stones. They can't. That way will open but until then, they are deadly to the ones not of this world." Mott blinked. "I'm very tired." Just like that, he closed his eyes and sagged in Reece and Jones' grasp.

"Okay, that passing out bit wasn't me." Aisling stepped back as Reece and Jones dragged Mott to a sofa.

"Can weird replica people have a disagreement? Aren't they sort of like robots?" Maeve pushed Mott's arm back on the sofa when he flung it off.

Bart shook his head. "The ones that infiltrated Area 42 were extremely realistic in behavior. They could think and reason. However, in this case, I'd say they acted that out. They wanted Mott in the neighborhood that vanished. He probably was supposed to go with the rest wherever they were taken. That explosion on the door wouldn't have hurt anyone unless they were right in the doorway. But he took off for the stones instead."

"He hadn't figured out what they needed, or they wouldn't still be looking for him. But they wanted him to be body snatched with the rest of that street?" Aisling dropped into a chair. "We need to find out who or what took those people. And the ones from here."

Avebury's great henge was huge. If that thing became

a passageway through the veil, the invasion forces would be massive.

"Agreed." Caradoc had been looking over Mott's computer pads. "He was looking into transformative mutation between species on this one, the power of standing stones in general and unique properties of the Avebury stones specifically on the second, and missing persons in the U.K. for the past two hundred years on the third."

"Good to know he was multitasking." Jones peered at the pads as well. "Not sure how that helps us."

"We need to look at this from multiple points, not unlike what Mott was doing." Bart nodded to Aisling. "Do you have your collapsible board?"

"I do, but we tried that at Dailten's place, it was a mess." Aisling pulled the laptop case for the board out of the pile of luggage.

"Because we weren't looking at multiple sources." Caradoc grinned and help her set up the expanding board. "How many centers do you think? Three? More?"

Bart nodded. "Your mother is one. Garran and Surratt replicas."

"Whoever your mother was working for when she killed Aisling," Reece added. "They might have been from the other side, but we can't count them with her. She made a deal of some sort from what Harlie had said. There's a larger fish out there. Or fishes."

Aisling nodded in agreement. "Whoever freed the ghanloughs. Although that could have been Nix. Plus, Neasa said that there had been some odd things happening that side of the veil. Including something draining magic and life-energy. It was bad and we were only over there for a few hours this time."

Caradoc added the people listed. "Do we think whoever was after us and called in those thugs and the attempted Malifithri in the Tesco parking lot was part of one of those, or another item?"

"Item," everyone said at the same time. Aside from Mott, who started snoring.

One by one they added items until Caradoc hit the big one. "The High King and Queen of the fey."

"Unless they had some sort of deal with someone on the other side of the veil, like your mother does, I think they are on their own with their own agenda," Bart said.

"The vallenians and the family boxes. Including the destroyed ones. What were the family names again?" Reece had his phone out.

"Hthia and Wolinshea," Aisling responded.

Reece started swearing. "Both families live in different parts of the US. The Hthia family were killed in a single car collision yesterday morning. The second family, the Wolinshea, was in a fire at an impromptu family reunion. No survivors."

CHAPTER THIRTY-ONE

"I'D SAY THE vallenians are stepping up their threat level. If we don't do what they want us to do, they'll just keep picking off families." Maeve watched the storm. "And I don't think that storm is natural."

"Considering that one of those boxes belongs to our family, that does increase the threat." Caradoc moved to the window. "Yeah, this can't be natural. Can water-mages control rain?"

Aisling swore as she and the rest crowded to the window. "Are those rain spears? How would you even do that?" Most of the rain appeared normal; heavy, but realistic. However, there were long, pointed shafts of rain, and they were stabbing what remained of the swamp goblin bodies as well as the dead wasps. With enough force to obliterate them.

"Damn it. We should have taken samples. Someone who might or might not be working with a water-mage is covering their tracks." Caradoc scowled out the window.

"But not damaging the rocks." Reece pointed to one of the boulders the commune seemed to keep as yard décor. The spears turned to normal water the minute they hit the stone.

"Hopefully our car is safe. And they don't seem to be coming in here." Caradoc pulled out his phone and started scrolling local news. "No sign of any attack rain. Lucky us."

"Yet." Maeve shook her head. "We're looking at the end of times, aren't we?" As she spoke sirens echoed in the distance, but they were too far away to tell if they were coming from the village of Avebury.

"Damn it." Bart shook his head. "We can't warn people. We need to get this sorted."

"I think the vallenians might be a place to start. They're marginally on our side and seem to see me as a way to save this world and their own." Aisling held her ghau pendant up. "You too, Bart. They trapped you with one of these, there must be a reason. Even if the vallenians don't have the power the old stories told us, they know more about what in the hell is going on than we do. I'm not sliding into the apocalypse without a fight."

Bart shrugged and held his pendant as well. "I feel kind of silly. They don't seem to be answering."

"I don't think they're used to being called. Put some magic into it."

"Wait, you're going to call vallenians here? Maybe we should talk about—"The rest of Caradoc's comment was lost as Aisling fell into a black void.

And landed on her ass with a dazed looking Bart sitting next to her.

"Oh dear. I really don't think you're supposed to be here, either of you."The voice was familiar, and a moment later Stella's Aunt Jilan came into view. "Where were you aiming to go?" As before, wild trees surrounded them— ones not of earth nor of the other side of the veil that Aisling had seen.

"Is this Isfyden?" Aisling thought about getting to her feet, but her legs were like jelly. Bart wasn't getting to his feet either.

"Yes. No. Depends. It's a difficult concept to say the least. But it is a place that you two shouldn't be in." Her long silvery hair was twisted into an even more elaborate display around her head than before.

"Aren't you dead? Sorry, that trip jostled my manners. I'm Bart. Stella says you died ten years ago. She seemed fairly sure of it."

"Again, I will have to be vague. I do apologize. And my niece is correct, I was mostly dead. Caught up in a magical ambush in the deep forest." She scowled and her fingers twitched as if she was remembering a spell.

"And? Not to be pushy, but this is the second time I've been tossed here and found you. I think there might be a reason." Aisling's legs were feeling less jelly-like, but she stayed seated.

"I believe those vallenians are up to something. They can't cross here; did you know that? They and the xpenc don't get along." She gave a laugh that sounded just like Stella. "Well, most beings can't get here. Which is why your visiting is odd."

"We were trying to reach them. Both of us have the ghau pendants and I thought it might make them show up. Back on earth. They're being cryptic and killing people. All supposedly to save both worlds." Aisling briefly told Jilan about the dystopian threats and the attacks on two of the family boxes. And the apparent results.

Jilan kept her face neutral up until the destruction of the two families whose boxes had been destroyed. "That's not possible. Well, it shouldn't be. My people, the changelings, weren't high in the fey government during the crossing—it was all elves. But we all knew about those boxes. They were designed to protect the higher families, yes, but it was more on a spiritual, esoteric level. Not on a physical one."

"My theory is the vallenians destroyed the boxes and then killed those families to make a point. They seem to like doing that," Aisling said.

"And since it looks like their ability to complete these

tasks on their own seems to be slim, they have others working for them to do it." Bart shook his head. "Just made that connection. They didn't even do their own dirty work on the other side of the veil; I doubt they were doing it on ours."

"This is not your place." The voice was deep, gruff, and familiar. Aisling froze as a coldness enveloped her soul. It sounded like the voice she'd heard when Reece and the other precogs were dying a month ago—the one that was shocked she was alive.

And the one that had ordered her mother to kill her when she was five.

"You must make them leave." Even though the voice wasn't attached to anything that Aisling could see, she knew that bit was directed at Jilan.

"Xpa, pah. I didn't bring them here. What have you done?" Jilan shook a fist at the sky. No more words, but an odd popping sound followed. "Good, they're gone. That's not good that the xpenc know you. They can't hurt me, but I fear they might hurt you. We need to get you out of here."

Jilan looked off into the distance, then turned back to them with a frown. "The xpenc are gone, but I fear the vallenians have broken into here. At least something that feels like a vallenian is here. That's never happened." She started backing away. "I am sorry, but I can't meet them— not yet, and not here. Hopefully, whatever is coming will give you answers." She spun around and was out of sight before Aisling or Bart could respond.

"That was interesting." Bart slowly got to his feet and held out his hand to help Aisling up.

"Thank you." She dusted the dirt and pine needles off her jeans and looked around. Nothing but the odd pine trees were in sight. "I wonder if we can use Harlie's ghau spell to locate others?" She kept her voice low, but it seemed that even on earth the vallenians could find out whatever they wanted. If the vallenians were limited in their worldly interaction, they might have seeded the ghau pendants on others.

"That might work, it found me. Sort of." Bart kept looking around the forest as well.

"It found your copy, but Harlie thinks it was because the essence of the ghau muddled the spell of the duplicate. Where are they?" She didn't point out that she had no idea how they were going to get home if the vallenians didn't show and Jilan didn't come back.

There was another odd popping sound, like someone opened a vacuum sealed case. Then four vallenians stood in front of them. Male, as always. Aisling briefly wondered how an all-male species propagated itself.

Then again maybe they just appeared out of thin air when they needed more.

"You shouldn't be here." The foremost one tilted his head as he peered down at her. "Why are you here?"

"We were trying to find you." Aisling took a step forward. Yes, Bart also had a ghau, but she seemed to be the vallenians' special project.

"We do not come when called." There was some annoyance there, but Aisling kept her smile to herself.

"You left destroyed clan boxes at my feet. Now those families have been killed. You keep telling me that if we don't solve the problems, both our worlds, and I would assume whatever this one is, will be destroyed." She took another step forward. "We can't save anyone if we don't know what in the hell is going on. And killing entire families to make a point is vile."

The vallenians didn't move, didn't turn to each other to discuss, nothing. All four stood still and watched her and Bart.

Finally, the front one nodded. "*We* did not destroy the clan boxes. Nor did *we* kill the families of those boxes. They were given to you to find the connections before it is too late as we are limited in what we can do. We don't care of your world—it isn't ours. But if the veil falls, all worlds suffer."

Aisling wanted to ask about the place they were in right now, but all four vallenians looked agitated.

"Connect the pattern and close it."

Before Aisling or Bart could respond, the world went black.

"Damn it. That's a rough way to travel." Bart got out of the mud they'd both landed in and shook off as much of it as he could. "At least the stabbing rain stopped."

"But we got no useful information from them. Do we really believe that they had nothing to do with the destroyed boxes?" She watched her step. She had good night vision, but they were at the far end of the camping area and the rain had left a lot of destruction.

"There was a lot of emphasis on 'we' in their statements. I think they were involved. But it might not just have been to make a point." He glanced around. "Weren't there cottages at this point? Or am I just disoriented?"

"We probably both are." Aisling froze as she cleared a clump of trees. The cottages, the ones the Ckiong had moved into, were burned rubble. The smell of burnt plants, buildings, and flesh made her gag. "How long were we gone?" She started running toward the reception building, but like the cottages, it was nothing but cinder. She ran to where the car had been parked and almost threw up.

It was still there. Untouched.

This could be another of the vallenians' lessons, but it was too real. They'd run over the remains of the swamp goblins as they raced for the car.

She pulled out her phone. There was a signal. She tried calling Reece, then Caradoc, then Maeve. Calls went nowhere. She tried Harlie.

"Aisling? Where are you? I can't reach anyone. There's been attacks—"

"Harlie, they're all gone. Bart and I went to Isfyden, or somewhere. We…"

Bart took her phone from her hands as sobs tore through her. Unlike the other images from the vallenians, this had a visceral punch. She knew they were gone—all of them.

"This is Bart. It looks like something destroyed the entire camp. Caradoc's car is still here." He put it on speaker.

"Oh my god. Get out of there. Run. Just get—" Harlie's voice ended in an explosion.

"No!" Aisling grabbed her phone tried punching his number in again. Then the world went sideways and she passed out.

"Aisling? Are you okay? You and Bart vanished and then we found you outside, unconscious." It was Reece, he was alive.

Aisling flung open her eyes and grabbed him tight enough to cut off his air. She released him when he patted her arm.

His gray eyes were worried as he brushed her hair back. "It's okay, you're safe now, both of you. Were you crying? And can you release your phone? We couldn't get it out of your hand."

She winced in pain as she released the phone, her hand was going to hurt for a while. But the sound of rain outside was wonderful to hear.

"Make way, tea will heal them." Maeve came out with tea for Aisling and Bart.

Bart sat up but shook his head. "I need something far stronger than tea."

Maeve smiled and held up a bottle of whisky. "Thought you might. We only found you both because Aisling was screaming. Even while unconscious. You both look like crap."

Most alcohol didn't affect elven physiology, but it might take the edge off for a brief while. If Aisling started drinking nectar, which could get elves drunk, she feared she'd crawl into the bottle and never leave. She'd used that to deal with her mother for almost two years, and that was before she realized how vile the woman really was. Even the potential end of the world wasn't enough to have her dive back into that.

"Whisky for me too, please."

Maeve smiled and made sure there was a nice amount in both teacups. "Okay, take some sips, get fortified, then talk. I've never heard of someone being able to scream when unconscious, and you sounded like you'd lost everything."

"I had." Aisling took a few sips; the tea and whisky relaxed her, but she still felt cold inside. And she couldn't stop looking at Reece or the others. The feeling of them being dead, knowing deep inside that they were gone, was still a presence in her mind. She didn't know if she'd ever completely move past it.

"I can start," Bart said as he set his cup down. Yes, these people were his friends, but he wasn't as close to them as Aisling. The small nod he gave her said he knew it had been far worse for her than him.

Reece hugged her closer and Maeve quickly added more whisky to Aisling's cup as Bart filled them in on everything. Down to Harlie's end over the phone.

Aisling rubbed her arms. "It was so real. It had to have been those damn vallenians. It was just as real as being right here is. You were all gone."

Caradoc reached over and gave her shoulder a tight squeeze. "Maybe the car was left behind, but we all ran away. And the explosion you both heard was the phone line, not the others."

"Thank you. And thank you, Bart, for telling them. I don't want to think about those minutes ever again." Aisling wasn't going to explain the tear in her heart when she'd seen his car. She knew in that reality, whatever it was, they hadn't gotten out. They'd all died.

CHAPTER THIRTY-TWO

EVERYONE WAS QUIET, lost in their own thoughts. Maeve kept watching Aisling with weepy eyes and making sure everyone had tea and whisky.

Finally, Aisling pulled out of her terrors long enough to realize Mott was gone. "How long were Bart and I gone? Is Mott working in one of the back rooms?"

"Who?" Caradoc looked up.

She thought he was joking, but she saw the same look of confusion on everyone's face except Bart.

"Where is Mott?" Bart got to his feet and Aisling followed him.

This had felt real, but then so did that horrific scene they just went through. Was this another reality? One where Mott Flowers didn't exist?

She and Bart ran for the back rooms, the last place Mott had been headed before they vanished. There were three converted storage areas, and he wasn't in the first two. Aisling ran forward and hugged him when they opened the door on the third.

"You're okay!"

Mott smiled at the hug, but looked confused. "I've only been in here an hour. What might have happened to me?"

Aisling grabbed his hand and pulled him behind her. "Come with us."

The others were talking in the front room but hadn't followed Aisling or Bart. Aisling stopped right before going out and kept Mott behind her. "Bart, can you go ask them about Mott?" she whispered. This might not be an altered reality at all.

He shrugged, but stepped around her and again asked if they'd seen Mott. More mutters of asking who that was.

Mott's eyes were huge when Aisling pulled him into the room. "Now do you remember?" She didn't go far from the hall in case her theory was wrong.

Everyone looked at Mott in surprise, blinked rapidly, then passed out.

Aisling ran to Reece, but he, like the rest, was coming around already.

"Damn, what was that?" Jones shook his head as he sat up. "I feel like I got hit with a bat to the back of the head."

Bart had gone back to Mott. "Do you know who this is?"

"It's Mott, of course we do. In that weird dystopian future, did he not exist?" Caradoc started swearing and rubbed his forehead. "Wait, in our world he didn't. Damn, that's a nasty, evil, and tricky spell. I can feel myself not having a clue who he was when you asked. Seeing him broke the magic. That's Harlie level spellcasting. Or higher."

"Wait, you all forgot me? And there was a dystopian future?" Mott stumbled forward and took a seat. Maeve quickly gave him some tea and whisky.

Bart summed up everything and Mott kept drinking.

"How did they make you forget me? Was I in the destroyed world you and Aisling came back to? Why me?"

Aisling settled next to Reece again. "I originally thought that this was maybe another twisted reality when none of you knew who Mott was. Then realized it might have been a spell left behind by our duplicate Garran and Surratt.”

“This is seriously not good. If we forget who he is again, they could come get him and leave without a problem. But how could two duplicates have that much magic?” Caradoc shook his head. “The real Garran and Surratt are both heavy magic users, although they hide it. But can that transfer to replicas?”

Mott kept sipping his tea until he realized everyone was looking at him. “Oh. Yes, well the research I did hadn’t indicated that transfer of magical ability was possible. Duplicates, even those extremely realistic Xilen, which aren’t common by the way, shouldn’t be able to copy magic.”

Aisling didn’t like that he said shouldn’t and not couldn’t. But there was something else there. “Do we have any way to find out when the switch was made? Did the real ones even come to the UK?”

“I looked into that.” Jones looked around and nodded. “Yeah, you all and your researching got me thinking. According to a reliable source in California, they both were body scanned before they flew over here. The scan came back as originals.”

“They have a body scan for duplicates? No one told us, and obviously they haven’t shared it with the London office. I know Mott has his blue box and those slivers, but it’s limited.” Bart narrowed his eyes. “I’d like to know who your source was.”

Jones shook his head. “Not that I don’t trust everyone in this room, because I do, but there is too much risk, as we just saw with Mott. I trust them with my life, but we need them to stay safe.”

“Then the real ones are possibly here, somewhere in the U.K., and being held as prisoners. Unless the ones running around are them, but possessed. If the scan in L.A. is just for duplicates, they might not pick up the possession. At least I don't feel so bad that we might have been dealing with fakes for the entire time." Aisling had been sure she'd be able to tell if she was met with a duplicate—especially people she knew well, like Garran and Surratt. It had been disturbing to think that wasn't the case.

Mott scowled into his teacup. "Actually, my invention with the box and the slivers is more robust than how we're currently using it. I could make a body scan too, probably even scan for full duplication. Just figured having something simple would be handier."

"Not to mention that your program allows us to see who might have been changed."

"That's one thing," Maeve said. "Can those slivers stay in a body that's been duplicated?" She looked around. "Mott's is for possession, isn't it?"

"True. And if these full body scanners can pick up a switched body, they might not pick up a possessed one. Those could have been the real ones but already possessed." Mott shook his head. "I don't know what would happen to the slivers if the body they were in was duplicated. I would guess that the slivers wouldn't duplicate." His shrug said it was seriously just a guess.

Aisling yawned. After their adventure into altered dystopian land, she didn't know if she'd ever be tired again. Apparently, she could be. Maybe jumping back and forth between worlds, then thinking everyone you cared about was dead, wore a person out.

"Look, unless we have anything else to go over right now, I think we need sleep. And I think we all need to stay together." Aisling shook her head as people looked ready to disagree. "Think about it. You all forgot Mott. Completely. Hopefully, no offense, Mott, it's just a spell on him and we can resolve it. But what if it's on all of you? What if we forget who everyone else is once we're out of sight for a period of time and shoot or throw a spell before we realize who people are?"

Caradoc nodded. "Good point. I'm texting Harlie what happened. I don't want to call as he might actually have gone to sleep. Then let's bring all the bedding out here."

The rest of them started moving things, but Mott just brought out his computer pads and notes and set things up on the table. "I'm not really much of a sleeper, and this way I'm still with you all." He scowled. "I'm going to track down whatever spell they put on me." Mott often worked hard to keep people from noticing him. But it was a different thing completely to have that happen against his will.

They'd settled in on the floor and sofas, no one was going to sleep well tonight, but everyone agreed this was the best precaution. Aisling would have liked to remove all the guns, but there would be no way to stop the magic users if they misjudged and still forgot each other.

Not to mention, there could be worse threats than forgetting out there. If any of them came through that door, it could be vital to have weapons on hand. Aisling snuggled into a pile of blankets next to Reece and put her head on his shoulder.

"I'm not going to vanish in front of you, you know," he whispered when she continued watching him.

"You did though. You all did. I won't keep bringing it up, but that feeling is never leaving my soul." The terror and pain at realizing they were all gone was still bouncing in her psyche.

"Your screams were horrible; I can only imagine what you felt. But we're safe. We're together. We will get through this." His words were so convincing—he believed in them—that she gave in and went to sleep.

She woke up at some point later to a dark room and for a moment panicked. But Reece was sleeping quietly next to her, and when she focused, she could hear the soft breathing of everyone else. Even Mott's computer pads were turned off and the dark lump on the table was most likely him where he fell asleep. She didn't know what time it was and didn't want to disturb Reece or the others to check. The curtains hadn't been completely closed and it still appeared dark outside. If they could get more sleep, they should get it.

She rolled over to try to get some more sleep herself, when she heard a soft voice. She didn't sit up, but focused on where it was coming from. It had been so faint that it could have been one of her friends talking in their sleep.

Then it came again. It was more than just sleep muttering, and almost sounded like it was saying her name.

The third time it was clear. The voice was outside, and it was repeating her name. She stayed where she was while she got her heart to settle down. The voice almost sounded like her own, once she really listened. She debated just putting a pillow over her head and ignoring it. But things had been too terrifyingly weird so far to ignore anything at this point.

She carefully got out of the blankets, grabbed her gun, and stepped over her friends' sleeping forms. They'd all just slept in whatever clothes they were in, but her shoes were too far to get quickly. She didn't plan on going outside and her socks would suffice.

Taking a deep breath, the voice had called three more times, each time only her name. She unlocked the door, braced it with her foot, and opened it a few inches.

The rain hadn't come back, nor had the puddles gone away. That storm had been quick, but intense, and obviously saturated the ground.

There was no sign of anyone. Then the largest puddle

rippled and the voice, now sounding less like her own, but still female, came from it.

Crap. What she wanted to do was shut the door and go back to sleep. That wasn't an option. Neither was getting help. Something deep in her mind said that anyone else she brought out here would die. Could be really good mind mojo on the behalf of whoever was behind this. Or could be her own instincts or lingering terror of that place where everyone was gone.

Regardless, she wasn't taking that chance. She stepped out of the doorway, with her gun ready, and a relocation spell in her mind. It wouldn't hurt someone it was used against, but could throw them back about thirty feet. Then she could hurt them.

The puddle rippled again. "You came. I didn't know if you would."

Aisling almost shot the puddle because she now recognized that damn voice. "What do you want?" She kept her voice low; if her mother could call to her through a puddle there was a good chance that she could hurt others if they came out.

A watery face appeared in the puddle, confirming it was her mother. She looked older than the last time Aisling had seen her—a lot older. But she stayed silent.

"Again, what do you want?"

"Aren't you glad that I'm still alive?"

"No."

"But I can help you. We can save everything."

"No. Did you call through that puddle just to get me on your side? *What. Do. You. Want?*" She knew her mother was on the other side of the veil either working with, or for, forces that were trying to destabilize that side of the veil in their efforts to bring it down and take over everything. But there was no advantage in letting her know that Aisling and the others were aware.

"I want to help you."

"Wrong answer." Aisling gave in and shot the puddle and hit it with her relocation spell. It wasn't really her mother, and probably didn't hurt her at all, but it felt good. The puddle exploded when the bullet and spell hit. The oddness she'd felt when she first heard the voice vanished as well.

The front door flew open and Jones, Reece, Maeve, and Bart came barreling out with guns drawn.

Aisling held up her gun then tucked it in her waistband. "It was just me. Mom paid a visit." The chill of the air hit her and she rubbed her arms. "Can we go back inside?"

They went in, but the looks from everyone weren't good. She didn't blame them, but told them what happened. And her reasons for not waking anyone else.

"It could have been a trap," Reece said. He sat next to her, but looked the most upset at her actions.

"Oh, it was. Just not an immediate one. She was limited in what she could do right then. I felt it. But for some reason she thought I'd believe her and join her in whatever she was planning." Her mother was a lot of things, none of them good, but delusional hadn't been one of them before.

"That's sloppy. And not at all like her." Caradoc didn't look as pissed as Reece, but still annoyed. He probably wanted to run through the puddle before she destroyed it.

"I agree." Bart focused on the issue, not Aisling's reaction. "That's not anything I would expect from someone with her profile. And what was she expecting?"

"Maybe she *was* hoping you'd bring more of us out?" Maeve shrugged. "That woman is insane."

"She is, and I need to text Harlie that too." Caradoc looked at his watch. "It's four a.m."

"I think we need to get some sleep, even a little more before we move on tomorrow." Bart nodded to Aisling. "I know why you didn't involve us. I get it. But I'll be moving my bedroll over by the door. We need to stick together."

Aisling nodded. "Fine. But if she shows up again and you all get sucked into the void, it's not my fault." She took off her soggy socks, and climbed back into her pile of blankets. Her mother hadn't done that on a whim, there was a plan behind it. Aisling needed to figure out what it was before another part was sprung.

Aisling heard the others talking quietly, but didn't bother to listen. It was a weird situation, and she knew she'd been right to exclude them. Her mother probably couldn't drag her or Caradoc through to the other side, or whatever she had been planning. But she could have gotten all or some of the others.

Holding her friends hostage for her to come back through the veil was something her mother could and would do. Rolling over, she drifted off to sleep.

———◆———

The sounds of slightly muted chaos invaded Aisling's slumber. Once she'd woken enough to sort out that they weren't under attack, she opened her eyes. Reece was gone and his blankets had been picked up. Everyone else, aside from Mott who was still snoring on the table, was quietly packing, or, from the sounds, in the showers.

"Planning on waking me? Why are we heading out so early?" She rolled out of her blankets and stretched.

"We tracked a signal; I found a way to see where the holes were in the veil. We need to test things away from Avebury." Caradoc went to the table and gently shook Mott. He grumbled and hit Caradoc's hand, but didn't wake up. "Eh, he doesn't have much to gather, but Bart and I were able to track and remove the spell of forgetting. It was on Mott only. But it's taken care of now."

He held up a computer tablet. "I couldn't sleep after your adventure last night. Neither could Bart. We used my gizmos and his ghau pendant to find weaker spots in the veil. Not sure what will happen when we get to one, but I think we need that data. It will allow us to develop a plan for shutting down the ones here when the attack comes."

"Where are we going?" Aisling was pretty sure that Avebury, even with all its weirdness, wasn't ready to crack yet, but it would be good to know.

"About an hour north of here. A small gnomish village called Rosenpur. There were smaller signals around Avebury and one or two rips along the henge, but they're weak compared to this. I do think Avebury will be the focus when the attack happens, but it would be best not to disrupt things here if our technique for closing the rips doesn't work."

When Mott finally sat up, he looked awake enough that he'd probably been listening with his eyes closed. "For now. If we don't stop it from opening—boom— those stones are going to let everything come through. And I might point out that since some of the creatures from that side can't survive unassisted here, we probably won't do well when both worlds merge. Just because you've gone over there for a short time, doesn't mean that long term exposure would be good for you." He got up and stumbled to the kitchen.

"All the points he made are valid. And once we can confirm what I think we're seeing, we'll have a better idea as to our timeline for resolving this. And hopefully a way to close the holes in the veil before they get large and stable."

"How'd the ghau help?"

"It focused Caradoc's gizmos. Extremely disturbing. It lifted in the air and it felt like it was communicating to the tech. And it added another line." Bart lifted his pendant to show her. A new line, this one deep blue, was etched around the rest. Aisling's didn't have that one. Yet.

"Good to know that they can do something useful." That wasn't fair though, they had helped a few times. She just felt they should be doing a hell of a lot more if they were going to hang around. Aisling gathered fresh clothes and was turning toward the showers when a thought struck her. "Bart and I speculated that the vallenians might have given their gifts to others on this side to hedge their bets. If you reach Harlie before we head out, can you get the spell from him on how to find other ghau?"

Caradoc nodded as he pulled out his phone. "The Hyithalin nothaer tribusrt? I might know that one, but I'd want to talk to him about it. You should memorize it too. It's fairly simplistic."

Aisling nodded, then went for the showers. She turned on the water cautiously, but no strange water hugs came from it. Still, she showered quickly and got out.

Reg, Grundog, and Fieath were in the front room when Aisling returned. Even Mott was packed up.

"What you've told us is disturbing," Reg said to Bart and Caradoc. "Especially as my people will still be convening here. We believe this will be a focus of a battle and your words support that. I think we need to stay in close communication."

"Agreed. We seem to have also picked up allies within the Lazing and I'm hoping to find some of the Area 42 people who helped with the fight in London," Bart responded.

"I thought you folks weren't connected to them anymore?"

Bart grinned. "We're not. Too messed up at this point. Staying clear of them until things are settled is the wisest direction. Not to mention, I'm not completely sure they don't have me listed as dead or missing. But these people might be on the outskirts now as well. Especially if the London office is as disturbed as it appeared."

Caradoc had been fussing with two of his small electronic toys. Neither was more than a few inches in diameter and they both were extremely thin. "Let me finish these. I only have two, besides mine, ready right now, but they could come in handy." He closed the backs on them and handed one to Reg and one to Grundog. "In case the phone systems go down, and there has been enough instability that that's probably coming, these will reach us. They're almost indestructible and have a cloak-mimicking effect once placed. They won't be invisible, but put them on your clothing and they shouldn't be noticed." He ran his hand over his shoulder and a similar disk appeared. "Like fancy walkie-talkies, press them, speak a name, and talk. They have a long range, but not long staying power and will need to be off to automatically recharge after ten minutes or so."

Reg turned his over, then nodded and clipped it on his shirt. Grundog didn't even hesitate, and just put hers on. Both gizmos disappeared even though Aisling knew they were there. There was a damn good reason why Caradoc was as rich as he was.

The trolls moved some of their people into the reception area as Aisling and the others loaded luggage into Caradoc's car. Reg followed them out and talked car envy with Caradoc for a few minutes. Grundog came out as well, but went to Aisling.

"Tell Stella hello, and to be wary of interactions with her late aunt. I didn't say anything when you told us about her earlier, but I had an odd feeling. Something is wrong."

"That's an understatement, but I get what you mean. You don't think the person I've seen is really her aunt?" Aisling hadn't sensed anything scary about her, but not all bad beings looked evil. Her mother was a poster child for that.

"Not sure." Grundog scowled at the swiftly moving clouds overhead. "But I felt a chill in my bones. Fieath said to never ignore those, even if we're not sure what caused them."

"Thank you. I'll pass that along to her." They were trying to keep communications between the two groups minimal for now, at least until they all had a better idea of who was doing what to track them, and how much Aisling and the others were targets. But it could be crucial for Stella to know about it in case her aunt, or whoever it was, came for her.

Reg nodded to everyone, then paused before he and Grundog turned to go back to the building. "I'd like to say I hope when we next see each other this has blown over, but I'm not that good of a liar."

"Agreed. Stay safe, trust no one, and use Caradoc's gizmos if you have to." Bart shook Reg's giant hand and they climbed into Caradoc's car.

Aisling looked around and smiled as Caradoc turned the car around and drove out.

"What's that smile for, sister mine?" Caradoc asked as he glanced in the rear mirror. "You look smug."

"Not smug so much as an odd feeling, but not a bad one. We're a family leaving camp after our trip." She really felt it. She'd never been close to any of her real family aside from Caradoc and Harlie. But as they drove out, she had an overwhelming feeling of comfort. They might be fighting to stop the end of the world, but she was with the right people.

"I'm going to turn this car around if you kids don't settle down!" Caradoc shook his fist at the mirror and laughed.

Reece squeezed her hand. "I know what you mean."

Maeve turned back to her with a smile. "Me too."

The trip out of the commune was almost scarily uneventful. Aisling found herself waiting for something to blow up, charge them, or throw them into another realm.

The waiting bit sucked.

"You *can* relax sometimes, you know," Reece said.

"I know." Aisling leaned against him. "We've been running for so long that I've forgotten how to do that. Have we heard back from Harlie yet? I need to get a warning to Stella." Grundog had sounded disturbed enough that even though the being they assumed was Stella's aunt hadn't crossed to this side yet, she should be prepared.

"Only confirmation of odd weather disturbances continuing out there, wherever they are." Caradoc got them on a busier road. "He was impressed at you shooting the puddle, by the way. But he feels there will be more attempts from her and you need to be ready."

Aisling looked to Reece. "See? How can I relax with that going on? But I doubt that she'll leave you two alone. Especially if she can't reach me."

"You're not helping, Caradoc." Reece put his arm around her and rubbed her shoulders. "It's okay, we're all here."

"Now *you're* not helping. I keep having flashbacks to your *not* being here." Aisling gave him a quick kiss. "That's not true, it's my own head to blame. There are just too many pieces to this, and not enough of us to figure it out."

"Hopefully we'll find some answers once we get to Rosenpur. If we can get a handle on shutting the small holes in the veil, Mott and I can extrapolate that to come up with ways to shut the big one when it hits."

"You don't think there's any chance that it won't come to that?" A chill went through Aisling. The end that she and Bart had seen was because the veil had fallen.

"No. I think at this point, we need to figure out how to fight back once it happens."

CHAPTER THIRTY-THREE

———

THE REST OF the trip to Rosenpur was silent as everyone processed that. This had gone from figuring out what was happening to finding a way to stop it. That it was now a 'how to shut it down once it happens' situation wasn't good.

But part of Aisling felt relief. Maybe deep down inside she hadn't believed that they could stop it, and taking this tactic was better.

"Still no word on the missing people of Avebury?" Jones asked as he watched the countryside roll by.

"No," Caradoc said. "Harlie said he and his team swung by on their way out of town, it's still being completely ignored by the rest of the people in town. No one walking down that street, looking at the houses, nothing. I told him our plans and he said he's been working on the non-tech side. No followers yet from what he and the others can tell."

"That's cheery. Who took those people? Why? And I know I'm not a magic user, but keeping others from noticing seems like a terrifying amount of magic." Maeve shook her head. "What if Avebury and that commune aren't the only places it's happened? Maybe it's spreading?"

Mott had been focusing on his pads but looked up. "I think the action along the veil, and the rips in it, might be what's feeding these disappearances. If I'm right we should see some similar areas around Rosenpur. And the locals won't know."

"Which brings up the point, are we able to see past it because we weren't there when the people were taken? Or something else?" Reece shook his head. "If that's the case and it is happening in larger towns, ones with more people coming from outside, someone would notice the abandoned neighborhoods."

"Good point. I'd be surprised if whoever is doing this has targeted any areas of size for that reason. I'd say they were trying to create duplicates of the missing people. But if none of them have come back? That theory doesn't fly." Bart shrugged.

Aisling's phone rang and she glanced at the caller. "Damn it, it's Garran. I know we need to keep stringing them along, but every time I answer I'm afraid that I'll give something away."

"Might as well see what lies they'll give us this time. We'll be harder to track since we're moving." Maeve patted Caradoc's arm. "Not that your blockers aren't working, but more defense is better."

"True." Aisling put the phone on speaker and nodded to the others. "Hey, Garran."

"Where are you all going?" It still sounded a little like her friend, but less than before.

"To find Mott. Isn't that where you're going?"

"Then why are you almost to Rosenpur?"

Aisling kept her swear words to herself but looked around to the others for ideas. Maybe Garran had tagged Caradoc's vehicle when they were together, but there was no way they accidentally figured out that they were heading toward a remote gnomish village.

Caradoc looked in his rearview mirror and started swearing. Maeve followed his view then pointed to Aisling's phone.

Aisling looked back but wasn't sure what they saw. At

first. She grimaced when the sports car came into view. "We had a tip that Mott had relatives there. Why are you guys going there?" Lying about where they were was pointless.

"Ah, same. We were on our way north when a tip came in. We can meet up there." Garran ended the call as he and Surratt passed them.

Bart pushed Mott down in his seat even though the windows were tinted. "Damn it. They can't find Mott with us."

"And if we try and pull over or change direction, they'll know we're onto them." Caradoc slowed down.

"They can't find me." Mott's eyes were wide as he clutched his pads. "They got in my head before. They can't do it again."

"We'll figure it out. Damn, I wish Harlie or Stella were here. Although who knows if the possessed or duplicates can see through glamors or not."

This time Bart's phone rang, he scowled at it before switching it to speaker and answering. "Surratt?"

"Damn it, glad we got through. There's a car ahead of you, they look like Garran and I—they're copies. Even down to the car. We just escaped and are a few cars behind you. Don't interact with them. They want to kill you." Then the call cut off.

"There is another sports car exactly like the one that just passed us back a few lengths. What the hell is going on?" Caradoc had continued to drop his speed but was now picking it up again.

"The real ones escaped, which means the others aren't possessed, they're actually duplicates." Mott looked around. "Isn't this good?"

"Unless they're both copies or possessed? Or the ones behind us are the fakes and the front ones are the real ones?" Jones shook his head. "I don't think we can assume anything at this point."

Caradoc hit something on his dash and a hands-free phone appeared on his nav screen. Harlie's voice came a few moments later.

"Caradoc? Did you find anything in Rosenpur?" He sounded like he'd been walking quickly, or that he'd been extremely focused on what he had been doing and had been startled at the call.

"Garran and Surratt. Two of each." Caradoc returned to slowing down as cars started dropping speed ahead of them. He explained about the two pairs, including the same car.

"Interesting. I would like to hear what happens. But right now we're being chased in a field." He still sounded like he was moving, but his tone was more out for a quick stroll than being chased.

"What? By who?" Aisling leaned forward. They didn't know where Harlie and the others were, but they had to find them if they were under attack. Rosenpur could wait.

"By what, actually. We found more contaminated rapeseed plants, a huge farm of them. No dogs from the other side of the veil this time. Just a massive bull. Who doesn't like strangers."

"This way! I can't keep the hedge open for long!" Neasa's voice came through the call along with answering shouts from Stella and Dailten. Harlie must have been bringing up the rear.

"Why aren't you using magic?" Especially if the bull was from this side of the veil—Harlie should be able to stop it.

"They added magic blocking spells to the rapeseed. If you go near the plants it gets on you. Explains why they have a non-magical bull!" Harlie's voice went up at the last word and scrambling was heard.

"Drop it!" He yelled to the people he was with. "Okay, that wasn't fun. But we did get plenty of samples. Offhand,

I'd say they've been far more modified than the prior ones. Probably even more than just magic blockers."

"Harlie, I know you want to find your answers, but you all need to get those spores off immediately," Caradoc said.

Harlie laughed. "Thank you, little non-magic-loving brother. Never fear, Dailten is neutralizing all of them except for the small amount that I've got sealed away. I promise that I won't examine it without full protection."

Caradoc swore and slammed on his brakes as both lanes of cars ahead of them came to a stop.

"What's happening?" Harlie asked.

"I don't know, everything has…shit. Everyone hang on, going off-roading!" Caradoc yelled and made a sharp turn of the wheel.

As a fireball hit the front of the line of cars.

The sports car behind them also zigged out of the line, as well as a few other cars. Many were caught in the explosion.

"Can we go airborne? This would be the time." Maeve clutched the dash as Caradoc fussed with controls on the dash.

"It won't engage. Damn it. Could just be this new program, or someone disabled it. Hang on!" He took off across the fields. Luckily this field was large, but there was a very solid looking short stone wall in the distance.

The line of cars continued to explode until the line was broken as the cars further back followed Caradoc's lead.

"Garran and Surratt from behind us, whichever ones they are, are still following." Bart continued to watch out the back.

Aisling had been looking as well. Most of the cars that had escaped the line and gone this way stopped when the explosions were no longer a threat. The sports car kept following them.

"Did those flames just go out completely on their own?" Maeve twisted to see behind them.

"Yes. At least a dozen cars were on fire, they're all out now," Jones said as they heard sirens in the distance.

"Is everyone okay?" Harlie's voice from the car speaker was a start. From the reactions around her, Aisling wasn't the only one who'd forgotten about him.

"Yes, but that was close and people died." Caradoc turned to the left to follow the line of smoking cars from a distance. "And it looks like a small, familiar sportscar was the first to go."

"Someone didn't want them talking to you." Dailten's voice replaced Harlie's. "Which would be even more interesting if they were the duplicates."

"True. The other set is still following us. We're continuing on to Rosenpur. Will contact you once we have something."

"Agreed," Harlie responded, and they both ended the call.

"It's good to know that you two hang up on each other too. I was afraid it was just me." Aisling had grown to like them both just ending calls. If something was extremely bad, they said good-bye. But it had taken some getting used to.

"Eh, just easier. Okay, boss man. How do you want to play it with our friends?" Caradoc hooked his thumb behind them where Garran and Surratt were still slowly following. Caradoc's SUV was better adapted to driving across the field than the sports car. While its progress was slow, it was making it.

If that really was Garran, Aisling was pretty sure he wasn't getting a deposit back on that rental.

"That's a damn good question." Bart turned to Mott. "You need to stay in the car and down low in the seat. Can these windows be made darker?"

Caradoc nodded. "I can do it as I lock the car. It'll

blackout everything. But Mott? You need to stay inside. No matter what you think—stay inside."

"What if the car catches on fire?" Mott watched as they passed the smoky ruins of cars on the road.

"Then you can get out. Otherwise, stay put. Oh, give Aisling your possession box and the slivers."

"You think they'll let us check? And basically tag them?" Aisling asked as Mott dug through his bag to find the items.

"They won't have a choice. I'd like to get it taken care of before we enter the town though." Bart leaned forward from the seat in the back. "What about over there right before that big tree? Far enough from both the road and town."

Caradoc moved to the tree and parked. "If they show as non-possessed, are we letting them know we have Mott?" He turned back to everyone.

"No," Mott responded first. "It's my skin. These might, or might not, be the ones who grabbed me, but I can't take that chance." He looked around. "I don't think we can keep them with us either, even if they scan clean."

Aisling watched him as he clutched his important possessions tightly. She had a feeling that if things didn't go as he wanted on this, he was going to bolt. She wished they had time to try to go over all the things that might have happened to him when he was taken.

Bart paused, then nodded. "Agreed. Even if we're sure these are the real ones, we need to keep Mott hidden. For now." From the look on his face, Aisling wasn't the only one who thought Mott was a flight risk.

CHAPTER THIRTY-FOUR

M OTT WASN'T A fighter, not by a long shot. His technique for dealing with a crisis was to run away. Which didn't do much for his nerves as he'd gotten used to having armed and magic-wielding people protecting him. Hence the freakout when he was hiding in the Avebury stone henge. But he was willing to risk it now if it meant staying away from whoever grabbed him.

Everyone got out of the car, aside from Mott, who had managed to drop into the floor space between seat rows and looked like he wasn't planning on moving even when the windows went black.

Garran got out first, with Surratt following. Both looked like themselves, but Aisling had no doubt that the ones who'd just probably died in that car explosion had looked like them as well. This non-battle battle was hard enough without trying to figure out who was who they were claimed to be. She shuddered to think what would happen when the veil fell.

"This isn't Rosenpur. Good to see you all though." Garran looked toward the road. "The rest of your crew in another car?"

"Harlie, Stella, and Dailten had other errands to run." Bart stepped forward. "You know how those magic spiritualists are."

"Agreed. Now why are we not going into town? And

why were you heading into this town originally?" Surratt stayed closer to the car than Garran, but he was also more paranoid than Garran.

"I'd like to know what happened to you. We all would. How did you know about the duplicate yous? And, before we go further, I'd like to make sure you're not possessed." Bart waved Aisling forward. Mott or Stella usually used the blue box, but it wasn't hard.

"I need you to open the box." She held it to Garran then stepped back.

He shrugged, held open the box, and didn't even look startled when Mott's voice said, "clean, not possessed."

He handed it to Surratt. Who paused and looked at all of them. Aisling felt the tension increase. The odds that one of them was possessed and not the other were slim, but not impossible.

Surratt paused while looking at Aisling, then nodded and opened the box. "Clean, not possessed." He shut it and handed it back.

"Almost done. Just need to place these slivers in you, we all have them. They'll let us know if you become possessed." She held up the slivers and this time both quickly nodded. The marks went into their cheeks, flared, then became invisible.

"Now can we go into town?" Surratt glared equally around the group. He liked to be equal with his annoyance.

Bart folded his arms and shook his head. "I'd rather hear what happened to you two before we go in."

"Who took you?" Reece had never worked for either Garran or Surratt, but he'd worked with them. And he still didn't look like he believed they were really them— regardless of Mott's toy.

"The people we thought we'd shaken." Garran's jaw clenched as he spoke, which was about as far as he was going in showing how pissed he was about that. "The hench people of the High King and Queen. They grabbed us when we were heading back to your flat. They wore all black, including hoods, so I couldn't tell you who they were beyond that. Aside from the fact that at least one is a terrifyingly strong magic user. If I hadn't seen the vid of Maeve cutting off his head, I'd say it was Nix."

Maeve had kept her eyes narrowed as they spoke. "If you couldn't see them, how do you know who they were working for? Or that they were the same ones who followed you?"

Surratt stepped forward. "They weren't the same people—both groups were working for the royals. As for how we knew this time? They took us to the dungeon under the royal palace. It could have been a ruse, but if so, it was a damn good one. I felt the royal lineage as we were taken inside."

The palace of the High King and Queen was imbued with a unique essence of power. They'd had a dozen high magic users spend two years putting the magical lines into the building when it had been first built. Or so it was said in primary school. Designed to intimidate everyone else, in the past ten years, there'd been talk about disengaging the lines as a show of equality with their subjects. If this really was Garran, then obviously that had never happened.

"You saw them?" Aisling was thinking of the vallenians dropping off the royal family box to them. To her.

"No, we were left to our cells. Aside from a few gnome scientists who drew blood a few dozen times."

"How'd you get out? Those dungeons are inescapable." Jones stayed the furthest from them, but he looked the least upset. Rather, his face was its normal neutral, with a side of deadly killer. Aisling was sure he had at least three weapons in immediate reach and a dozen more easily obtainable.

"That's one of the things we wanted to talk to you about," Garran said. He appeared calm, but also wasn't approaching anyone else. "They'd stopped taking our blood, and dropped to leaving food and water only once a day. Then a day ago, there was a major issue in the palace. Both royals were freaked out and shut everyone out over something. The guards vanished and we were able to escape through a sewer pipe. We didn't call in case you were compromised. Then we found our duplicates."

"Did you blow them up?" Caradoc pulled his gaze away from the road they'd left. He'd probably been trying to figure out how both the explosion and the rapid suppression of the flames had been pulled off.

Aisling wondered if it had been the discovery of their missing family box that threw the royals so off.

Surratt shook his head. "No. Another thing we were going to ask you. But did any of you do anything to upset the royals?"

"Nope." Bart shrugged. "We've been looking for Mott. Did run into Reg and some of his people though."

Aisling relaxed. She had hoped that Bart wasn't going to tell them about the royal family box, not yet anyway. He was longtime friends with Garran, but even if this was truly him, the fewer people who knew about the current location of the fey royals' family box the better.

Garran watched Aisling. "We thought maybe they'd found out about the second royal line."

"First of all, I have no idea how that could happen, unless they have friends on the other side of the veil. In which case, they probably already knew. Secondly, if that lost line is legit, then both Harlie, Caradoc, and our ten siblings, are further up in line. So stop looking at me like that." She knew why Neasa focused in on her, Aisling was the first one she met. But everyone else needed to drop it.

Garran shrugged. "Just a hunch. So, what's happened in the past week, and what are we looking for in Rosenpur?"

Bart looked around the area and scowled. "Too much

to talk about now; we can fill you in once we check this town out. We're looking for rips in the veil. Things have gotten worse. Aisling, Reece, and Jones made another trip through the veil. Caradoc is pretty sure there will be a major breach in the not-too-distant future, and we're trying to stay a step ahead of things. Step one is to make sure we can close these rips when the big one hits."

Surratt scowled, but that was sort of his resting face.

Garran started laughing. "You're finally getting to use that college dissertation you got rejected? Took a few decades, but at least it's something."

Aisling had been watching Bart, and his shoulders visibly relaxed at Garran's words.

Bart and Garran had known each other for an extremely long time. Garran knew about Bart's abandoned area of study on veils decades ago—hopefully it would have been too deep of a memory for a duplicate to have access to. Aside from Mott, who obsessed on knowing everything, few people knew of it. Bart's presented paper had been rejected and his Ph.D. retracted.

Bart laughed. "Took long enough, and not the way I would have liked. But yes. And it does look like the veil *will* collapse. We were able to track down Rosenpur as a location of some smaller rips in the veil. Like I said, we need to find out how to stop them."

They were keeping the information simple and not diving into too many things. And Bart hadn't lied. He simply implied that it was the group that figured out where the veil weakness was.

"You're giving up on getting Mott back then?" Surratt spoke first, but Garran nodded.

"We do think that he might be hiding in Rosenpur. I got a call and the hints indicated he was here." Caradoc did his best Bart impersonation as he folded his arms. "Mott also indicated that it was you two who grabbed him, by the way."

Garran frowned. "It wasn't us. Like I said, we never even made it to your flat. But the ones who replaced us might have been able to move fast enough to get him. If Mott hadn't simply wandered off."

"No, he was taken from the flat. The door was shattered, even though it looked like it wasn't real. Like someone wanted us to think it had been a break-in."

"We found some of our things when we broke out, but not your keys. Those copies could have taken him by just walking in. Is that why they were going to Rosenpur?"

"Yes. We think they were following us," Caradoc said. "But they might have had information beyond what we have. Information that we've now lost." From the way he was watching Garran and Surratt, Caradoc wasn't sure about them being themselves nor that they had nothing to do with the other two being blown up.

Aisling thought that Dailten had been right. Whoever was handling the other Garran and Surratt pair didn't want them to speak to their group.

"Can we stop this fencing and just go get your resident mad scientist back? Especially if the veil is planning on crashing." Garran shook his head. "I took enough veil studies to realize that I don't want to see that happen. But I know we need people like Mott if it does."

"*When* it does. It's not an *if* situation anymore." Caradoc nodded. "Let's go then. First test shutting a veil rip, then track down Mott. We can get back on the road once we're past the wreck and the rescue vehicles. Follow me." He quickly got into the driver's seat and everyone else got in as well.

Aisling was the last and she turned to see Surratt in Garran's car, but Garran stayed next to the driver's door watching her. She gave him a small smile. "I'm glad you're back." She really hoped he was the real thing—she needed him and Surratt to be.

"I'm glad you knew I was missing." He still looked

like he wanted more answers, but instead of asking, he nodded, and got into the car.

Aisling hopped in Caradoc's car to find Mott in the back with Jones and Bart, asking a dozen questions per minute.

"They know I'm here? You gotta let me out." He went so far as to try and climb over Bart to get out, but Jones grabbed his belt and pulled him back into the seat.

"First of all, jumping out of a moving car is stupid. Secondly, they'd see you and would probably grab you before we could. Thirdly, don't do things like that, it pisses me off." Jones had been lightening up in the past few weeks, but he was back into full secret-assassin-tough-guy mode.

Mott watched Jones carefully as he put on his seat belt and settled back in his seat. "You all think those are the real Garran and Surratt, then?"

Aisling looked from Mott to Jones and back. They always treated Caradoc like the Mott handler, but Jones might be a better option. "I think they're them, and the box said they weren't possessed."

"I hope so." Mott shrunk back on himself. "How are we handling me?"

Bart patted his shoulder. "I want to keep you hidden for now. Have them focus on the rips in the veil first. But until we're sure, and have a clue as to who blew up the other car, you should stay put. Caradoc and I can search for the rips."

"I'm good with that."

Caradoc glanced back. "And, so no one takes my vehicle, I'm disabling it when we park. There's going to be an increase in the alarm level if anyone opens a door or the hood."

Mott gave a one-sided shrug. "That doesn't affect me. Staying right here."

Aisling had a good view of the side of Caradoc's face as

he turned back onto the road. His grin said he knew he'd squashed Mott's plans of possible escape.

The road into town was more awkward than it could have been. People from within the town were coming out and walking closer to the wrecks to see what happened. The police, paramedics, and coroners blocked most of it.

They got past them with Garran almost on their bumper. That was an extremely Garran thing to do, and made Aisling feel better about that being the real him.

They pulled through the town with Mott giving them directions. Even though Caradoc and Bart had figured this system of tracking the veil rips out, Mott had streamlined it.

In about two minutes.

Mott bounced as something appeared on his pad. "Okay, just past that pair of farmhouses, that's where the veil should be ripping. Oh, and it's a biggie. The hole is massive enough to swallow both of those farmhouses. I'll send it to your pad, Caradoc."

Technically, Caradoc and Bart should be able to pull it up without a problem on their own. But this might speed things up.

Caradoc parked with Garran and Surratt pulling in next to them.

Bart turned to Mott. "Duck." The doors opened and everyone except Mott left.

Aisling heard him muttering to himself, but she had to admit, no one would have seen him.

Caradoc hit the window tinting the moment he locked the car. At Garran's raised eyebrow, he shrugged. "We've got equipment in the back. I don't need to tempt someone to try and break in."

"I didn't say anything. Oh, I wanted to ask Harlie, but maybe one of you have heard of this, the xpenc? Some mystical entity from the other side. They were somehow involved with our being taken, but I don't think they were actually on this side of the veil. Neither of us had heard of them, but the name made the royals nervous. Extremely nervous. Before whatever happened to make them close in on themselves."

"No, but you're right, that could be something that Harlie, Stella, or Dailten know. They're all on the mystical side. Is it a person? Group?" Caradoc glanced to Bart, but kept his face neutral. Aisling had told all of them about running into a voice of an xpenc, and what it meant. Clearly, there were still some things Caradoc and Bart thought should stay hidden for now.

Surratt had been watching Caradoc's car, then shrugged. "No idea. It was just something involved with the royals and is extremely magically powerful."

She thought Caradoc was going to reach for his phone, but instead he swung his computer pad forward.

"Here's where the rip is." He held up his screen against the area in front of them. "If what Bart and I calculated works, it will shut this rip and give us a basis to work with to shut down others."

"What if it's not?"

"It'll be fine." Bart grinned and patted Garran's shoulder.

"I didn't trust you when you said that in college, I sure as hell don't trust you now." Garran pulled out his gun, then muttered a few words and a spell ball appeared in his other hand. "Anything you said would be fine usually blew up in our faces."

"Fine." Bart shrugged, but also pulled out his gun.

"I'd feel better if I knew what might be coming through whatever we're facing." Maeve had her gun out the moment she stepped out of the car.

"No idea. But hopefully this will work." Caradoc's smile wasn't big enough to support his words. He clearly had doubts.

"Then find Mott after? If he's hiding from his attackers, shouldn't we find him first?" Surratt also had his gun out and seemed to have a spell twisting around his wrist.

Caradoc shook his head. "Pretty sure that Mott's safe. This thing is already destabilizing. We need to know if this will work. Not to mention, I think these people would rather they didn't get sucked through to the other side of the veil if it expands."

Aisling had both a spell and her gun out, but nothing happened. She wasn't completely sure, but she figured there would be some visual disturbance if the veil sprung a leak. It had previously.

"Shouldn't there be something?" Reece asked as he took two steps closer to the still normal looking area.

"It's right there. Damn it, this is going to get messy if we can't see it without this scanner." Caradoc stepped in front of them all and lifted the computer pad so that they could see it. An angry, gray disk fluctuated between the farmhouses.

Aisling didn't think that the almost flame-like edges were good.

"This might be a good time to shut it." Bart sounded calm, but his body was tense.

"I want to get more data; we have to find a way—" Caradoc's words were cut off as the space in front of them exploded.

CHAPTER THIRTY-FIVE

CARADOC WAS BLOWN backwards the furthest, but no one remained where they'd been. Even the cars lifted briefly off their tires.

The explosion, or whatever it was, vanished almost immediately.

Aisling and Maeve reached Caradoc at the same time. He was flat on his back with his eyes closed, but still holding the computer pad.

"Caradoc!" Maeve looked hysterical as she yelled his name.

Aisling looked him over for injuries, but didn't even see any scratches. His hands and face were pink though—like a bad windburn from skiing. "Come on, you're fine." Aisling tapped his cheek.

"Ow." He still didn't open his eyes, but did lower his arms.

"Seriously, if you're fine, you'd better open those eyes, *now.*" Maeve still looked scared, something she hated, which made her angry. She also looked as, if he didn't open his eyes and sit up immediately, she was going to start shaking him.

"I'd listen to her." Aisling looked around. They weren't that far from the center of town, yet no one had come out when the explosion hit. In fact, she could see people a few blocks away carrying on as if nothing had happened.

Caradoc opened his eyes and slowly sat up. Maeve still looked ready to chastise him, but hugged him fiercely instead.

"Is the rip closed? And if that explosion is what's going to happen each time you close something, I'd say you need to go back to the drawing board." Garran walked closer to where the rip in the veil had been. "It smells like fire and freon from an icemaker. Did you freeze it?"

Bart glanced down at Caradoc, then followed Garran. "Not really, but you're right. According to my pad, it's closed."

Aisling joined them, leaving Maeve to deal with Caradoc. "You're sure?"

Bart held up his pad. "Yup. There are a few smaller ones a short distance from here, none larger than a soccer ball. This one is closed. But we can't explode them all."

"No, but you can all turn around slowly with your hands up." The voice was low and serious.

Aisling had already put away her gun and dropped her spell, but she raised her hands and slowly turned. Bart and Garran did the same.

The rest of their friends did it as well, aside from Caradoc and Maeve who were on the ground.

The speaker, and his friends, wore all black clothing, including hoodies, and had the lower part of their faces covered.

Aisling mentally pulled in a spell. If these people were the ones working for the royals who had grabbed Garran and Surratt, she wasn't letting them take her or her friends in.

"Aisling, Reece, and Bart?" A female voice this time came from a few steps behind the original speaker. One that sounded familiar. She pulled her mask down. It was Narissa the Area 42 flying fey who'd helped them out before.

"What are you doing?" The leader didn't take his eyes off Aisling and the others, nor did he lower his mask or his weapon. "They could be fakes."

"Mate, we can't operate on the premise that everyone has been replaced. Not to mention, they closed one of the veil rips. That sounds like the people who saved London to me." Narissa didn't step forward, but she did holster her gun.

"They caused a massive backlash. The waves went all the way back to Avebury." Judging by the height, or lack thereof, this speaker was a gnome. He and another similarly sized person next to him had smaller versions of the computer pads Bart and Caradoc had.

Caradoc started to get to his feet, but remained sitting when their leader shook his head. "What kind of backlash? It vanished almost immediately."

"A psychic wave, that most people wouldn't even notice, but we did." Narissa came forward. "You had some mystics with you before, where are they?"

Aisling's phone rang. "Probably on the phone. Do you mind if I answer it?"

The leader shrugged, but didn't lower his weapon. Narissa rolled her eyes at his behavior.

"Harlie? What's wrong?"

"I was about to ask you the same. You're in Rosenpur, I take it? We just got a nasty chill from there."

"Yup. We were testing our ability to close a veil rip. It shut it but we had a brief explosion." She looked to the two gnomes still typing on their pads. "A not-so-good one."

"Not surprising that we felt it then. It hit all of us. Is Caradoc handy?"

Aisling handed her phone to Caradoc who stayed on the ground. He briefly explained what had happened and that friends of Narissa were holding weapons on them. Then he did a lot of nodding and hung up the phone.

Aisling took her phone back, but obviously whatever Harlie had been saying to Caradoc was going to wait.

"You know, we are all on the same side. Both Jones and I are Area 42." Reece stepped closer to the leader, but stopped when he raised his gun.

"Area 42 fell three days ago," the leader spat out. Chances were the people facing them were all former Area 42 agents, but from what she could see of their faces, they had no remaining loyalty.

Aisling wasn't surprised at their complete fall, and from the looks on her friends' faces, neither was anyone else. Area 42 had been the most powerful, and most secretive, agency in the world. And clearly one that had to be taken out if someone was planning an invasion of this world. Most likely the road to destroying them was started long before the Area 42 building in Los Angeles had been sucked through the veil.

"And that doesn't mean they're bad, or duplicates. Damn it, we need to work with others." Narissa stepped closer to the leader. "We can't do this alone."

He tilted his head, then finally shook it, holstered his gun, pushed back his hood, and dropped his mask. An older elf, with short gray hair and a face that probably had looked tired before Aisling was born. "I'm Tobias. I was in the London home office when it fell a few weeks ago under Nix's attack. Thank you for saving us. But you can't keep doing whatever it was you just did."

"My brother said the same thing, actually." Caradoc got to his feet and dusted himself off before continuing. "The wave that knocked us over, and closed the rip, also disrupted psychic lines. If we'd done it during a larger rip, or when the entire damn thing falls, we could have destroyed the magic, and possibly the minds, of a few hundred thousand fey."

"Harlie is a wise man," Narissa said. "But you did this without him or the other mystics' help?"

"We did. Unfortunately, it appeared that someone was profiling us, so we sent them off in a different direction. But they're going to meet us to fix this thing," Caradoc said.

Tobias nodded to the rest of his people and weapons and magic were put away, but no one else dropped their masks. "You said *when* the veil falls. It's certain then? We have a few more pockets of cleared Area 42 former agents throughout England, Scotland, Wales, and Ireland. We're staying separate for the same reason you split from your brother and the other mystics. But we figured it could still be repaired."

"No, at this point the veil will fail. And we have to assume that there are people on this side and the other, who want that to happen." Bart nodded to Garran and Surratt. "We need people to help us fight back."

"We can't cover everywhere. If that veil falls, we've lost." Tobias shook his head. "I was a veil tectonic researcher once I left being a field agent. That was always our worst-case scenario."

"We're trying to mitigate the results when that happens." Aisling looked around at the grim faces. "You have some experts here, how about you brainstorm some tactics?" She was about to mention Mott, and if she had to, she would. They were running out of time to be careful. She also wasn't sure that this was the time to mention that the veil would need to be shut for good. Even though no one wanted it to fall completely, with good reason, it seemed that having it never be able to open again disturbed people. Her too.

"We're moving out soon, but will set up a secure line with a few of you. After we compare notes of the veil rips. Do you have access to any other groups?" Tobias waved over the two gnomes.

Bart told them about Reg and the Ckiong as well as

the Lazing—with the caveat that they weren't sure how many of the Lazing were on their side.

Caradoc, Bart, Garran, Tobias, and the two gnomes, closed ranks and compared notes on the veil. Jones, Reece, Narissa, and pretty much the rest of Tobias' crew talked about what happened to Area 42. Judging by their faces, it hadn't been a clean ending.

Maeve, Aisling, and Surratt stood back and watched.

"You two ready to come back to the LAPD after we've saved the world?" Surratt hadn't turned to them.

"In a heartbeat." Aisling said. "Wait, maybe we should be hard to get. You and Garran did bench us."

He turned with a shrug. "Not me, I was dead." He tried to keep a straight face, then let a smile crack through. "I hope we all survive to go back to our boring lives."

"That would be nice." Maeve gave a sigh and continued to watch Caradoc.

Aisling smiled. Maeve might claim to want to go back to boring, but Aisling knew she'd go wherever Caradoc did.

Surratt's phone rang. He paused when he saw the caller, but Aisling couldn't see who it was. "Speaking." He listened for a few minutes, nodding as he did. "Agreed. Thank you for telling us." Then he hung up and slid his phone back into his pocket.

"And?" Maeve asked when he didn't say anything.

"And that was one Satoshi of the Lazing. He said that Harlie said Garran and I could help them, and that we were trustworthy. Cardiff has fallen."

"Fallen? As in gone? Under some weird dome like Nix put over London? Been swallowed by the veil?" Maeve narrowed her eyes. "You're too calm to have just finished talking to a Lazing."

Aisling leaned forward to see Surratt's face. "Nope, he did. He's got that smug twitch. But I agree about what in the hell happened to Cardiff?"

"It's been covered in a dome, like the one you all fought off in London, according to Satoshi. Smaller, not even covering the entire city, but Satoshi and his people need Garran and me to help."

He still looked smug. But Aisling couldn't figure out why Satoshi hadn't reached out to them or called for Harlie to help them, not just point them to others. And just what special skills Garran and Surratt had. Garran didn't use magic much, and since Surratt was pretending to be a magicless human instead of the changeling he was, she had no idea what his magic level was. But all changelings were powerful. Obviously Harlie was aware of whatever unique skills they had and told Satoshi about them.

"Let's wait until they're done. Oh, and you might as well let Mott out of that car. He's dying of curiosity. Even though he's afraid of us." Surratt didn't look toward Caradoc's vehicle, nor Aisling or Maeve, as he spoke. But his smile was larger.

Aisling caught herself before her look of surprise showed. That answered one question. "Telepath?" Rare among any fey, but being a true telepath could explain why Surratt had been so good at his job.

He gave an almost real smile. "Something like that. Strong emotions mostly, but stronger than an empath. It's complicated. And Mott is sending them all over the place. I noticed his when we first got out of the car back in that field." He looked toward the street. "And we might have gathered some attention from the locals. At least their law enforcement."

Two police cars cruised down the road. They didn't appear to be aiming their way, but pulled up behind Garran's rental car.

The others stopped their conversations, Reece and Jones held their phones up to Narissa and two others before coming over. They were connected now, better than just having phone numbers.

Tobias did the same with Bart and Caradoc. The entire former Area 42 group vanished before the cops got out of their car.

"Is this your vehicle?" The first cop, an older satyr, asked Bart as he nodded toward Garran's car.

"Nope, it's mine. Well. It's a rental." Garran flashed a smile, but his eyes were flat. "What can I help you with?" He drew himself up to his full height.

"We had a report to be on the lookout for that car. Then we find it as the inciting point for a flash spell that destroyed five other cars and killed six people." The satyr walked around the edge of the car. "And yet, this looks to be the exact same vehicle. I think we need all of you to come to the station with us."

Aisling knew that wasn't going to happen, but was clueless how to do it without hurting the five officers now drawing guns and spells.

Reece and Jones moved closer to the police while Caradoc's car started a full alarm attack. Mott came racing out of the car with an odd stick gun that he pointed at each cop, while yelling some completely nonsensical words.

Simultaneously, a helicopter came overhead and started lowering as if to land. On one of the cop cars.

Stella, her tiny face almost lost in the massive headgear, waved from the pilot's seat, sending the helicopter over a few feet, but then she adjusted.

Whatever weapon Mott had used, all five cops collapsed. Which was probably a good thing as then Stella did land…on both empty cop cars.

"What in the hell are you doing?" Surratt yelled at Stella as he ran over to grab Mott as he tried to make a dash for the farmhouses.

"Flying," Stella said. "Not bad for my first time, eh?"

She got out along with Harlie. Neasa looked passed out in the back seat, and Dailten wasn't in there at all.

A flapping of powerful wings announced Dailten's arrival. "Please tell me you intended to land there?"

Stella looked at the cars and shrugged. "I wanted to make sure I didn't hit a veil rip. I figured if the cars were in that spot, the rips probably weren't." She turned back to the helicopter. "Probably want to let Neasa sleep; she didn't enjoy takeoff."

Garran peered inside. "A dryad? Aren't they all dead?"

"Long story, but no." Aisling hugged Harlie, Stella, and Dailten. It had only been a few days, but it felt much longer.

Surratt came forward still holding Mott by the collar. "Look, we found him."

"You can't take me back!"

"Mott, it's okay, these really are the correct Surratt and Garran." Aisling sent a pleading look to Stella.

Stella nodded and walked over to Garran first, then Surratt. Her smile was genuine. "Yup, they're them. It's okay, Mott." She was one of the few people in their group shorter than Mott, and that, combined with a love of her baking, made her the least threatening for him.

He visibly relaxed. "Thank you. Oh, the officers aren't dead. I rigged a stun gun up while you were all talking out here." He peered down as the satyr twitched. "Not sure how long it will hold them though."

"I think we've got what we came for, and hopefully some ways to deal with that aftereffect. Shall we head out?" Bart nodded to Garran as he moved to Caradoc's car.

"The Lazing called and need Garran and myself to head to Cardiff. The city is under a suspiciously green dome. Came up from a weird crack in the city center." Surratt looked down at Mott. "You're not going to run? Because I could take you with us."

Mott shook his head. "I'm staying with them." He didn't look as freaked out about being held by Surratt as would have been expected, but he also looked ready to be let go.

Surratt gave him a narrowed-eyed look, then released him.

Caradoc held up his phone to Surratt and motioned for the others to do the same. "I already gave them both my gizmos, but let's lock the phones as well."

Harlie, Stella, and Dailten joined in and got their visually disappearing gizmos pinned on. Caradoc had restocked his supply quickly. There was no idea how to know how many they would need.

"No reason to wake Neasa, we'll lose her again when we take off," Dailten said as she peered inside the chopper. "Where are we going?"

Mott had been fussing with his pads but looked up. "Back to Avebury. We need to fix the feedback problem and shut down a rip without that happening. I feel more confident of doing that in Avebury now. The veil will still fall, but closing rips along the way will help us shut it for good."

Garran and Surrat went for Garran's car. "I'll be changing this vehicle out for something else as soon as I can. It's not good that our friends were warned to be looking for it. We'll be in touch."

They tore off before anyone could respond.

"If Cardiff is covered like London was, shouldn't we all be going?" Maeve's family had relocated to Bath, but that wasn't too far from Cardiff.

"We need to shut down the bigger problems. Not to mention, there would have been a good reason Satoshi reached out to Surratt," Bart said.

Harlie just nodded, but didn't explain why he'd recommended them.

"But why back to Avebury? Or, better yet, why couldn't

we have stayed there to do this test?" Aisling had felt like she was missing something since she came back from visiting the other side the first time. It was only getting worse.

"I didn't want to test it there because there had been too many openings. But I think once we get our feedback issues resolved that's where we need to be." Caradoc looked around. Still not a lot of people noticing them, but a helicopter sitting on two cop cars might draw attention. "We probably want to leave."

Stella flipped her flight headgear back in place and trotted to the helicopter.

Harlie gave Aisling a tight hug. "Stay safe, I can't get a solid feel on what it is…but something is going to happen."

Aisling tried to laugh, but his deep brown eyes were serious. "To me specifically?"

"Yes." He hugged her again, then started for the helicopter.

"How did you guys get that thing, anyway?" Bart asked.

Harlie gave a small smile. "You don't want to know. We'll find the best location and set this thing down away from it. See you in an hour or so." His dark eyes lingered on Aisling, but then he ducked into the helicopter.

Dailten nodded, then lifted, her broad gray wings easily taking her out of sight.

Reece came next to her as they got to Caradoc's car. "What was that about?"

Aisling rubbed her arms as a chill hit her. "I don't know. But something beyond everything we know about has him worried."

Reece gave her a hug. "I won't let anything happen to you."

She gave him a quick kiss. "Thank you." They got into Caradoc's car.

"Too bad we lost flying ability. We could catch them in

the air." Maeve hung onto the dash as Caradoc spun out and hit the road.

"Actually, this might be better." Mott looked up from his collection of pads. He'd even recruited Bart and Jones to each hold one up as he worked. "The information from your friend Tobias should take care of the feedback." He scowled. "I'd almost say it was deliberate, this feedback issue. Like someone knew what we were going to do and wanted us to be the weapon to destroy all the magic users."

"How could they?" Reece asked.

"How could they be doing anything?" Bart looked at the pad he was holding, then shrugged. "I understand veil tectonics better than most, and I'm not sure how the other side is doing what they're doing. Or even this side. Mutated rapeseed plants? Cities being held in stasis? I'm in over my head."

"And we have little time to figure it out, which I think was the plan." Caradoc went off-roading as one or two of the destroyed vehicles were still blocking the road. "We've been running after solutions this entire time. I think it's time we bring the problem to us."

"Why does that make me nervous?" When Aisling had been a kid, Caradoc often had plans. Ones that usually got her in trouble.

"It's nothing. But let's face it, Avebury is the crux. We get things sorted there and winning the battle will be easy."

Even Maeve gave him a dubious look at that.

CHAPTER THIRTY-SIX

———◆———

THE TRIP BACK to Avebury passed uneventfully. Everyone seemed lost in their own thoughts or projects. Or, in Aisling's case, trying to avoid thinking. Harlie wasn't the best at social niceties, but he'd been more worried than she'd ever seen him.

"Harlie was probably just worried about his little sister. He hid his feelings in research while you were lost, but he was frantic," Reece said.

She dropped her voice. "You still haven't had any future feelings?" Reece was a far weaker precog than Harlie, but there could be differences in how they worked.

He ran his hand through his hair. "Not a single one. That could also be an attack from the other side."

"You're a cheery pair." Maeve had been looking out the window, but looked back with a sigh. "But we're almost there, so hopefully we'll find some answers."

Harlie's number popped up on Aisling's phone without it even ringing. "Where are you?"

"We're near Silbury Hill. The hill is giving off odd readings, both externally and internally. Might as well drive in, there's no one walking the stones." He cut off without saying goodbye, which was hopeful.

Aisling looked around as they passed through the town. Few people were out and the ones that were seemed to be all heading into houses. Something was warning them. Aisling just hoped that it was on their side. They'd known this was where things would go down, but they still thought they had more time to plan and gather forces.

That felt like it wasn't going to happen.

They couldn't drive all the way through, but they got close enough to see Harlie and the rest. Neasa still wasn't under her glamor. Harlie hadn't said anything before, but Aisling thought maybe he'd dropped it when she passed out. Right now she was looking around the area, but wasn't hiding. She waved at Aisling and crew, but kept watching around them.

Aisling didn't blame her. The feeling of something coming was making the hair on her arms stand up. Something was wrong.

"This is the spot?" Bart looked at Silbury Hill and the nearby stones. "And what is that?" He pointed to an extremely tall rod that hadn't been visible until they were almost upon it.

"Along with whatever Mott has come up with, this should help us deal with the feedback when the veil rip is closed. Harlie, Dailten, Neasa, and I made it." Stella shook it for emphasis. The thing didn't budge and must have been extremely deep in the ground. "Neasa and Harlie, mostly."

"And it should help bring whoever we're looking for to us." Dailten grinned. Caradoc wasn't the only one who wanted to stop chasing.

"We still don't know who it is. How is that stick going to bring out people here who might be working toward destroying the veil?" Bart kept glancing back to it, but he was also keeping an eye on the open spots around them.

Neasa didn't stop her surveillance, but nodded. "I helped make it. Not only will it pull anyone associated with the other side here, but also from Isfyden who might have crossed over. The distance isn't strong, but it should work. I don't believe all the ghanloughs who attacked your city before went back or died. I also don't believe they were alone. Those mutated yellow flowers we found, for instance. On this side they cause problems, but from what I sensed, they could become horrific weapons on my side of the veil."

"Then it's not people on your side trying to destroy the veil?" Maeve asked.

Neasa shook her head. "No, there are many there, beyond the ghanlough, who want to take over this side. But they might not know of those flowers. I would say those were created by ones who won't be hurt by them. They were never strong, mostly castoffs from our world." She paused and looked sad. "When the other fey fled, they left us in shambles. Harlie, Stella, and Dailten have told me of what you were all told. That there was a deadly danger on my side and that everyone had to flee. The only dangers were the members of the High Council and the royals. They'd destroyed other races and the vallenians were gathering to fight them off."

"The vallenians did chase them off then," Aisling said. "The royals kept their myths close to the truth. Just forgot about the bit of the vallenians trying to stop them from killing others." It explained why vallenians, and the other Old Ones, were said to be dangerous killers.

"No offense, but from what I saw, your world wasn't very advanced. Was it that way when the rest of the fey left? I'm still not understanding why they fled; couldn't they have fought back against the vallenians?" Bart shrugged. "Not that I'd want them to have won."

"They saw a great future on this side of the veil. There was a chance for more magic here since the humans had never tapped it—and as far as we knew, couldn't. A seer from the former royal family saw power beyond imagining if they opened the veil and left. He was the one who led them to their deaths when they refused to follow his actions, and to the memory loss of your father."

Neasa had continued looking around as they spoke, but froze now. "There are beings here, who shouldn't be on this side." She started shaking. "Something's wrong. Have you heard of the xpenc? They were banished to Isfyden before your people came here. *No*." She dropped down and started rocking. "They've found me."

Aisling and the rest looked around, but there was no one coming for them. "Garran and Surratt said the xpenc had been involved in their kidnapping by the royals. But they didn't know anything about them. Why would they be after you?"

"No. Not me. Everyone. They will unleash the Biotáille olc, they will consume this world and then all the others." Neasa's eyes were wide and she stared ahead blankly. "They want your soul." The look she flashed Aisling's way was full of terror.

Harlie had stayed back, but he and Stella approached Neasa now. "How can they release the Biotáille olc?" He kept his voice low and Stella dropped down to put her arm around Neasa's shoulders.

"They will forge a new world of pain and violence. When the one who is forgotten takes up their power, and in vengeance destroy all—the Biotáille olc will be released."

"I guess that's easier than the rituals they tried." Aisling shrugged when Neasa looked to her. "Years ago, I had a run-in with people trying to bring forth the Biotáille olc via ancient rituals. It was horrific."

Neasa's look softened. "What happened?"

"I lost a close friend. But I stopped it." It was fifteen years ago, but still not what she ever wanted to face or think about again.

"But how do we know who's going to be their focus?" Reece stepped next to Aisling and took her hand.

She'd not told him what happened that solstice fifteen years ago, but she was grateful for his support.

"There's no way to know until they attack." Neasa didn't get up. "I need to go back to my people. *Now*. They must be warned."

Mott walked past her a few feet, toward the hill. "I'm not sure exactly how you got here, but I think I can get you home."

Harlie shook his head. "But if she's supposed to be here…"

"Maybe she was here to help with the pole and find this out," Caradoc said. "Having her people help from their side when the veil falls could be a major advantage."

Harlie reached down and helped Neasa to her feet. "Then you should go." He smiled and crossed his right wrist over his shoulder. "I will always be your friend."

She repeated the move and the words. "Thank you, all of you. My people will be ready when the final battle comes." She stood alongside Mott.

"We still can't see the rips well, although maybe you can. There's one right…there." Mott pointed to the side of Silbury Hill. Aisling couldn't see anything, but Neasa smiled and ran forward. Then she vanished.

"I hope we see her again and that she's okay." Aisling started to step back when the world folded out from under her feet and everything went black.

Aisling woke up expecting to be somewhere else. Beyond the veil or wherever Stella's aunt was, or in an alternative time. She was startled to see Reece, Maeve, her brothers, and the rest all clustered around her, looking exactly as she had before she passed out.

"What happened?" It looked like she had only been out a few moments, but she felt stiff and out of sorts as she tried to sit up. Like something had hit her hard. Reece helped steady her, but she stayed seated on the ground. Getting on her feet would take longer. "How long was I out?"

"You were only unconscious for a few minutes, but there was nothing around to indicate you were struck. We couldn't wake you." Harlie peered down at her closely. "How do you feel?"

"Everything hurts. And I have a massive headache." She let Reece finally help her to her feet and looked around. "Are you sure I was only out a short while? The ground is a lot more chewed up than I thought." The ground was slightly damp but did look like a lot of people had been moving around. A lot. Churned up grass stuck up in odd tufts.

"Looks the same to me," Maeve glanced around. "Maybe you didn't notice before. Pretty much Neasa went through the veil, you gave a meep, and collapsed. Nothing has happened since then."

Aisling stopped dusting the dirt off her legs. "I don't meep. I'm not even sure what that sound would be."

"I was watching you," Bart said. "Your eyes went wide as you stared where the rip in the veil is, then you made a meeping sound, and collapsed. Sorry, but that's what you did."

Aisling narrowed her eyes. She would have thought that she'd remember something. But she had just watched Neasa leave, then darkness. "Well, I have no idea what happened. Maybe something snuck through the tear? None of you felt anything?" She had figured that if they did, they would have said something. Still, it was disheartening that they all shook their heads.

Mott held his pads up. "It could have been something we didn't see coming through the rip. You have had the most adventures through it. You might be more susceptible."

"Now that that's taken care of, shall we close this rip?" Caradoc had his pad out.

"I thought we were going to see about calling some of the people from this side, who should be on that side, first?" Aisling's mind was still sluggish, but she was pretty sure that had been the plan. She pointed to the staff stuck in the ground. "Isn't that part of what that thing is for?"

There was a collective pause, then Bart nodded. "Ah, we changed direction when you were out. The staff will help deal with the aftereffects of closing the rip first. Then we'll call our enemies to us."

Aisling narrowed her eyes. Her head was a massive jumble of pain, but that made no sense. If they got their enemies to come to them, sending them back through the rip before they closed it would be more logical. But Mott was already starting to do whatever he was planning, so she'd have to trust them all on this.

She called up a spell that Harlie had taught her to push back an attacker, just in case the rip didn't close cleanly.

Mott and Caradoc both stepped closer to the base of the hill, their fingers flying as they entered whatever they were using to close the rip.

Without warning, the rip exploded open. Even Aisling could see the broken veil as the gap expanded to obscure Silbury Hill.

Dozens of ghanloughs, alari, logazins, and others came charging out as if they'd been waiting for that moment. Had they misjudged Neasa that badly? There were no dryads in the group, but the timing was suspicious. Had the dryad betrayed them?

Aisling's friends were quickly engaged in heavy fighting, and from the sounds of gunshots, ammo was quickly being used up. The veil flared and more beings could be seen running in slow motion to join the fight.

Red and black clouds boiled overhead, sending stinging rain and lightning strikes that didn't look in the least bit natural.

Aisling used her spell, but it only slowed the attackers

running her way. Her gun worked but she was quickly overwhelmed and couldn't reload. She was down to hand-to-hand fighting with one of the evil swamp goblins. He held an elaborate, but nasty looking dagger, but she managed to break the arm wielding it, then his neck.

She grabbed the unusual dagger and looked up just as a giant snapped Bart's neck.

Chapter Thirty-Seven

"NO!" AISLING YELLED and tried to reach her friends. But all of them were now too far away. Bart's body was tossed aside as the giant went for Jones and snapped him in half. No matter what magic she used, or how many attackers that she killed with her new dagger, Aisling couldn't get to her friends.

One by one they fell. Maeve and Reece were the last and Maeve yelled for help before she was stabbed through the chest by a massive pike.

Aisling screamed, but they were gone. All of them. She turned to the attackers and started killing even as she was sobbing. Magic, the dagger, she didn't care how she destroyed them. Her grief and rage were too much to deal with. This had been real. She *felt* her friends all die.

The attackers through the rip were slowing down, but appeared to be standing aside for something larger to pass. Aisling waited. Everyone on this side was now dead aside from her. She'd destroy whatever came through.

The creature was startling, but would have been more so if they hadn't run into the weird mutated Queen Bellaquora. Like that one, this monster was a familiar face combined with the partial body of the spider-like krilaze.

This time it was twice as large, appeared to have an elven top half, and a krilaze bottom. And was her mother.

"You have done well." The voice was definitely her

mother and the thing scuttled to her. "I am sorry two of my children died, but they weren't strong enough to rule. You are."

Aisling didn't respond until she mentioned Caradoc and Harlie. Then she lunged for the mutated creature. "They were a thousand times better than you!" She got a solid stab into the thing's shoulder before it flung her away.

"Not unexpected. But you will learn to love to rule. That is why the xpenc made us kill you all, the children of our pledge. Did you know that? We sold the souls of a generation to gain dominance over the new world by obtaining the spells from them that would make the humans weak. Only then to find out that *you* were to be the one to lead us to control so much more. The xpenc knew." She darted forward with lightning speed and skewered Aisling with her clawed foot in the same shoulder where Aisling had stabbed her. "I had you brought back to life for that and your powers. Nothing more."

"You're not even you anymore." Aisling kept low and had the dagger out as she circled around. She was fast, but the elf/ krilaze combination was faster than her.

"I'm better. The xpenc know ways to make us all better. Stronger. Better killers. The people taken from this world are already being transformed. Nothing can stop us." She darted forward again, but this time Aisling slapped her with a spell that sent her flying over Silbury Hill.

Aisling raced after her. Using her magic, and the odd dagger, she knocked her mother over and started stabbing.

It took her a moment to realize that she was no longer fighting back.

Aisling raised the dagger, it was dripping with blood, most of it green from the creature that had been her mother, but it needed more. There would be nothing to stand in her way—no one would block her from finishing this.

"Aisling! Stop!" Reece's voice was distant and faint.

Aisling shook her head. Reece was dead. She'd felt his loss before, and she felt it now. This time she'd seen it. She saw all of them die one by one, and there had been nothing she could do to save them. There was no one left that she cared about. No one she loved. She would follow power, make the world she wanted.

"Aisling!" Maeve this time. Her voice tinny, like it was coming from an old speaker far away. Red and black clouds grew heavier, and the lightning more frequent.

"This is what must happen!" There were piles of bodies around her, all the swamp goblins, ghanloughs, giants, and more were dead because of her. The bodies below them, her friends, brothers, and innocents, were all dead because of the woman on the ground before her. And the vile creatures who had pulled her strings. She would find the xpenc, and she would destroy them. Regardless of the cost. There was nothing left for her.

"Aisling! Come back to us! Stop this!" That was Caradoc and Harlie. Then many voices, some she recognized, others that she lost in the noise—all yelling the same words.

She paused. She'd watched them die. Unlike that image of before, where she and Bart had seen the aftereffects, this time she saw and *felt*, each one of them be killed. Nix had been the vilest person she'd ever known, but he was nothing compared to the xpenc. Her friends died in pain and terror and she'd been helpless to stop it.

"I will do this!" Still sobbing, she started to bring the dagger down for the final stroke. The thing before her wasn't her mother, not anymore. But it had led to the deaths of too many.

"Look up!" A chorus of voices shouted out from the dead around her.

The voices were fading more and soon they would be gone. Even though Aisling knew they were dead, hearing those voices one last time was important. She paused and looked up.

Where there had only been flame-filled clouds, a few small patches of blue sky appeared. The lightning strikes were fewer, and the burning rain vanished.

"The fight isn't over. If you kill her, you will let the Biotáille olc free to ravage even more than they already have. They are trying to use you." Reece sounded closer now, his voice strong.

Amazing what the heart could create when it was breaking. She looked away from the sky and started shaking. "You are dead. You're all dead. I saw you die. I'm doing this for you."

"What if you're wrong?" Maeve this time and her voice was also stronger.

"You could be doing what they want you to, sister mine." Caradoc's voice was so loud behind her that she jumped, expecting to see him standing there.

The thing before her took advantage of her distraction and lunged for her throat. Aisling lost her dagger as she fought to break the hands cutting off her air.

"Heal her." That was Harlie.

Aisling shook her head. She didn't want to heal this thing, she needed to kill it. Even if she was going mad and hearing the voices of her dead friends and brothers arguing with her.

"You need to." Stella and Dailten echoed each other and she felt a mental hug as well.

"No! It has to die! This thing killed you all!" She'd blocked the hands grabbing her throat, but she and it were matched for strength and rolled over the bodies of the dead as they each tried to gain the upper hand and kill the other.

"If you love me, heal her." Reece's voice was soft in her ears.

"Damn it! That's not fair! You can't use them against me." She sobbed as she fought back.

"Do you love me?" Little more than a whisper, but pure Reece.

Aisling shook. "Yes." She changed her tactics from trying to kill the being who wore the face of her mother, to healing. A brief flash of what this woman had caused almost had Aisling turn the healing around to hurting, but Reece's presence was too real in her mind.

The result was instantaneous and brutal. Her mother's injuries healed, but she screamed in pain as the healing destroyed the evil souls that had been inside her and the modification of the krilaze she'd been blended with. Her mother came back, but she was dying.

Her eyes narrowed and she looked like she wanted to kill Aisling, but had no strength left. "You were supposed to be the one. They said you would destroy this world and the next, and give us power beyond knowledge." She coughed. "They didn't know how much of your father's blood you carried. I failed." One more gasping cough, and she died.

Aisling rocked back as tears flowed harder. So much pain, suffering, and loss. And for what? There were no more mental calls from her lost friends, but a light normal rain started to fall. She looked up, the flame clouds were gone, replaced by heavy, dark rain clouds. The cleansing rain grew heavier and a wind picked up.

"What now?" She raised the ghau pendant and shouted into the air.

No answer from her lost friends or the vallenians, but the wind picked up. She got to her feet and let the rain wash over her. She could see the rip in the veil as it closed. Not that it mattered that much, no new creatures had come through in a while.

One by one the bodies of the swamp goblins, ghanlough, and the other invaders vanished. Including her mother. She wanted to bury her friends, or at least bid them farewell, but their bodies vanished also.

Aisling got ready to follow through the veil. Finding the xpenc on her own wouldn't be easy, but if they went to ground, it would be on the other side. She had Caradoc's gizmos and enough anger to fuel a hell of a lot of magic.

Then Reece appeared in front of her.

He was a ghost, or at least transparent, and he looked like crap. She would have thought if someone turned into a ghost, their injuries would fade. He looked like he'd been beaten regularly for days. But his smile was genuine.

"Don't go, you need to find us."

"You're dead. All of you. I *saw* it happen." She folded her arms. Arguing in a heavy rainstorm with her dead boyfriend wasn't on her agenda. But ghost or not, it was good to see him. It felt like he and the others had died years ago, not an hour or two. "I need to finish this. I saved this world, but not for me."

"They got in your head. We were captured, those were Xilen copies you saw die. We're trapped and injured, but all of us are very alive."

"Okay, for the sake of argument, how are you projecting yourself here if you're not dead?" She swung her hand through his waist. It went through easily. "And how did all of you yell at me?"

His laugh was definitely Reece's. "Your brother. Your communication device still works, so does his and our kidnappers never saw it. It won't last much longer, so you need to come get us now."

Aisling looked through him as the holes in the veil between the standing stones closed on themselves. The great henge of Avebury would look normal fairly quickly. They hadn't succeeded in shutting the veil for good, but once it was back to normal, it might be harder for her to track the xpenc. Crossing now would increase the chances of her reaching the xpenc and destroying them.

Then she returned her focus to Reece. If this wasn't a trick, and there was a chance that he and the others were alive, she had to take it. "How? How do I find you?"

"Caradoc says to use the Hyithalin nothaer tribusrt spell. Track Bart's ghau." He flickered. "The power is almost gone. I love you. Find us." He vanished.

Aisling turned her face back up to the rain. It felt like it was cleaning her of the past few hours. She found the dagger half buried in mud. What she wanted to do was throw the vile thing as far from her as she could. But something in the back of her head stopped her. She did know she didn't want it touching skin and she didn't have a sheath for it. She tore off the bottom of her shirt, wrapped the blade tightly, and stuck it in the top of her boot.

Then she lifted her ghau and cast the spell. She wasn't used to it, so it took a few more tries than she wanted to admit.

But then her ghau started tugging her out of the empty field.

The ghau seemed certain it knew where to go, but Aisling wasn't so sure. She also didn't think the pendant had the slightest idea that she needed to be able to travel on the ground, not just float over it like it did.

It first pulled toward a gift shop, an empty one since the fire rain had cleared out everyone in Avebury. Then it suddenly zigged to the left and down the road. At least the nice empty road was easier to go down than scrambling over walls and around buildings, aside from the giant-sized new potholes where the fire lightning had struck.

The ghau sent her down to a familiar neighborhood, the one with the missing people. She stopped outside of the street, ignoring the insistent tugging from the pendant. There wasn't a chance this was a coincidence. They hadn't found the people who had lived here, nor the ones missing from the commune. Her mother indicated they'd been taken beyond the veil. Were her friends now with them?

The ghau didn't like her interfering with the spell and practically dragged her down to the second to the last house. The one that not long ago had lost its doorway.

"This is interesting. Okay, pendant and spell, lead on." She stepped through the door and was slammed into another reality strong enough to drop her to her knees.

CHAPTER THIRTY-EIGHT

CONSIDERING THAT THEY'D checked out the entire house before leaving earlier and found nothing, this was startling.

She got to her feet and dusted off her knees. It looked like a medieval dungeon. She was pretty sure that nice people in Avebury didn't put those in their basements. It was also a hell of a lot bigger than the footprint of the house she'd entered. A portal of some kind, obviously. But no way to tell to where.

Torches lined the heavy stone walls, adding spooky ambiance, but not much light. Aisling hit the light on her phone and continued down the corridor. The ghau wasn't reacting anymore and the spell seemed to have vanished. It must have felt this was close enough.

Or this was a trap and both the ghau and the spell had been blocked by it. She paused to reload her gun, then slowly kept walking. The place was silent and all she could hear was the crackling of the flames from the torches. She shoved down the bolt of terror that this was a setup. That Reece and the others were really dead, no matter what she thought she'd felt from that image in the field. If that was true, she'd deal with it. But right now, she needed answers.

Massive walls of iron-barred cells lined the path as she turned a corner. The first ones were rusted and mostly empty. She looked away quickly when she noticed at least two had skeletons—neither looked small enough for elf or human.

Then she heard an argument. It was low, and at first, she thought it might be guards. She cut off her light and crept toward the cell with her gun drawn.

To find Caradoc and Mott sitting in the far corner of it, debating something.

She wanted to shout. Up until this moment a part of her didn't really believe they were alive. Her heart pounded in her throat as she watched them. There had to be guards here, somewhere, and she didn't want to attract them. She knocked on the bars tentatively. They weren't made of fey-killing pure iron, but a safer substitute.

"Aisling!" Caradoc jumped to his feet when he saw her and ran to the door. "Reece swore he could get to you, but I wasn't certain. You have to get us out. All of us."

"I can't believe you're here. I saw you die. But you're alive?" She kept her voice down even though Caradoc was talking normally. "As for getting you out, I'm not exactly sure how to do that. Where are the guards?"

"No guards for the past three days." He nodded. "Yup, another time dilation trick. We were taken five days ago, they even let us watch as the Xilen were made and sent out to be slaughtered." His blue eyes held tears that he kept back.

"That fight was a few hours ago. I watched you, *them*, die." She squashed down the terror and pain that came with that image.

"They were messing with your head. Remember when you passed out right after Neasa left? All of us were knocked out with a nasty spell, not just you. It was five days ago in reality, but just an hour or so for you. You were left behind and the Xilen were put in our places then they woke you up. Because they knew exactly the worst thing for you to go through—us being killed and you unable to save us. Near as I can guess, someone needed you to kill our mother violently."

Mott nodded from his corner. "But our guards have been gone and we need to rescue everyone. We need to get out." He wasn't panicking, not completely, but it was there at the edges.

"Who else is here?" She needed to know, but was terrified to ask.

"Everyone." Mott came closer but stayed behind Caradoc and flashed her a small smile. "I'm glad you survived."

"Thank you, I'm glad all of you survived." She stopped. "You *all* did survive, right?"

"Yes. We're all down here. Along with what sounds like most of the people from that block as well as some of the commune. No sign of Reg or his trolls, so I think they're still free."

"Some? What happened to the rest?"

"Harlie thinks they were taken to the other side and killed. But obviously he's just working on instincts."

"Aisling?" Reece called out from a few doors down.

Her breath stopped when she heard him. "Hold on you two, let me see him." She needed to figure out a spell that would unlock those doors, but she needed to see him first.

"Oh!" A ton of emotions slammed into her when she found his cell. As she'd seen when he sent his image to her, he was beaten up. Caradoc and Mott hadn't been, but they were less likely to physically fight back. Reece, Jones, Maeve, and Bart were their fighters. She stared at him, afraid to move closer.

"I told you we were alive." Reece was alone in his cell and came up to the iron grating. Aisling grabbed his fingers. The bars were too narrow for anything else. But she didn't want to let go. Tears flowed down her face. He was alive.

"I know…but I watched you die." She wiped away the tears with her free hand. "I promise not to keep saying that, but it was horrible." That was the understatement of the millennium. She'd thought that weird sideways alternate future jump where everyone had been destroyed had been traumatic. It was tiny compared to watching them be slaughtered.

"I know." He squeezed her fingers. "The beings who did this counted on your reaction to seeing us killed. They knew about the altered reality that you and Bart had seen. They needed you to kill in a mindless fury."

"Why did they beat you up though? I thought they knocked you all out?" His face was a mass of varying bruises, some older than others.

"Our fears of the High Council finding out about my unique talents were unwarranted. They already knew it was happening to many hybrids long before I was born, but had been keeping it secret. They were trying to get me to shift forms so they could figure out how to stop us. There are far more magic using fey-human breeds than thought. All have just been hidden."

"Damn. But you're okay? You'd tell me if you were really hurt, right?" She needed to get him, and the others, out of the cells. Aside from his bruises, he looked fine.

"I promise. Bruises, nothing broken. And I never changed form."

Aisling stared at his face. Beaten or not, it was a wonderful sight. "Now we need to get all of you out of here." She took a deep breath and looked around. The cells were ancient, but extremely solid looking.

"I have some ideas." Harlie called out from a few cell doors down.

There were a lot of cells down here, but there seemed to be no logic as to how people were put in. Some, like Reece, Jones, and Maeve were in solitary, others were with people from their group. Further down the long curving pathway, more voices could be heard. There were probably over a hundred villagers and people from the commune here.

Harlie was in a cell with Bart. "I think that you, me, and Caradoc can cast a spell and blast open all of the doors."

"How? Don't we need to be close to each other? You and Caradoc are pretty far apart, space wise." She watched Bart, but he hadn't moved beyond nodding her way and rubbing his head. "What's wrong with him?"

Harlie's face fell. "He fought hard and is just now coming around. They worked hard to get that ghau off him. Someone who took us was terrified of it." He watched Bart for a moment, then turned back. "We have to break out of these cells, but the spell between the three of us will be tricky. We'll use these bars to act as invigorators for the spell. Caradoc will anchor his end; I'll reach to the end of the cells with my mind and anchor this end. You stand in the middle." He smiled and nodded like that resolved it.

"And what? What spell? Why didn't you use magic to get out before? What do I need to do?" She kept from laughing, but an hour ago she wouldn't have thought she'd ever be getting exasperated about her far too smart older brothers. It was an amazing feeling and one she'd never take for granted again.

"I'm going to cast a gifhu spell of unbinding. One, point of fact, that Satoshi's grandmother, Kana, taught me over a thousand years ago. I couldn't use it before as it requires more than one person, and these cells are warded against magic from the inside. You being outside of them allows us to work through the spell on the doors. It is easier to share the spell directly than teach it to you. Place your head as close as possible to the bars."

She did and was rewarded with a flood of information about the spell, most of which flowed right through her and almost dropped her to her knees. But the important part, what she needed to do magically as the supporting tier, was clear and relatively simple. It was almost like a healing spell in the way it worked. The gifhu spell would unbind not the locks, but the hinges of every cell in this place.

"I got it, I think. Might be a good idea to warn everyone down here though, they need to stay away from their doors," Aisling said. Harlie was brilliant but didn't always include the person in the equation. Not all the doors would fall forward.

"I got that!" Caradoc yelled. A moment later his amplified voice echoed down the long corridor. The people who'd taken them took their weapons, blocked their magic, but there was no way to take away all of Caradoc's gadgets. "Everyone step away from the cell doors. Danger! Step away from the cell doors!"

Harlie closed his eyes, then nodded to Aisling.

She went to the opposite side and between Caradoc's and Harlie's cells. She had line of sight for both. Harlie started muttering the spell, Caradoc joined in, and then Aisling found herself saying the words. What had seemed like skimmed information of the spell flowed through her. There was an odd pressure, like waiting for something to adjust. Then a loud bang followed by the sound of dozens of heavy cell doors falling off their hinges.

Reece ran and grabbed her in a hug that lifted her a foot or two off her feet. Considering she was only a few inches shorter than him, it was impressive.

Not caring that including their friends and dozens of total strangers were around them, Reece lowered her and kissed her like he was never letting go.

The kiss was almost enough to push out the mental pain of watching his duplicate die.

Coughing behind them ended it, but they both pulled away slowly.

"I know you've been through a lot, but we still do have

a world to save." Caradoc and the rest surrounded them.

Aisling didn't say anything, just ran from person-to-person, hugging. Maeve looked at her mid-hug and wiped away a tear. "You look awful, love. Just saying." Which made Aisling hug her tighter.

"Great, everyone's out of their cells, but how do we get out of here?" Aisling asked as no exit suddenly presented itself.

Bart looked down both ends then back to her. "Thought you'd found a way down here?" He still looked pale, but more like himself. The lines on his neck showed where force had been tried against the ghau. The only good thing about their enemies working so hard to get it off was that they feared something it could do.

"No. I was following your ghau, when it led me to that house of Mott's in Avebury. As soon as I went through the front door, it dumped me here."

The Avebury villagers wandered around in confusion once their cell doors were blown free.

"Did they know anything about getting down here?" She lowered her voice.

"I don't know," Harlie said as he watched them mill about at either end. "They never spoke to us."

Stella shook her head. "They feel like they were spelled. Not just against magic, although there are a fair number of magic users in that group. But something more. I think they were locked in stasis spells."

"Nicer for them than being aware, but we're back to how do we get out?" Maeve asked.

"That's a very good question." Caradoc nodded and looked around. "I think I can rig a version of the spell we just did against one of the walls."

"And what if we're underground?" Bart waved around—definitely sounding like himself now. "We don't know if there's anything open around us. We could just let in tons of dirt."

Aisling watched as Bart's words trickled to some of the villagers. Fear crossed many faces. If Stella was right, they'd been in stasis this entire time and had no idea what happened or how long they'd been gone.

"Where are we?" An older satyr came forward. He had the distinguished bearing of a village leader, maybe even mayor.

"We're not sure," Bart said as he stepped forward and extended his hand. "I'm Bart, part of a US/UK task force. I'm afraid we're just as unsure as you, but we're working on getting everyone out."

The satyr shook his hand and motioned to the people around him. "I'm Lyxin, unofficial town mayor of Avebury. Thank you. If you need magic users, we have quite a few on our street. The commune also had many and I see some of their people here too."

"Thank you. Does anyone have a clue as to where this place is? Rumors? Thoughts?" Bart raised his voice to carry to most of the people. Once it had been determined that there weren't any exits at either end, most of them had returned to the center.

There were mumbles, but nothing that sounded like a real answer until a teenager came forward. They had so many clothes on, that it wasn't clear if they were male or female. They looked human, but there could be wings folded under the oversized jacket.

"It looks like the Tronxian Gambit." They looked around at everyone from under a mass of red hair. "The massively multiplayer online role-playing game? Visiting Under the Veil scenario?" The tone in their voice was exasperated at the blank faces around them.

Finally, Stella perked up. "Sorry, was thinking about something else. I love that game." She looked around, pursing her lips and squinting as she turned. "You're right. It does look disturbingly a lot like the dungeon from that stage of the game. Hard to notice that from inside a cell. They could have made this look like any dungeon, but they went for one from a popular game? Anyone else think that's weird?"

"Anyone else wonder how that helps us?" Jones shrugged. "Unless we're in the game right now, I'm not sure how knowing this place was modeled after it is going to help."

"*Could* we be inside a game?" Maeve looked around and shook her head.

"I think they just made it look like it. But if it's more than just looks, we should be able to hit the main goon block and it will let us out." Stella and the teenager echoed each other on the last line.

Stella darted around the center of the corridor. "The blocks will be here, somewhere. We find the pathway, defeat the goon, and we're out."

Caradoc turned to Bart. "*Now* are you okay with me blowing a hole in the wall?"

"No. The same reasoning stands. Although I'm not sure about this being modified after a game. Who does that?"

Mott had been watching Stella, the teen, and three more people marching around in huge strides, trying to trigger the steps they were looking for. Then his eyes got big. "The fey High Queen. She loves this game."

That stopped the searching for a moment as the players all started muttering about who might be the queen's persona.

"That does help. There has been research into using premade scenarios for spell enhancement. If she's a regular user, setting this up would take less magic than creating a new holding area." Stella stopped looking for the invisible blocks and instead pointed to the end then turned to Aisling. "That's where you came in?" At Aisling's nod, she whistled for the other four gamers. "We're probably dealing with a troll invasion scenario. Which means the secret entrance is where Aisling was dropped in."

The players, and a few others who just wanted to join in, or had been keeping their online game playing habits on the down-low, followed Stella as she jogged to the far end.

Dailten nodded and looked up into the completely lost ceiling. It was so high that nothing beyond a vague darkness could be seen. "Flyers, come with me. We need to see what's up there." She released her wings and a dozen flying fey joined her. Most had their lamps on their phones on, one or two, who appeared to be campers, had small flashlights. They were quickly only seen by the lights they carried as they spread out and flew in slow patterns in the darkness.

"Damn, using a game to trap people is twisted. Whatever the reason, we need to get out of here. The holes in the veil are still open," Maeve said.

"I know you were just coming through my tech, but you missed a damn good fight. After I killed everything that went after you, and helped my mother die without releasing the Biotáille olc, the rips started closing. At least the ones in Avebury."

"That's good, because we need to—" Harlie's words were cut off as an explosion came from the far end of the corridor.

Right where Stella and her gamers had been searching.

CHAPTER THIRTY-NINE

E VERYONE RAN OVER to pull away the rubble. Stella had gotten a spell shield up that kept her people from being squished. But it appeared to be slowly collapsing and was already pressing down on them.

"There's something messing with magic down here," Stella yelled as she fought to keep the spell up.

Aisling cast a spell to lift the rubble off the spell shield, but the spell felt heavier than it should. "Get them quickly!" She would be more impressed with her spell casting if it weren't that the ghau felt warm and was most likely lending support.

They pulled Stella and her people out just as Aisling's arms started shaking. It felt as if the weight of the rocks and stones was now coming full to her. She dropped them just as Caradoc got the last person clear.

Just in time for the ground to start rumbling.

If she were in L.A., she'd say it was a rolling earthquake, but the loud drumming sounds weren't earth driven.

"Get back! It's the trolls!" Stella looked shaken, but had her hands up to cast a spell.

Aisling stumbled back to them. She was used to trolls like Reg and Fieath. Even when she had lived in Alaska, most of the trolls only pretended to be less civilized than they were.

The three coming through the hole in the wall didn't look to be playing.

"Classic troll minions." Stella shook her head. "They're blocking the way out."

"I'm having a hard time with someone trapping us all in a version of a game." Aisling shook out her shoulders and loosened her arms. She doubted there would be any hand-to-hand, but better to be ready for it. She still had the swamp goblin dagger in her boot, but using that would be a last resort.

"It actually is sort of genius," Mott said. "The energy to create something like this from scratch would be massive. Much easier if it already exists and they ran an evergreen spell through it. They could have killed all of us at any time."

"Then why didn't they? Trust me, I can't tell you how glad I am that you're all alive. But why didn't they?" That was a thought Aisling had been trying to repress.

"They were keeping us until you let loose the Biotáille olc by violently killing our mother. We would have been the first victims. Because you tried to heal her instead, you broke that. Not a normal way of getting the Biotáille olc new bodies, but I think we can guess what their plans were." Harlie didn't seem the least concerned as the trolls slowly marched forward. Nor that he and the others had been intended to be fodder for evil spirits bent on taking over the world.

Aisling shook her head, she needed to find a way to channel her brother's calmness. Without having to spend a few hundred years in a cave in Nepal.

"I'll take the first round. That magic suppression in the cells left me needing to kick some ass magically." Caradoc flashed a grin to Aisling—he was definitely getting back into using magic. Before anyone could respond he sent a simple but powerful blast spell at all three trolls.

They exploded far too easily, but were quickly replaced.

"Isn't that cheating? Does she know what we're doing?" Maeve scowled at the trolls.

Stella shook her head. "Probably an automatic program. Like Mott said, simple and would keep us out of the way."

"Depending on how many fronts the royals are fighting, they might not realize that Aisling failed to do what they wanted yet," Reece added. Like Maeve and Jones, he had his guns out.

Aisling hadn't noticed they were all still armed until now, and had been ready to hand her own weapon to one of them. "They let you keep your guns?"

"They blocked them within the cells just like the magic. And our cell phones, but I checked—those are still blocked." Reece shrugged. "Trust me, I fired a dozen shots into that door. Came out as ghost bullets. Did nothing. But the gun feels normal now." He fired one shot at an approaching troll. It collapsed when his bullet struck it in the forehead.

The people from the block and the commune were still milling around behind them.

Bart turned to them. "If any of you are heavy magic users or fighters, come forward. The rest of you probably want to go as far back as possible."

Mott started to go back, but Jones blocked him.

Bart nodded. "Good grab. Not you, Mott. We need you, Stella, and the rest of the gamers for advice. We've killed four trolls and they're just being replaced. How do we stop this?"

A group of fey moved forward as the rest of the crowd went back. Aisling knew that they needed to figure out how to beat this with brains, not magic and bullets. Even with more magic users they would be too exhausted to fight if the trolls kept replicating. And there was no way to know if the rips in the veil were still active—the veil hadn't completely collapsed yet—and in here they had no way of knowing what was going on outside. Things could be falling apart outside while they were trapped.

"Normally, the troll invasion comes much faster. But it does look like there's a never-ending supply this time and that's not normal." Stella stayed near the front with her gamers and continued watching the trolls. "Ha! There, in the back. There's a replicating machine."

"A what?" Caradoc took down two more trolls, but turned back to her. "That's not a thing."

"Ahh, it is if you're creative and have a lot of magic." Harlie looked grim. "They're using death magic to power this entire thing. Probably other things as well." He lowered his voice. "I think we know what happened to the people who were taken but not locked up here."

"Damn it. Can we stop this thing? Can I blow it to hell?" Maeve looked like she really wished she had some explosives with her.

"I think we can. We'll need our flyers back though." Harlie was already doing calculations in his head, ones that showed themselves as he wrote in the air with his finger. They faded too fast for Aisling to read, but he kept nodding as he did more.

Stella turned and yelled at the ceiling. "Dailten, bring your people back down here!" At first such a loud voice coming from the tiny changeling was surprising. But owning a loud diner could account for that.

Dailten dropped out of the darkness with a look of disgust on her face as she and the other flyers swooped down. "Absolutely nothing up there. Aside from the fact that the ceiling looks like this might have once been a bomb shelter, so we're probably not in some odd realm." She looked to the trolls marching forward only to be shot or spelled, and then having new ones pop up. "That's fun. Troll simulacrum whack-a-mole?"

"That's what it looks like. The High Queen, or whoever is behind this, set things up, then just left them running.

Tells me they are thin on resources, which is good for us in the long run. But we'll run out of bullets and exhaust the magic users before they stop." Stella pulled Dailten over. "See through there? In the game, there's a notice on the wall just above that empty throne. You hit that and the game is over."

"You mean the escape will appear?" Aisling squinted around the troll heads. An old-fashioned scroll hung about twenty feet up the wall. Even with her elven eyesight, she couldn't make out the words on it though.

"Hopefully? I have no idea. But it's the best shot we have. Especially if Dailten didn't find anything of use up there."

"Nothing." Dailten held up her hands to the distant throne—that could barely be seen past the trolls slowly marching through the entrance. "How much force are those trolls using?"

Stella pointed to where a crumpled and broken elf body was up against the wall. A gamer had thought he could make it past the trolls. One of their clubs caught him and sent him flying. "What would be expected. Only take the flyers you think can handle it. If any of you miss, that's what will happen."

"Got it." Dailten turned to the other flyers, and motioned for two younger pixies, a male and female, to move back. "I'm sorry, but I won't be responsible for you two. You need to stay out of this."

The pair both looked ready to argue, even though they were both so slender that a strong breeze could snap them, until Dailten pointed to the dead fey against the wall.

"Understood." They both nodded and stepped away.

"Good. I'll need you both to keep people calm back there." She pointed toward the milling mass behind them. People weren't freaking out yet, but that could be the result of the stasis that they'd been in for the past few days. If they panicked and ran forward, too many would die before they could be stopped.

Aisling nodded as the trolls kept marching forward. "Okay, so what do we do, while the flyers try to dart in there?" The constant line of trolls meant that the stone arch was mostly always full. They'd have to time it exactly. To get past them the moment the trolls fell, and before the next ones appeared. They didn't seem to move fast unless they were filling the spots of the fallen—then they were exceedingly fast.

"We keep killing trolls," Caradoc said as he fired a spell and destroyed a pair of trolls. "The ones in the center, right under the arch, will give our flyers the most room. I think we all need to be ready to move forward and take the fight to the trolls as the flyers take off."

Bart nodded. "You'd make a good Area 42 agent. And I don't mean that in a bad way." He laughed as Caradoc looked offended.

"They couldn't afford me." Caradoc gave a haughty look, then broke it by grinning.

Dailten and another harpy charged the trolls as two more fell under the barrage of magic and bullets, but neither of them could clear it before the trolls were replaced. They pulled up at the last moment and circled back around.

Everyone who was fighting moved forward and the trolls were replaced faster. Dailten and her flyers managed to refrain from getting smashed, but they also couldn't get through.

"This is taking too long." Aisling had thought that the spell behind this, using parts of an online game, was almost funny. But it was designed to keep people trapped, eventually wearing them down—and no living guards were required. Sneaky and annoying.

"*Do you want to die?*" The voice in her head was soft, even though the words were shocking.

Aisling looked around frantically, but no one else had reacted to the words.

A vallenian appeared next to her, but unlike prior times, he looked more like a ghost. "*Do you want to die? You will. All of you will. You need to work with the ghau. Both of them. Your world will burn. You're out of time.*"

The ground shook with more than just the trolls, knocking her off her feet. By the time she recovered, the vallenian was gone.

"Damn it. Bart? We need to use the pendants." She cut through her friends to reach him.

"To do what?"

"Not sure, but one of our vallenian friends just reached out to me. They said we have to use the ghaus to end this. Whatever is happening outside isn't good." As she spoke, she pulled out her pendant. Looked normal to her. Then it shocked her hand. "Damn it! It bit me." Reece looked over at her yell, but she waved him off.

The rest of their friends continued to move forward slowly as the flyers kept trying to stay close enough to the walls of trolls to zip over when the trolls fell, but remain out of reach of their clubs.

It was hard to tell in the weak light, but her ghau now had added about three new lines and seemed to be crackling with light blue arcs bouncing around it. She looked over to see Bart holding his out by the chain. Probably a safer idea.

"Whatever is going on, these things are pissed. I feel like I need to charge those trolls with my bare hands." He shook his head. "Stop it, you possessed pendant."

Aisling hadn't put the feelings into words yet, but those fit. "Sounds odd, but I think that's what we do. Stick together, keep firing, but let's do it."

Bart turned and yelled. "Everyone fall back! Flyers be ready." He was almost as loud as Stella, and it worked. Everyone made a path.

Aisling felt her ghau shake and burn, but she didn't let it go. She had been planning on funneling a spell through it as they ran, but the ghau had its own ideas.

Bart ran alongside her, and both their ghaus acted like living beings. Pissed off living beings. They shot arcs of electricity at the trolls, knocking them down the instant they appeared. Aisling helped with a few spells as they ran, and Bart ran out of bullets.

He also yelled as he ran. She wasn't sure how that would help, but Aisling joined in.

Dailten and the flyers with her swooped in with everyone else charging behind.

The scroll they had to hit would have been better for the flyers, it was closer to thirty feet high, rather than twenty feet up, but swarms of bats came out to disrupt the flyers, pushing them back even if they made it past the trolls.

Aisling felt a pressure in her boot. That damn dagger. She hadn't been sure what to do with it, but this worked. She grabbed it, dropping the fabric covering it, then leaped in the air and threw it.

Her ghau and Bart's both reached out and gave the dagger a shove so that it not only hit the notice, it went through it, shattering the wall behind.

The world started shaking, the ceiling tumbling down around everyone, then everything vanished.

CHAPTER FORTY

THERE WAS A flash of nothingness. A bright light. Then they were all on the street.

And everyone who had been fighting the trolls found themselves still running or flying for a few moments. Most avoided running into anything, or at least didn't hit too hard.

"Are we really out? Or is this another trick?" The harpy flying with Dailten pulled a massive loop to avoid slamming into a house.

Bart dropped his ghau back into his shirt. "I think so. Aisling? Do you sense anything? See any of our friends?"

Her ghau had settled down, but its stunt left a nice burn mark in its exact shape on the palm of her hand. She glared at it, but then also dropped it into her shirt. "I don't sense anything, and not a single vallenian in sight or in my head. But that can't be good." She pointed up to where a massive collection of black, red, and orange clouds were forming a distance away. If anything, they looked more foreboding than the ones that had vanished when her mother and her minions disappeared.

"Is that where Silbury Hill is?" Reece asked as he came over to them.

"No, that would be that way." Mott also came over and pointed to the left, then to the right—directly under the clouds. "That's where what's left of the commune was."

As they watched, the clouds vanished.

"You all saw that, right?" Aisling didn't think it had been one of those possible future images the vallenians kept flinging at her, but there was no way to be certain.

Murmurs of agreement came from around her and a chill wind picked up.

"I did. We have to get the civilians out of here. It might be gone now, but it could come back." Maeve looked around and brought the satyr town leader over. "Things look better at the moment, but this world is still under attack. You need to take anyone who can't or won't fight somewhere safe." She looked over as a group was heading toward one of the houses. "Not in this area. Nor anywhere near the commune. Maybe get completely out of the area."

"I have a farm a few miles from here. I'll take any who want to leave. I'm too old to be much use in a fight anymore. But some of these people lost loved ones, and they will fight."

About half of the rescued people went with him, and they collected anyone who'd gone into the houses. The ones remaining were mostly commune folks, but there were town folks who wanted a chance to fight back as well.

Bart gathered them together. "You don't know us. And most of us aren't even British, but we're facing a full attack on this world from beyond the veil. One that's focused here, in Avebury. But if we fail here, the veil will collapse and there are some deadly things that will be coming through. We could all die. Last chance to leave." He folded his arms, watching with a carefully neutral face as people muttered among themselves.

But no one left.

"Okay. What we're going to do first is find a place to set up as a base camp. We need to get more organized as to how to stop this. Hopefully get some more people, but it might just be us. If we can properly close the rips in the veil, my friend here assures me it will close everywhere." He turned in Mott's direction. Mott's shrug wasn't much of a pep talk.

One older elf stepped forward. "I know not everyone has magic. I'm a weapons collector and can provide knives, daggers, swords, whatever you feel comfortable using." He very carefully avoided looking at the humans in the gathered group, but they were the ones who could be at a major disadvantage. They all nodded and followed him to a small yellow cottage along with a few fey.

"I'm still not completely sure what we're doing," Maeve kept her voice low as the rest of the crowd waited for those getting weapons to return.

"Not sure either." Mott gave a tight smile. "But Caradoc, Bart, and myself should be able to throw enough tech at the rips to stun them. Harlie, Stella, and Dailten, along with the mystics Harlie is talking to, will hit the rips from their level. The staff that we left near Silbury Hill will keep the veil rips close by." He glanced around with a frown. "Which might be a scary thing. Everyone else will have to defend us." His brows were drawn low and he seemed on the edge of a meltdown.

"It is scary. But we can shut it down. Shut the rips, close the veil, and save the world." Caradoc came to Mott's side. "You're the smartest person I know, we need you."

Mott just watched the people chatting among themselves, but he finally looked away and nodded. "Okay, but you take me with you afterwards if you move here. Deal?"

Caradoc laughed. "You got it."

The elf came out of the yellow house, leading a group armed with pointy weapons. Aisling almost felt bad about leaving that dagger behind. Except she had an impression that thing wasn't good for anyone. There were mythological weapons that could suck souls, and she had a bad feeling that thing had been one of them. Looking back, she realized that the swamp goblin who'd attacked her with it hadn't fought well at all. His sole purpose might have been for her to pick up and use the dagger. Damn it. And she fell for it.

"We need to be ready for anything. I wish there were more of us…" Bart shook his head. "I think the goons who grabbed me rattled something in my head." He pulled out his cell phone, hit a few keys that were too short to be a number, then relaxed when it was picked up.

"Narissa, thank the gods. We're gathering to defend Avebury—" He stopped as the other person started talking. "No, we're not dead. Damn, how many copies of us did those bastards make?" He quickly filled her in, then ended the call.

"Narissa and Tomas have found more former Area 42 agents, but they saw a bunch of us die in a fight in a small town right outside London. Not us, obviously. So, there might be more copies wandering around." He held up his hands as everyone started talking at once. "They're heading this way, but it will take about an hour. Their reinforcement will be damn helpful. The heavily armed and heavy magic using kind."

"It's already getting dark, and we do need to wait for more fighters. Is there a place we can use as a base camp near here?" Bart turned to the locals.

The elf who brought the weapons stepped forward. "There's the new town hall. Massive and mostly empty building on the edge of town. Has a storage building too, but as far as I know the storage place is locked."

The rest of the locals nodded, and a few more had joined. Either people who just found out, or some of the ones who left had second thoughts. She knew there was a damn good chance none of them would survive. But they were needed to keep the enemy away from the tech and magic folks so they could do what needed to be done.

———◆———

Bart turned as the elf led them down the road. "Has anyone been able to reach Reg?"

Stella had her phone out, but shook her head. "There's something blocking it. Even Caradoc's tech isn't going through." Her face said what her words didn't—they might not still be alive. They'd stayed at the commune even though there had been numerous attacks there. Grundog had been Stella's friend for a few decades, and Aisling knew by the set of Stella's face as she handed her phone to Caradoc, that she wouldn't rest until she knew what happened to Grundog and the rest of the Ckiong.

"We need to plan with what we have then. Narissa said they also have another group of sixty MI-6 agents enroute from London and were trying to reach another group in Glasgow. The problem is that, like Cardiff, more incidents are popping up worldwide. People are trying to defend where they are." He looked around. "We need a way to reach more fighters."

Harlie had been walking in the middle of the group, but quickly caught up. "Maybe Stella could contact her friends outside of London? Jili and Arthero? I don't recall a lot of what happened down there, but they were preparing for something big."

Jili and Arthero were a pair of prepper elves that Stella knew. They'd tried to help Harlie when he collapsed a few months ago, but found themselves overmatched. Still, they might be willing to come up and help the fight.

Stella snatched her phone back from Caradoc with a grin. "I have a feeling they have a nice sized group behind them too. The elven preppers are a unique group and have been waiting for something like this." She danced away from the walking group and was quickly explaining the situation to someone on the phone.

She came back as they approached two huge buildings. "They have a group already heading this way. They were staying behind to get as many people up here as possible but will be bringing about fifty magic users when they head up."

"They knew where to come? Good on them, but still kinda disturbing," Maeve said.

Mott looked giddy. "Elf preppers? I can't wait!" He looked around the fields. "Will the ones they already sent be here soon?" He hadn't been in the UK when Harlie had gone to them.

"Probably." Stella frowned at the buildings as they came closer. "How did we miss these? They're massive and not far from the road."

One of the locals turned around. "That was the plan when they were put in. The town council felt they didn't match the image of Avebury, so there's spells on them." He shook his head. "None of us voted for them to be installed, by the way."

Mott had been focusing on his pads as they walked but patted his pockets and looked up. "Would having the L.A. Area 42 command codes help? Maybe tap into their communications and get more agents? There have to be more here and in Europe than just two hundred." He held up a plastic card with a tiny chip in it. "I knew this might come in handy at some point."

Mott had stolen a copy of all Area 42 command codes and passwords right before the L.A. Area 42 building was ripped out of this world. He'd never said where he hid it.

Caradoc laughed. "You've had that thing with you all this time? I think you and I should be able to get in and send an alert." He looked toward Bart. "If that is acceptable?"

"Hells yes, break in. Many might not be able to get here in time, but some can."

Caradoc froze. "My car. If it survived that battle out near the hill, I want that thing back." He held up his hand before Bart could finish shaking his head. "You don't know when it will come in handy—especially if I can fix the flying portion."

"We can go with him, make sure he doesn't decide to wander off, right Jones?" Maeve smiled broadly.

Reece looked ready to help, but Aisling pulled on his arm. "You can drool over it when he gets it back here." Reece was a car junkie just like Caradoc. The temptation would be too strong to try and fuss with it where it currently was. Not to mention, she still almost felt sick to her stomach at the thought of Reece being out of sight.

Something she was going to have to deal with before the real fighting began.

Bart put the kibosh on getting Caradoc's car until they got everyone into the town hall building. He might not be a precog, but he looked nervous and kept watching the darkening sky as they walked.

The town hall was as expected. Not exciting, large, full of folding chairs and tables with a partially built stage at the far end. The town folks were set up in a corner to work on weapons training. Luckily, most who took the swords already knew how to use them. Apparently there was a large reenactment event not far out of town.

The warehouse, oddly built adjacent to the town hall, was massive and had no distinguishing features, nor any windows.

"What was this for?" Bart tugged on the door, but it wouldn't open.

"No idea. It was paid for by regional leaders. None of our own people were involved." The man who'd suggested coming over pulled on the doors as well and scowled. "I thought it would be empty, but not sure why it's locked if that's the case."

Reece started to go for the door, everyone always has to try something that's locked, but grabbed his head and stepped backwards. "Harlie?"

"I'm feeling it too. Get back, but it's all around here." Harlie had dropped to his knees along with half of the mystics he'd been working with. The rest of them looked ill. Stella wasn't holding her head but she kept blinking rapidly.

Aisling grabbed Reece and started pulling him away. "Those of you not affected, get the other mystics away. If you're feeling odd or have a sudden pain in your head, back off." There were a few humans in the group who were reacting, and there was a chance some of them were like Reece. There was something in that warehouse that was designed to hurt precogs or other mystics. Or at least make them stay away.

Aisling kept tugging on Reece until he finally stopped her about a hundred yards from the warehouse. That seemed to be the good point for them because all the precogs and mystics immediately looked better once they got there.

Bart followed them. "We have to find out what in the hell is in there. Obviously, Mott wasn't the only one to realize Avebury was a weakness in the veil. But whoever we're dealing with on this side was prepared. I need you folks to stay back or go into the town hall. If you start feeling bad when we blast that damn door open, you keep moving away until you feel okay again." He glared around the group, but settled on Reece. "You're in charge of them." With a sharp nod, Bart marched back to the warehouse.

Aisling finally let go of Reece's hand.

"I'll be fine." His crooked smile almost reached his eyes.

"I know…I just. Damn, now I know how you felt when I came back." She hadn't completely appreciated the pain Reece had felt at her month-long disappearance, until now.

"And I was only gone less than an hour to you." He gave her a soft smile.

"You were *dead*, that balances out the time difference." Aisling grabbed him and kissed him hard. Then rocked back. "Stay out of trouble."

"You too." He rubbed her arm.

Aisling followed Bart back to the others and the warehouse.

Caradoc and Mott were scanning the wide doors, the metal sides, and the ground close to the warehouse. Both kept nodding and muttering to each other, but neither looked happy.

"That's great you two, any clues?" Maeve had stayed with them. She had her gun in an unclasped holster and a borrowed short sword, she didn't trust that there was no danger around.

Probably a good assumption.

"I think so." Caradoc looked up, then pointed to two sections near the roof. "There's an odd weakness along the very top of the walls. The rest of this thing is made from extremely thick, highly treated galvanized steel. Won't know until we get in there, but I'd say at least five inches."

Mott nodded. "Or more. It is blocking most of our scans." His tilted grin accented the word, 'most.'

"Okay, so what isn't it blocking, and is it the warehouse or the contents?" Bart didn't say 'I told you so' to Caradoc about not getting his car yet, but clearly, whatever was going on was in Caradoc's area of expertise. Mott was brilliant, but didn't always work well in groups unless he had someone to direct him.

"It's not blocking the waves emitting from a ton of

alopoxilyn hyto. Probably a few tons based on the size of this building," Caradoc said.

"Wait, wasn't that the stuff those rapeseed plants were combined with? That was also in that weird fog that almost made Jones and I shoot each other? Why are we still standing here?" Maeve took another step back from the warehouse and looked strongly like she was debating dragging Caradoc away with her.

"The same chemical, but it might not be dangerous." Caradoc's weak smile showed that even he didn't believe himself. "To be fair, the chemical itself isn't dangerous. It's when it's combined with other elements. It acts like a booster."

"So, there could be a few tons of the rapeseed plants in there? Or that manufactured baois fog?" Bart shook his head as both Caradoc and Mott nodded. "Damn it. We need to find out what it is without letting whatever it is loose. Any ideas?"

"If I can get my car," Caradoc said, "I can use it to go in through the roof. The sides of this thing are coated so we can't get up them. But if I can get my car's aero component fixed, I might be able to get up on the thinner roof with a reverse kilon vac and get a sample."

"A reverse what? Do you have one of those in your car, too?" Maeve's eyebrows vanished into her hair.

"No, I'm designing it." Mott had pulled out two more computer pads from his pack, strung their holders around his neck, and was working between all three. "Just a few minutes or so, the parts should be easy to find once I figure them out. Oh, and I've set up a repeating pulse on all Area 42 frequencies. We can't see responses, but it has all the information in a general agency distress call." He grinned. "I used your name, Bart."

Bart started to say something, then shut his mouth and nodded.

"Might be easier to use the helicopter that I borrowed.

It's behind the gift shop. I'm not as affected as some of the mystics, so I checked on them." Stella had come from the town hall but waved to it. "Don't worry, they're all working on fencing practice and the magic users are working on spells. Dailten is watching them."

"That would probably work better. Not that having your car wouldn't be helpful, but what if you can't make it fly?" Maeve asked.

Caradoc looked ready to argue, then finally shrugged. "Agreed. We don't have much time. Get your chopper, Stella. Mott and I will put together the reverse kilon vac."

Stella looked far too giddy as she ran off. Jones looked to Bart and followed her when he nodded.

"Sorry, I don't want anyone going off alone if we can help it. So don't any of you get ideas." Bart glared equally around the group.

Aisling went back to Reece, Harlie, and the rest of the mystics as they watched from the edge of a lawn. She quickly filled them in.

Reece looked annoyed, most likely because he wasn't involved. Harlie looked concerned.

"Is Caradoc certain he can protect everyone from whatever is in there? I know he and Mott know their tech, but anything with alopoxilyn hyto added can be extremely deadly."

"You know Caradoc, he says he can. But I don't get the bit with the altered rapeseed. Which side made it? If it's deadly to beings from the other side of the veil like Neasa said, why would people working for them make it?" Aisling asked.

Reece shook his head. "Either a double cross, or it's been changed enough that the plant Neasa said was deadly to her people, isn't anymore."

"Or it's only deadly to some of the population on the other side of the veil, and not all. Our mother was working with a specific group, the xpenc. Maybe they found a way to protect their own?"

A loud popping sound rattled Aisling's brain. Everyone was shaking their heads and rubbing their ears. Everyone except the small white-haired changeling who now stood in front of them.

"Good to see you, dear. Thought you might be dead by now. Where's my niece?"

CHAPTER FORTY-ONE

"HELLO, I DON'T believe we've met. I'm Stella's Aunt Jilan." She held her hand out to Harlie. "You must be Harthinatle. I'm very glad that you're not dead, also." She grinned around at the entire group of mystics. "All of you. You could have been dead had things taken a different turn. And sadly, still could be. But you're not right now. Isn't that great?"

Aisling hadn't been certain of what to think of Stella's late aunt the first two times she met her, she was even less sure now. She thought she was on their side, but as she still didn't know how Jilan was alive, it was hard to tell whose side she was on.

"Now, just where did you come from?" Bart asked with a reassuring grin as he was the last to shake her hand.

"Interesting question, and good of you to ask it." Her smile dropped. "I didn't die ten years ago, although it appeared that I did. No body found, that's always a clue. But I was trapped in the Isfyden plane. I shouldn't have trusted the xpenc when they said they'd save me from the assassins sent to kill me in that damn Slovenian forest." The annoyance on her face completely resembled Stella.

"You're working with the xpenc?" Aisling thought she'd disliked them. "Is that how you got here?"

"No. They came to me, not in person, they couldn't cross over then. Still can't, technically, but they have enough minions now to not need that." She folded her arms and scowled. "Where was I again? Oh, they grabbed me ten years ago, dumped me in that wretched place—that they live in by the way. Never have seen them though. I got back here by following the trail your ghaus left when you came through the last time." She winked. "The vallenians might have had a thing or two to do with that. For which I'm grateful. Since I was from this world, and alive, I might have been helping the xpenc keep their plane viable." She frowned.

Aisling wasn't sure how to process that, but her concern was cut off at the sound of an approaching helicopter. Actually, a bunch of helicopters. At least fifteen, of different sizes. All of them following Stella's borrowed chopper.

Stella waved madly out the window, then led the helicopters to a field. Jones was in the front seat of her chopper but didn't wave. He did look slightly concerned.

"How did she find more?" Bart kept watching Jilan, but was shaking his head at Stella.

"Oh, she's tricky, my niece!" Jilan beamed proudly as she continued waving.

Stella came jogging over to them as the rest of the helicopters landed. "I found some of Bart's friends. They were all circling south of here and when I lifted, they spotted me. They're Area 42 folks and they said more are coming." She stopped in her tracks as she saw her aunt. "What are you? Do the rest of you see this?" She looked ready to pull in some magic and blast Jilan.

"It's me, lovey. Long story, not dead, trapped, and your two friends and their fancy gifts from the vallenians led me out. It really is me." Jilan had started to step forward, but stopped when she saw Stella curling her hand for a spell.

"How?" Stella released her spell, but still looked doubtful. "Come here. I can tell if you're really Aunt

Jilan, you know." She held out her arms for a hug, but it was more of a challenge than a gesture of kindness.

"I would hope so. That spell was one of the first things I taught you when I started training you." Jilan didn't hesitate as she stepped into Stella's embrace.

Stella hesitated, then hugged her harder. "Damn it, I've missed you. Things have gone in the shitter, just like you always said."

"I missed you, too. One time I wished I'd been wrong." Jilan kept one arm around Stella and turned back toward Bart and the others. "The groundwork for what we're currently facing started about fifteen years ago. It took me a few years to build up enough proof of it, which I stupidly sent to the High Council. I was attacked not long after that, and was saved by the xpenc—although I had no idea who they were." Her grin turned feral. "But I'm back now. The High Council and the royals better watch out."

The group from the helicopters approached slowly, scanning the mismatched group—who mostly didn't appear to be agents.

Bart stepped forward. "Thank you for answering our call. I'm Agent Barthlinio Churchill and we have a crisis."

Bart took the agents, at least fifty heavily armed people, off to one side to review the situation. From the frowns and nods that she saw, Aisling didn't think any of them were surprised.

Stella and Jilan turned back to Aisling and the rest after watching the agents. "We need to set up another landing area. Before they realized that I wasn't one of their agents, they told me more choppers are coming in. Rig fives they called them? Jones seemed impressed. We will need more room."

Reece whistled. "Damn, that's impressive. Rig fives are high-speed troop transports. They're massive helicopters and can carry up to fifty people." He turned to Jones. "Any clue as to how many or from where?"

"Once I gave my ident as an agent, they were more forthcoming." Jones shook his head at Stella. "There are thirty coming in from all over Europe. Each one is full and loaded with weapons. It looks like all the European Area 42 offices have been taken over or abandoned in the past week. She's right though, we need a much larger area for them to set down. The first ones should be here within ten minutes if their ETAs were on target."

"I can help with finding land." Jilan patted Stella's shoulder. "You need to go fly your machine." She glared at the warehouse. "There is something vile in there. We must stop it." With a nod, Jilan took Jones' arm and led him off.

Caradoc and Mott were still building something, but Caradoc had looked up when the helicopters came in. He came over to Aisling and Reece. Reece was being good and staying away from the warehouse. For now. Bart had the right idea of making Reece in charge of the mystics. He would risk his own life, but would think twice about risking the lives of others.

"Any time now? We're getting reinforcements, but we need whatever is in there taken care of before we leave," Reece raised his voice to be heard by Caradoc.

"I think we have a working prototype. Okay, not a prototype, we don't have time for that." Caradoc held up his pad. "I know you can't go near it, but this is it."

Aisling laughed. "It seriously looks like an old vacuum."

"It doesn't look that bad." Caradoc tilted the weird item toward him. "Whatever. It'll do the trick, and let us sample what's inside, without letting anything out. But I need someone else to help me use it up there."

Reece started to speak but both Aisling and Caradoc cut him off.

"Not you."

"Whatever is in there could really mess you up, then what would happen?" Aisling was trying not to worry too much, but it was pointless. "I'll do it. Besides, elven reflexes are faster."

Caradoc and Mott brought the odd thing to the helicopter as Stella took the pilot seat.

"I'm going too." Mott sounded defiant as he looked around. "Boss, pilot, muscle, and ground support. I'll be the brains in the back."

Caradoc shrugged, then handed his computer pad to Mott, and waved for him to get in first.

Aisling shook her head at being called muscle, but he wasn't far off. Reece gave her a kiss, then she climbed in next to Mott. Caradoc shut them in as he got into the passenger seat.

Stella's grin was a bit too manic for Aisling's liking as they lifted.

"Oh! The first Rig five is here!" Mott twisted around next to her, trying to get a better look. There were three, the other two were further back. At their size they were noticeable even at a distance. "Can we check them out when we're done?" He yelled to Caradoc.

"After we save the world?" Aisling responded first.

"Of course!" Mott looked far more confident of that happening than she felt.

If Caradoc heard him, he didn't respond as he was motioning to Stella where to hover. Mott held up a pad to Aisling. It was a scan of the warehouse. The roof was significantly thinner than the walls. Caradoc took the reverse kilon vac and leaned out as they got lower. The helicopter was too heavy to land on the roof, but Stella was doing well at keeping it steady and as close as she could get.

"Aisling, grab the end!"

Aisling leaned forward and stabilized the reverse kilon vac. They all had Caradoc's masks on—improved—but she still wasn't happy about the chances of whatever they were checking getting out.

Caradoc hit a few toggles and the front end of his toy extended a long snout to the roof. The front end of the machine cut, and sealed, a small hole. Caradoc counted out loud to twenty, then hit a few more toggles and retracted the end. The hole in the roof was left sealed.

"Boss! We've got readings! That thing is filled with rapeseed plants that have been coated with anti-magic!" Mott yelled as Stella tried to pull away. The helicopter shot straight up instead.

Helicopters weren't magic powered, but like most things, they had a few magic components. And they were all dead.

"Hang on!" Stella yelled as she fought with the controls.

"Damn it! We shouldn't be affected, it's sealed!" Caradoc yelled as he hung on the capsule that was the basis of the machine and contained the samples.

"Unfortunately, this chopper doesn't agree!" The helicopter stopped going up, then went drastically down. "I'm going to suggest that all helicopters have mundane redundancies. I can't even figure out what's going on." Stella pulled hard to get the steep decline to stop. It did slow down, but the helicopter was still out of control.

Aisling's phone rang.

"What's going on up there? The Rig fives are asking if they need to shoot you down." Bart was yelling, but it was only because the phone went through her headset that she heard him.

"We're out of control. That stuff in the warehouse is anti-magic modified rapeseed plants. All the magic elements in this thing are fried. Can the mystics do anything? The flyers? Someone?" They were too high to safely abandon the chopper. And low enough to become a menace to a lot of buildings.

"Aisling?" It was Harlie's voice now. "Dailten and some

flyers are trying to stay under you, we're going to try and catch you."

"What?!"

"Just tell everyone to hang on!"

Aisling did that, forcibly taking Mott's computer pads away from him. She had no idea how in the hell a bunch of mystics and flyers were going to catch an out-of-control helicopter, but they didn't have many options.

"When I say cut, tell Stella to kill the engines." Aisling repeated it, but she could almost feel the disbelief from the others around her.

"What? We'll drop!" Stella stopped yelling as Dailten rose next to her side of the helicopter and gave a thumbs up. "You'd better not drop us!"

Aisling doubted Dailten could hear her, but she flashed a smile and dropped down again.

"Cut!" Harlie yelled and Aisling echoed.

Stella cut the engines and the blades went still. Mott started praying to something. Caradoc started swearing, and Aisling just held on.

They dropped, then there was a jolt, like something shook the helicopter as if it were a toy. Then they dropped again. Each drop brought them further down, with the catches in-between being rough. But at least they hadn't gone splat. Yet.

CHAPTER FORTY-TWO

THE LANDING ITSELF was more of a controlled crash than an actual landing. The flyers could only stay under them for so long and the mystics didn't have as much control as they'd hoped. The landing skids both snapped, and the helicopter lurched over to the left even though Stella kept trying to control it until the end.

The helicopter started shaking again and Aisling was afraid it was going to blow up. Then the door next to Stella opened, Dailten peered in, and pulled Stella out. It took longer to get Aisling and Mott out, but by then Caradoc was helping as well. Mott had reclaimed his computer pads and had to be dragged out with them.

They were in a field, one that had a number of much larger helicopters on it in the distance, and a bunch of heavily armed agents running toward them.

Bart and the rest of their people were racing out to them as well, but were still a distance away. The agents would get to them first. Aisling wasn't looking forward to explaining what they'd been doing to a bunch of freaked out Area 42 people until he got there.

She threw her shoulders back and stepped forward. Caradoc was behind her, but she needed him and whatever he'd collected to stay out of sight.

Dailten and another harpy came up behind her.

"Just for support," Dailten said as she turned to Mott and Caradoc. "You two should stay back."

Stella joined Aisling and the harpies as they marched out to the agents.

"What's going on? We almost shot that thing down." The leader was a gridgen, a race of small fey who used to control the mines. He sounded like he was from Switzerland, but his accent was soft. He managed to glare down at Aisling, Stella, Dailten, and the other Harpy, although even Stella was taller than him.

"Our helicopter had technical difficulties. But we're fine. Thanks for asking. I take it you're all Area 42?" Aisling mentally held a few spells at the ready, but she wasn't expecting all the agents to raise their guns at her words.

Dailten stalked forward, her wings slightly extended. "Seriously? You were coming here to join a group trying to save this world—did ya think we didn't know who and what you are?"

"Where are the agents? Who sent out the call?" The gridgen ignored them and looked around.

Aisling would have been insulted that he didn't think that she or her friends looked like Area 42 people, but she then decided that wasn't a bad thing. Her view of Area 42 had crumbled in the past few months.

"Right here!" Bart yelled as he, Reece, Jones, and Maeve ran up. Bart was panting heavily, but he made it. "Lower your weapons!" He held up his badge. "International Internal Affairs, Agent Barthlinio Churchill. Stand down."

Jones and Reece also flashed their badges. Maeve didn't show her MI-6 badge, but jogged over to Caradoc and Mott. She kept her hand on her gun and was watching the clump of agents.

The leader narrowed his eyes as he looked at the badges, then motioned for the others to lower their weapons. "Thank you. It's been a rough week. These are all yours?

Gotta say, I've never seen a controlled landing quite like that."

Stella did a curtsy. "Thank you."

"He didn't say it was good." Dailten shrugged.

"We don't have a lot of time. There's going to be a massive opening of the veil here, hopefully not for a few days, but we can't count on it. The veil is going to let some vile creatures through and if we don't hold them here, until my mystics and tech-heads can shut things down for good, this world will fall." Bart looked up as two more of the massive Rig five helicopters came in. "We're going to have to brief folks as they come in, but right now go with my people and agents Larkin and Jones will fill you in."

He motioned to the new copters. "I'll greet them."

Aisling walked back with the Area 42 people, but stayed off to the side with Mott, Caradoc, and Maeve. The agents were probably all legit, but more than a few shot questioning glances at the container Caradoc carried and Mott's collection of computer pads.

They let Reece and Jones and their collection of Area 42 agents drift slowly ahead.

"So, what did you find? Something we can use, I hope?" Maeve had removed her hand from her gun, but like Aisling, she was still watching the agents ahead of them.

Caradoc shook his head. "The plants we were worried about are in there. A hell of a lot of them. I don't see how that can help us though. We didn't pick up on any explosives, but there could be a reason the roof is so much thinner than the sides."

Aisling swore as the implication hit her. "And it's tall enough to act as a funnel. That plant dust would cover everything for a few hundred miles if there was enough force behind it."

"But wouldn't that hurt whoever set it up as much

as our side? It kills magic, right?" Maeve asked as they slowed down more.

"It depends." Mott had appeared to have been lost in his own world but clearly had been listening. "These could have been even more modified than before—or whoever set this up already had a way to protect their own. What would happen if there's a fight in this area, and all magic users on this side are disabled?" He shook his head and drifted back to his pads.

That was horrifying. Yes, they had weapons, but the majority of Old Ones from the other side were magic users. Removing magical abilities from the people on this side could allow the invaders to bowl right over the defense. Aisling's side needed to engage the attackers long enough that Caradoc and Harlie could both get their jobs done.

"Now, don't everyone freak out." Caradoc patted his canister. "We've got more details to get out of this stuff, and I'm sure we can find a way to turn it around."

Aisling happened to glance over at him as he spoke. He'd be more believable if his smile actually made it to his eyes.

The group went silent as they approached Avebury's town hall and everyone was lost in their own thoughts. Reece nodded to Aisling and the others as he led the new Area 42 agents to the others who were already forming groups, many were setting up tents. The town hall was a good staging area, but there were already too many people to stay inside once night fell. A small unit of them had gathered off to the side, and Aisling spotted Narissa. The winged flyer was still in a functional business suit as she looked around. She smiled when Aisling came over to her.

"Good to see you, Aisling. I was beginning to wonder if this was the right place." Narissa shook her hand and watched the new people coming in. "How did you reach the European agents?"

Aisling shrugged, even now there were things most people didn't need to know. Mott's secret access to the inner workings of Area 42 technology was one of them. "Not completely sure. The brainiacs worked with Bart and pulled it off. There is another group of Rig fives coming in soon."

Narissa watched the tent set up, then turned back. "What exactly are we fighting? No one has read us in, by the way."

"Sorry, we had a helicopter issue." As quickly as she could, Aisling filled Narissa in on the plan—and the stakes.

Narissa's eyes went wide. "Avebury is going to be the make-or-break place? We've had a lot of doomsday scenarios, but I have to say that Avebury wasn't at the center of any of them."

"We only knew because of Mott." Aisling hooked her thumb to where Mott and Caradoc were busy arguing over something on one of the pads. "He's got a brain that most of us can't understand. But it looks like he was right about the location." She noticed Joli and Arthero and about forty or so fey, setting up their own camp near the town hall. "Other groups predicted it as well, it appears."

Stella nodded to Aisling and ran to greet them.

"We fight to protect the mystics and tech folks, so they can close the veil entirely. I won't lie, we have no idea how many will be against us. There could be way more beings coming through the rips in the veil, and possibly ones already on this side, than we can handle."

Narissa slowly nodded and watched as more Rig fives landed. "Any more that you've reached?"

"We have a group of Ckiong who were last seen not far from here, but we haven't been able to contact them." Aisling was hoping Reg and the others were just cut off, but fine. She was also hoping that Neasa had been able to rally people on her side of the veil. "There's a chance more will trickle in during the night. But we might be it."

"Thank you for being blunt. Tobias went to recruit some more agents he'd heard about, but we've lost contact with him." The look on Narissa's face said she figured he wasn't coming back.

"We're sure there have been people working on this side of the veil for the other side for a while. Including the High King and Queen and High Council."

"Damn." Narissa shook her head. "Tobias thought they were somehow involved. But couldn't prove it. That might have gotten him killed. Do we have a clue what they're doing or why? They already held a lot of power."

"We think there's someone manipulating them from the other side." Aisling told her about her mother and the mysterious xpenc.

"I knew who your mother was. She spent a lot of time in London. Can't say I've heard of xpenc before." She narrowed her eyes. "Unless you mean Xi Paulians? Old children's story of monstrous beasts who were sent far away when they lost a fight with the vallenians. Long before we crossed here. But they all died."

"Probably the same, but I'd guess they didn't die. They have been prisoners in the Isfyden plane."

"We're dealing with myths and stories, possibly the end of the world, and less than a thousand people to fight back." Narissa looked around. "So be it. I'll inform my team and go speak to the other agents. Good luck."

"You too."

Aisling looked for Reece, but he and Jones were still explaining the hell that was about to happen to another group of Area 42 agents. Bart must have stayed at the field and just sent new agents over as they landed. She knew Area 42 had fallen apart in a spectacular way, but to be fair, the entire world had been under attack and no one had known. Except for Stella's aunt.

Aisling had planned to see what Caradoc, Mott, and now Harlie, Stella, and a few other mystics were so focused on, but she now wanted to find Jilan.

She walked around the edges of the staging and tent areas. There was no idea how long they had before the first wave hit, but they all needed places to rest and train tonight. No sign of Jilan. Aisling found her further out by the standing stones.

And she was talking to one of the stones quietly.

Aisling slowed down but continued to approach. It could just be an odd eccentricity, or Jilan might not be who they thought.

Jilan's voice sounded so much like Stella's when she laughed, that Aisling really hoped she was Stella's aunt, and was on their side. An image appeared in front of the standing stone, as Aisling moved closer.

The High Queen of the fey.

CHAPTER FORTY-THREE

"AND WHO DO we have here?" The high queen's voice was so confident that Aisling figured she knew damn well who Aisling was.

Jilan turned to face her, but where she'd been laughing a moment ago, her face was now still and emotionless. If Aisling hadn't heard her, she would have said Jilan was in a trance.

Aisling ignored Jilan and focused on the High Queen. "Why are you doing this? What possible benefit could you gain by causing the veil to fall and destroy this world?"

"Why did you kill your mother?" The image wavered and Aisling realized that it wasn't mystical, but rather a hologram that had its emitter at the base of the standing stone. Most likely the royals were hiding in a bunker somewhere.

"That thing wasn't my mother. But I killed it to keep whatever you're doing from happening." Aisling felt her pendant grow warm and an almost irrational urge to kill the person behind the hologram rose in her. Then she recalled who was responsible for her going through that hell of watching all her friends being murdered. It wasn't an irrational urge at all.

Aisling turned to Jilan, but she stood still, vacant eyes looking out over the stones. "What did you do to her?

Why won't you fight your own battles? Setting up a game scenario to keep everyone trapped? How'd that work out for you? Trying to get me to release the Biotáille olc into this world through my mother? Failure. Now taking over Jilan? If you wanted me to come here, you should have picked someone else. I barely know her." Aisling folded her arms and calmed her rising anger. Anger seemed to help her magic. But it could also make her miss things.

"If you must know, I was aiming for her niece. She has more abilities than we knew, and the xpenc wanted her. But I'm sure taking you will work just as well."

Aisling took one step backwards, but the hologram grabbed her hand and a glow came from the stone. But if they had a way to pull someone through the rock to them, they could come back the other way too. Aisling switched the hold on the queen's hand so that she had control and jerked the image forward. She was almost as startled as the High Queen when both she and the High King tumbled through the stone and landed at her feet.

Jilan gave a sigh, then folded to the ground. Most likely because the spell holding her was broken.

Aisling had never seen the royals in person, but she'd seen enough images to know they were currently in bad shape. Both looked gaunt and sick. They stumbled backwards, but couldn't go back through the stone, as her pendant became visible.

"You're working with the *vallenians*." The king spat out as he crawled behind his queen. It was good to know that their loyalty to each other was as strong as the loyalty they had to their people. They might have been together for a few thousand years, but they were each in it for themselves.

Aisling held the pendant high. It honestly felt like it was purring. "Not really, but they gave me some gifts. And this one doesn't like either of you for some reason." She wasn't sure what all the ghau could do, or was planning on doing, but it really was pulling toward the royals.

The queen was clearly the stronger of the two, and she got up a shield around both with a flat smile.

Damn it. Too bad Caradoc hadn't been able to get his car back yet. The shatil bag—that happened to have the royal family box in it—was in her backpack. Which was in his car. If the destruction of the other two family boxes were any indication, if she could destroy the royal box, the king and queen would die. She had no idea who was next in line for the throne, and she didn't care, as long as they weren't on the same side as these two.

The ghau started bouncing in her hand, then leaped to the other hand where it had left the burn earlier. It wanted her to do something. She just wasn't sure what.

Jilan was still on the ground but conscious and rubbing the side of her head as she sat up and glared at the king and queen. "You two need to die. Preferably painfully and slowly. But, since my young friend here doesn't seem to be patient, I think we'll just go for fast." She turned to Aisling. "They are responsible for letting the xpenc gain a foothold here. The shatil bag has their box, yes?" She grinned when Aisling stepped back warily. "It *was* my bag; we still talk sometimes." She turned to the king and queen. "Yes, I think it needs to be here. Now." Jilan muttered the spell so fast that Aisling only caught a few words. Then the black shatil bag dropped at her feet.

"I could call it to me because we're friends. But only you can do what needs to be done with what's inside. Well, you and your necklace there." She handed the shatil bag to Aisling.

The king was still partially behind the queen, but both looked confused. To be fair, even though she didn't look healthy, the magic coming from the queen for her shield was impressive. And they appeared to be trying to figure out what a bag could do to them.

Aisling opened the bag, checking to make sure she had the right box. The Lazing were still on their side from what they could tell. She didn't want to destroy the wrong box and risk that.

"Let us go back through the stone. You can't break my shield, not before the heavens open and you all die. If you let us go, I will protect you." The queen was trying to weave a comforting tone to her voice—but her spell would have to be a hell of a lot stronger to convince Aisling not to destroy them.

Aisling snorted and pulled out the royal family box. "Ya know? I don't think so. You two were involved in the death of my father's family. You led the fey through to this world, for no reason other than greed, not caring how you destroyed the ones left on the other side. You and my mother set up the sterilization spell on the humans. All backed up by your friends, the xpenc. Your reign of terror ends now." She kept the ghau in her hand with the burn mark and focused on destroying the wooden box.

"No! You can't, we'll do anything!" The king yelled as the box caught fire.

"You should have thought of that a few thousand years ago." Aisling focused on the box and it fell to splinters at her feet.

For a moment, nothing happened. Then the ground under the king and queen collapsed, and the standing stone they'd been at fell on top of them.

Jilan stepped forward and held out her hand over the stone with her eyes closed. Then she opened them and smiled. "Not sure how the vallenians did it, but they're dead. Thank you for saving me."

Aisling held up the bag. "Can you put it back? It's got one more box in it. I don't think we want to risk damaging that one."

Jilan took the bag and nodded, said a few words, then it vanished. "Back where it was. I'm glad it came in handy."

They marched back to where their forces were gathering. In the small town they looked like a serious force to be reckoned with. But the reality was that they had a roughly a thousand people facing a possibly massive invasion twenty times their size.

Caradoc ran up to them. "There you both are. We've had some developments."

Aisling started to tell him about the king and queen, then closed her mouth. She'd tell him if they survived this. If they didn't, it didn't matter. "What happened?"

"We found explosives around the sides and base of the warehouse. They were heavily masked with spells and buried deep. And put in when the thing was built. They're also controlled by someone remotely." He took a deep breath. "I don't know if I can shut it down." That was a hard thing for him to admit.

"Can you tell when they're supposed to go off?" Jilan hadn't paid much attention to the warehouse as they walked, but she was back to glaring at it now.

"No. They have redundancies around redundancies. It would take days to figure out how to override it. We don't have the time. Mott's scans are showing three large areas of veil weaknesses—all surrounding the henge stones. We probably have about twelve hours before the rips open." His eyes were haunted as he looked at the warehouse. "I think we can guess when that thing will explode."

Jilan rubbed her hands together. "I have plenty of magic, but it wouldn't be helpful in a fight. But this warehouse issue might be something I can do." She looked to Aisling. "You believe me when I say that I wasn't there of my own will?" She stood tall with her chin up, she honestly needed to know.

Aisling smiled. "I do. If you can stop that from exploding, please do so. There's enough anti-magic and potentially poisonous material in there to wipe out a few miles around us."

Jilan pointed to Mott. "He's the one with the information?" At both of their nods, she scurried over.

"She wasn't where of her own will?" Caradoc watched Jilan and Mott for a moment, then turned back to Aisling.

So much for not telling him. Aisling quickly summarized the visit with the royals as they walked to join the mass of people picking up supplies and dinner.

"Wait," Caradoc stopped and grabbed her arm. "You killed the…*them*?" There were too many people around and even a whisper could be picked up by some fey.

"Well, technically, I destroyed their box. I have a feeling the xpenc might have helped them get here and rule things, but the vallenians control those family boxes. They were who actually killed *them*. If we survive, we should probably bury ours in ten feet of cement to protect it."

Caradoc started walking again. "Or when we close the veil completely, the vallenians might not be able to influence anything anymore. You might even lose your pendant."

People were getting food then either going to their tents or into the town hall. Most of the strategy planning was done. In the morning the teams would take their positions around the henge.

Aisling smiled and patted it. As annoying as it was, it had saved her ass again. She might miss it when it left.

CHAPTER FORTY-FOUR

THE EVENING PASSED quickly as food, supplies, and weapons were spread around and more troops came in. They now had closer to fifteen hundred fighters and magic users, but against what could be thousands of assorted monsters coming through those rips when they opened, they would still be outmatched.

Bart continued to remind people that their goal was to keep the tide of invaders back long enough for Harlie, with his mystics, and Caradoc and Mott to shut down the veil for good. A lot of speculation was made on whether it would work, and even if it did, what would happen to the Old Ones on this side.

Bart ignored all of those.

Aisling and Reece took a tent near the town hall after Caradoc brought his car back and they could get their luggage. Not terribly romantic, since Maeve, Caradoc, and Mott ended up having to join them. Eighty MI-6 and Closen agents arrived via a pair of buses and space was needed. More were expected throughout the night.

Mott fell asleep clutching one of his computer pads. For someone who insisted he didn't sleep much, he dropped off damn fast.

The tent wasn't huge, but there was enough room for them to spread out. Maeve and Caradoc cuddled together murmuring to each other. Aisling and Reece did the same.

She couldn't think about tomorrow. She and Reece, along with all the others out there, were basically cannon fodder to protect the ones trying to close the veil.

"We'll be okay. I know it." Reece smiled and gently touched the side of her face.

"You sensed something?"

His smile dimmed. "Not officially. But we have to be. We have something good. We deserve a chance to see it through without disasters all around us. I love you." He held her tight.

"I love you too." Aisling embraced him tightly as well. She hoped his view was right and that the growing pit of terror in her gut was wrong. With her face buried against his shoulder, she finally fell asleep.

A bullhorn and what sounded like the clanging of a hundred pans jolted Aisling awake. Reece was up and had a gun in his hand and pointed to the entrance of the tent immediately.

Then the words from the bullhorn became clearer. "Rips forming in the henge, gather in your squads. Grab food, ammo, and head to your assigned stations." It was Bart's voice, but repeated itself so specifically, that it must have been a recorded spell.

From the rushing of feet outside the tent, it was effective.

Mott sprung out of bed and ran out of the tent—it was a good thing they'd all slept fully dressed. Reece took off after him.

Caradoc, Maeve, and Aisling followed.

"This is it then." Caradoc looked around the organized chaos of their encampment. Bars and other easy to carry food and water were available. Along with more weapons and ammo.

"It is." Maeve looked at both. "Neither of you get killed today. Do you understand?" She looked furious, but Aisling knew that was her reaction to terror.

Aisling grabbed her in a hug. "I promise. Caradoc?"

He enveloped both in a hug. "I won't lie. I'd be a hell of a lot happier if you two weren't involved. But as that's not possible with two of the fiercest people I know, I'll just repeat what Maeve said. Stay alive."

Aisling stepped back as the hug ended. "And keep whatever comes through the veil off your backs." She looked around. Harlie was animatedly talking with twenty other mystics. "Keep an eye on him too. He often forgets to."

"You got it." Caradoc laughed as Reece and Jones came up with an embarrassed looking Mott between them.

"I was confused. All better now." Mott joined Caradoc. Together the two would use their tech to add another prong to the attack of the mystics.

Jilan and Stella came up just as Caradoc and Mott went to gather supplies.

Jilan looked to Maeve and Aisling. "This might sound presumptuous, but I think one of you might have something I can use. A scroll? An ancient one in fact."

"How did you come up with that?" Maeve was already gearing for a fight. There were only a few people who knew about the scroll that she and Harlie had been trying to translate. It was currently held in Aisling's clan jewelry box in her luggage.

Stella looked embarrassed. "Harlie told Dailten and me about it." She glanced to Aisling. "In case he didn't survive, he wanted others to know. He thinks it will be important at some point. I told Jilan when she started asking about it."

Aisling shook her head and turned to Jilan. "How could you know about it? That opal charging box is sealed."

"Oh, it is. It is. But I sent out a searching spell while trying to sort out that warehouse. It bounced back. It's up to you two. I can feel it, but couldn't get it out of the box. And Maeve would have to gift the scroll to me to understand it."

"Harlie tried that." Maeve still looked prickly, but not as hostile. "It didn't work."

Jilan looked around. "He is stronger than me, that's true. But my magic, combined with my nature, gives me an advantage." She briefly flashed into the likeness of Maeve. "If you tell the scroll to focus on me, it will."

Maeve watched her for a few moments, then turned to Aisling. "Get it. None of us might survive this, and if that cursed paper can up our odds, I'm game."

Jilan changed back to herself, and they went into Aisling's tent.

Opening the opal box, and seeing her clan earring, the trail of rubies almost made Aisling ill. That was what was left of her mother. She'd find a way to destroy the earring if they made it through this. She handed the scroll to Maeve, then started to shut the case.

Stella stopped her. "That is your clan, yes?"

"Past clan. But yes."

"Put it on." Stella was earnest.

"What? No. I'm not shouting that information around. Nor reinforcing any connection to *that* woman." Clan jewelry was worn by the highest families at formal events as a status symbol. Not at a battle for all known existence.

Jilan tilted her head. "My niece sees more than many. I agree that the power of the jewels can help you."

Aisling watched both, then sighed and put on the earring. She already had her hair back in a braid for fighting, so the rubies would be extremely noticeable. "Not sure what this will do, but here we go."

"The clan jewels go beyond the veil, it might help." Jilan gave a shrug, changed back into Maeve again, and the transfer of the scroll was made.

Judging by Jilan's nodding and murmuring, she could understand it. "I'll be at the warehouse. Stay safe, all of you."

They followed her out only to find Reece standing suspiciously like he was on guard.

"Everything okay?" His gaze went to her clan earring, but he didn't ask.

"Hopefully." Maeve's eyes narrowed as Jones took position with a group of agents. "Ya know, no one has ever mentioned that man's given name. Even you just call him Jones. We have no idea what we're facing, and I feel I need to know."

Reece looked to his friend and at first looked like he wasn't going to answer. Then sighed. "Do not tell him I told you or that you know it. Both of you promise." When they nodded, he lowered his voice. "Aristotle. It's a fine name, but he hates it. I mean, really hates it. He got Area 42 to officially list him as only Jones."

"Bah, quirky, but not as weird as I hoped." Maeve shrugged. "Shall we get this thing started?"

A massive cracking sound hit and the ground shook. Another alarm went off and the mystics raced for the standing stones.

Bart barked orders and the bulk of the fighters, along with Caradoc and Mott, raced off. The veil was ripping again. This time the gaps could be seen from a distance as massive hordes came through.

CHAPTER FORTY-FIVE

WHIRLING DUST DEVILS came through above the rest of the enemies—alari. Hel-pixies flew overhead, only noticeable as dark clouds. Giants also. It was hard to tell all the species, but as Bart got everyone moving, she knew that wouldn't be the case for long.

Bart went with the last group heading toward the stones, after giving a nod to Aisling, Maeve, Stella, Dailten, Reece, and Jones. This group would drive down the road and check the commune for the trolls first, then come at the field from that angle and join the rest of the fighters. If the trolls had been attacked and there were survivors, they had to at least check.

Reece parked outside of the commune to keep the car safe if there was something wrong. They jogged in.

Stella looked like she might be ill as she ran. Her best friend, Grundog, had been with the Ckiong when they went missing. Dailten flew overhead, scouting the terrain.

They ran into the ruins of the commune, but the reception building they'd stayed in was nothing but rubble now. And so were the cottages the Ckiong had been staying in. There was a chance that if the rest of the Ckiong had shown up, they chose another place to plan their attack from. They might not have been here when whatever this was happened.

Maybe if she kept telling herself that as they slowed

down to look in more areas, she'd believe it. Not only would have the full might of the Ckiong people be invaluable in this battle, but Reg, Grundog, and Fieath were good people. So were their friends.

Reece looped around the massive pile of a destroyed outbuilding. The sounds of battle were getting louder, even though Avebury wasn't that close. "They aren't here. We need to join the battle without them. There are fights being reported across the world, they might have gone somewhere else." He turned to Stella. "I'm sorry."

She looked ready to cry or scream and start blasting things. But she nodded. "We fight for them."

They quickly got back in the car, aside from Dailten who flew ahead.

Parking and running closer brought swearing from everyone. The confrontation was already not going well, as the attackers coming through the veil easily doubled the defenders.

There were three rips in the veil, all visible and all massive. They'd feared that, but had hoped for them to only have one huge one. Harlie and his mystics needed to work with Caradoc and Mott to safely close the rips and shut that section of veil.

Which meant they could only focus on one rip at a time.

Bart and a heavy contingent of fighters were working on protecting the magic and tech users. The rest of the fighters were simply fighting to keep the enemies at bay.

Aisling fought with both bullet and spell, but there were just too many beings to fight against. Then the ground shook. Something massive was running toward them through the nearest rip. Neasa with about eighty dryads, good giants, and good swamp goblins, among others, came racing through. They all had a mark of bright green on sashes across their chests—most likely to help the people on this side recognize who was good.

Then the sunlight hit a few of them—they were wearing Trileium-embedded sashes. The rare metal had powers beyond any metal on this side and seemed to be acting as a shield as well as identification.

Hopefully.

She'd briefly questioned Neasa's allegiance when the attack against the Xilen copies of her friends happened. Once she was calmer, she realized that wouldn't have been the case.

Neasa fought her way to Aisling and clasped her arm. "Well met. We weren't sure if we would make it."

"No vallenians?" Aisling never thought she'd be looking for them, but they were powerful and supposedly on their side. And extremely distinctive.

"They can't leave our side of the veil anymore. They have been weakened by trying to keep the xpenc out of our plane. They never let anyone know. But they said to send you this." Neasa reached out, took Aisling's ghau pendant in her hands, and whispered a few words that Aisling couldn't make out.

"That should help." She released the pendant. "Or so the vallenians said. The ghau now has all the strength it had on the other side when it was made long ago. But they said be wary of absolute power, as it doesn't always cut the way we want. And that it was now connected to your soul." She shrugged. "Whatever they meant by that."

Aisling looked at the pendant. The entire thing had dozens of lines of color, so thin they blurred into one. It also felt heavier now. "Thank you. And thank you for your timing." She wasn't happy about the connected to her soul bit, but they needed any weapons they could use. They had to keep fighting until the rips could be shut and the veil closed for good.

The Old Ones brought by Neasa were fighting the attackers on a scale people on this side of the veil couldn't do. There was still a lot of hard fighting, the bad giants were doing their best to smack down flyers with their clubs. But the tide was slowly turning. They just needed to shut down those rips.

Mott moved toward the closest one and savagely punched buttons on his pad. With a triumphant yell, the rip closed. Violently. If the veil was an active participant in this war, it wasn't happy about the rip being shut. Caradoc nodded in approval and they made their way to the next one with Harlie and his mystics following.

A blast of wind slammed into everyone within a hundred yards, knocking smaller fey off their feet and some into the air. Including Mott.

Aisling grabbed him as he flew past. He had his eyes tightly closed and he clutched his computer pad with so much force, it looked like a race to see whether his arms or the tech would break first.

A muffled explosion came from behind as Aisling set him on his feet. She spun around as a massive dust cloud extended high over Avebury and rapidly spread out.

"Damn it, Jilan didn't shut the explosion down." She'd almost forgotten about the warehouse and its contents. The fighting was too spread out and there was no way to warn their magic users about the rapeseed dust. If their magic fell, but somehow the ones from the other side were protected, things were going to go from bad to tragic immediately.

Mott pulled on her arm and pointed to the sky. "Umm, that's not rapeseed dust."

He was right. Thousands of tiny, brightly colored flowers started falling on the battlefield and beyond.

Aisling shook her head. That was impressive. Jilan couldn't stop it, so she changed the poisonous rapeseed dust into tiny flowers. And judging by the lack of impact on nearby magic users as the flowers landed on them, she'd changed the properties of it too.

Transmogrification was a tricky magic and one really only successfully used by higher level changelings. And that scroll of Maeve's might have helped since whatever it was originally intended for, changing things was its goal. It was a good thing Jilan was on their side and an extremely good thing she was powerful.

The flowers drifted around the combatants and soon covered the field. Stella wasn't too far away and Aisling heard her laugh as the flowers hit her.

It was a brief cheery moment in a rough couple of days.

But one that didn't last long. Even though there were only two rips open here, now, there was a new rush of ghanlough charging through the largest of the remaining rips. They were racing further into the fighting, managing to break up all the groups of defenders. Bart and the other leaders were trying to keep them together, but it wasn't working.

The fighting became more brutal.

Aisling was too busy trying to keep an eye on her friends, and she missed a swamp goblin charging behind her. Its blow missed her, barely, but as she swung back, she instinctively grabbed its arm. Her healing magic could be used as a weapon, although she didn't like doing it. But the swamp goblin had startled her and when she grabbed him she sent out the anti-healing magic.

The creature screamed and exploded as Aisling jumped away, shaking her hand. She'd felt a jolt from the ghau pendant as the magic flowed from her. But was it that or herself that killed him? That was a brutal reaction for whichever did it.

Aisling shook off her fear at what just happened and swore as she looked around. It appeared that the scenario with the duplicates of her friends was going to happen again—for real this time. Everyone was separated and fighting on their own. Even the people from the village and the Area 42 agents were pinned down individually or in small groups.

Garran and Surratt had shown up with a mixed group of Lazing and agents—but it wasn't large enough to make a big impact.

Then a roar came from the far end of the field, where the blasted remains of the commune sat. The trolls had survived.

She had no idea where they'd been when they ran through the commune before, but she was extremely glad to see Reg, Grundog, and Fieath leading a few hundred furious trolls. Some even in war paint.

Reg led them, but Grundog yelled and shot off in a different direction as Stella's magic started to fail. She'd been holding a partial shield up around the mystics trying to close the rip, but it was weakening. She and Harlie were back-to-back, but he wasn't doing much to defend his side. Grundog literally ran over the two alari who'd been attacking her friend. Then stomped on them for good measure.

A portion of the trolls followed Grundog, killing as many of the enemy as they could as they ran. Reg led his group to where Reece was cornered, and Fieath took the last third down the middle to the wavering black mass that was the final rip.

Grundog sent the trolls with her down the direction she'd been going, then picked up Stella and Harlie and ran back to Aisling. "He's hurt." She gave a tight smile, then ran back into the fight. Some fighters didn't want to step back and fought side by side with the Ckiong trolls. Others gladly pulled out of the melee for a reprieve. They were injured and exhausted and at this point might be more of a hindrance than an asset.

"Good timing from my friend, eh?" Stella had blood dripping from a nasty gash on her arm and some marks on her face. Harlie looked dazed. Aisling had seen him fling a spell that got deflected and it looked like the attacker had hit him with it. It would explain why Stella had been having to protect both.

"Harlie? Are you okay?" Not that there was much they could do right now if he wasn't. The trolls had saved them for the moment, but there were more enemy fighters coming through the rips. They had a reprieve, nothing more.

"What? Yeah, I'm fine." He tilted his head oddly and the scowl on his face went against his words.

Stella marched up to him and pulled his head down. "Nope, pupils are dilated. Not fine. Can you heal him?"

Aisling wasn't sure what she could do. Head injuries were tricky and there was too much chance of making it worse. "If it's just a slight concussion, maybe?"

Dailten landed near them. "Most of their flyers are down, but that doesn't mean they won't have more coming in. Narissa and her airborne agents are helpful, but many aren't as trained in aerial battle as one would hope. And apparently Area 42 doesn't believe that flyers fight." The dark gray feathers on the back of her head ruffled in annoyance indicating what she thought of that. She nodded to Harlie. "How is he?"

"Hopefully, soon to be better." Aisling nodded and moved closer to her brother. "Harlie? Can you focus on anything else that might be wrong? I'm going to do a general healing, but if you have something serious?"

"I don't think so. I did get a concussion once when I lived in Nepal. This sort of feels like that."

Aisling studied his face to see if he was lying, but there wasn't time for waiting. The rest of his mystics were still working on closing the remaining rips, but he needed to be with them. She put her hands on either side of his head and reached for her healing magic.

It wasn't there.

She tried again. The anti-healing had worked. The rest

of her magic worked, why not this? She reached for the ghau, but there didn't seem to be energy there. It helped her destroy someone, but not save her brother?

"Get mad at your mother?" Stella suggested hesitantly.

"That's a good idea. But. I. Can't." There was a block around her healing magic. Whether it was a deliberate last act by her mother, or the result of healing her, Aisling's healing magic was cut off.

She squashed the panic down and focused on anger about everything they'd been through. She wasn't sure, but it felt like her clan earring was helping her. These bastards were not taking her family. That seemed to work. Channeling her magic through different angles, she reached into Harlie's mind. He would be fine. She gave him enough healing to heal the concussion.

Finished, she rocked back on her heels and looked around them as the fight had moved on. Reg and his trolls had balanced the battle, at least on this side, but Reece was now further away from them. He was using his borrowed sword like an expert, but a giant raced up behind him.

"No!" Aisling yelled as the giant's club missed Reece's head, but got his shoulder and sent him flying. Her ghau pendant flared both in pain and brightness and she felt a jolt of power come from it. She didn't grow wings, but lifted into the air as if the pendant was flinging her. She landed hard next to Reece.

He wasn't breathing. She quickly tried to channel her healing magic like she'd done for Harlie, but terror suppressed it. She couldn't grab ahold of anything to heal.

A popping sound came from next to them and Satoshi appeared inside what looked like a small veil rip. "Might my companion assist?" He moved out of the way and a cloaked shachen mage stepped forward.

Garran and Surrat had come back with some of the Lazing, but clearly not many of them.

She started to move away to give him room, but the powerful, and extremely secretive, shachen mage took her hand and pulled her back to Reece. His magic flowed around hers and whatever the ghau was doing, and together, they got Reece's heart to start.

Reece gasped, but was breathing.

"We stopped the attacks on your cities as well as ones throughout this world. We cannot be more help here." Satoshi nodded to Reece.

"Is that a rip in the veil?" Aisling was clutching Reece tight enough that he had to have her release him, but color was coming back into his face.

"It is…our payment." The shachen mage spoke haltingly. "We will keep the power for ourselves." He nodded and both he and Satoshi vanished into the small rip. It closed neatly behind them.

"I'm glad to be breathing, but do they have the power to travel with those things?" Reece had only caught their leaving, but that was enough. His face was pale from more than briefly dying.

The Lazing were sometimes allies and sometimes enemies. That power could be terrifying if they went back to being enemies. Unless once the veil shut for good, those pockets vanished. But something in Aisling's head said that wasn't the case. The odd rip they'd come through felt different than the others.

"I'd say they found a way to win their fight and gain more power." Aisling brushed the hair from his face.

"How did you get here? I saw you; you were at the other end of the field." Reece stiffly sat up. He might no longer be dead, but he was still in pain.

"I'm not really sure." Aisling lifted the pendant. The vallenian in her head said it was now tied to her soul. Maybe he meant it literally. The flying or being flung over to Reece had felt natural, but not something she could call up again.

Not something she was explaining to Reece in the middle of a battlefield.

"I think the trolls are turning things around," Reece said. The fights were switching slowly. Harlie, his remaining mystics, Caradoc, and Mott were working on the last rip. Aisling hadn't even seen that there was only one remaining, but that was great to see. The fighters needed to protect them a little longer, then this could be stopped.

Aisling helped Reece to his feet, but his color was coming back and his shattered shoulder was fine now. There was no fighting close by, but that could change quickly.

"How much ammo do you have left?" Aisling asked. Reece's sword had been lost when he'd been flung and she doubted he would have been using it if he still had bullets.

"Nothing." He laughed. "As you already guessed." He stepped back where a dead human lay and took their sword. "I'll hold my own. I really do wish my fey ancestors had been something other than swimmers though."

"I think that—" Aisling's words were swallowed by an explosion and another rip, this one red and savage, burst open. Monsters came through. There was no other way to describe them. Massive monsters swinging tree-sized staffs. They didn't care which side they killed.

Aisling almost threw up as a horrific feeling overwhelmed her and the ghau shook so hard, it felt like it was trying to scream. She'd never seen these nightmarish things, but she knew without a doubt what they were. "Get away! It's the xpenc!"

CHAPTER FORTY-SIX

AT FIRST EVERYONE stayed still. Aisling wasn't sure if it was a spell from the xpenc, or just seeing monsters from nightmares coming to life froze them in place. The xpenc might have been working behind the scenes before, but they weren't now. There were about twenty, possibly more coming through the rip. All were easily twenty feet tall, almost like a nasty combination of massive dryads, swamp goblins, and some sort of sea monster. Each one had two arms and four tentacles.

The lead xpenc picked up two giants, with no green trillium on them, so she hoped they were bad ones, and smashed them into a bloody mess.

Interestingly, the rest of the bad side yelled and ran in the wake of the xpenc. Aisling thought that if the people you were fighting for were killing your side, running away would be a better idea.

Everyone was exhausted and many were injured. Which was probably why the xpenc came through now, less resistance.

Trolls, giants, elves, and humans, all fell under the onslaught of the xpenc. The ghau started tingling. This was what it had been made for. Why it was given to Aisling. And why it was going to make her fly.

She lifted into the air with surprising ease and charged

the closest xpenc. They were still too close to the rips in the veil. Harlie, Caradoc, and the others needed time to shut them and seal the veil for good. She needed to distract the xpenc and send them far from the area. Flying was odd, but slamming into the side of a xpenc and breaking it in half was kind of awesome. By the time she'd destroyed four of them, all the xpenc were targeting her.

Hoping that it was enough to give the others time to close the rips, she flew south. Open water might be a better battlefield against these monsters. And less chance of collateral damage. She just needed them to follow her.

Her magic felt stronger than ever and while flying was new, she was able to fly circles around the massive xpenc. Her clan earring was channeling power to her in a way she'd never heard of before. But she would use it.

She had no idea how long the fight went on. The xpenc were powerful, but so was she. And she was growing stronger.

Using magic, Aisling grabbed two xpenc in front of her and, channeling the ghau in her mind, shattered them. She tossed the remains aside and looked around. There was only one left, a snarling, tentacled beast that even the most creative horror movie couldn't come up with. She smiled. This was the leader, there might be more beyond the veil, still waiting in the Isfyden, but this was their ruler. Instinctively she knew if this one fell, they all would.

She patted her ghau. It wasn't instinct so much as the connection between them.

"Why?" She hovered in the air, far enough that it couldn't reach her with its waving tentacles.

"Why? You are nothing. All of you are nothing. We will win and remake the worlds."

"Hmm, not a great answer. But if that's what you're going with." She raised her hand to strike him down as she had the rest of his people. And found her magic blocked.

There had been no stopping her magic just minutes ago, and a quick glance at the sky said she'd been fighting the xpenc for an hour or more. How could her magic be blocked now?

She dug into anything magical she could grab. An odd, darker feeling magic flowed around her and she used it to fly toward the xpenc. It flung out a pair of tentacles at her. Perfect. She grabbed them both and using whatever the new magic was, plus the ghau, she used her anti-healing on the xpenc.

It didn't die immediately, but managed to pull her closer as it yelled in pain and struggled to fight back.

She reached forward and grabbed the sides of its head, again slamming her anti-healing into it—reinforced by the pulse of hatred from the rubies in her earring. The odd new magic flowed around her, embracing her as she destroyed the xpenc. It hadn't been upset at first, she could see inside its mind, and the idea of someone being stronger than it was foreign. But as she dug deeper in, it began to realize its fight was over. She used the xpenc's own magic as a final push and destroyed it.

Aisling felt the power flow through her as she flew higher and drifted toward the ocean. She did it, she'd channeled the power from the xpenc, and used it and the ghau to destroy them. They couldn't harm anyone again. She'd often envied the fey who could fly, and now she knew that was right. The power of being above everyone was a wonderful feeling.

Controlling everything was even better.

The High King and Queen were already dead, and no one would notice her completely taking over until it was too late. The blood of the lost prince showed itself to be powerful with her—she would claim the throne.

People who didn't agree could be removed.

"Aisling!" It was Reece with a loudspeaker, one magically enhanced judging by the volume, but he was small below her and easy to ignore. "Come back!"

She reconsidered. "This is where I'm supposed to be. You can rule by my side."

"No! You're out of control! They're still manipulating you!" As he yelled, Reece ran to a chopper that was sitting on the beach. "You'll die!"

The helicopter flew up alongside Aisling and she debated smacking it out of the air. "No, this is who I was meant to be." She flew higher and further away from the coastline. The ghau pendant seemed warm, and was fighting her clan earring. She debated ripping the ghau off. She could tell that it would come off this time. But there could still be a use for it, it held power and the xpenc were right to have feared it. She would use it.

The helicopter pulled closer, and she could see that Jones was flying and Reece was leaning out to her.

"If you keep going like this, you'll be destroyed! I'm coming to get you."

Aisling almost laughed. "You can't fly."

"I know." Reece took a deep breath and with a nod to Jones, Reece jumped out of the helicopter toward Aisling.

The shock and terror of him leaping out of the helicopter jolted Aisling back into herself. Luckily, she could still fly. She grabbed Reece as he started to fall and slowed him down.

"What are you doing?" She had to yell as they were still falling, albeit slower. She couldn't keep them in the air. Whatever power had been messing with her mind had also been what was giving her flying strength. And it was gone.

He grinned. "Saving you."

Aisling couldn't stop their descent. Whatever evil mojo that last xpenc had hit her with was fading. Which was good and bad. They were plummeting toward the English Channel, but at least she didn't want to take over the world now.

"We'll drown!" Aisling tried again to call on anything that would keep them out of the water, but even the ghau seemed to have forsaken her.

"Not if I can help it." Right before they hit, Reece changed. The fins she'd seen in the coastal waters of Los Angeles were back. The hands he grabbed her head with were webbed. He held her close, covering her mouth in a kiss as they dropped into the water.

CHAPTER FORTY-SEVEN

FREEZING WATER EMBRACED her, but so did Reece. He kept up the kiss and remained holding her, until they stopped their watery descent, then he met her eyes, nodded, and started swimming to the surface. She hung on to him as he swam up, the feelings of power she'd had in the air were completely gone now. Even the ghau felt dead. Her clan earring vanished when they hit the water. That saved her from having to find a way to destroy it.

Damn it. Had she followed through with those plans, she would have met a similar fate to her mother. After she caused the deaths of thousands, if not more. Hopefully the xpenc were really all dead now. They were dangerous beyond belief. They'd almost gotten her to carry on their work even after they were dead. She knew the clan earring had messed with that too—one last gift from her mother. Luckily, the ghau was stronger and kept it at bay.

They broke through the surface of the water and Aisling sputtered. Reece turned to her. "Are you okay?"

Aisling laughed as she treaded water. Right now, the coolness felt good, but she had a feeling that wasn't going to last for long. "Thanks to you. You do realize that in the state I was in there was a chance I wouldn't grab you. You shouldn't have taken that risk. I wasn't me." Now that things were settling, she was getting an emotional backlash. And feeling more than a little sick to her stomach.

"I knew you were in there somewhere. If I couldn't save you, I didn't mind if I fell." Those amazing gray eyes were sincere—and no longer worried her about what trouble they might be making.

Aisling kissed him, then started laughing. "And it was just happenstance that we were over the water?"

He shrugged. "That was a benefit, but I still probably wouldn't have survived if you hadn't slowed our descent. There were serious debates as to how strong you were."

She looked around. "I'd only been up there for a short while." Although it felt like it had been days in her head.

"They were quick debates." He looked up as Jones lowered the chopper. A rope ladder hung down as he hovered over the water.

Reece moved back. "Ladies first."

Jones looked at her carefully as she climbed inside. "I'm glad you're you again. I didn't want to have to try to kill you." That explained why he had the helicopter ready and at least some of the quick debates that had taken place.

The fact that he'd said 'try' was disturbing as it reminded her how strong she'd been in those moments. He clearly knew that he wouldn't have survived, but that wouldn't have stopped him from trying. "Thanks. On both counts." She buckled herself in as Reece climbed in and did the same as Jones took off back to shore. She hadn't realized how far over the water she'd gotten until now. The battle area was a mess, the damage done by the xpenc was something that literally changed the shape of the land. Huge gouges had been dug into the turf, and the bodies of the xpenc hadn't vanished.

"The veil is closed?" When she'd taken off after killing the xpenc, they'd still been closing the rips, but she'd been focused on world domination. That wasn't a feeling that was going to be easy to forget. Even though it had been enhanced by the xpenc, and reinforced by that damn clan earring, there had been a small part of her there too.

"Yup, while you distracted the xpenc, Caradoc, Mott, Harlie, his crew, Stella, and her aunt all managed to close the last rip here and seal it. According to your brothers, the veil as we knew it is gone. Neasa got her people back to their side just in time."

Jones lowered the helicopter to a clear spot of land. The number of dead were outmatched by the huge groups of people still alive and moving—but it was still too high. Aisling felt sick as part of her wondered if she could have done more to save them when her powers hit.

Reece reached forward and took her hand. "You couldn't have stopped it. We all knew what we were up against. You took out the xpenc, and that changed the battle completely."

"Thank you. I just…" She couldn't finish her statement as they landed and her friends and brothers came running up.

Harlie had the longest legs of all of them, and put them to good use as he got there first and grabbed her in a hug. "You're you! And alive! And very wet." He didn't let go even though she was obviously making his clothes soggy.

Soon Caradoc, Maeve, and the rest were surrounding her and moved in for hugs once Harlie finally let her go.

"We won?" She wouldn't call it a win, not with all the people who gave their lives. But it was better than the other option.

"We did." Jilan beamed. "And Isfyden, the third plane, is gone from existence. The xpenc kept it open through their magic. When you destroyed them, it disappeared." She put her hand on her heart. "I felt it here." That it might close when the veil did was one thought. That Jilan might be dragged back to it, was another. Aisling was glad that Jilan had survived and stayed here. She'd been fighting to save both sides of the veil before anyone else even knew there was a problem.

"Auntie is going back with me to Los Angeles. When Reg and Grundog came over here, they shut down the diner. I think it's time to get back to making food and living a simple life." Stella looked around as ambulances and medivacs continued taking the seriously injured away. "I've had enough adventures for a few decades."

Garran joined the group. He had one arm in a sling, but other than that looked okay. He hung back with Bart.

"Where is Surrat?" She'd last seen the two of them fighting a group of swamp goblins. But that had been before she took on the xpenc.

"Being dragged off in a medivac." Garran shook his head. "He is one stubborn man. Could barely walk, but kept fighting."

Bart nodded, but didn't say anything. The same could be said for most of the people with them. Instead, he pulled out his ghau by its chain from his pocket. "Mine came off when the veil closed. The vallenians are on their side for good now."

Aisling reached up and lifted her ghau over her head. The thing had been a pain many times, but it had also done some good. There was no doubt that everything the vallenians had done was for their own benefit, and that of the others left behind on their original world. But they had managed to save people here as well. With a smile, she put it in her pocket. No idea what she was going to do with it, but when she got back to her stuff, she'd put it in her opal charging box for safe keeping. She didn't need the box for her clan earring anymore. That traitorous piece had vanished when she hit the water. She rubbed her arms. "Ya know? It's getting cold out here, and Reece and I are still in wet clothes."

Bart and Garran grinned and waved to one of the larger

helicopters as it flew in. "Got that covered. We found a spot for all of us to rest and recover."

Caradoc laughed. "One that's set up for Area 42 intel. Resting involves figuring out where the world goes from here. They'll be looking for lineages to take over as the High Queen and King, not to mention most of the High Council." He turned to Aisling. "Wanna rule anything?" He didn't say more but the look on his face showed he knew part of the megalomania she went through.

Aisling stepped back into Reece's embrace. "Hells no. I just want to go back to being a cop in L.A."

Garran laughed as they walked to the waiting helicopter. "I think I can make that happen."

Aisling let herself and Reece drift behind as the others went on board. Garran wasn't the only one with injuries, but everyone was there. Against all odds, all the people she cared about survived.

Reece rubbed her shoulder. "We should get on board. But first," he didn't drop to one knee, but the look in his eyes was serious. "I don't have a ring handy, but will you marry me?"

"Of course, I will." Aisling wrapped her arms around his neck and kissed him to reinforce her answer. "But you had to wait for the world to almost end to ask?"

THE END

DEAR READER,

Thank you for joining me on the last book of the Broken Veil trilogy. This story arc is now done, but stay tuned as there are still plenty of issues on this side of the veil.

If you want to keep up on the further adventures of any of my characters, make sure to visit my website and sign up for my mailing list. *www.marieandreas.com/index.html*

You can also sign up on Amazon to follow me and they will keep you updated. *Marie Andreas Amazon*

If you enjoyed this book, please spread the word! Positive reviews are like emotional gold to any writer. And mean more than you know.

Thank you again—and keep reading!

ABOUT THE AUTHOR

MARIE IS A multi-award-winning fantasy and science fiction author with a serious reading addiction. If she wasn't writing about all the people in her head, she'd be lurking about coffee shops annoying total strangers with her stories. So really, writing is a way of saving the masses. She lives in Southern California and is owned by two very faery-minded cats. She is also a member of SFWA (Science Fiction and Fantasy Writers Association).

When not saving the masses from coffee shop shenanigans, Marie likes to visit the UK and keeps hoping someone will give her a nice summer home in the Forest of Dean or Conwy, Wales.

9 781951 506322